Big Shot

A Quirky, Small-town Mystery

Kirsten Weiss

MISTERIO PRESS

CONTENTS

ABOUT BIG SHOT

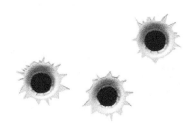

SMALL TOWN. BIG MURDER.

Hi. I'm Alice. The number one secret to my success as a bodyguard? Staying under the radar. But when a public disaster blew up my career and my reputation, my perfect, solo life took a hard left turn to crazy town. And to bodies. Lots of dead bodies.

I *thought* my hometown of Nowhere would be an out-of-the-way refuge to wait out the media storm.

It wasn't.

My little brother had moved into a treehouse. The town had the bright idea of attracting tourists with the world's largest collection of Big Things... Nowhere now has the world's largest pizza cutter. And lawn flamingo. And ball of yarn...

And then I stumbled over a dead body.

All the evidence points to my brother being the bad guy. I may have been out of his life for a while—okay, two blissful years—but I know he's no killer. Can I clear my brother before he becomes Nowhere's next Big Fatality?

Buy this fast-paced and funny mystery and start reading now!

Murder mystery game included in the back of the book!

COPYRIGHT

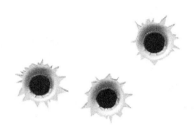

misterio press / paperback edition May, 2022
ISBN-13: 978-1-944767-79-2

To Charles, who wrestled a deer.

CHAPTER ONE

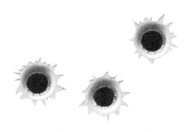

JUST TO BE CLEAR, it wasn't my fault.

It wasn't my responsibility either. But when your client slips you a mickey, there's a principle involved. Though after falling down a flight of hotel stairs, I wasn't entirely sure what that principle was anymore.

I staggered to my feet, lost the rest of my dinner in a potted palm, and careened through the door into the hotel lobby.

Guests turned to stare, and why not? My blond hair fountained out of a high, pre-makeup-removal ponytail. Camo pajamas and flip-flops completed my tipsy party-girl look.

I staggered deeper into the chic gray and white lobby. Lights glinted off the chrome chandeliers, and I winced at their dizzying starbursts.

My fist clenched on my phone. Or at least I thought they did. My fingers were a little numb. But I'd expelled most of the drugs, and I was going to catch my wayward client, Toomas Koppel, and surveil him until it hurt. Him. Hurt *him*.

That wasn't ego. I was well aware of my many flaws. But I also knew who I was and what I was. I was very, very good at surveillance.

Plus, I was an optimist. Personal protection agents, otherwise known as bodyguards, frequently were. We liked to think we were tough and cynical, since our job was to watch for trouble. But you didn't get into this business if you didn't think you and your client would survive it. Maybe that was why I'd been snookered by mine. I still had no idea why he'd drugged me, but I was going to find out.

I pushed through the hotel's revolving door, tripped over my own feet, and fell flat on the sidewalk.

San Francisco was a beautiful city in the summer and particularly tonight. Fog coiled low above the streets and blurred the outlines of the elegant buildings like something out of a Sam Spade novel. But not even Sam Spade would voluntarily lie on a San Francisco sidewalk.

A wary doorman in green approached. "Mm, may I help you, Ms. Sommerland?"

"Where'd he go?" It was the first time I'd tried out my voice since I'd been drugged, and it was embarrassingly slurry. I clambered to my feet and rubbed my bare arms, chilled by a gust of fog. It blotted out the stars, and ghostly wisps reached with coiling arms to the street.

"Who?" the burly doorman asked.

"The guy I was with. Toomas Koppel."

He pointed to the darkened street. My black Hummer glided past.

"Son of a..." I gaped at my swiftly vanishing vehicle. Shaking myself, I whirled on a valet. "How'd he get my car?" My Hummer was less than a year old, the first treat I'd had since my divorce. The thought of Koppel driving it made me ill.

The green-coated valet edged backward.

I exhaled, trying to get a grip. "Why did you give him my car?" I asked in a level voice.

"He had your room number," the valet sputtered and raised his hands in a helpless gesture. "You two were together."

My lips pinched. The entire hotel thought I was Koppel's mistress. I didn't *look* like much of a mistress. I'm a beanpole—too tall and too much lean muscle. But I'd been dressed to kill on the few occasions we'd been seen together. There were also our adjoining suites.

I scanned the street for a cab.

"Ms. Sommerland?" The bellhop pointed at my feet.

Red yarn trailed from the revolving door to one of my flip-flops. The yarn was the remains of a sweater I'd been knitting, and my left eyelid twitched. I'd been working on that sweater for *weeks*.

A silver-haired couple in formalwear emerged from a yellow taxi beneath the concrete awning. I yanked the yarn free and jogged erratically toward them.

The male half of the couple stuck his head in the open, front passenger-side door. He fumbled with his wallet and coughed, his mercury silk scarf dangling. "I know I've got a fifty in here somewhere..."

I squeezed through the open door and sat beside the cabbie. "I'll pay it. Follow that Hummer."

"But young lady, it's nearly fifty dollars," the man said. Judging by the suit, I guessed he'd come from a symphony or opera—both popular events on a Friday night.

The black-haired driver eyed me. "No one rides in front. And I don't go anywhere until I get paid."

I pulled my credit card out of the slipcover on the back of my phone and handed it to the cabbie. "Use this."

"I insist on paying." A hundred dollar bill dropped from his wallet to the sidewalk.

I leaned out and picked it up, handed it to the man. "Seriously," I ground out. "I got this." Straightening in the seat, I turned to the driver. "Let's go."

The cabbie's jaw stuck out mulishly. "Not with you up front."

"Fine," I snarled, and stepped from the cab.

The old man shook his head. "But—"

"Enjoy your stay in San Francisco." I hopped into the back and slammed the door. The cab smelled like pine freshener. "*Now* can we go?"

"Go where?" the driver asked.

"Follow that..." My Hummer was gone, and I bit back a curse. "Hold on." I pulled up the anti-theft tracker on my phone. "Go two blocks east and make a left."

He pulled from the curb. "So," the cabbie said brightly. "You're following someone?"

"Yes."

"Who?"

"A client." My client might be a blackmailer and all-around jerk, but he still got confidentiality. At least until he got to court.

I couldn't wait.

The taxi sped up. "What sort of client do you have to follow?"

"The kind who stole my car."

His shoulders twitched. "Ouchy."

I hadn't caught a whiff of trouble around Koppel until now. What was he up to? My stomach tumbled unpleasantly. Was this a run for the border? It made sense. Why else would he reject protection from the feds? Aside from the fact that he hated them with a red-hot passion.

I checked my phone. "Turn left at the next light." It glowed green, turned to yellow.

"I don't see a Hummer." He shot through it and past rows of Victorians, partially hidden behind gloomy cypresses. "All I get are taillights."

"Slow down. I don't want him to see us." It was after eleven, but that didn't mean much in this city. Koppel was driving too fast, weaving in and out of traffic. If he scratched my new car, I was billing him double.

"And you're getting too close again." I glanced down at my phone.

"Are you some sort of PI?"

I snorted. As *if*. "No. Personal protection."

"Uh, what now?"

"A bodyguard." Technically, my specialty was countersurveillance, watching for trouble from afar while the client's close protection team took care of any trouble that gets close. I was the early warning system. Tonight, that system had been compromised.

"Sure, sure..." His head bobbed. "You travel a lot?"

"Yes." I studied my phone. "Take the next right, at the church."

"Must be hard on relationships."

My gaze narrowed in the rearview mirror. My relationships were just fine. I didn't have any. And after my divorce eighteen months back, a little distance seemed like a good thing. I obviously couldn't trust myself to make good decisions in that arena.

He cleared his throat. "Why are you wearing pajamas?" he asked. "It doesn't seem professional."

A mini disco ball jiggled from the rearview mirror. I had to pick a critic, a disco fan, *and* a chatty Cathy? It wasn't my fault I was in pajamas. My usual dress code was business casual. "Can you just drive? And turn right at the light."

"Looks like he's heading to the bridge," he said. Horns blared. "Hey, I think a Hummer just changed lanes up ahead. That yours?"

To the Golden Gate? Then Koppel wasn't heading to Mexico. *To Canada?* "That's mine. Hang back. We don't need him to see he's being followed." The cabbie slowed in the traffic—still heavy even this late at night—and a horn blared behind us. "You're still too close."

The taxi slowed. "Lady, as car chases go, this ain't very exciting."

"It is for me," I said, grim.

We followed the blinking light on my phone all the way to Sonoma, where the light stopped moving.

My pulse accelerated. *Gotcha.* "Slow down."

I checked the clock on my phone. It was almost midnight, and we were nearing Sonoma's town square. The streetlamps glowed dully in the fog.

The cabbie sighed heavily. "If I go any slower, I'll get a ticket."

I bounced my heel. "My car's stopped. It's five blocks up and another two over."

We drove past low brick shops, arched windows dark, potted topiaries bracketing their doors.

"Over in which direction?" the cabbie asked.

"Right. Turn here." We were heading into the business district. Was Koppel meeting someone?

I switched to my phone's video camera. Slouching down, I raised it just above the door frame. That familiar adrenaline rush flowed through my veins. "I got you, you son of a—"

The cabbie cleared his throat. "Uh, I don't think you're getting your car back." The cab glided to a stop.

I jerked upright in my seat and sucked in a breath.

My Hummer was accordioned against the grill of a tomato truck. Tomatoes and pieces of scrap metal lay scattered across the Sonoma street.

I swore and leaped from the cab, my flip-flops crunching across broken glass. "Call nine-one-one," I shouted over one shoulder.

The door to the tomato truck snicked open. Its driver tumbled out, his seatbelt still hooked around one shoulder. It snapped free when his feet hit the reddened pavement.

"How many fingers am I holding up?" I gripped his bicep, steadying the man and held up three fingers. No bleeding. No visible wounds aside from the lump forming on his temple. The cab of the truck itself was dented but not badly damaged. The seatbelt had saved him, but he'd need to be checked out by the paramedics.

The truck driver groaned. "Three."

"You win. Help's on the way," I said. "Don't move. You're going to be fine." I squeezed his shoulder, hurried to my SUV, and started to reach through my broken driver's side window.

Abruptly, I withdrew my hand. My fingers curled inward. Toomas Koppel was dead. There was no question as to how. He *hadn't* been wearing his seatbelt.

The street smelled like burned rubber and marinara, and my stomach twisted. I focused on the scattered tomatoes instead of the car and what was inside it.

I'd never look at spaghetti the same way again.

The cabbie appeared at my elbow and whistled. "Damn." He shook his head. "I called nine-one-one."

I nodded and blinked rapidly. I'd known Koppel was a horrible human being from the jump. But after three weeks of building rapport and pretending to be the jerk's friend, my subconscious had gotten a different message.

I returned to the truck driver. The lump on his head had, if possible, grown bigger. So... *possible concussion.* I sat him against a rear wheel of his truck so he wouldn't fall.

The police arrived. I gave a young officer my statement. The cop looked at me oddly and told me to wait.

I walked across the street and called my boss, Buck Jackson. Terse, I explained the situation. The fact that my boss also happened to be my ex-husband had absolutely nothing to do with the edge to my voice.

"You were chasing him?" he shouted.

I jerked the phone away from my ear and winced. "I was *following* him, in a yellow cab—"

"Tell me you didn't panic him into speeding."

I stiffened. "Of course, I didn't. Koppel had no idea I was on his trail. I was following the tracker on my car."

Buck exhaled. "Okay, okay. Sorry. I know you wouldn't spook him. Now I want you to get back in that cab—is it still there?"

I looked across the street. The cabby was sitting on the hood of his yellow cab and talking to a cop. "Looks like the driver's being questioned." *Again.* A wisp of fog twined around a streetlamp. When there was a fatality, the cops liked to take their time. That was the way it should be. So why was my stomach jumping? A crow alighted in a nearby elm tree and cawed.

"Alice?" Buck was saying. "You still there?"

I pressed the phone closer to my ear. "Yeah." But I didn't *feel* here. The early morning mist gave the scene a dreamlike quality. None of this seemed real. For a moment, I wasn't even sure if I was real.

Was I in shock? I didn't think so. But I'd been in this business for ten years. I'd never lost a client before, even one who'd revolted me, even one I wasn't physically protecting.

"Koppel should never have been able to *get* to that valet, let alone get your car," Buck said. "Where was his other protection team?"

"Down for the night is my guess. They probably thought he was in bed." *With me.*

Buck snorted.

"We knew he didn't trust them," I continued, "or he wouldn't have hired us—your firm."

Toomas had had his own team of heavies surrounding him. And if anything looked off, I was to phone Koppel, not his team. It wasn't the way it was supposed to work, and my shoulders curled inward. I should never have taken this assignment. But Buck had asked, and I'd been trying to prove... What? That we were really okay? Just friends? No biggie?

"Are his guys at the crash scene yet?" Buck asked.

"No," I said, drawing the word out.

"Why weren't *you* watching him?"

I sucked in my cheeks and didn't respond, let the silence extend. Buck cursed, long and colorfully. It was an impressive display of verbiage for a man who rarely cracked a book. But like me, he'd had a lot of practice in the military. We hadn't met there—I might have been smarter about things if we had. We'd met on assignment in Marrakesh. People do all sorts of stupid things there. But at least we knew we could work together.

"Why?" he asked. "Why'd he run?"

Heart leaden, I watched three firemen in canvas coats extract the slender body from my SUV. "Probably to prove he could."

I squeezed my eyes shut. I should have seen it coming. Koppel had been arrogant and psychotically confident. It's why he'd relied on me and his own team rather than taking up the feds' offer of protection. Of *course* he'd think he could ditch his protection.

But a man was dead. A man I'd failed to protect, a man the justice system had needed alive, even if he was a scumbag. *Because* he was a scumbag. My stomach rolled again.

Across the street, the tomato-truck driver rubbed the back of his neck.

Buck groaned. "This is a disaster. Is the press there yet?"

My jaw clenched. *For God's sake.* Who cared about the press? "No." If I kept to single syllables, I wouldn't yell at him.

Though clusters of people with cell phones snapped pictures of the proceedings. And of me. It was tough to look inconspicuous when you were five-ten and wearing camo pajamas.

"And you gave your statement to the police?"

"Yes."

"Then get out of there," he said. "ASAP."

I blinked, certain I'd misheard. "Excuse me?"

"Get. Out. Of. There. They're going to pin this on you."

"The police? They've got the truck driver in custody, but judging by the skid marks, Toomas was driving like a maniac. My cabbie and I didn't get here until it was too late—"

"Finish with the police. Go back to your hotel. I'll let the FBI know where you are. They'll want all your surveillance footage. Don't edit it down to what you think they want. Give them everything. Then lie low, go home."

Another agonizing silence stretched between us. We both knew I didn't have a home to go to. I'd been living out of suitcases since the divorce, throwing myself into one job after another, recreating the stale, globe-trotting existence that had ended my marriage. And I guess trying to prove it had been worth it.

Buck cleared his throat. "There's something else you should know. Did Koppel, um, talk about his family?"

"A little. He said they were estranged."

"Estranged. Good word. Yeah."

Threads of panic squeezed past my helpless anger. "You're stalling. Why are you stalling?"

"So, his family... They're uh, mafia. Estonian mafia."

I burst out laughing.

"I'm not kidding," he said.

I wiped my eyes. "I know. I mean, Koppel told me. But he didn't take them seriously."

"Well, I do," Buck said. "And his team isn't going to want to take the blame."

Realization chilled my blood. No, they wouldn't want to take the blame. They'd want to blame me, the odd woman out, the person who *wasn't* part of their team. And I'd been first on the crash scene.

Plus, his close protection team didn't know about me. Koppel had insisted I stay undercover. But I couldn't be certain he'd kept that part of the deal.

"Take a vacation," Buck was saying.

I dragged my attention back to the conversation. "A what?"

"Is there somewhere you can lie low for a while? We need to keep you out of the public eye."

Hot anger flushed from my heart to my scalp, but my only movement was the tightening of my hand on my phone. "We lost a client. Forget the public eye."

"You *always* do this. You never took my company..."

Seriously, I finished in my mind.

He drew a deep breath. "Toomas Koppel was the key witness in the biggest underage girls and blackmail ring since Epstein. Everybody who's anybody wanted him dead. And now Koppel *is* dead, and the undercover BG who was supposed to be watching him *somehow* let him steal her car and get himself killed."

Since a lot of guys in protection found the term *bodyguard* mildly irritating in the industry, *BG* had become the approved substitute. "But—"

"No one's going to believe that. They're going to think it was murder, and you were in on it."

A news van with a satellite dish on the hood pulled up beside a store that sold over a hundred different kinds of olive oil.

I shook my head. "But the police—"

"Aren't you listening? I don't care what the local police think. No one cares what the police think. In about thirty minutes the rest of the world is going to think you're a conspirator to murder."

I turned away from the news van. *Maybe in less than thirty.* I rubbed the back of my neck, my stomach tightening.

"There's got to be somewhere you can go," he muttered.

"Put me on another assignment, maybe in Russia..." Or maybe not Russia. The Estonian mafia might be small potatoes, but they had ties to the Russians. "Latin America?"

He laughed hollowly. "An assignment? Don't you get it? No one's going to want a BG who took a payoff and let their client get killed."

My legs wobbled. I braced my hand on an ornate lamp post. A *payoff*? No one who mattered would believe that. I had friends in the industry, a reputation. "I didn't—"

"I know you didn't, but no one else is going to believe you just let him borrow your car." I could actually hear his quote marks around the word *borrow*.

"But it's not *true*." Despite the cool fog, sweat broke out on my brow. "I wasn't even his close protection. No one expected me to shove him out of the way of a bullet."

"So?" Buck demanded. "What does truth have to do with anything?"

My mind raced. I could fix this. There was always a solution, even if I hated it.

I swallowed, closed my eyes. "What about Afghanistan?" I'd gone there once to do a security training and nearly got dismembered by an angry mob with rusted farm implements. I'd gotten my client out, but it had soured me on the country.

But Afghanistan was the place that failures went to launder resumés the way the mafia laundered money. No one knew what went on in Afghanistan—they were too scared to check. Resumés came out clean.

He huffed. "Are you nuts?"

"I've worked there before."

"Yeah and look how that went."

I swallowed. There was one other place, but these days, it made Afghanistan look like a day spa. "Sudan?"

"No." He paused. "You're still gawking at the crime scene, aren't you?"

"Crash scene, not crime scene." I strode away from said scene and down a tree-lined street. "And no. I'm moving."

"There's nowhere to put you..." He trailed off as if he'd just gotten an idea. "Nowhere..."

I stopped short beside a mailbox. He couldn't think... "You can't be serious."

"It makes sense. I'm the only one who knows where you're really from. It's enough to stall the press for a couple weeks, and you can get there fast. It's only a few hours from the crime scene."

"*Crash* scene." I strode past a clothing boutique.

"And I'll know where to find you," he said, sounding more cheerful.

Nowhere. I shook myself. Okay. This wouldn't be so bad. All I had to do was lie low. How hard could that be? This would blow over, and my career would get back to normal.

But that was my stupid optimism showing. I had no idea what the real problem was. The accident had set something in motion much worse than I could ever have imagined.

CHAPTER TWO

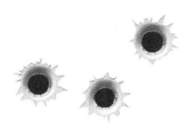

I WAS IN NEVADA early the next day. An illuminated billboard flashed past on the dark, mountain highway:

BIG THINGS IN NOWHERE

Despite the disaster that was my life, I smiled. A tangle of my blond hair escaped the cracked window of my rented SUV. I clawed it back inside and rolled up the window.

Every state has a Nowhere. Forgotten towns with empty storefronts, their only citizens old-timers with nowhere better to go.

Plus, my brother, Charlie.

It had been two years since I'd been back. That was too long, and I wasn't proud of my absence, though I was fairly sure Charlie would forgive me for that, or for showing up on his doorstep without calling. But there hadn't been time, and it was too early now, and he was a better human being than I was.

I crested the Sierras. A yellow, BIGFOOT CROSSING sign beside a tower of granite boulders flashed past. I frowned.

Did I really need to hide? The FBI, San Francisco *and* Sonoma PDs had agreed it wasn't my fault. The cause of death had been a tomato truck and reckless driving.

But I went over Friday night again in my head, searching for mistakes. Taking the job had been mistake number one.

But Buck had asked.

And now he was being overly cautious, sending me into hiding. There was no way this could rebound on his company.

I squinted into the rising sun, my hands clenching and unclenching on the wheel of the SUV.

This would blow over. Buck and I would do an after-action review, figure out what went right and wrong. We'd move forward.

Soon there'd be a new protection assignment, and I'd vanish somewhere slightly more glamorous. Ethiopia. Kazakhstan. Baku. Because my career *would* get back to normal. It had to.

I didn't have anything else.

My chest tightened. I'd never lost a client before, either.

I drove through a black-rock canyon, and I knew every twist and boulder. The tension in my muscles loosened. *Home.*

I passed another billboard.

Don't Miss the Big Things in Nowhere

Bemused, I drove on.

The town had great hiking trails, but the only thing *big* was the old silver mine. There'd been some talk of turning it into a tourist attraction. Maybe they'd actually done it.

I slowed, rounding the final bend. The tops of Nowhere's old-west brick buildings came into sight above the pines. A punch of longing surprised me.

I'd stayed away too long. Sure it was small and dying, but Nowhere had been home.

Nowhere, where nothing and no one changed. It had been a place I'd had to escape, to break free from, to break out of. It had been five years since my father's death and twenty years since I'd first left after graduating high school. Now I was back.

I turned onto Main Street, passing a scattering of neat Victorians. Back to Nowhere, where nothing and no one changed—

My jaw slackened. I gave a slow, disbelieving head shake. My SUV glided to a halt at the four-way stop.

Okay, something had changed. And just like the billboards had said, it was big.

Ahead and on my right, a giant coffee pot towered over the Sagebrush Café. The pot was in the Scandinavian style, with a stylized blue bird on the front.

Mechanically, my head swiveled left, toward the park across from the café where my brother and I had spent our youths. Its basketball court and swing sets had vanished. Now, pastel mushrooms and flowers the size of small trees sprouted from the manicured lawn. A Japanese-style wooden fence ribboned past a gravel path.

A horn blared. I glanced in the rearview mirror and sketched an apology wave to the red Tesla behind me. Letting up on the brake, I let the SUV roll forward.

Tires screeching, the Tesla passed my rental.

I pulled to the curb in front of the café and stepped from my car, a Mitsubishi SUV that I still hadn't mastered. Baffled, I crossed Main Street to the mushroom park. Pine trees towered behind the mushrooms.

The mushrooms, the flowers, were taller than me. I was a child again, when I knew the world was full of mystery waiting for me to explore.

Whoosh.

I leapt backward, but not fast enough to avoid the park's sprinklers, sputtering to life. Water droplets darkened the hem of my blue travel slacks. I had a lot of professional travel clothes—stretchy and tough to wrinkle.

"Aaaah!" A person in a white-rabbit suit wailed and raced past on the sidewalk.

I rubbed the back of my head. "No, this isn't strange at all."

Across the street, three beefy young men in over-priced hiking gear lounged against the Tesla, parked in front of a stationary shop, and laughed. Perversely, watching three jerks laugh made me feel better. They'd seen the rabbit too. I wasn't hallucinating.

The giant rabbit raced across Main Street and vanished behind an enormous green-and-white can of peas. It stood on the other side of a narrow alley between the park and a four-story brick building that used to be an old cannery. Even when I was a kid the place had been abandoned.

I looked at the giant mushrooms. The giant coffeepot. The giant peas where the rabbit had disappeared. Edging off the lawn and onto the cracked sidewalk, I gazed south down Main Street.

An odd, flamingo-pink bubble nosed past the top of a building toward the end of the road. Were hot air balloon rides a thing in Nowhere now too?

Slowly, I walked past the cannery. The old-timey brick structures from Nowhere's heyday as a silver mining town were still there.

I scanned the street for more changes. The feed store was gone, replaced by a knitting shop, and my heart gave a joyful hop. Nowhere had a knit store? In its window, beside colorful displays of yarn and knitwear, a sign proclaimed:

KNITWITS
WORLD'S BIGGEST BALL OF YARN
COME INSIDE AND MARVEL!

I kept walking. The pink bubble swelled. As I walked closer, I could see it was tipped with black... I reached the end of the building obscuring the object and stumbled to a halt, my skin tingling.

On the corner of Town Hall's wide lawn, a lawn flamingo three stories high stood.

Hands on my hips, I turned in place. This *was* Nowhere. Or maybe an alternate-reality Nowhere. I swayed. *Could* we be living in a simulation?

No. That *would* be crazy. I laughed nervously.

The flamingo squinted down at me. Whoever had developed the giant art must have decided you can never get too much of a good thing, because Big Things were everywhere.

I crossed the street to the bowling alley. Its unlit sign promised the world's largest bowling pin inside. Returning in the direction I'd come, I wandered past the world's biggest winged corkscrew, standing in front of a wine store. Experimentally, I lifted one of the corkscrew's wings. The worm turned smoothly.

"Good God." You could kill someone with this thing. If they laid down beneath the rim and let you.

I kept walking. All the shops were closed at seven AM. A spot between my shoulder blades heated, the flamingo's gaze following me. Shaking myself, I turned the corner, walking down an alley, and explored more of my old hometown.

All the big art—if you could call it that—seemed to be on Main Street. On the streets behind it, the two-story buildings were boarded up, their windows covered in paper.

Main Street was like a massive old-west false front. Behind its facade, Nowhere was still dying. I wouldn't say I was surprised to see it. I was surprised by how depressed the sight made me.

I returned to town hall and retraced my steps, taking more time to study the details of the changes. A sign in the cannery's windows promised rental spaces coming soon and the site of a new art center.

My gaze clouded. Nowhere had never been an artsy town. We'd had a rodeo and a cannery. Both of those had gone away, and then Nowhere had just had people, commuting to work in Reno, forty minutes away.

I stopped in front of the giant can. A small brass sign off to one side proclaimed:

WORLD'S LARGEST CAN OF PEAS

I laughed shortly. "Of course it is." Then I looked around to make sure no one had seen me talking to myself.

There was another sign, high in the cannery's second story window. I stepped backward onto the soft earth around the can of peas for a better look. My low heel caught on something, and I stumbled backward.

Normally, this wouldn't have been an issue. I was fairly light on my feet. But a howling mass of gray fur flew around the corner of the building at the same moment. I threw up my hands to protect myself and thudded into something hard and muscular.

Powerful arms wrapped around my chest. And since my hands were protecting my face, the arms grabbed a very sensitive spot. Two sensitive spots, actually.

"Watch it," a masculine voice rumbled.

I jerked away, and he released me. Embarrassed and indignant, I whirled and glared into a pair of green eyes full of mirth.

My gaze moved upward to his dark, curling hair. For the first time since the accident, I felt like I was in the real world. He was *real*.

He was also at least six-foot-two, because he was four inches taller than me. He looked like the Greek god of war—not the Ares from the marble statues, the one from that old TV show, *Xena, Warrior Princess* (my hero). The effect was in no way diminished by his white t-shirt and jeans stained at the knees.

"There are easier ways to get to know me," he said.

"I wasn't—there was a gray dog..." I looked around. The dog was gone. "He must have run off."

Maybe behind the can of peas the man had just rounded. I might have been a little off my game, but I wouldn't have missed a man like him walking down the sidewalk. He had to be the best-looking man in Nowhere. Granted, with a population Nowhere's size, he wouldn't have a whole lot of competition.

He raised a brow. "Sure there was. And you're supposed to stay off the grass." He pointed between my sneakers.

I looked at the bare earth we were both standing on. "The grass," I said flatly. "That we're standing on."

"Oatgrass."

I looked down again. Had my hometown gone completely insane while I was away? "Can *you* see this grass?"

His mouth twisted with amusement. "No one can see it."

Right. It was invisible grass.

"Seriously," he said. "You'd better move. Terrence gets salty when he sees people standing there."

I looked around. We were the only ones on the street. "Terrence isn't a giant white rabbit by any chance?"

"Nope, no giant white rabbits in town. Unless Harvey's come to visit."

The rabbit from that old Jimmy Stewart movie? "Does he visit... often?" How many imaginary friends did this guy have?

A wild-haired man rounded the can of peas. He wore paint-spatted clothing and was in his forties, a few years my senior. His watery eyes bulged. "Can't you read?" He jabbed his finger at a small wood sign stuck to the bottom of my shoe.

I lifted my foot and read it upside down.

KEEP OFF THE GRASS

"We just seeded." The first man smiled slightly, the skin crinkling around his green eyes.

"You could have led with that," I said, pulling the sign free.

"Well?" the wild-haired man demanded. I presumed he was Terrence. "Move!"

"Oh." I hopped backward and thudded into someone soft.

"Watch where you're going," a woman huffed.

I whirled.

My childhood neighbor and nemesis, Mrs. Malone, drew in a deep breath, then blinked. "Alice? Alice Sommerland?" A yellow track suit hugged the old woman's ample curves. It clashed with the sturdy brown purse slung over her arm.

I pressed my palm to my stomach. How had I not noticed her approach? Nowhere was dissolving my surveillance skills in a puddle of confusion. "Mrs. Malone," I said, relieved. "It's great to see you again." She hadn't changed a bit, right down to the one-inch white roots in her dyed-black hair.

Sure, she'd told my brother and me off more than once for biking too loudly past her house, or for playing too close to her property line. But that was then, and we were adults. She was the first person I'd recognized since arriving. I wanted to hug her.

"I'll take that." The green-eyed man plucked the sign from my nerveless hands.

Mrs. Malone sniffed, leaning on her cane, and clutched her purse closer. "I suppose you're here for the drugs. Tell your brother my driveway's cracked." The older woman turned and stalked into the park, the tip of her cane thudding rhythmically. "Fredo!" she shouted.

I blinked. *Drugs? Driveway? Fredo?* "Okay..." I watched her vanish into a stand of pines.

The wild-haired man, Terrence, scowled at the green-eyed Ares impersonator. "It's my *vision*."

"All right," Ares growled. "Though the Russian sage blooms longer than the lavender and is hardier."

"My *vision* is lavender," Terrence said.

"Sorry about the grass," I muttered and left them arguing about the landscape.

I wandered toward the Sagebrush Café feeling out-of-sorts. The life of a surveillance specialist wasn't as glamorous and exciting as the movies made it look. A car chase, a car crash, and a giant coffee pot were not all in a day's work. Had I been in an accident? Maybe I was in a coma, and this was all a bad dream.

I pushed through the diner's glass door. The same trio of old-timers that had always sat there perched on the same faded, blue barstools at the counter. A knot in my chest unraveled, and I smiled.

Then I halted on the checkerboard floor and rubbed my forehead. They *weren't* the same men, but I still recognized them. When I'd been young, these three particular men hadn't been that old. Maybe they'd just seemed ancient at the time.

A smattering of people I didn't recognize sat in booths and at tables. A TV ran silently, high in the right corner of the room, opposite the counter. Closed captioning ran across one corner of its screen.

My muscles re-clenched, and I forced myself to relax. It had been over twenty-four hours since my client's inglorious death. The media cycle must have moved on by now.

I walked to the counter and sat on one of the sky-blue barstools.

The elderly man on my right turned. His gray hair was close cropped, curls tight against his skull. He grinned, his brown eyes crinkling. He wore a faded blue windbreaker over his white, button-up shirt. "Well, I'll be damned. If it isn't Baby Alice."

The others turned, smiling. "Baby Alice? You're back."

My face warmed, my pleasure at seeing familiar faces muted by that stupid childhood nickname. I was five-ten. The nickname didn't apply. At all. "Hi, Mr. Washington."

"Are you back for the rodeo?" Mr. Washington asked. "I'm afraid you're too big for the mutton busting this year."

The other men guffawed.

My face warmed. "The rodeo's back?"

"You boys leave Alice alone, or she'll leave without buying any breakfast." Coffee-pot in hand, the owner, Molly Haanson, approached the counter. Her straight blond hair was bound up in a bun. There was more silver in it than the last time I'd seen her, two years ago, but she was still athletic-looking and smiling. And tiny burns from kitchen accidents still marked her hands and forearms. "What can I get you, dear?"

"Coffee," I said. "Black." Maybe caffeine would snap me out of it.

She turned over an empty coffee mug and filled it. Her blue dress was the same color as the coffee pot outside, and nearly the same color as her eyes.

"So what brings you back to Nowhere?" Mr. Washington asked. "Not the drugs, I hope."

"Uh, what drugs?"

"Marijuana," he said.

"Oh. No." Nevada had recently legalized marijuana. But I could get that anywhere in the state—not that I wanted to. I didn't think I could afford to lose any braincells.

"Never mind them," Molly said.

Mr. Washington sighed. "No one ever does."

The three men burst into laughter and slapped each other's backs.

"Charlie must be thrilled you're home," Molly said. "Where is he?"

"He doesn't know I'm here yet. It was sort of a spontaneous thing, and you know how he likes to sleep in." I sipped the coffee. *Heaven.* "What's with the giant coffee pot?"

"Nowhere's trying to be the town with the most record-breaking Big Things," Molly said. "We get tour buses now."

The coffee mug froze inches from my mouth. "Buses?" Slowly, I put it down. Nowhere had tourists?

I crossed and uncrossed my ankles. It didn't matter. No one would care about me. I hadn't been part of Koppel's close protection. It wasn't like I was news.

"Mr. Washington's son, Marques—you remember him?" Molly asked, her eyes glowing. "Marques Washington? He thought it up. Most of us thought it was nuts, but I have to give it to him, it's bringing people in. Most afternoons, the Sagebrush is full."

"That's great." Nowhere would be a ghost town without some new moneymaking venture, even if it was quirky. "And the rabbit?"

Her brown brows drew downward. "Rabbit?"

"I saw a white one running down the sidewalk." I gestured toward the windows with my mug. "About yea-tall." I raised my hand to shoulder height.

"Rabbits don't run down sidewalks," Mr. Washington said. "They hop."

"This was..." I brushed back my hair. "Never mind."

Molly bustled into the kitchen, and I swiveled toward the TV. The Reno Aces had lost to the Vegas Aviators. *Eeesh.*

A newscaster arranged his face into a solemn expression. A photo of me appeared on the screen. It was an old photo, one Buck used in the *About Us* section of his company website. I was smiling too hard in it, giving me a desperate air.

Caught off guard: Toomas Koppel's bodyguard claims she fell asleep when Koppel fled in her SUV before his "accident."

Heat rushed through my veins. I hadn't fallen asleep. I'd been drugged and had valiantly regurgitated said drugs to leap into action. And what was with the quotation marks? It *had* been an accident.

"Hey, Alice," Mr. Washington said. "That looks a lot like you."

I gulped my coffee and put a fiver on the counter. "You think?"

Okay. No big deal. This was my fifteen minutes of fame. *Or infamy.* I'd be forgotten soon enough.

The elderly man squinted. "No, it really does look like you."

I studied the picture. My brain did something funny, and for a moment, it didn't look like me, not even like desperate me. It looked like a stranger.

"Huh," I said, mouth dry, "well, I'll see you around."

"Say 'hi' to Charlie for us," Mr. Washington said.

I hurried from the café and got into my rental. *Okay. Okay.* Buck would deal with the press and set them straight if the FBI didn't. This would be okay. I picked up my cell phone and dropped it in the cupholder. *Stay cool, Alice.* When Buck had new information, he'd call.

I drummed my fingers on the steering wheel. Then I gave in and called my ex-husband. It went to voicemail. A hot burst of anger flared in my skull, bright enough to dizzy me.

"Take my picture off the website," I snarled. "It's all over the news." So there was little point now in removing my photo from the site. But the call made me feel marginally better.

I hung up and checked my watch. It was eight-thirty. Charlie would probably still be sleeping. But it was the time for normal people to be up and about, and he'd forgive me.

I stopped by a donut shop. It did not have the world's largest donut in its driveway, and that was a disappointment. It had, however, donuts piled high with children's cereal, chopped up candy bars, and crumbled cookies.

I scanned the glass cases filled with mutant pastry.

"Can I help you?" a man barely out of his teens asked.

"Have you got any chocolate old-fashioned?"

He blinked. "What's that?"

No *chocolate old-fashioned*? "Never mind." Progress had come to Nowhere. Progress could bite me.

"Our Big Donuts have chocolate frosting," he said helpfully. "One serves twelve people."

Of course they did. I ordered half a dozen of the most obnoxious-looking donuts they had and drove to Charlie's house. Our neighborhood was only a five-minute drive west of Main Street and in a low-maintenance residential neighborhood of ranch houses and rusted cars.

Parking on the street, I sat, my rental car ticking as it cooled, and I took in the house I'd grown up in. It had a fresh coat of beige paint, but otherwise, the ranch house looked the same. Good even. Charlie was taking care of the old homestead.

I smiled at the massive pine in the front yard. We'd built a treehouse in it when I was thirteen. I'd been determined to spend the night in it that summer, until the bugs had driven me inside.

Charlie had stuck it out and woken up the next morning covered in bites. I'd gotten in serious trouble for leaving a three-year old outside in a treehouse. And I'd deserved it.

I grabbed the pink box, walked to the porch, and rang the bell. Charlie would forgive a lot for donuts, even being woken early.

The door opened. A tall, gray-haired stranger stared out at me. "Yes?" He adjusted the cufflink on his white button-up shirt.

Who was this guy? I took a step backward. "I..." I shifted the donut box to my other hand. "Sorry, I'm looking for Charlie. Charlie Sommerland?"

"Oh. He moved."

My stomach bottomed. *Why? Where?* "He moved?" Why hadn't Charlie told me? He couldn't have moved far though. Molly had said he'd be excited to see me.

"He, er, sold the house," he said.

My insides tightened. Why would my brother sell the house without telling me? Not that he needed to. It was his house. But a heads-up would have been nice.

"Who is it?" a woman shouted from somewhere inside the house.

"I think he's staying in a treehouse on Big Sky Lane," the man said.

I took another step backward. My heel hit the edge of the wooden step and my ankle twisted beneath me. I steadied myself. "He's staying in a treehouse?"

"If it's those religious people," the woman yelled, "don't engage."

"It's someone for Charlie," he shouted over his shoulder. To me, he said, "It's a friend's treehouse. That's what I heard, at least."

"Oh. Okay." I edged backward. "Thanks."

I wrinkled my forehead. Why was my little brother living in a treehouse? He must have gotten *some* money for selling the home.

The man's brow wrinkled. "Wait. Haven't I seen you somewhere before?"

I froze. Had he been watching the morning news? How bad *was* the news?

He snapped his long fingers. "You're Charlie's sister, that mutton-busting girl, Alice."

"Wow." I braced one shoulder against a wooden post. "That old rodeo story will *not* die." I laughed uneasily. "And you—? I'm sorry, I don't remember your name."

"Why would you? You were just a kid, and I was a boring adult, and then we moved away. I'm Donald, Donald Rigby."

I still didn't know who that was, but I nodded. "Oh yeah. Mr. Rigby."

"You can call me Donald. So what brought you back to Nowhere?"

"A mistake," I muttered.

He chuckled. "There's a lot of that going around."

"Sorry, I came to visit my brother. I'm just... surprised he's not here."

"Donald?" the woman shouted. "Are you still talking to that church person?"

"I'd better go." I backed away. "It was nice seeing you again."

"Tell your brother no hard feelings, okay?"

"Sure. Okay." Baffled, I returned to my SUV. Once inside, I opened the box and ate a donut.

Then I ate another.

CHAPTER THREE

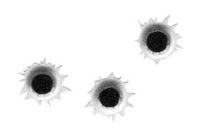

FOR A GUY LIVING in a treehouse, my brother looked pretty good. His blond hair needed cutting, but his new beard was neatly trimmed and did nothing to hide his open and honest face. And though he was ten years younger than me, deep laugh lines crinkled at the corners of his Capri-blue eyes.

I sat cross-legged on the wooden floor. The treehouse's peaked ceiling was too low for us to stand. A pine breeze flowed through the open window facing the street. It was the only thing that kept me from fleeing from the cramped treehouse, its corners piled with rucksacks and camping equipment.

He hadn't moved into a treehouse for the fun of it. My brother needed help, and he hadn't asked, and I hadn't been here, and guilt twisted my stomach. I should have reached out more. I should have known something was wrong.

"It's great to have you back." Charlie grinned. "I've got *tons* to tell you."

"I was surprised you sold Dad's house," I said carefully, but the words came out sharper than I'd intended. To cover, I picked up a nearby sword and pulled it halfway from its sheath. The blade was dull, so at least my little brother wasn't playing with sharp objects.

Charlie's smile faded. His gaze shifted toward the stack of medieval weaponry against one plywood wall. I had no idea what those were about either. I grimaced. More than the town had changed since I'd been gone.

"Um..." He canted his head. "I didn't exactly sell it."

"Are you renting it?" That made more sense. I slouched against the plywood wall.

"The town sort of..." He shifted on his sleeping bag. "They sort of took it."

"What do you mean they took it?"

"I sort of forgot to pay the property taxes."

My eyes bulged. "You what?"

"I was getting so much junk mail, I sort of stopped opening it, and I guess some notices were in there. It's not one of those regular bills that I can autopay."

A tide of anger rose in my chest, and I choked it down. The house had been Charlie's to keep or lose. Our father had left it to him, and I had no right to be angry. I hadn't been here.

I sheathed the sword, leaned forward, and set it with the others. "And so you're living in a treehouse. Like an adult."

He rolled his eyes. "You're one to talk."

"What's that supposed to mean?"

"And it's only for the summer," he said, "until I can get back on my feet. The treehouse is great, aside from the squirrels."

Something scampered across the roof.

"And between the theater and the town," he said, "I'm keeping busy with work. And the MBS has really helped. You wouldn't believe the connections I've made."

MBS? If one of those cults had gotten their hooks into him—

He clapped my shoulder. "This is perfect. You need to check out the MBS. You could meet all sorts of interesting people there."

"Thanks, but it's probably best if I don't. My goal is to keep a low profile."

"Oh." His boyish face fell.

I looked away. "Sorry. I should have explained... It's a work thing. But it's great to see you. It's been way too long.

So what's with all the weaponry? You're not planning an offensive to take back the house," I joked.

"Nah. I got home—or treehouse—late last night, so I couldn't drop off the swords and stuff."

He lurched forward on his knees and hugged me, nearly knocking me to the uneven floor. "It's great to have you back. You won't believe all the changes to the town. We've got a dinner theater now. It's haunted, but only the upstairs bathroom."

"Okay." I laughed.

"The equipment usually stays at the theater." He motioned toward the swords. "I've got to return this before our performance tonight, and then we can squeeze another sleeping bag in the treehouse for you."

"Thanks, but I've reserved a cabin at that place by the discount cemetery." The way my luck was running, the cabin would turn out to be haunted too. What do you mean *our performance?*"

He nodded. "Oh, yeah. I'm a player in the mystery dinner theater now too. You should come to a show. Our nineteen-twenties mystery is really popular."

"Sounds fun."

"There's tons we can do. There's a Japanese tea garden." His face fell. "But it's temporarily closed. There was an incident with the world's biggest koi..." He made a dismissive motion. "Water under the bridge. How long are you staying?"

"I'm not sure. Until things die down."

"What things?"

I swallowed the lump in my throat. *Get it over with.* "I was providing counter surveillance for Toomas Koppel."

Charlie gave me a blank look.

"He was a wealthy man with houses all over the world. He was famous mainly for hosting other famous guests along with underaged girls. But he got caught by the IRS not reporting his income—"

"Like Al Capone." Charlie's pool-blue eyes widened with delight. He sobered. "But why were you working for a guy like that?"

"So he could live to testify at his trial." So much for my big ideals. "There's speculation he got his income from blackmail. No one can figure out where else it might have come from. Unless it was his mafia connections."

"Mafia?"

I laughed shortly. "His family is Estonian mafia, but he wasn't."

"That doesn't sound good."

"It's no biggie. Koppel told me the Estonian mafia was like the Estonian Vikings."

"There were Estonian Vikings?"

"Exactly. There's good reason you haven't heard of them. In their entire history, Estonian Vikings successfully pillaged one village. Centuries later, the country's still dining out on the tale. Anyway—"

"Charlie? Have you got a woman up there?" a feminine voice shouted from below, her voice like a bell. "You know you're not supposed to have women up there. It's weird for me."

He stuck his head out the window. "Hey, Ivanna. It's not a woman. It's my sister, Alice."

I untangled my legs, squeezed beside Charlie, and waved out the window. "Hi."

An ethereal redhead, about Charlie's age and willowy as an elf, stood on the fading lawn with a book beneath one arm. She sucked in a breath. "Whoa, whoa, whoa. Your sister is Alice Sommerland? The *bodyguard* Alice Sommerland?"

My intestines spasmed. She knew about me.

"Uh, yeah," Charlie said. "But she doesn't like the word *bodyguard.*"

"There's a meme about you." She pulled a cell phone from the pocket of her painted-on-jeans and scrolled through the screen. "It *is* you!" She squealed. "Oh my God. I know a meme! There's a meme in my treehouse."

I leaned away from the window. "Meme?" My fifteen minutes of infamy might be worse than I'd thought.

"It's a visual joke people make online," Charlie said. "She's been out of the country a while," he said to Ivanna.

"I know what a meme is," I said. I just didn't know why there'd be a meme of *me*.

"Hey, throw it up here," Charlie said.

Ivanna tossed up her cell phone, and my brother caught it one-handed.

Charlie studied the screen and frowned. "I don't get it. This isn't you." He passed me the phone.

A constipated-looking Sergeant Schultz stared from the photo. Beneath, the meme read:

TOOMAS KOPPEL'S BODYGUARD

"That guy doesn't look anything like you," Charlie said.

And that... was unnerving. Ivanna knew I'd been on Koppel's protection team, and my picture wasn't even on the meme.

I gnawed the inside of my cheek. Random women in Nowhere, Nevada shouldn't recognize me. "This is not good."

"What? This?" Charlie pried the phone from my sweaty hand. "This is nothing. It's just a picture on the internet. It isn't even real. We're what's real."

"Yeah, well, it's not easy being a meme," I said and laughed shortly.

Charlie stared blankly.

"You know," I said, "like that talking frog... being green... Never mind."

"Okay, big shot," Ivanna shouted. "You come down here and give me a hug."

I glanced at Charlie.

"You'd better do it," Charlie said in a low voice. "Ivanna's a big hugger."

I climbed down the makeshift ladder, hammered into the pine. Ivanna hugged me, her book pressing into my chest, and I awkwardly patted her back.

"Oh, sorry." She sprang away and brushed off the cover of the pale pink hardback. "Welcome back to Nowhere."

"Thanks," I said, uneasy. The news couldn't be saying *really* awful things about me. Otherwise, she wouldn't be so happy to find me in her treehouse. "Good book?"

"It's a bestseller." She flipped the cover to reveal the title: *Your Job Doesn't Love YOU*. If the universe was trying to tell me something, message received.

"How long are you staying?" she asked. "I'm not sure if the treehouse can handle two adults—"

"It's okay, I've got a cabin."

"At that place across from the discount cemetery?" she asked. "Those cabins are sweet. I love that little creek."

Charlie hopped to the ground beside us. "Ivanna's our scribe."

"Scribe?"

"In the MBS." Ivanna beamed at Charlie. I glanced up at the treehouse. The way she was looking at him, I was surprised she hadn't invited him into her actual house. Charlie grinned foolishly back at her.

"Your networking group has a scribe?" I asked. Didn't they usually call them secretaries?

"It's not a networking group," Charlie said. "It's the Medieval Battle Society. And Ivanna's amazing. She does the calligraphy and illumination for our scrolls. She paints oil paintings—"

"Acrylic," she said. "It dries quicker."

"And she works at the theater too," he said. "Makeup *and* acting."

Ivanna blushed. "I'm still learning."

"No, no. You're great." Charlie beamed at her. "She's a real artist. She even did a comic book."

"I illustrated *your* comic book," Ivanna said. "It's not mine."

"I mean, I haven't sold it or anything," Charlie said modestly. "I wrote it just for fun. For the MBS."

I ground my palm into my forehead. *Oh boy.* My adult brother was living in a treehouse *and* making comics? "That sounds cool." I shifted my weight.

"Oh, hey, we should get going," Charlie said. "We'll see you around, Ivanna."

We said our goodbyes, and my brother and I walked to the street. "She's really amazing. She's got a master's in fine arts from some big school in New York."

"What does she do?"

"She works at the Sagebrush."

I stopped short. "She's got an MFA and she works at a diner? In Nowhere?" That was just sad.

"She's got other irons in the fire. Like me. Portfolio career, right? Hike at Snitz Creek?"

"Why not?" I was feeling sick from all the donuts.

We bought water bottles at a local minimart, then hiked our favorite trail, which lead along a creek and into the mountains.

Snitz Woods was on the other side of the discount cemetery. Hiking trails laced its forests, wound through with majestic, black-rock formations. A creek burbled through its narrow canyons. It also had great cemetery views. This had diminished its popularity among hikers.

The vanilla scent of sugar pines twined with the fresh mountain air. The smells took me straight back to childhood. And when we finally returned to the car, I felt lighter, more confident, and hungry.

We drove back into town and to the pizza parlor on Main Street, between the ice cream parlor and a stationary shop.

My mouth watered as soon as we hit the door. The scent of baking cheese and tomatoes flooded the dimly lit room, lined with red Naugahyde booths.

Making my usual ladies' room excuse, I confirmed the exits were clear and where I remembered. I rejoined my brother in a booth beside the world's largest pizza slicer, hung on a dark-paneled wall. We ordered a pepperoni from the smiling waitress.

Charlie waved at a man in his fifties, sitting in a neighboring booth.

The man squinted, rose, and walked to us. "Alice? Alice Sommerland?" Marques wasn't as tall as I'd remembered, but he was a good six feet. His graying, curly hair was still close-cropped.

I winced. "That's me."

He laughed. "You probably don't remember me, I'm Marques Washington."

The tips of my ears grew hot. Oh, I remembered him. He'd been the one to sit me on that fateful lamb during the mutton-busting competition.

Unless you're a lamb, mutton busting was the most charming part of the rodeo. Children rode the lambs like broncos. The goal was to stay on as long as possible. I'd been five when I'd tried my hand at it.

I forced a smile, my neck muscles tightening.

Baby Alice and the lamb are on the run! Norm has a lasso! Save Baby Alice!

I shuddered. *Stupid lamb. Stupid announcer.*

But because I'm a mature adult, I scooted from my booth, and we shook hands.

"I remember," I said. "I ran into your father at the Sagebrush."

He threw back his head and laughed. "I'll bet you did. He's stuck to that barstool like a barnacle. What brings you back to Nowhere?"

"She's on the run from the Estonian mafia," Charlie said. "But it's okay. They're not that dangerous."

A balding elderly man seated at the bar glanced over his shoulder at us. I frowned. He looked a little familiar, but I couldn't place him.

Marques laughed. "Gotcha. I mean, who hasn't been on the run from the Estonian mafia, right?" He clapped my shoulder. "Whatever the reason, it's good to have you back."

"Marques is the man responsible for the Big Things," Charlie said. "You know, the giant pizza cutter and stuff."

"What do you think of our town's new look?" Marques asked.

"It's sure different," I said politely. I hadn't quite gotten used to the Big Things. They were fun and quirky, and I usually enjoyed that sort of thing. But they left me with an unsettled feeling. My hometown had changed, and that was to be expected. I just hated that it had.

"The Big Things are amazing," Charlie said. "They're like the perfect tourist attraction because everyone..." He swiveled to face Marques and squinted. "What do they do?"

"People come to take their photos with them and post them online," Marques said. "The Big Things basically promote themselves."

I shoved my hands in the pockets of my jeans. "Uh, huh."

"How long are you with us?" Marques asked.

I leaned one hip against our table. "Not long."

The older man's face fell. I didn't look at Charlie. A tour bus wheezed past on the street outside.

Marques jerked a thumb toward the picture windows. "Tourism's going to save this town. They come for the Big Things, but they stay for the food and the hiking."

And then they fled to The Town of Hot Springs, the upscale town in the next valley. There was another town in Nevada with the same name, so our neighbors had added "The Town of" in front of theirs to differentiate. And also because they were snobs.

Okay, maybe I was a little jealous of Hot Springs. They actually had hot springs.

"And for the show of course." Marques grinned at my brother.

The bus squealed to a halt and the doors opened. An enormous man in a Hawaiian shirt squeezed from the doors and stood, puffing on the sidewalk.

I arched a brow. "They stay for the hiking?"

Marques scratched the back of his head and smiled ruefully. "That's the theory. But they do shop and eat. And it beats the alternative."

"Which is...?" I asked.

A waitress set two mugs of beer, their heads dripping down the sides, on our table. She strode into the kitchen, the doors swinging behind her.

"The silver mine." Charlie toasted me with his mug.

"What happened to the silver mine?"

Charlie took a sip, and foam stuck to his moustache. "We tried to turn it into a tourist attraction. You know, mine tours? But then there was the accident, and we had to close."

"Oh my God," I said, horrified. "There was a collapse?"

"No, no," my brother said, oblivious of the white foam. "Nothing like that. A Winnebago crashed into the entrance."

"It got stuck," Marques said. "We still haven't been able to pry it out."

"If we pull it out," Charlie said, "the entrance may collapse."

"Ah," I said. Had Nowhere always been a joke? I didn't remember it being so nutty when I was younger. Changing the subject, I asked Marques, "How are your kids, Tyrone and Janelle?"

The older man's face shuttered. "They're doing great. Well, I'd best be going. Charlie, I've got a job opening. See me if you're interested." He smiled tightly at me and strode from the restaurant.

I slid into the booth and picked up my beer. "Did I say something wrong?" I asked my brother.

"No, it's just..." He hunched forward, elbows on the table, and glanced around the pizza parlor. "He's a little sensitive about his kids. They moved away and never came back. I think that's why Marques is doing all this stuff for Nowhere. To bring them back."

"Wouldn't it be simpler if he just went to visit them?"

"Yeah," he said. "But... you don't get it. Nowhere's special."

"At least your job prospects are improving," I said brightly. "Maybe you'll be able to move out of that treehouse."

He snapped his fingers and pointed at me. "That proves it."

"What does?"

"The treehouse."

"What about it?" I asked.

"I needed a place to live, and Nowhere provided. That's what makes it so special."

"Wouldn't you rather have an apartment?"

"That's not the point." He clawed his hand through his longish blond hair. "Besides, I don't want to get tied down. You know how that is."

I shifted my weight. I *did* know. "So what are you doing for money? Does the theater pay, or is it a for-fun thing too?"

My brother sat up straighter. "I receive a share of the profits," he said loftily. "The theater's not every night, but like I said, I keep busy. I even roofed Gert's garage." He waved to the elderly man at the bar.

The gnome-like man wrinkled his nose, adjusted his thick glasses, and turned his back to us.

"You remember Gert?"

"Oh, yeah. The eastern European guy? Runs the antique store?"

"Yeah, he's cool. I mean, he's a little eccentric," Charlie whispered. "But he supplied most of our weapons."

"You mean the theater's?"

"The MBS and the theater's. We share. Hey, did you know MBS is an international organization? I mean, it's more than me and Ivanna. I couldn't battle her anyway. We're in different weight classes."

"Your battle society sounds fun, but—"

"It is. Whoa." He grabbed my bicep. "You should totally join. You must have all sorts of fighting chops."

"I really don't. But wouldn't you rather have a steady job?"

"The MBS isn't a *job*. It's a calling."

Of course it was.

If there was a better way to avoid people than off-trail in the Sierras, I don't know it. My brother and I spent the rest of the day hiking.

Afterward, I dropped him and his weapons off at the theater. Rosy cheeked and full of the virtue of outdoor exercise, I ate dinner alone at the Sagebrush. Charlie had offered to get me a ticket for tonight's sold-out performance, but I wasn't quite up for a show. When it finished, I took Charlie back to his treehouse, where I reluctantly left him. The temperature was supposed to drop into the thirties tonight, but Charlie insisted his sleeping bag went to minus fifteen.

I waved to Ivanna, who'd stuck her head out her door when my SUV had lit up her driveway, and I drove back to my cabin at the motel. It was an A-frame, with an open kitchenette up front leading into the bedroom. The bathroom had been wedged beside the kitchen area. The back had a sliding glass door with a small porch that mirrored the front. The night was still full of mosquitos, so I gave up on the idea of stargazing and gazed at my TV instead from the lumpy twin bed.

It was better to know than not know.

But I really didn't want to know.

Swallowing hard, I braced myself and turned on the TV. The screen remained black. I jabbed random buttons on the remote. Still no TV.

I sighed and set the remote on the stand. Maybe this was the universe's way of telling me ignorance was bliss.

The next morning, I woke at five, which was typical for a Monday morning but irritating since I wasn't working. I tried again and failed again to get the TV running. So I headed out the cabin's rear, sliding glass door for my AM jog. I warmed up beside the chattering creek. On the other side of the water, deer grazed between the headstones of the discount cemetery.

I hated jogging. I hated running in all forms. But it was the quickest way to burn calories and keep my heart in shape. And being able to move fast wasn't a bad thing in my line of work.

Besides, trail running kept things interesting. But instead of heading for the hills, I turned toward downtown. It was only a fifteen minute jog from the cabins, and I hated to admit it, but the Big Things were kind of irresistible.

I was tall for a woman. Things that were bigger than me made me feel small and delicate. Also, in spite of my resistance to Nowhere's changes, I loved weird places. I'd take a good roadside attraction or paranormal museum over the Met any day. Nowhere had changed, and I needed to get over it. And it seemed silly not to enjoy the eccentricity.

I jogged past the bowling alley. How big *was* the world's biggest bowling pin? After crossing Main Street, I wound beneath the tall metal legs of the giant flamingo. Its gaze still seemed to follow me, but maybe it felt a little friendlier.

I crossed to the oversized corkscrew and passed what had to be the world's tiniest apothecary shop.

At the giant coffee pot, I crossed the street to the park where I'd once played. I made a game of racing around the enormous, metal mushrooms.

Jogging across Main Street to the cannery, I slowed at the world's biggest can of peas. My thudding heartbeat turned heavy.

A man in a simple gray wool coat lay sprawled against the giant green-and-white can, and my heart turned leaden. So Nowhere had homeless people too.

I hesitated before walking toward him. The temp had dropped pretty low last night. And he had no blanket. I didn't want to wake a sleeping man, especially one who might be under the influence. And he'd have to be on something to curl up against the can like a dragon around its treasure.

Then I saw the knife. I stopped short and sucked in my breath.

He wasn't a homeless man.

He wasn't sleeping.

He was dead.

CHAPTER FOUR

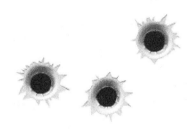

FINDING ONE DEAD BODY was bad. Finding another corpse two days later wasn't a great look. But I couldn't ignore the dead man, pressed against the can in a twisted embrace. Especially not when I knew him.

I called nine-one-one and took pictures of the body and the ornate knife beside it. Photography had become a bad habit. It was a surveillance thing.

A fire engine arrived. An ambulance. The mayor. And finally, the sheriff, since Nowhere still didn't have its own police department.

The sheriff—a grizzled, middle-aged man—eyed me and tapped his pencil on his notebook. His nametag said RANDALL. I hoped I'd never need to get that personal with him. "And you said you just *happened* to find him?" he asked.

Heat rolled up the back of my neck. He sounded a lot like one of the FBI agents who'd interrogated me in SF. "Yes."

"And you first met him yesterday?"

I glanced toward the body of Donald Rigby, sprawled between yellow crime scene tape and the world's biggest can of peas. "Yes." Another thing I've learned in my work. When authorities started asking questions, keep the answers honest and brief.

"Go over that again," Sheriff Randall said.

"I drove to my father's old house, thinking my brother would be there—"

"Why'd you think he'd be there?"

"My brother used to live there."

He raised his bushy eyebrows. "Used to? And you don't know where your own brother lives now?"

I stiffened. "He'd recently moved, and I'd been traveling."

The sheriff grunted.

"Mr. Rigby answered the door," I continued. "He told me where my brother was staying, and I left."

His mouth pursed. "But you got his name in that short encounter?"

"The Rigbys are old Nowhere residents. He recognized me, and we reintroduced each other."

"Not so old," Pete McGregor said. While waiting for the sheriff, I'd learned Pete had been elected mayor.

Pete was a tall man with a runner's body. We'd gone to the senior prom together, so I knew that body better than I should have. Not that I spent a whole lot of time dwelling on the past or anything. Not when twenty years had passed.

"He and Carmel moved away," he continued. "They recently moved back."

"I'd prefer to conduct this interview on my own," the sheriff said, voice tight.

Pete's nostrils flared. "And Alice only arrived in town yesterday. She's got nothing to do with this."

My face warmed. It didn't surprise me Pete knew I'd gotten in yesterday. Word spread fast in a small town.

"Thank you, Mayor McGregor," the sheriff ground out. "If you wouldn't mind, I'm sure Ms. Sommerland would like some privacy while we talk."

"Fine," Pete said. "But it's a waste of time. Donald was probably killed by a vagrant or one of those Hot Springs punks."

I managed not to roll my eyes. At least one thing hadn't changed—Nowhere still blamed everything on The Town of Hot Springs. Scapegoating the wealthy was all kinds of fun.

"Thank you, Mr. Mayor," the sheriff repeated flatly.

Pete hesitated.

The sheriff waited.

Finally, Pete limped a little way down the block and stopped to talk with a firefighter.

"You were saying?" the sheriff asked me.

I repeated my story a few more times. The sheriff copied down my contact info and let me go.

Pete waited for me on the corner of the mushroom park. He frowned. "Unbelievable. You bug out of Nowhere, and when you finally decide to come back, you dig up a body?"

"I didn't dig him up," I said, indignant. "He was just lying there." I studied the mayor. If anything, the years since high school had improved him, hardening his jawline and bulking out his shoulders. He was still an inch taller than me, and his sienna hair was as thick as ever.

"I'm mayor now. I can't just have bodies lying around town."

I stared at him. And then I laughed. "Yeah, bodies littering up the place *can* be inconvenient."

His mouth pinched, then quivered. He hung his head and chuckled. "Sorry."

"Forget it. I haven't been around awhile, but I'm going to go out on a limb and guess this morning isn't typical."

"Grab a coffee with me?"

I looked down at my sweaty workout clothes. "Only if we get a booth far from other diners."

"I'll see what I can do. But I'm sure no one will mind."

I wasn't so sure. Pete was so close, it was a mystery his eyes weren't watering.

We crossed the street to the Sagebrush Café, the only place open at seven AM.

The wild-haired man who'd shouted at me for killing his grass plants leaned against the brick building. He spat, narrowly avoiding Pete's loafers.

"That'll do." Pete held the door for me, and I walked inside.

"What's *that* about?" I asked as the glass door closed behind us.

"Long story."

And I very much wanted to hear it.

The café had a decent crowd, but we managed to get a corner booth. I slid into the side furthest from the other patrons. Pete motioned to Ivanna, and she nodded, grabbed a carafe.

Eyes glued to the front windows, Ivanna filled our empty coffee cups without spilling a drop. "What's going on over there, Mr. Mayor?" She jerked her chin toward the window and the police activity beyond.

Pete shook his head. She nodded and swished away, undoubtedly figuring she'd find out soon enough.

"I'd ask what brings you back to Nowhere," Pete said, "but I saw the news. You're hiding."

I gripped my warm coffee cup. "Really? What did—?" I shook myself. It didn't matter what people were saying. The FBI and two police departments had cleared me. I almost reached for my phone to call Buck, to find out what was happening with the investigation, and managed to restrain myself. He'd call when he knew something. I pulled my ballcap lower. "I'm not hiding."

"Sure you're not." He cocked a brow. "So. What really happened?"

"Koppel was driving too fast and crashed into a tomato truck. Wasn't that on the news?"

He shook his head. "Uh, huh."

"What's *that* supposed to mean? They did mention the tomato truck, didn't they?"

"They mentioned it, and that it was your car he was driving."

"Koppel stole it."

"Oh." He grimaced, looked at the linoleum table, looked up to meet my gaze. "I'm sorry about your father's house."

I scowled. "That's not your fault either." At least, it better not have been. I still had a hard time believing Charlie had missed those payments.

"So you're a jogger now," he said.

I leaned back in the booth. "Yes. It's awful, and I hate it."

He laughed. "I love it. The doctor says I can get back to it, but I've been dragging my feet. No pun intended."

"I noticed you were limping." I turned my mug on the table.

"I was biking and ate it on a trail six months back. Broke my leg, had to get a metal pin put in."

I winced. "Ouch."

"But like I said, I'm ready to get back to jogging. If you stick around, maybe we can—"

"Hey, Pete," Mr. Washington the elder shouted across the diner. "Who died?"

"No comment." Pete smiled and waved toward the counter. He turned back to our table. "Everyone will find out about Donald's death soon enough," he said in a lower voice. "But I'll let the sheriff break the news."

I bit my bottom lip. Would the press learn I'd been the one to find the body? No. I was being paranoid. Only the locals would care, and... "Do we still have a local paper?"

Pete snorted. "That went out of business years ago."

I shifted in my chair, the muscles in my legs twitching. But the longer the investigation dragged on, the more likely my name would come into it. "How good is this sheriff?" I asked.

"He's... you know..." Pete waggled his hand.

That wasn't encouraging. "Does he have much experience investigating murders?"

"Around here?" Pete barked a laugh. "No. I mean, not much happens in Nowhere. The occasional domestic violence. A guy killed his wife up in Little Dog, but that was pretty cut and dried."

So, not much experience. "This didn't look like domestic violence."

Pete glanced around. "We can't say for sure it was murder."

"Donald was stabbed in the back. The knife was on the ground beside him."

"Was it? They didn't let me get close enough to see." He smiled bitterly. "I don't have much pull with the county sheriff. Nowhere's not a priority."

"But Hot Springs is?" I guessed.

"Yeah. That's not to say the sheriff won't give this death his full attention," he added, his face tightening. "You deal with many murders as a bodyguard?"

"No. We try to keep our clients from getting dead." Until recently, I'd had a hundred percent success rate.

"I guess I can see you going into the business, keeping people safe. You did a good job taking care of your mother."

"That was a little different. She was sick."

"Yeah." We fell silent. My mother. His mother. But his mother had had a different kind of illness. "So I hear you got married," he finally said.

"And divorced." I wasn't proud of that failure. Maybe we'd been doomed from the start. Maybe two people who can't stay in one place just shouldn't have been married—or they'd needed to figure out a way to not stay in one place together. I tightened my grip on my mug. "Who would have wanted to kill Rigby?"

"Who knows? His wife? Someone who had a grudge?"

I stiffened. *Tell Charlie no hard feelings.* Would people think my brother had a grudge against Rigby? Would Charlie be a suspect?

Pete groaned and sat back in the blue-vinyl booth. "This is my fault."

I refocused on him, which was no hardship. Pete was easy on the eyes, and he knew it. "How do you figure that?"

"I invited Donald's company here. And then when I learned Donald was their point man... it seemed like fate."

"Oh?"

"Donald works—worked—for a big marijuana company. They were interested in turning Nowhere into a resort. A marijuana resort."

I sat back against the light-blue bench. Sure, weed might be legal, but the thought of Nowhere filled with rich stoners made me queasy. And the thought that Pete had proposed it left me floored. "Why would you want that?"

"Look around." He motioned toward the square windows and Main Street. "The town's dying."

"But—"

"Do you think these crazy sculptures are going to save it? The big-things tourists gawk and go. If we're lucky, they spend a few bucks in the shops and restaurants. This isn't Hot Springs. No one stays overnight."

"No, but—"

"Something has to be done," he said heatedly. "I'd be doing this town a disservice if I didn't explore all the options."

"But—"

"But what?"

But Pete's mother had a drinking problem. I couldn't believe he was promoting any kind of mind-altering substance. I sipped my coffee. "Don't you think it might change the character of the town?"

He shot me a look. "Seriously? We've got seven-foot mushrooms in the park across from the world's largest coffee pot. Marques thinks he's going to turn the cannery into some sort of artist colony and food court."

That was an improvement over a marijuana resort, but I took Pete's point. And it wasn't my town anymore to critique.

"You left, Alice, and so do most of our young people."

Stomach burning, I looked down at my hands laced around the white mug. I'd left Nowhere, and it had changed. That was life. But irrational annoyance swelled inside me. I sipped my coffee and said nothing.

"All the young people are leaving." He raked a hand through his thick hair. "And who can blame them? You of all people should understand. This town needs business, it needs jobs so people can live and work here and thrive."

It sounded like a speech he'd given before. I nodded.

Nowhere was cute, in a down-at-the-heels, old-west, small-town sort of way. But it wasn't Tahoe. And it wasn't The Town of Hot Springs. And it wasn't Doyle on the other side of the Sierras. If Nowhere wanted to survive, it needed to go big. *Heh.*

"So Donald Rigby decided to take a late-night walk down Main Street, and someone stabbed him." I sipped my coffee. "It was awfully cold last night for a stroll."

He arched a brow. "You're a bodyguard, not a cop."

"It's professional curiosity," I said haughtily. "And we prefer the terms executive protection or personal protection." But he had a point. There wasn't a whole lot of overlap between the two.

"How did you get into that business?" he asked.

"I was an MP in the Army." I shrugged. "It seemed a natural transition." And when I'd been an MP in the Army, I hadn't been detecting. I'd been the equivalent of a beat cop, cleaning up messes after the fact. And those years were far behind me. Murder was well above my paygrade.

"You're kidding." He sat back against the booth. "When?"

"Out of college. Four years in, and then I got into personal protection."

He shook his head. "Wish I could have seen that."

Ivanna stopped beside our booth and topped us up. She touched Pete's shoulder. "Anything else I can get for you this morning?"

"Not for me," he said. "Alice?"

"No thanks."

She smiled at us and moved off.

"I mainly talked people out of bad ideas," I said. "So who had a grudge against Donald?" My gaze darted around the diner. *Aside from Charlie.*

"Donald and I are—were—the face of that resort," he said. "Not everyone was happy with the idea of bringing it to Nowhere."

"I can imagine."

"Terrence Madoff—you met him outside—"

"The spitter?"

"Yeah," Pete said. "He's the artist who designed all the Big Things. He thinks a marijuana resort will turn his art into a joke."

I imagined rich and happy stoners giggling at the giant mushrooms. Terrence wasn't wrong.

"Marques wasn't happy about the idea either," he said. "He's like you—thinks it would destroy the character of Nowhere."

"I wouldn't say *destroy*."

"You didn't have to. Your expression said it all. And then there are people like Mrs. Malone, who don't want change of any type."

"I can't see Mrs. Malone stabbing a man to death. She's got to be seventy if she's a day."

"Ageist." He grinned and sipped his coffee. "Old people can be killers too. Anyway, I wouldn't worry about it. He may have been giving you grief, but the sheriff doesn't really suspect you. He can't."

I tipped my head, a fluttery feeling in my belly. I hadn't thought the sheriff had suspected me at all. "About that, is there any chance you can ask him to keep my name out of the press?"

"I don't have any control over the sheriff. Sorry."

I blew out my breath.

"But since the newspaper closed," he said, "there were no reporters on the scene to notice you. And I can't imagine why the sheriff would release that information."

Yeah. I was being paranoid. But I was supposed to be staying low profile. This wasn't that.

"For what it's worth," Pete said, "He's a reasonable guy. I'll see what I can do."

I twisted the dive watch on my wrist. Pete would try, but his message was clear: no guarantees.

The investigation needed to wrap up fast if I was going to stay under the radar. The county sheriff was as much an outsider to Nowhere as I was. What were the odds he'd figure this out? Murders went unsolved every day.

I nodded, glum. "Thanks. How's your mom doing, by the way?"

He grimaced. "She bugged out of Nowhere too. Moved to Clearwater, Florida. But she's doing good."

Tingling swept up my back. I glanced out the diner's front window. The handsome gardener stood beneath a giant mushroom across the street. He studied a computer tablet, but he was watching the diner. He wasn't bad at it, but he wasn't as good as me.

"You okay?" Pete asked.

I smiled. "I will be when this is cleared up."

I looked back out the window. The gardener was gone.

CHAPTER FIVE

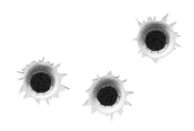

SMOKE COILED ABOVE MY cabin's back porch, snaking into the sunset over the western mountains. The air had a stifling feel to it, but maybe that was just my aversion to Mondays. Once the sun sank behind the Sierras, night would fall fast, and the temperature would drop.

I grilled steaks and buffalo wings on the motel barbecue. I wasn't a huge fan of charcoal, having been converted to pellet grills by my ex—who still hadn't called—but beggars couldn't be choosers.

Charlie leaned against the porch's splintered railing. "Are you sure Mr. Rigby was murdered?"

"He didn't stab himself." I flipped a buffalo wing. It looked done, and I shifted the wings to a plate on a low, wooden table by the railing. Undisturbed by our presence, a good-sized stag grazed on the other side of the nearby creek. I pulled my phone from my pocket and scanned to the picture of the knife.

Charlie took the phone and frowned at its screen. "The knife looks old, or like a replica. You should ask Gert, what with his antique store."

"I will." I hesitated. Why had I said that? My job was to *prevent* crimes from happening, not solve them after the fact. "Pete didn't seem confident in the local sheriff."

"You saw Pete?" He arched a blond brow.

"Yeah, but the big takeaway here is about the sheriff's competence."

"I guess I'm not surprised you two ran into each other. I thought you and Pete would stay together. You were a great couple, like Mom and Dad."

For a long moment, I didn't respond. Mom and Dad hadn't been that great of a couple. Mom had been unhappy and Dad oblivious. He wasn't home when she'd flown into her rages. He hadn't been there when I'd ridden my bike away to escape, only to hear her shouts echoing up the street, my hurt mingling with humiliation.

But Charlie was ten years younger than me. Things had been different for him, and there were things he hadn't understood growing up. And that was okay.

He angled his head. "Of course, I thought you and Buck would stay together too."

So had I, up until I realized I no longer had a marriage. I'd drifted. Buck had shamefacedly admitted he'd found someone else. That hadn't lasted long, but it hadn't been the problem either. *We'd* been the problem.

Charlie shook his head. "Buck was a real tool."

"It's fine. It wasn't all him."

"Uh, unless you cheated too, it was." He canted his head. "You're compartmentalizing."

"What?"

"It's separating conflicting emotional issues into different compartments, so you don't have to deal with them."

"Maybe. But when stuff goes sideways, you don't always have time to have an emotional breakdown on the scene." Compartmentalization came in handy in a crisis. "How well did you know Donald Rigby?"

"You're doing it again. Or just avoiding."

"Donald?" I prompted.

Charlie scratched his head. "Well, he stole my house."

My chest tightened. I closed the grill. "Did you say that to anyone else?"

"I didn't have to. It was obvious he took it." He rolled his eyes. "I mean, technically, the town took it, and then they sold it to him at a bargain price."

I smothered a groan. Charlie had access to old weapons and reason to want revenge. Though anyone who knew my brother knew he was too laid back to bother.

"Mind watching the barbecue?" I asked. "I'm going to make those margaritas."

"Sure." He plucked the long fork from my hand.

I went inside, moved my knitting off the counter, and got busy with the cabin's blender. If I were the sheriff, Charlie would be at the top of my suspect list, right next to Donald's wife. I'd also think it was a little too convenient that Charlie's sister had been the one to find the body.

I turned off the blender and walked to the open door.

Charlie had one arm around the neck of the stag, on the other side of the railing. His other arm gripped the deer's antlers. Orangish sauce dripped from the deer's mouth. A dark slash of fur above his eyes curved downward, like frowning eyebrows. The deer and Charlie seemed to be wrestling, and the animal had at least a hundred pounds on my brother.

"Uh, Charlie? What's going on?"

My brother grunted. "He's got a buffalo wing. Get it back before he swallows. It'll hurt him."

At least Charlie hadn't taken up a new hobby. "Deer don't eat..." But it obviously had. An orange-sauced wing was sticking out of his mouth. Even the wildlife in Nowhere were screwy.

And I'd no idea what chicken bones would do to a deer. I did know they could be deadly to dogs. Setting down the pitcher, I grabbed the deer's antlers.

"Get the wing!" Charlie released his grip and vaulted over the porch rail. He put the deer in another headlock, one hand on an antler. The deer tossed his head, rearing backward and dragging Charlie with him. My brother held on.

I made a desperate grab and yanked the wing free. "Got it!"

The deer changed tactics, lowering his head and pressing my brother forward.

Charlie swore and bumped against the rail, and I saw the problem. If he let go, the deer would gore him.

"Climb over," I shouted.

Charlie scrambled backward, tumbled over the rail, and slammed into the lidded barbecue. The barbecue skidded, tipped. Steaks, wings, and coals scattered across the wooden d eck.

The deer snorted and vanished around the corner of the cabin.

"Our steaks!" I grabbed the margarita pitcher and poured it over the white-hot coals. They hissed, steam rising.

I set the pitcher down and with the long fork retrieved a steak off the deck. *Dammit*. Those hadn't been cheap. "I guess we're beyond the five-second rule." I turned to my brother.

His hands were clamped to his right thigh. A crimson stain blossomed on his khaki slacks. He grimaced. "He got me."

"Keep the pressure on." Heart thumping, I raced inside and grabbed my first aid kit. I ran back to the porch.

"Let me see," I said.

He grunted and removed his hands. His thigh oozed blood where the antler had gored him.

I held open the door to the diner. Charlie, backlit by the Tuesday morning sun, hobbled inside the Sagebrush leaning on a cane. The urgent care clinic in Hot Springs had been reasonably priced considering its health-spa atmosphere. But they'd done a bang-up job on Charlie's leg.

The diner fell silent. The three old men at the counter swiveled to face us. It was eleven o'clock—after the breakfast rush and before the lunch rush. I'd hoped we'd avoid the hecklers, but the odds had been low. The old men at the counter seemed to be a permanent fixture.

"I heard you wrestled a deer and lost." The older Mr. Washington guffawed. His laugh morphed into a cough, and one of his buddies slapped him on the back.

"Hey," Charlie said, "we saved that deer from death by buffalo wing."

"Why were you feeding a deer buffalo wings?" Gert asked in a faint lilt. It was familiar, but I couldn't place the accent. He adjusted his glasses. His tan jacket was stained, his hands gnarled.

"We weren't." Charlie said. "He stole one off our deck."

"You've got a deck where you live?" Mr. Washington said. "That's one deluxe treehouse."

Gert coughed. "Deer don't eat meat."

"This one did," I said.

"I wouldn't have thought one would go for something spicy like a buffalo wing." Mr. Washington shook his head. "It's the end times, boys. Better load up on peanut butter."

I steered Charlie to the nearest open table, near the counter. I sat facing a window to the patio. The TV flickered at the edge of my vision, and I determinedly stared at the counter area. Watching for what the news might say about me was too tempting. My brother hooked his cane over the back of a chair and dropped into it.

Ivanna bustled to our table and poured us cups of coffee. "Did you really wrestle a deer for a buffalo wing?" She brushed away a loose lock of red with the back of her hand.

"Yup," Charlie said.

She squeezed his shoulder. "You're a true knight." Her gaze flicked to the television, tuned to a baseball game. "Coffee?"

We nodded, and she hustled away.

"You can't avoid every TV in Nowhere," Charlie said quietly.

"I'm not—" I clamped my mouth shut. I'd forgotten that Charlie noticed more than he let on. "I checked the internet last night, while you were with the doctor."

"What for?"

"I was looking for news on Koppel."

"Why?" he asked. "You already know what happened."

Heat flared in my cheeks. "I don't know why I looked." I fiddled with my mug on the table.

"What did the news say?"

There hadn't been any real news. It had all been opinion. The commentators had implied I'd sold Koppel out, looked the other way. It shouldn't have bothered me since none of it was true. A part of me had even felt I'd been reading about a different person, one that wasn't very likable.

Another part of me though...

Years ago, in New York City, two guys had tried to mug me. I hadn't been protecting anyone, they'd came after *me*. As an MP, I guess I'd been lucky, because New York had been the first time someone had seriously tried to hurt me. What had stuck with me most hadn't been my success in escaping. It was the sense that to them, I wasn't a real person. I didn't deserve to live in safety. What happened to me didn't matter. Live, die, disabled... I didn't matter. I'd been nothing to them.

I'd felt something like that reading those articles.

More concerning, there'd been a *lot* of articles. Koppel had been big news. People were interested. And my name was everywhere.

"They got most of the details wrong," I finally said. "But in fairness, no one asked me what really happened."

He leaned forward and mashed his finger into the table. "Isn't that their fault?"

"I haven't been making myself easy to find." And Buck wouldn't have given up my contact info. Not until he knew he could control the narrative. But would he ever be able to? "Buck should call with an update soon," I continued. He'd damned well better.

"Wait." Charlie tucked his chin. "Buck? What does your ex have to do with this?"

"The Koppel job was his. I was doing contract work."

"Wow." His blond brows pulled inward. "That must have been tough."

"Nah." I glanced toward the TV on the wall. It was hard not to stare at the flickering images. "The divorce was amicable."

"I thought he cheated on you."

And the betrayal hadn't hurt that badly. That was when I'd known it was truly over. I'm not proud of the failure, and it *was* a failure. I should have tried harder. But Buck hadn't wanted to, and I hadn't had the heart. "We're still friends."

Charlie cracked his neck. "They're like hypnotists, you know?"

I dragged my gaze from the TV. "Ex-husbands?"

"No, everyone out there." He motioned toward the screen. "They're all trying to make people believe their version of reality. But none of its real. It doesn't matter."

Ivanna stopped beside a table to chat with the handsome gardener, sitting with Pete. She studiously ignored the mayor. The waitress arched her back and shifted her weight, her hip brushing against Pete's arm.

Remembering the gardener's "accidental" grope, I narrowed my eyes. What was a gardener doing talking to the mayor? Granted, this was a small town. Being the mayor wasn't exactly a prestige job here. But...

The gardener had been loitering near that giant can of peas after I'd found the body. He hadn't struck me as an idle curiosity seeker. He didn't strike me as a simple gardener either, work shirt and dirt-stained fingernails to the contrary.

The bell over the front door jangled. Dressed for success in a white golf shirt and gray slacks, Marques Washington walked into the café. He smiled at Molly behind the counter, and the café owner raised a coffeepot in greeting. Marques patted his father's back then strode to the table where the mayor and the gardener sat.

"Last night I found gas cans outside my cannery," Marques boomed in his rich, velvety voice.

The gardener tilted his head, and Ivanna backed from the table. I tried to look disinterested.

Pete regarded Marques warily. "Okay. Sometimes people leave trash—"

"*Full* gas cans." Marques tugged down the cuff of his white dress shirt. "And yes, I already reported it to the sheriff, but I thought you should know."

"Property owners are responsible for any trash discarded on their property," Pete said. "I'm sorry it happened, but you know we don't have patrols."

Two of the old men at the counter ambled from the café, leaving Gert alone.

Charlie waved Gert to our table. Creakily, the old man crossed the checkerboard floor and sat in the free chair between us.

"You remember Gert, don't you?" Charlie asked me. "He sold me most of my medieval weaponry."

I leaned back, listening hard for more interesting intel from Marques. But he seemed to have finished. He crossed to the counter and sat. Ivanna walked around the counter and poured him coffee.

"Reproductions," Gert said. "What brings you back to Nowhere?"

"The Estonian mafia," my brother joked. "She was bodyguarding—"

"Charlie," I said warningly.

"Counter *surveilling* the brother of some mafioso, and he ran off and crashed into a tomato truck. Alice was right behind him. She was right *there*. It was on the news, but they totally screwed up the story."

I grimaced.

"I *did* hear about that," Gert said slowly. "Toomas Koppel."

Ivanna laughed too loudly at something Marques had said, and I glanced at the counter.

"But it's okay," Charlie said. "The Estonian mafia is like the Estonian Vikings. They were so bad at, um, Vikinging..." Charlie frowned. "Well, they were really bad."

"I'm Estonian," Gert said. That was why that faint accent had seemed so familiar. It was an echo of Toomas Koppel's. But that wasn't what made my scalp prickle.

The old man stared at me, his blue eyes arctic.

"Oh." Charlie blinked. "Well, your Vikings probably weren't *that* bad. You know how stories get exaggerated."

"And my associates would be very interested to learn where you are," Gert said to me.

"Associates?" my brother asked.

"In the Estonian mafia," Gert said.

Silence iced our table. Gert's gaze turned several degrees colder. I forced my muscles into relaxed alertness and expanded my awareness. Two exits, front and rear. A family of four behind us. Gardener and mayor talking animatedly in front.

"Heh, good one, Gert." My brother reached across the table and nudged me. "Gert's a real kidder."

"I don't think he's joking." I rested my hands on the table.

Gert nodded once. "Out of respect for your brother, who roofed my garage, I won't tell my associates you're here."

Charlie's muscles relaxed. "See. We can trust Gert."

"I'll have to kill you myself."

"What?" Charlie's eyes widened. "That's not funny. He's joking, Alice. Gert, tell her you're joking."

"But don't worry," Gert said, "I won't defile the body."

Charlie sputtered. "But that's..."

Gert rose, joints cracking. He reached behind him, brushing aside his stained windbreaker and exposing a Glock.

"Gun!" I launched myself at Charlie. The edge of the table struck one thigh. Plates and silverware crashed.

Charlie's eyes grew bigger. "Whoa—"

I slammed into my brother. His chair tilted backward, fell. I slipped my hand behind Charlie's head to protect it, and we landed hard on the linoleum. I rolled off him and to my feet.

Diners stared, open mouthed. The gardener sat frozen, a mug of coffee to his lips. Ivanna stood still, gripping a coffeepot.

Gert held a worn, leather wallet in his hand. "Give me a break. I'm not going to kill you in front of all these people." Shooting me a disgusted look, he tottered to the counter, left a bill, and wobbled out the door.

Warmth crawled up my neck and face. This was almost as bad as the mutton-busting disaster. Except then, an entire rodeo arena had been laughing. I almost wished someone would laugh now to break the silence.

Pete stood so fast his chair clattered to the floor. "Good one, Alice. The twenty's yours." He turned to the other diners. "Just a dumb bet, everyone. I didn't think Alice would do it."

"Yeah," I said weakly. "Heh."

Grumbling, the diners turned back to their meals, and conversations resumed.

"Uh, a little help?" Charlie wheezed from the black-and-white floor.

"I've got you, honey." Ivanna rushed to help my brother up. I set the table on its feet while Ivanna cooed over my brother and brushed off his t-shirt. Charlie stumbled a little, his arm coming around her, and she laughed. Judging by the look on her face, Charlie wasn't going to have to worry about wintering in the treehouse.

"Really?" Pete hissed at me and righted Charlie's chair.

"You don't have to do that, Mr. Mayor." Holding Charlie's elbow with one hand, Ivanna motioned toward the chair he gripped with the other. "I can clean everything up."

"I've got it," Pete said.

"He had a gun," I whispered.

"Everyone has a gun," Pete said. "This is an open carry state."

"I don't have a gun," Charlie said.

"He wasn't open carrying," I said. "He was concealed carrying. And he threatened to kill me."

"And concealed carry is legal with a permit," Pete said, "which I'm sure Gert has."

"Yeah." Charlie brushed off the front of his shirt. "Gert's cool. It's a good thing you tackled me instead of him. He might have gotten hurt."

Here's the thing. I'd seen that hard look in a man's eyes before. Gert hadn't been kidding, and he hadn't been cool.

Gert was going to be a problem.

CHAPTER SIX

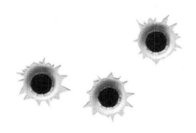

OVER IVANNA'S PROTESTS, PETE and I helped her clear up the broken dishes. It gave me something to do while I pretended not to notice the other customers' stares. In a small town, there's nowhere to slink away and hide.

Fortunately, a new diversion soon arrived.

The café's front door jangled open. A woman in a fitted black suit clacked inside on four-inch heels. She stopped beside the slowly closing door and adjusted the matching wide-brimmed hat that hid her face. She pointed a dramatic, beringed finger at the center of the diner, where Ivanna stood. "*You* killed him."

Heads swiveled to stare at Ivanna. She paled and touched her throat. Pete frowned.

The newcomer made a sweeping gesture, encompassing the entire café. "You *killed* him," she said more loudly and raised her head, exposing her face. She was in her mid-fifties and made up like a cover girl. Her full lips flattened.

A few people glanced at me and Charlie. We were nowhere near where she was pointing. Why were they looking at us? Did they expect me to tackle her to the floor too? I sat to make sure I wasn't raising any expectations.

The newcomer shook her fist. "This *town* killed my husband," she shrieked. She dropped her arm. "I just thought you should know." The woman pivoted and strode out.

Her voice had sounded familiar, but I wanted to be sure. I cleared my throat. "And that was...?"

"Donald's wife, Carmel," Charlie said in a low voice, confirming my suspicion.

I nodded. I hadn't recognized her, but when I'd been a kid, all adults had pretty much looked alike. But her voice, I'd heard in the background when I spoke to Donald at Charlie's old house.

"How deliciously dramatic," I muttered. True, the shock of a sudden death didn't leave the survivors at their personal best. But this had been performance art.

Charlie shot me a critical look.

"She's upset," Pete said. "I'm going to go talk to her." He followed Carmel out the diner's glass front door.

"Wow," I said. "That's government service in a small town."

"I think it's cool," Charlie said. "People take care of each other here."

I folded my arms. "Someone took care of Donald Rigby all right."

"That's not fair," my brother said, looking unhappy.

"I'll be right back." I rose and walked to the counter, where Marques sat. The gardener eyed me. I ignored him.

"Did you move those gas cans you found?" I asked Marques.

"Yes." He sipped his coffee and set down the mug. "I put them in my office. And yes, I wore gloves, so the sheriff can check for prints—if he ever bothers to get here."

"Where exactly did you find them?"

"They were behind the building. Near the rear door."

"Mind if I take a look at the spot?" I asked.

Marques shrugged. "I guess it can't hurt. Let me finish my brunch, and I'll take you there."

I returned to our table. Charlie ordered huevos rancheros. I ordered coffee. Smiling at my brother, I watched the gardener out of my peripheral vision.

He was easy on the eyes, but the gardener didn't do anything interesting. I wasn't sure what I'd expected from him. But that was surveillance. You watched. You waited. You recorded. And okay, I was surveillance, not a detective. But I was going to detect anyway.

Marques rose to go. I slid the keys to my rental across the table to Charlie. "Take my car," I said. "You can stay at the cabin."

"There's nothing wrong with the treehouse."

"There's everything wrong with it. For starters, you can't climb that ladder with an injured leg."

"Wha—" His face crinkled. "Oh."

I left money for the food plus extra for the damage. Marques and I strolled toward the cannery.

"You heard I found Donald Rigby's body?" I asked.

Marques ran a hand over his short, gray hair. "The whole town heard."

"What can you tell me about Rigby?"

He raised an eyebrow. "What do you want to know?"

"I heard he was behind a proposed marijuana resort."

Marques's expression hardened. "Yeah."

"What were the politics involved?"

"The town didn't want it." A piece of trash tumbled past his feet. Absently, he bent and picked it up.

"But the idea had traction," I guessed.

He dropped the paper in a nearby bin. "The mayor was pushing for it. Tax revenue." His mouth twisted.

"I guess it would have meant good money for the town." *And jobs.*

"It would have destroyed Nowhere. This town needs families. Who wants to raise kids in an environment like that? Can you imagine what sort of shops would take over in Main Street? Gone would be the knitting store, the bookstore, the toy store. We've put a lot of work into making Nowhere a clean tourist destination. Families can enjoy themselves and buy souvenirs to remember the nice time they had. All that effort would be wasted."

"Not entirely," I said. "I imagine the marijuana tourists would enjoy the art."

He snorted. "That's not why we built the Big Things."

"Is that why Terrence is so antagonistic toward the mayor?"

"Antagonistic?"

"He spat at Pete yesterday."

Marques sighed. "He shouldn't have done that. But Terrence is an artist with a temperament to match."

I wasn't convinced a giant pizza cutter qualified as art, but I nodded.

"He's intense," Marques continued, "but harmless. Terrence is actually first in line to get an apartment at the cannery." He motioned toward the four-story brick building.

"An apartment?"

"I'm turning it into a mixed-use space, with galleries for local artists on the bottom floor and housing on the upper levels. You ever heard of a business incubator?"

"Cheap rent for start-ups that's usually paired with consulting to help them grow."

"Same deal at the cannery. Low rent for artists and a place to live and sell their work. I want to make Nowhere a place for young, creative people again."

I gazed up at the four-story brick building. "Who owns the cannery?"

"I do."

The property couldn't be worth much. Nothing was worth much in Nowhere. But if Marques succeeded in making Nowhere a tourist destination, the old cannery's value might grow. Would the same be true if the marijuana resort succeeded?

"I'd no idea you were so connected to the art world," I said.

"My kids are both artists."

And if Ivanna was anything to go by, that wasn't an easy career path. I hoped his incubator succeeded in luring Tyrone and Janelle home.

We cut behind the world's biggest can of peas and walked to the back of the cannery. It was weedier in back, the sidewalk cracks deep enough for an Eldritch horror to crawl from.

"Are there actual peas in that can?" I asked.

"Yep. Dried. It's a bona fide can of peas." He paused. "You should have seen the pizza we had to make to prove our pizza cutter worked."

Marques led me to a tattered awning above a metal door. "There." He pointed to the concrete step. A dumpster stood beside it, partially hiding the step from sight.

I shifted my weight. Anyone making a reasonable search should have seen the gas containers. Why hadn't the sheriff found them?

"Do you know if the sheriff searched back here?" I asked.

Marques folded his muscular arms. "As far as I know, he didn't."

And he definitely should have. "How big were the cans?"

"Two gallon. Want to see those too?"

"I think I would." I wasn't sure what I'd find, but *not* taking a look just seemed sloppy.

Marques pulled a key ring from the pocket of his jeans and unlocked the door.

"Who would want to stop your project?" I asked.

"Aside from the mayor and Donald? No one."

I followed Marques inside a cool, brick hallway. "But why would they want to stop you? How could an art gallery hurt a marijuana resort?"

"Donald wanted *this* property for his resort," he said.

We emerged into a spacious room. Sunlight filtered through the papered windows and cast the massive room in a warm glow. A wide, metal staircase led up to an open hallway that wrapped around the second floor. Closed doors led off it. The upper floors had a raised gallery. Natural light streamed through skylights in the fourth-floor ceiling.

"Wow." Once the construction detritus was gone, it would be an amazing space.

"If you were a young artist," he said, "would you live here?"

"In a heartbeat." I saw the advantages of working close to home, not having to commute. Not that living here was in the cards.

"The apartments are going to be on the third and fourth floors. We'll keep the first two floors as studios. Come on up."

I followed him up the steps to the third-floor walkway that ringed the open space.

Bracing his hands on the iron railing, he gazed into the space below, littered with sawhorses and circular saws. "It's going to work," he said quietly.

"And no biggest piece of art in the center?" I pointed.

Marques laughed. "The can of peas is enough for now." He paused. "And what about you? What are you going to do next?" His expression turned serious. "I saw the news."

"I'll find a new assignment," I said tightly, then smiled and raised my chin. "I rarely know what comes next in this business. So for now, I'll enjoy my vacation in Nowhere."

He nodded hesitantly. The phone clipped to his belt rang, and he checked the number. "Sorry, I've got to take this. Do you mind?"

"Nope."

He walked along the railing, and I wandered the raised gallery.

I tried a door. It opened easily, and I peered inside. The room was simple—bare wood and brick with an industrial window. I walked to the chicken-wire window and peered past its panes.

A Jeep cruised past on Main Street below. The Sagebrush's giant coffee pot glinted in the late morning sun. The Sierras rose behind the low, brick buildings, and I inhaled the scent of fresh sawdust.

Nowhere might be dying, but it was beautiful. How had I forgotten that? My breathing slowed.

I left the room and walked up to the next level. A breeze wafted through an open window. It teased the loose strands of hair at my neck, and I shivered. On the opposite end of the gallery, a door stood open. I walked inside.

Windows dotted a brick wall. I stopped and frowned, my pulse speeding. One of the windows was broken, the chicken wire cut. I neared, my boots crunching on glass fragments.

Careful of the shards, I peered outside. Below, a fire escape crooked down the side of the building. This had been no accident. Someone had to work to cut through that chicken wire.

My breath quickened. Why hadn't Marques mentioned this?

Returning to the gallery, I leaned over the metal railing. I scanned the walkways below for Marques, but he'd vanished. A cold tide rippled up my spine.

Something crunched behind me, and I began to turn.

Pain jolted me from behind, knocking me forward. A hand grasped my ankle and pitched me over the railing and into space.

CHAPTER SEVEN

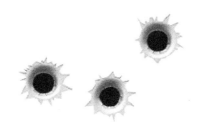

THAT MOVIE TROPE ABOUT near-death experiences running in slow motion? It was real.

I saw the concrete floor flowing nearer. I saw the bars of the metal railing glide past. I saw my hand reach out and grab one of the bars.

Then my arm tried to jerk from my shoulder. Pain screamed through muscles, ligaments, tendons. I dangled one-handed. My feet swayed over four stories of empty space.

Footsteps pattered against bare concrete.

Heart jackhammering beneath my ribs, I swung myself sideways, kicking my leg up and hooking the walkway's floor. Grunting, I levered myself up and through the railing. I lay gasping on the dusty floor.

The remnants of my fear morphed into anger, and heat flushed through my veins. My attacker hadn't come to the cannery just to push me over a railing. He'd had another goal in mind.

And I'd screwed up.

Below me, a door slammed. I staggered to a window facing Main and brushed construction dirt off my shirt. A tour bus puffed down the street.

Shoulders hunched, Mrs. Malone leaned on her cane and watched it go. From this height, she looked frail, vulnerable, and my heart pinched.

I shook myself. Mrs. Malone wouldn't appreciate my pity. Maybe she had a full and exciting life I knew nothing about. I scanned the street for anyone emerging from behind the cannery. No one did.

The old lady straightened her shoulders and marched away.

Footsteps sounded on the metal stairs, and I turned.

Marques huffed. "What do you think?"

"Is your office on this floor?" I asked more sharply than I'd intended.

"Yes. Why?"

I rubbed my palm, red and scraped and burning. "Someone tried to push me over the balcony." I pointed to the open door. "It looks like they broke a window and got in through the fire escape."

"What?" His brown eyes widened. "Who did it? Are you all right?" He looked me over, his gaze stopping at the dirt on the knees of my jeans.

"I didn't see him. He was behind me." Remembering that ankle grab, I shuddered.

He pulled his cell phone from his belt. "I'm calling the sheriff again."

"Let's see what the intruder came for first." I massaged my shoulder. I needed ice or I'd be in a world of pain tomorrow. "Where's your office?"

"This way."

We walked to the office at the south end of the building. The door stood open.

Marques stopped short inside. "The gas cans. They're gone."

So the guy who'd tossed me over the balcony *had* come for the evidence. I stared out the office window. Outside, the giant flamingo stared back at me. "That's that then."

Marques did call the sheriff again. And the sheriff arrived three hours later. *Three. Hours.* I suspected businessmen in Hot Springs didn't have to wait so long for his attention. But in fairness, the emergency had passed. There was no reason for speed.

And at least the sheriff himself had come rather than sending a deputy. He met us on the ground floor, scattered with tools and equipment.

Sheriff Randall raised a skeptical and bushy eyebrow. "He pushed you over the rail," he said, expression dubious.

I sat on a sawhorse and forced myself not to cross my arms defensively. *Act relaxed.* "Push plus an ankle pick."

He shook his head. "And you managed to catch the rail and haul yourself back."

"I try to stay fit." Also, I'd gotten really, really lucky. I shuddered.

"And you came here to look at two abandoned gas cans," he said flatly.

I felt a vein pulse in my forehead, a rhythmic twitch I hoped he didn't see. "Yeah, well." I shrugged. "I was curious." I half laughed. "Look, I know I'm not a detective—"

"That's for sure."

"But I found the body. I met Donald the day he died. I was—"

"Curious."

"Yeah. It just seemed a little strange that there'd be two abandoned gas cans so close to the murder scene."

His face shuttered.

"Doesn't it?" I asked uncertainly.

"You can go."

I hesitated, realized sticking around wouldn't gain me anything, and fled outside.

The summer day had cooled, the sun lowering toward the western mountains. Uncertain, I looked up and down the wide street. A tour bus rumbled past. Tourists headed for their next destination leaned sleepily against the windows.

My stomach growled. What I needed was comfort food. I crossed Main Street to the pizza parlor, one of three businesses in the brick building, and stopped in the doorway, my eyes adjusting to the sudden change in light.

Charlie waved to me from a booth, and I made my way to them through the pepperoni-scented air. A slight, pretty, young woman with longish, near-black hair sat opposite him. She wore an oddly thick, gray shawl over her slender shoulders.

"Hey," Charlie said. "Want to join us? We can't finish our combo."

I glanced at the woman. She wasn't wearing a shawl; it was a blanket. "Sure." I squeezed in beside my brother, and he shifted over.

"This is Lilyanna," he said. "Lilyanna, this is my sister, Alice. Lilyanna's in the MBS, that's the—"

"Medieval Battle Society," I said. "I think I'm catching on."

We shook hands across the table. Lilyanna's grip was firm, and pain flared through my palm, its skin roughened by my grab for the railing.

I forced a smile. "It's nice to meet you." I waited for an explanation about the blanket. The parlor's A/C was on, but it wasn't *that* cold.

"You too." Lilyanna blushed and stood. "I'll see you tomorrow, Charlie." Pulling the blanket tighter, she hurried from the pizza parlor.

"Was it something I said?" I asked.

"No, she's fine."

"What's with the blanket?" I slid from the booth and took Lilyanna's vacant seat.

"It's weighted," my brother said. "A security thing. I mean, psychological security. Lilyanna's got a portfolio career like me. She's a player at the theater too. And other stuff."

I scratched my cheek. "Which is so stressful she needs a security blanket?"

"No, it's not that. I'm just explaining why she had to go tearing out of here."

When he didn't elaborate, I said, "I thought I'd talk to Donald's wife, Carmel."

"No, no. It's pronounced *car*-mel, like the candy."

"Thanks for the head's up." I held out my hand, palm up. "Can I have my keys?" I didn't feel like walking to her house.

"Sure." He dug in the pocket of his board shorts and slid the keys across the table.

"You okay getting back to the cabin without the car?" I nodded to the crutches, leaning against the table.

"Oh, yeah. I've got a buddy who can give me a lift. Why do you want to talk to Carmel?"

I pocketed the keys. "Condolences, mainly," I hedged. At least, condolences would be my excuse. The scene she'd made at the Sagebrush had felt staged. And that made me curious.

"Carmel's not at home though," Charlie continued. "Right now she's at the Viking bar."

"The Vi—" I paused. "Let me get this straight. Nowhere doesn't have a medical clinic. It doesn't have a supermarket. But it's got a Viking bar?"

"Where else are you going to find indoor ax throwing? And mead?"

Okay, I'd always wanted to try ax throwing. And mead. "Good point. Who needs groceries? How do you know she's there?"

"I just finished installing purse hooks beneath their bar." He grinned. "Thanks to my portfolio career, I can throw axes there free, anytime I want. Except on evenings or weekends."

"Is it hard?" I snagged a slice of pizza, loaded with meat and dripping cheese.

"Throwing axes?" He squinted at me. "I guess. I'm not very good. I think it all has to do with distance. What are you doing tomorrow afternoon?"

I slid from the booth and stood. "Washing the cabin's back porch. My shoes are sticking to it since we dumped that pitcher of margarita."

"*You* dumped it. Uh, hey, I was thinking... Since you're a body—executive protection specialist and all, you might want an executive protection gig here."

I took a bite of the pizza. The sauce was spicy and as good as the toppings. "Someone in Nowhere needs protection?" I canted my head. "And they can pay?"

He tugged at his t-shirt. "Um, I don't know about *pay...*"

"No thanks." I turned to leave.

"Lilyanna's being harassed at one of her gigs by some guys from Hot Springs. Sorry, The 'Town' of Hot Springs." He put the word in air quotes. "I promised I'd help her out tomorrow, but with my leg..." He raised his cane and thumped it on the thin carpet.

"If this is happening on the job, why isn't her employer taking care of the problem?"

He pressed himself against the booth's back. "Yeah. Well. It's not that simple. She's sort of freelance."

Oh, *this* should be interesting. "Go on."

"She's Captain Rabbit. And she's amazing at it. She loves the kids, but these guys—"

"Hold on. What's Captain Rabbit?"

"You know, the mascot for that slushie company?"

I nodded, not because I knew anything about slushie mascots, but because she must have been the rabbit I'd seen when I'd first arrived.

"She's got this great rabbit costume," he continued, "and she stands outside different convenience stores. But there's these rich jerks from Hot Springs—"

I made an empty-sounding laugh. "No."

"No what?"

"No, I'm not guarding a slushie mascot."

"But it's what you do."

I took another bite. "I'm on vacation, and my specialty is countersurveillance."

"Well, yeah, but—"

"I don't do close protection anymore."

"But you guarded that Saudi princess."

He'd remembered that? I was touched.

"And Lilyanna needs your help," he continued.

"It sounds like she needs *your* help."

"How am I supposed to help anyone with this leg?" He stuck his wrapped leg into the aisle.

"It is a puzzle. Tell your friend to stay inside the store. Odds are the guys giving her trouble won't bother her where there are video cameras and trigger-happy cashiers."

"She can't stand inside the store. The whole point is she has to stand *outside* to attract customers. Come on, Alice. Just do it for me."

I raised a brow. "And what's in it for me?"

"Are you kidding?" He slapped his palm on the wooden table and rolled his eyes. "We're going to do this again?"

"Do what?"

"I ask you for a favor. You say what's in it for me. Then we bargain, and I blackmail you into it, or you blackmail *me* into something. You always do this."

"So do you," I said, indignant. He'd been an expert at extortion since he'd caught me climbing out a window to meet Pete. I'd done his homework for a month to keep him quiet. Since he'd only been seven at the time, it had been easy. But who knows what damage that missing homework had done to his childhood development?

"But I do it because it's fun," he said.

"That's why I do it. It's the—"

"Principle of the thing," he finished for me. "I know."

"Okay then. See ya." I stuffed the rest of the slice in my mouth and headed out the door.

The Viking bar was on the next block, wedged between the wine bar and what appeared to be a speakeasy. I still couldn't believe Nowhere had multiple bars. When I'd been a kid, Nowhere had been snoozeville. Now it was... weird, but interesting.

I pushed through the meadery's arched wooden door and blinked in the gloom.

Wooden shields lined the blond-wood walls, and tables and chairs in matching wood filled the room. It was after four o'clock, and the bar had a lonely air.

A man in a Viking helmet and a pale, red tunic morosely polished a beer stein. I ducked my head. Brass purse hooks lined up neatly beneath the bar.

THUNK. I started, realized the sound had come from another room, and straightened.

"Can I help you?" the bartender asked.

"I was just checking to make sure you had purse hooks. I never drink in a bar without them."

He beamed. "Really?"

I nodded. "These are A-plus."

A woman whooped in another room.

"Ax throwing?" I pointed toward the sound.

"Yeah," he said. "You can take a look if you want."

I followed the thuds to a wide room with targets on the far wall. Two parallel lines, one blue and one red, had been painted on the floor. The red line was closer to the targets. I guessed you weren't supposed to cross it. A few high, round tables stood at the rear of the room, away from the targets.

At the blue line, Carmel aimed an ax, cocked her arm back, and threw. The ax landed center target. *Yikes.* She laughed and grabbed a foaming stein of beer from the high table beside her. A generous portion slopped onto the wood floor.

"Carmel?"

She turned to me. "Yeah?" The widow had been dressed for chic mourning when she'd stormed the Sagebrush. Now she wore a tight white t-shirt and painted-on suede pants.

"I'm Alice Sommerland." I waited for a reaction, but she only stared at me. "I... found your husband's body. I'm very sorry for your loss."

"Oh, yeah," she said in a bored tone. "You're the one who offed that Koppel guy."

I folded my arms, my neck stiffening. "He drove into a tomato truck."

"Sure." She turned and picked up another ax from the table and aimed. "It's okay. If you did kill Koppel, he totally deserved it. Did he put the moves on you?"

"No." Koppel had been weirdly respectful. If I hadn't known what a creep he was, I might have even liked him. Hey, I was as vulnerable to charm as the next woman. I edged to the side.

She turned, a hand ax slung over one shoulder. "Want to play? It's like darts."

It didn't look like darts. But I nodded. People loosened up more easily when there was a shared activity involved. Or at least that had been true when I'd been dating back in the dark ages. Buck and I hadn't really dated. We'd just happened.

"You'll have to get your axes from the bartender," she said. "And I'll have a beer."

Dutifully, I trotted to the bar and paid for axes and two beers. I returned to the ax throwing room.

Carmel belched. "I'll go first. To demonstrate." She tossed three axes into the target, dead center. It was a good thing she hadn't suggested playing for money. "That's one round. We each get three rounds with three axes."

I wrinkled my forehead. "Is there a trick to this?"

"It's all in the wrist. Chalk's over there." She pointed to a small, round table. A gray wedge of chalk lay atop it. "So what was Koppel like?"

My face tightened. I didn't want to talk about Koppel. I wanted to talk about her husband. But it looked like Koppel was going to be the price I paid for Carmel's time. Plus the beer and axes. "He was charming," I said.

"That makes sense."

I rubbed the chalk between my palms, stepped to the blue line, and mimicked her two-handed, overhead throw. The ax bounced off the wall and skittered along the floor. I puckered my lips.

"That happens," she said. "You just gotta figure out the right spot to throw from. Try again."

I threw my other two axes and got similar crummy results. Carmel threw, and her ax thunked into the target. *Note to self: do not mess with Carmel.* At least not while she was near any axes.

"So if you didn't kill him, who did?" she asked. "Koppel, I mean."

I stretched my mouth into a smile. "He did it to himself. He was driving too fast and lost control." Why was she more interested in asking me about Koppel than about her husband?

Not liking how good she was with those axes, I didn't bring up her husband again until she'd won three games.

"Loser takes the axes back," she caroled and wobbled into the bar.

I collected the axes and joined her at the bar.

"Loser also buys the next round," she said.

I grimaced. I'd already bought a round, but rules were rules.

We sat at the bar and nursed our beers. Behind us, four people in medieval costumes sat around a wooden table and played a card game.

"I'm sorry about your husband," I repeated lamely.

"Yeah. Well. Don't be. He was a bastard."

Oh, really? "I'm sorry he was a bastard then."

She hiccupped. "Whatever. It's over now."

"Is it?"

She swiveled to face me, and her eyes narrowed. "What's that supposed to mean?"

I'd put my foot in it. I fumbled. "I just meant they haven't caught the guy who did it yet."

"Huh. I'm only surprised no one killed him sooner."

"Oh? Why?"

She belched. "He was like Koppel."

"A blackmailer?"

"A charming rogue."

Huh. "What do you think he was he doing by the cannery so late at night?"

She shrugged. "He told me he had a midnight craving for nachos. I guess he was lying. Again."

"He went on a nacho run at midnight?" I could get nachos in Nowhere? At midnight? The changes in my hometown weren't all bad.

"No," Carmel said, "he left the house around eleven-thirty. But he would have *gotten* the nachos by midnight."

"Do you have any idea who might have wanted him dead?"

Her laugh was hard and flat. "Oh, yeah."

"Who?"

"Are you going to finish that beer?"

"Why?" I asked. "Do you want it?"

"I don't trust people who don't drink."

Oh, come on. Reluctantly, I took a gulp. She stared. I chugged to the bottom, set down the mug, and smothered a burp. I didn't drink on the job as a protection specialist. Was this normal in detective work? Because it didn't seem very professional.

She motioned to the bartender. "Another round."

I blinked at her empty stein. How had she finished her own beer so fast?

The bartender brought us two fresh steins. He was a pro. There was hardly any head on the tops.

"Sho—" I shook my head. The beer was hitting me harder than I'd expected, but I hadn't been training for it like Carmel. "So who do you think killed your husband?"

"Oh," she slurred, "I know things."

Yes, and what *things?* I bounced my heel on the footrest. This was what I got for interrogating someone over drinks. Not that I was in much better condition. I should have left the keys with Charlie. I'd have to walk back to my cabin tonight.

I switched tactics. "What was he like?"

"Who?"

"Donald."

"Oh. Up to no good. Losing money we didn't have."

"Gambling?" I hazarded.

"The idiot." She downed the beer and banged the mug on the slick, wooden bar. "Another round, barkeep!"

He set two more beers on the bar. I clutched my stomach. This was just stupid. There was no way I could drink it. I shoved mine toward Carmel. "Thanks, but—"

"Are you trustworthy or not? This beer is made right here, in Nowhere. What kind of person doesn't drink local beer?"

She watched me force the beer down then slid the other stein toward me. "Skoll!"

I took a sip. "You were saying about gambling?"

"What?"

The card players at the nearby table roared. One pounded the table with the hilt of his short sword.

"Donald's gambling," I shouted.

"Have another beer."

My so-called interrogation went on for two more teeth-clenching rounds. I couldn't figure out if Carmel was just looking for a drinking buddy, or if this was a plot to put me under the table. But Carmel learned more about Koppel and countersurveillance than I did about her dead husband.

She also had somehow achieved a plastic Viking helmet. I think one came free with every ten mugs of beer.

She adjusted the horns and slid off the stool. "Magic mushroom time!"

Oh, hell no. Were those legal now too? "No, Carmel. That's not—"

She staggered out the door.

Halfway to embalmed, I followed. If she was going to try to drive home, I was at least going to stop her. I'd had enough fatal car crashes in my life. Outside, night had fallen and the drop in temperature felt delicious against my skin. I must have spent four hours throwing axes and drinking beer, and I was a little overheated.

Carmel zigzagged across Main Street and stumble-jogged the two blocks to the mushroom park. She disappeared behind a spotted toadstool.

By the time I caught up with her, she'd clambered into the low branches of a nearby pine.

Stomach churning, I glanced around the park for deputies or officious rangers but the streets were empty. "Carmel, be careful."

She climbed higher and inched out on a branch above an enormous metal mushroom. "Come on. It's easy." She waved and fell off the branch.

I gasped.

But Carmel was either very lucky or very acrobatic. She landed on the violet mushroom, crumpled into a heap, and sat up. "Come on. It's a great view."

Making room, she slithered toward the edge, and I sucked in another sharp breath. The top of the mushroom was a good eight feet off the ground. If she fell, she could really hurt herself. I'd never had to deal with an inebriated client, but I'd heard stories. None were good. But I climbed the tree. Inching out on the branch, I swung down and landed dizzily beside her.

I sat before I could fall down. Maybe I'd earned one of those Viking helmets too. I should have asked the bartender.

"Sit, sit," she said.

"I am sitting," I complained. The park spun. It was irritating.

"Groovy." She set her helmet on my head and slithered sideways, vanishing over the side of the mushroom.

"Carmel?" I shouted after her, my voice shrill.

Laughing maniacally, she ran down the street. I swore and hiccupped. Carmel had been lucky she hadn't broken an ankle. At least she'd left the helmet.

I peered over the side of the mushroom. The ground looked far, far away. My head spun. There was nothing to grip on the edge of the mushroom so I could dangle and drop.

Sure, Carmel had done it. But Carmel struck me as one of those fortunate people who careens from disaster to disaster unscathed. Recent experience had amply demonstrated I was not one of those people.

But if I could grab the branch, I could climb back the way I'd come. Carefully, I stood and stretched for the pine branch. It was two inches too high. I stood on my toes. My fingertips brushed rough bark. Lowering onto my heels, I rubbed my hands together. No biggie. I could do this.

I jumped. One hand closed on the branch. *Ha!*

I blamed what happened next on my prior injury from getting thrown over the railing. The branch scraped from my grasp. My feet hit the mushroom and skidded from beneath me. My butt landed hard, knocking the wind from me. I was sliding.

I sucked in a breath, my heart lurching. "Oh, my G—"

"Oof," my landing pad said.

I tumbled to the ground in a tangle of arms and legs and rolled onto my back. I stared up at the night sky. That hadn't gone the way I'd planned. But I was down, and the landing hadn't been bad at all.

The gardener propped himself on one elbow and cocked a dark brow. "If you wanted to get to know me better, all you had to do was ask."

CHAPTER EIGHT

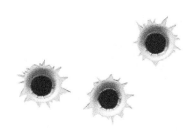

IN THE MUSHROOM'S MOONLIT shadow, I picked up the helmet, which had tumbled to the ground, and scrambled to my feet. I stumbled over a pinecone and windmilled my arms for balance.

The gardener brushed off his jeans, stood, and wrinkled his nose. "You smell like Valhalla."

"I just got..." I straightened and looked around. Carmel was long gone, along with the shreds of my dignity. I brushed off my jeans. "Who *are* you?"

"Arnie Smith."

He didn't look like an Arnie. Or even an Arnold. He looked like a Slate or a Liam or a Jared. But we couldn't help the names our parents stick us with. *Alice* was coming back in fashion, but it hadn't been when I was growing up.

Skeptical, I eyed the muscles bulging beneath his t-shirt. "And you're a gardener." He looked more like a bouncer. Who'd once been a model. But he *could* have gotten those muscles lifting sacks of manure.

"It beats the gym." He crossed his arms, an effect I was pretty sure he knew made his muscles bulge. "And you're... a Viking?"

I put the helmet behind my back. "I'm Alice. Alice Sommerland."

He snapped his fingers. "Hold on. You're that bodyguard."

My stomach plummeted. *Him, too?* "Executive protection."

"Whatever." His gaze burned me. "Wow. Alice Sommerland. So what really happened to Koppel?"

My fingers twitched. "A tomato truck. A tomato truck is what really happened." Despite the chill evening air, a bead of sweat trickled down my scalp.

He leaned against the mushroom stalk. "Yeah," he drawled. "I know it was a tomato truck, but—"

"You're not from around here, are you?" I interrupted before the conversation strayed into tinfoil hat land. I was already sick of that place.

"Nope. I'm from Reno. Marques hired me to do the landscaping for the Big Things."

I almost told him I was from Reno too out of habit. Then I remembered that had never been true. "And you're doing a little night gardening?"

"Nah, I knocked off work a couple hours ago. I stopped for a pizza before heading home. What are you doing out here?"

"Climbing mushrooms. Have you been working in Nowhere long?" Was I being obvious about my interrogation? It felt a little obvious.

"Three weeks," he said.

So he was a stranger to Nowhere, an outsider. Thus, he probably didn't have any reason to want Rigby dead. *Thus?* The meadery had done something to my brain. I rubbed the back of my neck.

"Why are you looking at me that way?" he asked.

"What way?"

"Like a wolf eyeballing a chick in a red cape."

"I'm not," I said. "It's the mushrooms. They make everyone think in terms of fairytales."

"I'm not sure *Alice in Wonderland* qualifies as a fairytale, but I take your meaning. So what about you? You local?"

"I used to be," I said. "I'm visiting."

"When did you get into town?"

The beer was still working its way through my system, and my gaze drifted. I pulled it back to him and glared. What was he interrogating *me* for? I was the one doing the interrogating.

"Recently," I said.

"Ah." He shoved his hands into the pockets of his jeans. "Did you know the guy who got killed?"

My stomach knotted. "Not really." This wasn't idle conversation. He was fishing. But for what? Why? What did he have to do with Rigby's death?

"It's funny," Arnie said. "The town doesn't seem too busted up by Rigby's murder. And you'd expect they would be, this being such a small place."

He was right. The small-town murder should have sent shock waves through the community. Conversations at the café should have been muted. People should be regarding me—a relative stranger—with suspicion. But they weren't. Life was going on as usual. And that was... strange. I stared at the lawn.

"I heard he and his wife moved back here recently," I said. "Maybe that's why the response has been lowkey."

"His wife..." He glanced up at the violet mushroom. "*That's* who the other woman on the mushroom was. What were you two doing up there?"

"It seemed like a good idea at the time," I muttered.

He didn't respond.

Something rustled in the nearby pine. A hostage negotiator once told me that saying nothing is a great interrogation technique. People don't like conversational gaps. The urge to fill them is nearly irresistible.

I was having a hard time resisting it, but my inhibitions had been lowered. I shouldn't have had all that beer.

"We met in the Viking bar," I finally said, giving up. It was true without giving anything away. And it lent verisimilitude to why we'd been up on the mushroom. *Heh.* And I could still remember words like *verisimilitude*.

"I hear the world's biggest throwing ax is next on the list for Nowhere," he said.

"I think that is a fantastic idea. Nowhere needs a giant throwing ax."

He laughed, a rich, rolling sound. "If no one's died by corkscrew yet—"

"I know, right?"

"How are you getting home?"

"I'm walking," I lied. Because I wasn't going home yet. First, I wanted to see where *he* went.

"I'll give you a ride."

Ah, no, that wasn't going to work. "I meant I'm taking a rideshare." Did those even exist in Nowhere? If they didn't, I was in trouble. Not because I couldn't find my own way home, but because I was in no shape to drive.

He looked up and down Main Street. "I'll wait with you."

Augh! Did my suspect *have* to be chivalrous? Because it was really inconvenient. Though in fairness, I still wasn't sure if he was a suspect or just a suspicious stranger.

I dug my phone from my pocket and sent for a rideshare. The good news was one was only five minutes away. The bad news was it was going to be a long five minutes. I didn't trust Arnie. And I didn't trust myself not to give away information I shouldn't. For all I knew, I already had.

"I hear you're Charlie's sister," he said.

I took a step backward and jammed my hands in the pockets of my jeans. How'd he hear that? Earlier, he'd acted like he'd only just figured out who I was.

"Marques told me Charlie's sister was in town," he continued. "I'm guessing you're her."

Okay, so that wasn't a huge deductive leap. Or was it *inductive*? I always mixed up those two. "Yeah."

If I kept my words monosyllabic—another excellent word—I couldn't give too much away.

Something rustled in the bushes. A stag emerged on the lawn. It stopped and stared accusingly.

"The deer around here aren't shy." Arnie cocked his head. "Maybe the Big Things *are* getting to me. This deer looks like an angry cartoon character."

"It's the dark fur over its eyes. It looks like cartoon eyebrows." Or did deer have hair? *Whatever.*

The stag ducked his head and passed beneath the giant mushrooms. He vanished into the pines.

"How's Charlie doing?" Arnie asked.

I stared after the deer, then shook myself. "You know him?"

He shrugged, an odd, catlike movement. "It's a small town."

Even after multiple beers, I knew that wasn't an answer.

"I heard he's living in a treehouse," he said.

"Not anymore. He's staying at my motel."

"That place by the discount cemetery?"

Dammit. Why hadn't I kept to one-word answers? Now he knew where I lived. I'd only been in Nowhere for three days and already I was losing my edge.

"What's the deal with that cemetery anyway?" he asked. "What's the discount?"

"Two for one plots."

He canted his head. "That *is* a pretty good deal."

"Unless you only need one." *Like me.* Gray sadness weighted my chest. I shook myself. I tended toward self-pity after too much alcohol and a divorce.

An SUV approached. I studied it then pretended to check my phone. "Nope, that car's too big to be mine. So how'd you get into gardening?"

"My father was a landscape architect."

Becoming a gardener seemed like a comedown from landscape architect, but I was too polite to say so. We stood in awkward silence until a blue Honda Accord glided to a halt in front of us.

"This is mine. Bye." I slithered into the car, set the helmet on the seat beside me, and shut the door.

Arnie took a step back but didn't seem in any hurry to move on.

The seventy-something driver turned to me. Her long, gray hair was bound up in a braid. "Hi. You Alice?" Her voice had a bell-like quality to it.

I hoped I didn't get sick in her car. I nodded.

"We're going to the airport?" she asked.

"No, I need you to take a detour first."

"It doesn't work that way. I'm paid by the destination, which you plugged into the app."

"I'll give you a hundred dollars plus whatever's on the meter."

"There's no meter." She shook her head. "Whatever. It's a deal."

She fiddled with her cell phone. "Where to?"

"Drive to the next block and turn right at the corner."

The car drove slowly down Main Street. I looked out the rear window. Arnie still stood on the sidewalk, watching. We turned the corner.

"Okay," I said, "stop here for a minute."

She did, and I stepped from the car. I walked to the corner and peered around the brick building.

Arnie ambled down the street. The lights on an SUV flashed, and he climbed inside.

I hurried back to the car and got in. "Okay, we're following the blue Ford Explorer, but we need to keep well back. Circle the block and take Main Street—odds are he's headed to the highway."

"Right-o."

Soon we were following Arnie down the winding, mountain road. His taillights flashed around a bend and disappeared.

"How far do you think he's going?" the driver asked.

I leaned forward. "Reno, I think." I paused. She was keeping an ideal surveillance distance. "You're good at this."

"This isn't my first rodeo," she said, and I filed that remark away for later exploration. She glanced in the mirror. "You look familiar."

No, *no, no*. My rideshare driver could *not* know who I was. Who paid attention to the TV these days? Wasn't corporate media dead yet? "I have one of those faces."

"No, you don't. I'm sure I've seen you somewhere before."

"I grew up in Nowhere."

"No, that's not it. Wait." She snapped her fingers. "You're the bodyguard who let that dirtbag get killed."

I stared fixedly out the car window. "I was only countersur—" *Oh, why bother?* I sank lower in my seat. "He stole my car."

"Doesn't seem like a good reason to kill him."

"I didn't kill him. It was an accident."

She snorted. "Convenient accident. Now the big fish are going to get away. All those politicians and CEOs..." The driver shook her head.

A hole opened in my chest. I'd wanted the big fish to see justice too. It seemed they rarely did.

"So what are you doing here?" she asked. "Are you trying to clear your name?"

"My ex—my company's working on that. The thing is, I wasn't Koppel's bodyguard. I was countersurveillance. It was just bad luck he decided to steal *my* car..."

She angled her head. "Hm."

I gnawed my bottom lip. "Okay, we had adjoining suites, so it was easier for him to drug me. And then all he had to do was tell the valet he wanted my car, and the guy just gave it to him."

"Why?"

"He had my name and room number. The hotel staff had seen us together. I played his girlfriend at dinner one night. The adjoining suites were to help sell it, and..." And why was I telling her all this?

"Uh," I said, "I'd prefer it if you didn't let it get around you gave me a lift. I'm trying to keep a low profile until my company can get the word out about what really happened."

"I'm no narc." She shook her head. "I never believed what they were saying about you on Twitter anyway. No one could be *that* stupid."

"Thanks," I said uncertainly.

"And you don't look like the kind of person who'd take a payoff."

"Thanks," I said with more feeling.

"So who do you think killed him?"

I held my breath for a long moment, then exhaled. "It was a tomato truck."

"A tomato truck is never just a tomato truck," she intoned. "There were ex-presidents he had the goods on. CEOs. Congress critters. Movie stars—not that *they'd* care."

Numb from alcohol and the general zeitgeist, I sank deeper into the car seat. The truth—a tomato truck—was as exciting as the DMV. People would believe what they wanted to. I crossed my arms and gazed out the window. It didn't matter. Once the truth came out that I'd been an innocent observer, my life would return to normal.

A leaden feeling quivered in my stomach. I realized I was sobering up fast.

"Look," I said, "there are easier ways to fake a murder than death by tomato truck."

"Oh?"

"Like pushing the car into a gulch..." My throat squeezed. Why had I brought that up? Because my father had died in an accident, when his car had gone over a nearby cliff? He'd swerved to avoid a deer, and then swerved again to avoid an oncoming station wagon rounding a bend. That second swerve had gone too far, he'd lost control. Nowhere was dredging up all sorts of bad memories.

"Are there any gulches in Sonoma?" she asked.

"There are plenty of places to drop a car," I said with more certainty than I felt.

"Hm."

"The real question is why did he leave the hotel so late at night, and alone? He stole my car—"

"Because if he'd taken a cab or a rideshare, there would have been a record."

I nodded, then realized she couldn't see me in the back seat. "Exactly."

We joined the stream of taillights on the highway and headed north toward Reno.

"You think whoever he was meeting is connected to this part of Nevada?" she asked. "Is that why you're here?"

No. "It's a theory," I said, noncommittal.

She made a low whistle. "I'm Perella, by the way."

"Alice."

"I knew that."

"Oh. Right." I looked out the window. Darkness flashed past.

We followed Arnie into Reno. He'd been driving at the speed limit, so it took us almost exactly forty minutes to get there. He crossed the river walk, passed a cluster of modern office buildings, and continued into a darker, dingier part of town. Here, the squat brick buildings were boarded up, windows papered over. It reminded me of the backside of Nowhere, and that was even more depressing.

Arnie turned into a down-at-the-heels five-story brick building. His car vanished into its underground parking garage.

"Stop here," I said, and she pulled to the sidewalk. I gave her a hundred. "Can you wait?"

"Yeah, I'll wait."

"Ah, mind if I leave my helmet?"

"I'm not going to steal it, if that's what you're worried about."

"Thanks." Breathless, I hurried across the street to the office building. I stumbled on the sidewalk, and forced myself to slow, steady myself.

Surprisingly, the doors were unlocked. No guard met me in the lobby. Either this was a better part of town than I'd figured, or the tenants were irrationally optimistic.

I waited by the elevator and watched the arrowlike dial swivel above it. The elevator creaked and groaned as it crept upward. The arrow stopped at the number three.

I dashed up the stairwell—there was no way I was chancing that elevator. Gripping the handrail, I took the stairs two at a time to the third floor.

Frosted glass doors lined the carpeted hallway. I paced down the hall and stopped at a door, its pebbled glass lit from behind.

RHODES INVESTIGATIONS

Taped in the bottom right corner was a Help Wanted sign. Well, a three-by-five index card with *help wanted* scrawled on it.

I knocked and walked inside the office.

Arnie—if that was really his name—half sat, one leg dangling, on the corner of a scarred wooden desk. It was the type of desk that should have a buxom, sharp-eyed receptionist behind it. He held a stack of mail in his hands.

His emerald eyes widened briefly, and I was gratified to see I'd surprised him. But he recovered quick enough.

"We should talk," he said.

CHAPTER NINE

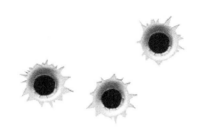

I CONSIDERED AND DISCARDED several responses, like, *Ah ha*. And, *Well, well, well*. And even, *What's a nice private eye like you doing in a place like Nowhere?* I settled for, "I take it you're not a gardener. Or even an Arnie."

The office matched the promise of the building's exterior—bland and old, with beige walls, a map of Reno on the wall, and thin, gray carpet. It also smelled like pine. I guessed the plastic air freshener on the desk was the culprit. A single closed wooden door stood at one end—the inner sanctum?

He cocked his head toward the reversed name on the pebbled glass door. "The name's *Rhodes*."

"Yeah, I got that from the name on the door." Honestly, I had.

"Fitch Rhodes."

"Alice Sommerland." I dropped into a chair against the wood-paneled wall. The chair fought back, a spring pinging.

"I already knew that. You're the bodyguard who got Koppel killed."

"I didn't—" *Why bother?* "I was having a bad night."

"A stunning understatement."

"It's more believable than you as a gardener."

"Is it?" he asked. "Where'd you learn to run a tail? That's not a typical bodyguard skill."

"My specialty is countersurveillance. Sometimes we get runners. Clients who want to sneak off. We don't want another Princess Di scenario—"

"Were you involved in that too?"

My jaw tightened. *Save me from wannabe comedians.* "How old do you think I am?"

"Early forties?"

"Late thirties," I snapped. "I'm just saying, we don't want to spook someone we're tailing into reckless driving."

His smile was condescending. "Is that what happened with Koppel?"

"If that was what had happened, do you think..." I sputtered. "Of course it wasn't what happened."

The PI waited, his expression politely expectant.

"Not that it's any of your business, but he stole my SUV. By the time I found a cab, the only way I could trail Koppel was using the anti-theft tracker in my car. I didn't even witness the accident. I got there too late."

"That wasn't in the news." He motioned me onward. "But do go on. I find myself oddly fascinated."

He was the last person I wanted to spill my guts to. But if I was going to get his story, it only seemed fair I told him mine. "I wasn't supposed to be guarding Koppel. I was countersurveillance. He had his own close protection team."

Frowning, he straightened on the desk. "He had his own team? You weren't part of it?"

"Koppel said he didn't trust them. He wanted an outsider watching for trouble."

He raised his eyebrows. "And you went along with that?"

I clawed back my hair. "It *did* seem like a bad idea at the time."

An air conditioner rumbled, a ghostly breeze wafting across my skin.

He shifted on the desk. "Then why'd you take the job? The guy was a creep and a blackmailer. Why protect Koppel?"

"Because I wanted to see him take the stand," I said hotly.

Yes, Koppel was a lowlife. He'd deserved to be dropped into a dark hole and forgotten. But the rich politicians who took advantage of his estates and underage girls were worse. They were still out there, enjoying their lives. They needed to be called to account. Now, they wouldn't be.

"So you volunteered to watch him." Fitch's green eyes narrowed.

My blood pounded in my ears. "No. Are you kidding me? Koppel was gross. But he asked my ex—" Why hadn't Buck called yet? "He requested a female bodyg— protection specialist—"

Fitch raised a brow.

"I was the only one in the firm available, and like I said, I wasn't his close protection. He had another team for that. I was usually at a distance, watching. Hasn't the news reported any of that yet?"

"No. But you *have* made the international news, at least in Japan."

I pushed aside the question of whether I was big in Japan. At least my hometown was still a secret, or the press would have caught up to me by now. Or maybe they didn't care about my side of the story. Maybe the facts weren't high priority.

"You speak Japanese?" I asked, stalling while my brain caught up with the ramifications. If this was international news... this was bigger than I'd imagined.

He shrugged. "Why were you the B team?"

"You know, it's just possible I was the A team."

"If he didn't trust his team," Fitch said, "why not just fire them? Why hire you?"

"Who knows? Koppel wasn't exactly known for his frankness."

"*Was* he being watched?"

"Not when I was there." And if I sounded confident, I was. I wasn't good at a lot of things—amateur detecting being high on the list. But I knew surveillance.

"And then you returned to your hometown and stumbled over another dead man. It seems a little self-defeating."

"Rigby's got nothing to do with Koppel. Finding him was just bad luck."

He gave me a long look. "You seem to have a lot of that."

"And you just *happened* to be hanging around, pretending to be a gardener, when Rigby was killed?" I pressed my lips flat.

"No," he said, "I'm on a case. And I'd prefer it, as a professional courtesy, if you don't blow my cover."

I was growing tired of spilling my guts and getting zip in return. "What's in it for me?"

"No professional courtesy then?"

"I found Rigby's body. I'm the stranger in town, even if I did grow up there. That makes me a suspect. How can you expect me not to mention you to the cops? You've been lurking around like a serial killer."

"You know many serial killers?"

"And don't tell me you're not involved," I continued. "You're involved. You've been watching me and watching Carmel. You're in this somehow."

"How'd you know I was watching you?"

After everything I'd just said about surveillance, that was just insulting. I cocked my head and arched an eyebrow. The A/C fell silent.

"Fine," he said. "But given your reputation, can you blame me for not taking you seriously?"

Generally, I counted on it. It made countersurveillance easier.

"Three weeks ago," he said, "a woman came to my office and hired me to watch Rigby. She said he was blackmailing her. Dirty photos. My job was to get them back and destroy any digital copies he might have saved on external servers."

I crossed my legs. It didn't make my seat more comfortable. "Who hired you?"

He shook his head. "I can't tell you that."

"Client confidentiality?"

"Client big fat liar. She doesn't exist."

"She hired you online?"

"No. In person." He pointed. "Sat in the same chair you're sitting in now. She paid in cash—said she'd been blackmailed once and didn't want to leave herself open to more."

I wrinkled my nose. "Bummer."

The detective shrugged, his t-shirt moving in interesting ways. "Trust isn't a big part of this business. I didn't take it personally, and I don't mind getting paid in greenbacks."

"So you took the job."

"Marques was looking for a gardener for his Big Things, and I was in. I made one email report to my client last week—mainly background on Rigby. Her response was brief."

"I'll bet it was."

"And then you found Rigby's body. My client stopped responding. The phone number she'd given me was disconnected—I'm assuming a burner phone."

"Did she have an address?" I asked.

"The address she gave me was real and inhabited by a family of five."

"And you got stuck holding the bag." I sighed and flicked my foot. The story was straight out of a Sam Spade novel—dark and twisty and hard to believe.

"Yeah. I have this theory—more of a hypothesis—that she meant to frame me for the murder. But then you came along and found the body instead."

"*Would* you have discovered it?" I asked. "In the normal course of things?"

"I would have been one of the first people poking around that nonexistent flowerbed." Fitch crossed his arms, muscles bulging. "It's enough to make you lose faith in human nature."

"There's a lot of that going around."

Fitch shifted on the wooden desk. "But I'll admit this is the most interesting case I've had in years. I get set up by a hot dame, and then a disgraced bodyguard—"

"Executive protection specialist."

"Disgraced executive protection specialist connected to the crime of the year turns up?"

"It could be a movie," I agreed. "Think of the visuals. The body. The renaissance dagger. The giant can of peas."

"The disgraced executive protection specialist." He eyed me.

"I'm only temporarily disgraced." The FBI *had* to be releasing a press statement exonerating me soon.

Fitch rubbed his ear.

"You said you found some background on Rigby," I said. "Care to share?"

He hesitated. His emerald gaze met mine, and something caught in my chest.

"You've got no client to protect," I said, "and Rigby's dead. What's the harm?"

"The harm is you're a suspect in two murder cases."

"I told you, Koppel wasn't murdered. And I'm pretty good at noticing things. I noticed you."

He threw up his hands. "Gambling. The guy was in hock up to his neck. End of story."

That lined up with Carmel's comment that Donald was losing money they didn't have. "Carmel doesn't seem like the long-suffering wife type."

"People are funny," he said. "It's the best part of being a PI—the endless parade of human foibles."

"And you've got no idea who this mystery woman who hired you is?"

"Not yet," he said. "She was five-five in heels and a hundred and thirty pounds or less."

I nodded. It was easier to add fake pounds than subtract them. She may have put on a few as part of her disguise.

"She presented as a brunette," he said. "but that could have been a wig. What's your connection to Rigby?"

In the achy chair, I uncrossed and recrossed my legs. "He lived in what used to be my father's house."

"Right. I heard your brother wasn't happy about losing it to the town. He and Rigby got into a shouting match a couple weeks back."

I bit back a curse. If Fitch was competent, he could be a problem. "My brother is what is commonly known as a slacker. He doesn't have the focus or the energy to commit murder."

"And yet, Rigby was killed with a knife straight out of a Ren Faire. And your brother has an impressive collection of antique bladed weapons."

A door slammed in the hallway outside.

Dammit. He might *be* competent. "And you know this bec ause..."

"Treehouses aren't particularly secure."

That stupid treehouse. "My brother's in a group called the Medieval Battle Society. Charlie's not the only one in town with old weapons. Gert Magimountain sells them out of his antique shop on Main."

"Oh yeah, the crypt keeper with the mob connections."

I shifted, uneasy. "He's actually got mob connections?" That was mildly concerning.

"Word is he was an enforcer back in the day. Now, he's probably just what he seems—an old guy with an antique shop." Fitch cocked his dark head. "What's wrong? Your eyes look kind of glassy."

I rose and gestured with my thumb toward the office door. "I'm temporarily unemployed and running a meter. Thanks for the intel."

"Thanks for keeping your mouth shut."

Mug of coffee in hand, I stood on the motel cabin's rear porch and felt sorry for myself. The mountains and the jagged black rocks were the only parts of Nowhere that still felt familiar. Sun turned the low mist over the discount cemetery golden.

It was peaceful. It was Wednesday. I was starting to consider the cemetery's two-for-one deal.

A movement stirred the mist.

I stilled, my grip tightening on my mug.

A stag emerged from the fog. The animal stopped, stared.

I cocked my head. It looked a bit like the deer from the park last night. I frowned. It *couldn't* be the same deer I'd wrestled the buffalo wing from. Could it? I squinted.

It had the same dark slash over its eyes. *Was* it the same deer?

It made sense. It had shown up for take-out chicken wings, so the cemetery and motel were in its territory. So it wasn't weird at all that the deer had come back, or that it was eyeing the human and potential food source. It wasn't like it had recognized me, specifically.

Eyes on the stag, I took an uneasy sip of my coffee. It's not like deer held grudges. They weren't cats.

"Chicken bones can't be good for deer," I told it. "It may not feel like it now, but we may have saved your life."

Gaze fixed on me, the stag lowered its antlers and pawed the ground. The animal feinted, charging into the stream and stopping. I backed to the sliding glass door and slipped inside the small cabin.

Charlie snored on the couch.

I edged aside a brown-checked curtain. The stag hadn't moved. I'd swear the deer was surveilling my cabin. He wasn't being very covert about it either. And I was saying that as something of an expert in the field.

I let the curtain drop and shook Charlie awake.

He groaned and slapped my hand away. "Ten more minutes."

"Wake up. We've got trouble."

"Is the sheriff here?"

"Not yet, but when he hears you were arguing with Rigby, he will be."

His blue eyes drifted lazily open. "Where'd you hear that?"

I sat on the arm of the couch. "You saying it's not true?"

He yawned. "Well, yeah I yelled at him. He stole my house. *Our* house. It was a garbage move."

"Your house, not ours." But the loss still hurt. I told myself it was just a house, just a building, but of course that was a lie. The home you grew up in was never just a house. It was memories, shadows of people you'd loved and lost.

"But you grew up in it. You must feel something for the house, for this town." He folded his arms, tugging up the blanket.

"Right now, all I'm feeling is worried. You make a great murder suspect."

"Come on. The sheriff knows I wouldn't kill anyone."

"Does he?"

Charlie rolled over and pulled the beige blanket higher over his shoulders.

I pinched the bridge of my nose. "Tell me everything you know about Donald Rigby."

"I'm telling you," he mumbled into a brown cushion, "you're worrying over nothing. I didn't kill Rigby."

"I know you didn't kill him, but we need to be able to prove that to the sheriff."

"Innocent until proven guilty, remember?"

"And since I'm assuming you were alone and sleeping in your treehouse when Rigby was killed, you don't have an alibi. Unless Ivanna can verify you were there?"

He rolled over to face me. "I didn't see her when I got back."

My heart shrank, my chest heavying. No *alibi then.* "Tell me about Donald."

"No."

"No?" I said, outraged. "What do you mean, no?"

"I'll tell you if you help me protect Lilyanna at the minimart."

"We don't have time for Captain Rabbit."

"Then I'm not telling you about Donald Rigby." His face got that stubborn look I remembered from childhood. I'd never been able to budge him once he got that look, but I tried anyway.

"Charlie, you could be in real trouble."

"How are *you* going to get me out of it? Last time I checked, you're not a lawyer *or* a PI."

"Fine," I said, resigned. "I'll guard the rabbit."

CHAPTER TEN

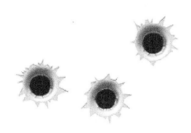

THE CONVENIENCE STORE WAS jammed between a dry cleaner and a laser skin and hair clinic. The strip mall, on the outskirts of Nowhere, clung to the side of the mountain highway opposite a looming wall of black stone. The white rabbit and I stood on the parking lot's baking asphalt. I waited for Buck to pick up the phone.

My brother cooled his heels in a folding chair in the shade of the convenience store and noshed on a burrito. For a minimart burrito, it looked good. Once I had a chance, I intended to try one myself.

BEEP. I took the phone from my ear and frowned.

Buck had declined my call, and it was hard not to take that personally. Maybe he was just in a meeting. Or avoiding me.

Boiling anger prickled my scalp. Buck had always been good at avoiding the rough stuff. Physical danger he was great with. But the emotional side of things, comforting a panicked client, dealing with his own mother's death, had been another story. Then it had been shut down, deny, evade. Had that been one of the reasons I'd imploded rather than exploded when he'd confessed his infidelity? Because I'd known there wouldn't be much point? Had I made things too easy for him? I exhaled slowly. It was too late to throw a tantrum about it now.

Lilyanna waved at a passing station wagon. "Thanks for doing this," she said, her voice muffled beneath the rabbit suit. "I know it's not your usual job."

"No problem," I lied, pocketing the phone. It wasn't that rabbit protection was beneath me. Lilyanna was light years more worthy than Koppel had been. I just didn't like close protection.

Forget the movies, where diminutive women kick men twice their size across the room. Hollywood might be able to break the laws of physics and biology, but I couldn't. Even with my muscles and training, the average guy had more speed and power than I did.

It was depressing, and the reason why I favored weapons and hitting first.

That said, hanging out at a mini mall beat chasing Koppel across wine country. And it wasn't like any of the guys I worked with would ever find out I'd been protecting a rabbit.

A bead of sweat trickled down my back. They'd better not find out.

"I like to keep busy," I said. "Tell me about these guys who've been bothering you."

"I know they're only punks," Lilyanna said. "Rich college kids with nothing better to do. But... it's no fun."

I knew an understatement when I heard one, but I didn't press. "What kind of car do they drive?"

"A red Tesla." The rabbit bobbed its head.

Teslas weren't as abundant in Nevada as in California, and I wondered about the car I'd seen when I'd first arrived in town. "They got anything against you personally?" I tightened my ponytail. "I mean, do you know them?"

"No. They just think pushing around a person in a rabbit suit is funny. They've never hurt me, but it's still scary." She patted her big head. "I've got no peripheral vision."

"Yeah," I agreed. "That would be scary."

"Charlie's been great though. He hangs out with me here and keeps the guys from making contact. Your brother is really, really awesome. Did he tell you he's a knight in the MBS?"

"No, he didn't mention the knighthood." But I could see Charlie as a knight. He'd always been a champion in the chivalric sense. When I was in high school and some students had been giving me lip outside the house, he'd charged out to defend me. Of course, they'd laughed at him. He'd been a scrawny six-year-old. But I hadn't forgotten.

"That's so Charlie," she said. "He's modest. But becoming a knight is a big deal. You have to know all sorts of things about weapons combat."

"You do?" I glanced sidelong at my brother, sitting in the shade. If the sheriff found out my brother knew his way around a knife...

My hands grew damp, and I rubbed them on my jeans. Why would anyone bother to try and frame a rando PI from Reno? It didn't make sense. Not when my brother had done a bang-up job putting himself in the frame.

Unless Fitch had been lying about the mysterious woman and the frame-up. But again, why? It was a crazy story. Good liars stuck close to believability.

"Not just combat," Lilyanna continued, "but the whole chivalric code. I mean, no wonder he couldn't go through with burning down his old house."

Everything stopped. My heart. My breath. My brain. "What?" I croaked.

"No one was in the house at the time. It was right after the town seized it." She shuffled her... feet? Paws? "He went a little crazy. Charlie didn't tell you?"

A crow fluttered onto the mini marts roof. It lifted its wings and cawed.

I swayed, dizzy. The house's plumbing had never been in good shape. Our father had often joked about burning down the house for the insurance money. After Mom had gotten sick and the bills had added up, I wasn't so sure if he'd still been joking. "Hold on. You're saying Charlie *tried*—?"

"No, not really. Some of the guys from the MBS figured it out and talked him down. But he wouldn't have gone through with it. He was super embarrassed afterward."

Some of the guys? More than one? It was only a matter of time before the sheriff heard. I shook my head, dullness settling in my chest. I should have been home more. I could have stopped him.

I'd failed my brother.

My fists clenched. "Excuse me for a minute." I walked toward the convenience store.

My brother looked up and winced in the sunlight. "Hey." He adjusted his board shorts and scratched his bare leg.

"You tried to burn down your house?"

"I wouldn't say *tried*. I mean, I didn't actually light anything on fire—"

"Did you bring gasoline?" *Say no. Say no.*

"Of course not. Gas is expensive. I just... I know it was dumb, but I just... stood there, looking at the house. And then the guys showed up—"

"You..." My hands turned clammy, fear squeezing my chest.

Charlie hadn't brought a gas can. He hadn't been serious. But he'd been shooting off his mouth in a small town. *Everyone* would know. But I hadn't known. Heat flushed through my body. I closed my eyes and breathed slowly because I had no *right* to be angry. But I was. At myself.

An image of five-year-old Charlie, on the roof and determined to jump onto our mom's minivan, rose before my eyes. Terrified, I'd tried to stop him, but he'd jumped and broken his arm. I'd been furious with him, my parents with me.

"Look," he said, "I didn't *do* anything. I was in a bad place, but arson's totally not the knight's code. I mean, what if a tree had caught and set a neighbor's house on fire? It wouldn't be right."

My brother was a suspect, in danger of being arrested, and he didn't even see it. And he never would, because in his world, people were basically good, and things worked out for the best.

"You—"

A red Tesla zipped into the lot. Three muscular young men in short-sleeved button-up shirts and shorts emerged from the car. They *were* the guys from my first morning in Nowhere.

Captain Rabbit froze.

"That's them," Charlie whispered. "Those are the jerks who've been harassing Lilyanna."

"Let me borrow that." I grabbed the cane from my brother's hand and strode toward Lilyanna.

Charlie struggled to rise and collapsed back into the lawn chair.

The three men approaching Lilyanna had clocked some serious gym time. They were roughly the size of mountain trolls.

"Hey, Captain Rabbit," the biggest shouted. "What's wrong? You look like someone unplugged your slushie machine."

The smallest—smallest being relative—catcalled.

Insides jittering, I held the cane loose at my side. Canes made great weapons. You could take them anywhere without question. The hooks could be used in surprising ways. And Charlie's was sturdy enough to do real damage. I looked forward to being old enough to carry one wherever I went. I did not look forward to taking on three grown men. But if all went well, I wouldn't have to.

"Hey guys." I waved. "What's going on?"

The largest one's jaw jutted forward. "What's it to you?"

I shrugged. "Nothing, really. I mean, I get it. It's boring around here. You're looking for something on the wild side of... Hot Springs?" I guessed.

"The *Town* of Hot Springs," the biggest one said.

I rolled my eyes. Only someone from Hot Springs would call it The Town of Hot Springs, at least seriously. It was so pretentious. And not relevant.

"Hey," I said, "I'm not judging. I've got nothing better to do than spend my day at a strip mall either." And suddenly, I realized that was true.

But this was only temporary. My heart caved inward. Was it temporary? I hadn't heard from Buck since I'd left San Francisco. And... Japan? The Japanese press were talking about me?

I straightened. No. Everything would be fine. I hadn't done anything wrong. And yet... Buck hadn't called. The FBI hadn't announced I wasn't involved. And I was still in Nowhere.

I rubbed the back of my head with my free hand. "It's like... your life has taken this hard left turn, and there you are, at the strip mall. With nothing better to do, because..."

My gut turned to lead. Because maybe I *wasn't* on vacation. Maybe this wasn't going to be a short-term stint of unemployment. What if it was long-term? The unfairness left me breathless.

"No one remembers the people you've helped," I said slowly. "Or that you've had over a decade of success under your belt. No, now you're just another screw-up on the internet. There's no forgiveness. There's just..." I glanced back toward the dusty store fronts, plastered with paper signs.

The three men shuffled their feet. Charlie grunted and levered himself out of his chair.

Heaviness settled beneath my ribs. "There's just the strip mall," I whispered.

The men shifted their weight and glanced at each other.

Heat flushed my face. What was wrong with me? "Sorry." I laughed shortly. "I'm babbling. I'm not sure why... um, you *do* know there's a girl in that rabbit suit, right?"

The biggest blinked. "A girl? We thought..." The three men looked at each other.

"A girl?" the biggest repeated. "Why didn't she say anything?"

My grip tightened on the cane. "Why should she have to?" I asked.

He pinked. "Sorry."

"If you want to apologize," I snapped, "buy some slushies."

"Yeah. Right." The smallest nodded.

The three shambled into the mini mart.

"Extra-large," I shouted after them.

"They didn't know I was a woman?" Lilyanna braced her paws on her hips. "What did they think I was?"

"I would guess they thought you were a guy."

She tugged her floppy ears. "They *wouldn't* know. I'm not supposed to talk to customers."

"You never said *anything* to them?" I asked, incredulous.

"It's against the rules."

"You're talking to me."

"But you're not a customer, and I know Charlie." She motioned toward my brother, hobbling toward us without his cane.

"If the rules put you in danger," I said hotly, "it's time to break the rules." It had taken me my first car chase to figure that out. I'd automatically begun to slow for a red light, the bad guys in hot pursuit, before realizing how fatally stupid that instinct would be for me and my client. Especially since there'd been no cross traffic. I'd followed my training and skipped that light and three more before screeching into the parking lot of a police station. That instinct hadn't troubled me since.

"I hate breaking rules," she said. "Besides, that's what..."

"That's what?"

She glanced toward Charlie and grasped her paws together at her chest. "I shouldn't have been in that bar in Doyle when it happened. The abduction."

Abduction? I stared, aghast, and took back every crummy thought I'd had about her little quirks. No wonder she'd been freaked out by the Tesla guys. I should have volunteered to help her instead of giving Charlie a hard time. I was scum. I was dirt. I was lower than dirt. "I'm sorry, I didn't know."

"Hey." Charlie panted, limping. "Hey. What happened?"

"Your sister was great," Lilyanna said. "All she did was talk to them. I didn't even know you *could* talk to them. I mean, those guys are worse than the grays."

"The grays?" I asked. Was that a sports team? Did Nowhere have sports now?

"You know, the grays," Charlie said. "Lilyanna was abducted."

I blinked. "By... wait. What does that have to do with gray?"

"Not gray," he said. "*Grays*. Aliens. She was taken by aliens. That's why she wears a weighted blanket and is Captain Rabbit."

Briefly, I closed my eyes, and I swallowed. "Yes," I said. "That explains everything." I'd been protecting a rabbit who thought she'd been abducted by aliens. And no one from my work life would hear about this. *Ever.*

I glanced around anxiously. A windowless black van cruised past, and I relaxed. Right now I'd take a creepy murder van over a press van. Getting quizzed about Koppel was one thing. Having alien-abductee protection splashed about on top of it was a whole different level. And bringing my brother into it would be worse now that he'd made himself a suspect.

"The weight of the costume is a stress reduction technique," she said. "A friend from Doyle who runs a UFO B&B suggested it. Well, first she suggested a weighted blanket. But we realized any heavy costume would work."

Aliens. My brother a murder suspect. A slushie rabbit. What had happened to my life?

"Lilyanna's from Doyle," Charlie said. "And she's older than she looks. It has to do with light speed travel—"

Angry heat rushed from my chest to the top of my head, dizzying. I thrust the cane between Charlie's arm and body, grabbed the tip, and pulled, forcing him to bend over.

"Hey!" He scrunched up his face. "Ow! Injured man here."

"I don't want to hear it, Charlie," I said. "There are things I need to know and things I don't need to know. And maybe Lilyanna wants to keep her alien abductee experience private." And I knew I wasn't making sense. Lilyanna had just told me about the abduction. But... *gagh!*

"Actually, I prefer the term *contactee*," the rabbit said. "And the whole town knows. But thanks."

A supernova went off at the front of my cranium. "Sorry," I ground out. "Contactee." I returned my attention to Charlie. "What I do need to know are things like, oh, I don't know, I didn't pay the taxes and am about to lose my house. I could have helped you." *And he's a suspect in a murder investigation!*

He winced. "You weren't here."

My chest tightened. I slid the cane free, releasing him. "You're right," I said heavily. "I wasn't here." And I should have been. I never should have stayed away so long. My misplaced anger evaporated in a wash of shame. "I'm sorry."

He rubbed his shoulder. "Nah, it was a cool move."

That wasn't what I was sorry about. I stared at the scrub-covered hillside on the other side of the highway. "Is there anything else I need to know?"

"We've got another show tonight at the mystery theater," he said. "I'm playing the one-eyed man. It's a 1920s theme."

"That's terrific, Charlie." I handed my brother his cane.

"That cane move was amazing," Lilyanna said. Can you show me how to do that?"

"I knew you could wrestle." Charlie punched me lightly in the arm. "But I had no idea you were so good with weapons. You *really* should join the MBS."

I covered my face with my hands. *The MBS.* He was on the verge of being arrested, and *that's* what he was thinking about?

Lilyanna rested a paw on his arm. "Not now, Charlie."

CHAPTER ELEVEN

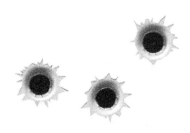

WATCHING FOR TROUBLE AT a strip mall was like watching for kids at a carnival. Trouble was everywhere. Shifty looking characters buying liquor and cigarettes. Rambunctious teens. Idiots driving too fast.

I stood outside the shop's front door. Its glass was plastered with ads for 12-ounce beer and ultra-barbecue chips. A parade of sketchy and—since the day's temp had hit the nineties—pungent characters wandered past. The Tesla guys weren't coming back, but Lilyanna had me for the afternoon. I liked to give value for money. Plus I still felt bad about my outburst and the cane.

"I don't know what you've got against the MBS," Charlie said, sitting in his folding chair. The shadows had shortened, and he crossed his legs.

The rabbit waved at a passing SUV.

"I don't have anything against it," I said. "It sounds... fun. I mean, crazy, but fun. I'm just not going to be around long enough to join."

Charlie looked at his frayed sneakers and turned his cane in his hands. Lilyanna waved at a passing black van.

A middle-aged man in a long apron emerged from the store.

"Hi, Mr. Graham," Charlie said.

The grocer smoothed wisps of graying hair across his scalp. "Hi, Charlie. Sorry, but you two need to go."

"Go?" Charlie asked.

"You're scaring off my customers."

"But we haven't done anything," Charlie said. "I mean, not since my sister drove off those guys from Hot Springs."

"And I'm glad she did," Mr. Graham said. "But they're gone now, and you're still here."

"They might come back," Charlie said.

Mr. Graham folded his arms over the swell of his stomach. "Goodbye, Charlie. And thanks, Baby Alice."

My hands twitched. "Just Alice." *Please.*

"By the way, my wife wanted me to ask if you teach self-defense," the shop owner said.

"Oh," Charlie said. "Alice is awesome at that. She's got like a triple-black belt or something."

I rubbed my forehead. "Your wife?"

"That's Mrs. Graham," my brother said helpfully.

"I texted her the video," the grocer said. "Do you teach self-defense?"

My stomach bottomed. "You texted... what video?"

"Of you taking down Charlie." He chuckled. "That was the best thing I've seen in the parking lot all year." His expression turned grim. "You wouldn't believe what I've seen out there."

"I thought your video cameras didn't cover the parking lot," I bleated.

"I shot the video with my phone through that window." Mr. Graham motioned to a window covered with discount flyers.

Sweat beaded my forehead. "You didn't post it online?"

"No, of course not."

The muscles between my shoulder blades relaxed. I was safe. None of the guys from work would see it, and neither would the press.

"I posted it on My Neighbors," he continued.

"That's, um, online." Charlie turned to me. "You know, where neighbors share info about plumbers and complain about stuff?"

I groaned. But My Neighbors was private. The odds that Buck or someone in the press would find that video were low. I mean, how many people followed the Nowhere chapter of My Neighbors?

"Her church group wants lessons." Mr. Graham said.

"Oh, hey." Charlie grinned at his phone. "We're on YouTube."

"What?" I snatched the phone from his hand.

There I was, locking up my brother with a cane. I glanced down at the title. The video was labeled Nowhere, NV. "Oh, sh—"

"That's probably Mabel from church," Mr. Graham said. "She's got a lifestyle account."

"Yeah," Charlie said. "It's Mabel's account all right."

I blew out a slow breath to stay calm. This would be fine. The account only had... I checked the video. *Twenty-thousand followers?* My pulse banged in my ears. I had to get out of Nowhere before the press picked this up. But how could I with a murder hanging over my brother's head?

I swallowed and returned the phone to Charlie.

Okay. No problem. All I had to do was clear up this murder business, and then I could leave. And if anyone knew what was going on in Nowhere, it was the town's queen bee, Mrs. Malone. She must have clocked the murderer by now. I'd just charm her into telling me the town's secrets and be on my way.

Charlie claimed he had some MBS business to take care of, so I dropped him at the theater and continued alone to Mrs. Malone's house. She lived in a red-painted wood cabin. Blue, purple, and pink petunias overflowed the boxes in its front windows. A NO SOLICITING sign glared from beneath a frosted, diamond-paned window.

I climbed the two steps to the front porch and knocked on the door.

As a kid, it had seemed like a fairytale house with its elaborate front garden and crooked thickets of scrub oak. Then our mother had gotten cancer. Charlie and I had spent miserable afternoons here, waiting.

Mrs. Malone had done a good thing, taking us in when our parents were at the hospital. But as a twelve-year-old I hadn't appreciated it. I'd just known my mom was sick, I couldn't be with her, and the fairytale cabin was a prison.

After a minute or two, a bulky shadow darkened the window. Mrs. Malone opened the door and leaned on her wooden cane.

"Yes?" she asked in an icy tone.

I tried not to stare at the inch of white roots in her ebony hair. "Hi, Mrs. Malone. Is this a bad time?"

"Yes." She started to shut the door.

"Wait. Please. It's about Donald Rigby."

Mrs. Malone paused, the door halfway shut. She squinted at me through her reading glasses. "What about him?"

"You may have heard I found his body?"

Mrs. Malone opened the door wider. "Yes," she said cautiously.

"Who do you think might have wanted to kill him?" I blurted.

She arched a brow. "This is your investigative technique? Going around and asking people who killed Rigby?"

"Well, no. I mean, I'm not investigating."

"Of course you're not. That would take diligence and dedication, neither of which you possess."

I smothered my irritation. I *was* diligent and dedicated, in countersurveillance. "It's just... I've been away so long that I don't know this town anymore."

"What do you expect when you've been playing around overseas all these years?"

I frowned. *Playing?* I'd been paid well for my services. "I wasn't playing—"

"Running from your responsibilities. Hopping from country to country like an Amish teen on *Rumspringa.*"

"What? No!" I'd had an expense account. Executive protection was serious work. And why were we bringing the Amish into this?

"It's high time you got a real job," she huffed.

"I *have* a real job, and that's not the point. You know everyone in this town, and... I'm feeling a little lost, that's all."

Her brow furrowed. "Oh. I hadn't considered how that must *feel.*"

Ha. I knew I could sweettalk her. Or had that been sarcasm? "And finding a body right after my arrival... Well, you can imagine."

Mrs. Malone sneezed. "Yes... Yes, I suppose I can." She nodded thoughtfully. "Come inside."

I followed her into a dark-paneled dining room lined with bookshelves. The house hadn't changed since my childhood, and a cape of cold depression settled on my shoulders. "Okay, who—"

She sneezed again. "Wait here." She turned smartly on her sensible heel and left the room. Her footsteps quieted on the stairs.

The cuckoo clock ticked on a wall. I wandered to a bookshelf. It was lined with true crime books, so that was different. When I'd been a kid, they'd held classic mystery novels. Those books had been my salvation. Nowhere didn't have a library, just the bi-weekly book mobile, which only let me check out two books at a time.

But true crime... Little wonder Mrs. Malone had let me inside. The opportunity to hash over a murder in Nowhere must have been too good to pass up.

Muffled footsteps sounded on the floor above, rattling the chandelier. I ran one finger along the spines and examined the titles. America had *way* too many serial killers.

Mrs. Malone walked into the dining room carrying the ugliest dog I'd ever seen. "I have a solution," she said, eyes watering.

The dog was small and gray, and those were the only two points in its favor. Its eyes bulged, cross-eyed. Its teeth spiked outward in different directions.

"You have a solution to Donald Rigby's death?" I asked, bemused.

"Of course not. Today, forty percent of homicides in America go unsolved."

"Really?" That didn't say much for my chances at figuring this out.

"In the sixties, only ten percent went unsolved," she continued. "That implies either policing has deteriorated, or a terrifying number of innocent men were jailed in the sixties. I suspect the latter. Here. Take Fredo." She shoved the snaggle-toothed dog into my arms.

The animal growled.

"Okay," I said, "but—"

"Fredo used to belong to a family in town. When they moved last week, they abandoned him in their home. I do not hold with abandoning pets. If you cannot care for a pet properly, you have no business adopting him, even if he does have behavioral issues."

Fredo wriggled, clawing my arm.

"No," I said, shifting, "but—"

"Unfortunately, I cannot keep him. I was on the verge of taking him to the shelter when you arrived. It's a kill shelter, and I suspect Fredo will not be long for this world if someone doesn't adopt him."

"Probably not, but—"

"Good." She backed me toward the open front door. "You're lonely. He needs a home. Problem solved."

"But I can't take Fredo," I yelped.

"You said you're lost and lonely."

That just sounded pathetic. "I didn't say I was lonely." I edged backward onto the wooden deck.

"You believe in murdering dogs?"

Fredo gnawed on my navy t-shirt's sleeve.

I pulled my sleeve free. "Of course not—"

"Then I don't see what choice we have," she said. "I just told you if you don't take him, he'll be killed."

"That's not—"

"I'm sure you two will get along swimmingly."

A bead of sweat slithered down my back. "I can't have a dog. I'm staying in a motel."

"The cabins by the discount cemetery?"

I nodded.

"That's all right then," she said. "They're dog friendly. You just have to pay an extra fee." She shut the diamond-paned door in my face.

"But I can't have a dog," I said to the closed door. Personal protection specialists didn't have dogs. I was on the road too much for a dog. "I'm leaving Nowhere in a week."

A bolt clicked shut. The gray dog howled and writhed in my arms. I struggled not to drop him, ducking and sidestepping to keep hold.

A streak of red bulleted downward. A flowerpot shattered beside my left boot. I gaped and looked up.

Gert leaned out the window and his wizened face peered down. He grimaced, the sunlight flashing off his glasses. "Missed again."

CHAPTER TWELVE

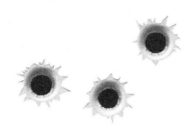

ANNOYED AND EMBARRASSED, I glared up at the open window. "Again?" He'd tried to kill before, and I hadn't noticed?

The old man slammed the window shut. A latch clicked, and the red cabin's front door popped open.

Mrs. Malone jammed a coiled leash between my chest and Fredo. "You'll need to walk him twice a day." She sucked in a breath. "What did you do to my flowerpot?"

"I didn't do anything to it. Gert Magimountain tried to drop it on me. Do you know you've got a hitman upstairs?"

"Don't be ridiculous. Mr. Magimountain doesn't throw flowerpots at people. And it's just like you to shift the blame."

Fredo choked on my sleeve. I pried it free with a tearing sound.

"What's that supposed to mean?" I transferred the animal—I still wasn't convinced it was a dog—to my other arm.

"You haven't exactly taken responsibility for that horrible man's death, have you?"

"It wasn't my fault," I said, voice rising. "Wait. Which horrible man are you talking about?" I didn't know why I asked. Neither death was my fault.

"That Koppel person."

"Oh. You heard about that."

"Everyone heard about that. Don't think you can return to Nowhere and coast on your junior-rodeo glories. That's *another* thing you quit."

"That's not the—" I grimaced. "Gert Magimountain tried to drop a flowerpot on my head."

She shook her finger at me. "Don't try to blame Mr. Magimountain. I expect a new flowerpot, young lady." Mrs. Malone stepped backward and slammed the door.

She hadn't denied knowing Gert was upstairs. In fact, she'd seemed to take it for granted. What was he doing there? They couldn't be dating, could they?

The dog howled and coughed, choking. I extracted another piece of navy fabric from its mouth.

This dog had to go.

I called Charlie. "Hey," I said when he answered. "Are you still at the theater?"

"No, I'm with Lilyanna in the picnic area at Snitz Woods. You know? The one near the highway?"

"What are you doing there? I thought she was working."

"She's off now, and we've got MBS."

I clipped the leash on Fredo's collar and set him on the porch. "You realize that sounds like a disease."

"Ha ha, very funny. Why don't you join us? You can meet the gang."

It wasn't a bad idea. One of them might want a dog. "I'll meet you there."

I found Charlie and a dozen other people of various genders and ages near the picnic area, shaded by pines.

A slender knight in full armor leaned against a picnic table. Sketch pad in hand, Ivanna sat on a bench and doodled beside the knight. I assumed it was part of her official duties as scribe.

"Oh, cool, my sister's here." Charlie hobbled to me and gave me a hug. "Everyone, this is my sister, Alice. And she didn't kill that Estonian guy." He paused, apparently just noticing Fredo on his leash. "Wow, that's an ugly dog."

The knight creaked to standing and clanked toward us. "I told everyone what you did with that cane." Lilyanna's voice echoed from inside the helmet. "Thanks."

I shifted the leash in my hand. "No problem. How do you feel about pets?"

"I love them. I've got a comfort dog." Lilyanna motioned toward a tawny, short-haired, mid-sized dog tied to a small pine. The dog panted happily.

A portly man in a tunic, a sword belted at his waist, shook my hand. "I saw the video. Impressive cane technique. Ever thought about quarterstaff?"

Remembered shame, which is the worst kind, heated my face. "You saw the..." *Already?*

Snapping at Charlie, going after him with a cane. I'd never attacked an innocent civilian before. I was supposed to protect the innocent. But the people I'd protected lately weren't all that guiltless. Toomas had only been the worst example.

"During the Renaissance," the man continued, "the quarterstaff was part of the curriculum of Europe's top fighting masters."

"I thought this was a medieval battle society," I said.

"It was important during the medieval period as well."

Ivanna slipped from the bench and tucked the sketch pad under her arm. "Hi, again." She nodded toward the guy with the sword. "And that's Rob."

Rob flushed. "Sorry, I should have introduced myself."

"Charlie should have introduced you." Ivanna laughed and glanced at me. "Are you sure you and Charlie are related?"

"Since birth," I said.

Ivanna shook her head. "You never know. I used to date a guy who found out his daddy wasn't his daddy."

"Trust me," Charlie said. "Our parents were solid."

I shifted my weight, uncomfortable. Fredo gnawed at my ankle.

"I heard you found Rigby's body," Rob said. "People are worried." *Good people.* People who *deserved* protection. Maybe, just maybe, I could provide that in some small way.

A rotund woman with graying hair nodded. "That jerk owes me a hundred stags."

My ears pricked up. "Donald Rigby did?"

"Hey, Gladys! Are we practicing or what?" A man in a motorcycle helmet and padding shouted from a nearby clearing.

"Sorry." The gray-haired woman, Gladys, bustled over to the man and drew a rattan sword from a cane stand.

"What did she mean about Donald?" I asked Lilyanna.

She shrugged, her armor creaking. "No idea. Want to practice with us?"

With all my traveling, it had been a while since I'd been in a dojo. Lately, all my practice had been in a mirror. But Gladys might know something. "I think I'd like to practice with Gladys."

The older woman whacked her partner on the helmet with her rattan sword.

Lilyanna lifted her visor. "Do you know sword?"

"A bit." I'd trained mainly with sticks and staffs because the odds of having a sword on hand were low. But in my old dojo, swords and sticks utilized the same basic techniques. It made training more efficient.

"Then I'll introduce you," Lilyanna said. "Gladys is dying for a female partner who can fight back."

"Give her hell." Charlie gave me a thumbs up, and Ivanna snorted a laugh.

Half-dragging Fredo behind me, I followed Lilyanna toward the combatants.

"Women weren't supposed to fight in tournaments," Lilyanna said. "It's not authentic. But recently, the MBS changed the rules. They had to acknowledge that if you're invaded, you're going to defend yourself. So they created a special women's league."

"Do you always practice in full armor?" I asked.

"Oh, no. I don't fight. The armor's because of the grays."

I tugged at the collar of my t-shirt. "Right. The aliens. Sorry, I'd forgotten."

"I don't."

An uncomfortable silence fell.

Lilyanna broke it. "But thanks again for helping me out earlier."

"No problem. What do you think about this Rigby business?"

Lilyanna paused. "Well... Donald wasn't the nicest person, was he?"

"You knew him?" I tilted my head.

"Not really, it's just..." She lifted her metal-covered arms. They clanked when she dropped them.

"Because of the marijuana resort?" I asked.

"Just because you can do something, doesn't mean you should do something," she continued. "Where did you get that dog?"

"He's a rescue. He could be a great companion for your dog."

"Oh, I... No. I couldn't."

I sighed. "I had to give it a shot."

"He's kind of cute, in a super-ugly way. What happened to your sleeve?"

"Fredo. Fredo happened."

"Who's... the dog? The dog's name is Fredo?" She laughed.

CRACK.

The man practicing with Gladys yowled and leapt backward, shaking his hand. "Watch it."

"You're supposed to have padding there," Gladys grumped.

He scowled. "I do."

"Want a new sparring partner?" Lilyanna asked brightly.

Gladys turned to eye me. Her partner flipped up the shield on his motorcycle helmet.

Gladys frowned. "I don't—"

"Great idea," her partner said. "I'm going to get some ice. And a beer." He strode toward a picnic table, where other members of the MBS were practicing knife thrusts.

Gladys blew out her breath. "You know sword?"

"I haven't studied medieval or Renaissance techniques," I said. "But I've had some weapons training."

"Grab one then." She nodded to a trio of rattan swords propped against a scrub oak.

I tied Fredo to a nearby pine, retrieved a practice sword, and swung it experimentally.

"Do you have protective head gear?" she asked.

"Nope."

"All right. No head strikes then. Got it?"

I nodded. "Got it."

Lilyanna grinned. She clanked to a nearby boulder and sat against it.

"En garde." Gladys made an awkward salute with her sword and rushed me.

I hopped backward and managed to deflect her strike. She pivoted and attacked again. I barely had time to parry. In spite of her bulk, Gladys was good. We were both panting after five minutes of intense sparring.

"So," I gasped. "You heard I found Donald's body?"

"Yeah. What's up with that?"

"I'm not sure."

"Between that Koppel guy and Rigby, you're not having the best luck." Her sword whizzed down in a vertical strike.

I side stepped and blocked. "What's Rigby's story?"

"He opened a hiking store years and years ago. They sold a lot of shoes, put the shoe store out of business. And then Donald's store closed, and we didn't have a shoe store or a hiking store. So he and Carmel left for better pastures."

I frowned. Pete's father had owned that shoe store. *Poor Pete.* His family had had the worst luck. "You mentioned he owed you some money?"

"The man was a cheat." She thrust the sword toward my chest, and I parried, slipping sideways. "He wasn't bad when he first lived here," she continued. "But he wasn't gambling then."

"How did he wind up owing you money?"

"I live across the street from Charlie's—the Rigby's house now. He was in his driveway one day, trying to pay a plumber. His credit card wasn't reading, and the guy didn't take checks."

"And you offered to help?"

She nodded. "Donald didn't have enough cash to pay the whole bill, so I lent him a hundred stags. I didn't think the reason his card wasn't working was because he wasn't paying."

"Yikes." I ducked, raising my sword, and hers skimmed off mine.

"The gambling must have started before his return to Nowhere." She attacked in a flurry of diagonal strikes. "I'm just surprised Carmel came with him."

"I suppose everyone has their breaking point though." I planted my foot in her stomach and shoved her backward.

"Oof. You think Carmel killed him?"

Not really. Stabbing her husband beside a giant can of peas seemed off, even for Carmel. Bludgeoning him in the bedroom looked more her style.

But I shrugged. "The spouse is always the most likely suspect." I was sure I'd read that somewhere.

"If she didn't kill him years ago, why do it now?" Gladys drove me backward with a flurry of strikes.

Fredo strained against his leash and barked, interested. My heel struck a tree root. I'd trap myself if I wasn't careful. I somersaulted, coming up behind her, and whacked her in the butt.

"How the...?" She turned and laughed. "Unfair!"

"Sorry," I said innocently. "Is that outside league rules?" I rested the tip of my rattan sword on the ground. Panting, I leaned on it.

"It's legal, I think." Red faced, she pointed her sword at me and wheezed. "You'll have to show me that move later."

Fredo growled. I turned to follow the dog's gaze. A massive stag stood in the forest, thirty feet away. It stared at us intently.

I ran my thumb along the rattan sword's hand guard and edged backward.

Gladys shook her head. "They've got no fear of humans anymore. Some hunter's going to take advantage."

I tugged down the hem of my t-shirt with one hand. "That would be a shame," I said slowly. "We should go."

Charlie hobbled up to us. "Hey, that kinda looks like the deer that gored me."

And we weren't far from the scene of the attack. My rental cabin was only a long walk across the cemetery. Could it be the same deer?

"Would you mind giving Lilyanna a ride home?" Charlie asked. "We came with Rob, but he had to leave early."

I studied the big deer. It stood, unmoving. "Sure," I said. "No problem."

"Cool. Keys?"

I dug in my pocket and tossed him the keys to my rental.

"We'll load up." My brother lurched away.

"It's weird." Gladys rubbed her chin. "If I didn't know better, I'd swear that stag saw you as a threat. He's not taking his eyes off you."

"He must be impressed by our sword technique."

"He shouldn't be too impressed. I'm only a middling fighter. You should see some of the others."

Gladys and I gathered up her equipment and Fredo, and we walked toward the parking lot.

"Did Donald owe anyone else money?" I asked.

She shook her head. "Probably, but no one's complained to me."

The remaining MBS members were loading their cars when we reached the shaded parking lot. I slowed. My small SUV was loaded to the brim with cloth bags, presumably filled with fighting gear.

"Hey, everybody! Everybody?" Charlie raised his hands and hobbled toward me. The others turned to look.

"This was my sister's first day practicing with the MBS. I say that makes her an honorary member."

"That's not how this works," Gladys said.

"It's okay," he said. "I know what I'm doing. Alice, as an honorary member, I'd like to present you with your first MBS badge."

I cleared my throat. "Ah, that's not—"

Charlie pinned a brass badge on my safari jacket. I turned the thin metal ornament between my fingers. A knight on horseback charged, lance lowered. The pin was so Charlie it hurt my heart. "Thanks," I said instead.

The remainder of the group applauded politely and wandered to their cars.

"How much did you two bring?" I motioned toward my car. Canvas and faux-leather bags pressed against its windows.

"Since Rob had to leave early, he couldn't take the shared equipment like he normally does. We had to put it all in your car," Charlie said. "He's the one who brings the protective gear."

It was a squeeze, but we managed to fit Lilyanna in the front seat, with Fredo at her feet. Waffle, Lilyana's dog, sat strapped into a harness between us. Charlie sat on Lilyanna's lap.

So *much for chivalry*. "Charlie," I scolded.

"It's okay," she said. "The armor distributes the weight."

Lilyanna gave me directions to her apartment, her voice echoing in the armor. We set off, winding down the mountain highway.

"Jeez!" Charlie jerked sideways, jostling my arm.

Lilyanna tumbled into me, and the car swerved across the median.

I wrenched it back. "Charlie!"

"Your dog peed on me." He scowled.

"Good." But I glared at Fredo. He'd just spent several hours in a forest, and he thought the car was a good place to relieve himself?

A siren blatted behind us, and I checked the rearview mirror. A sheriff's SUV tailed close behind, lights flashing.

Smothering a curse, I pulled to the side of the highway. Of course a cop would be around to see me swerve. I dug past Charlie and Lilyanna to get the registration from the glove box.

The sheriff knocked on my window, and I rolled it down.

He looked past me into the car. Or at least I guessed he did. It was hard to tell with his mirrored glasses. "That's a lot of people in your front seat," he said.

"We're just coming from MBS," Charlie said. "That's the Medieval Battle Society."

Lilyanna waved, armor groaning. "Hi, Sheriff Randall."

"I know what the MBS is, son," he said. "You got any weapons in this vehicle?"

"The dog," I said. "It's loaded."

His expression didn't change.

Oops. I'd thought it was funny. "We only have training weapons," I said meekly. "They're in the back."

"Step out of the car, please."

Gripping my license and the rental docs, I climbed from the small SUV.

He walked to the rear of the car, and I followed.

"License and registration?"

"The car's a rental." I forced a smile and handed him my documents.

The sheriff studied them. "How long are you planning on staying in town?"

"A week or so, I think." As long as it took to make sure my brother wasn't going to be blamed for Rigby's murder.

He walked to his vehicle and slid inside. After a long five minutes, he returned.

"Okay," he said, "I'll let you off with a warning."

My shoulders relaxed.

He handed me my paperwork and returned to his car. "People in these parts don't like strangers causing trouble."

I nodded. "Who doesn't hate strangers? They're the pits. Always asking for directions. Looking for lattes..."

The sheriff lowered his glasses to stare.

"I won't cause any trouble," I said.

He grunted, returned to his car, and drove off. I got back inside my rental.

Charlie clapped my shoulder. "See? No problem."

My stomach rolled. It *was* a problem. Sword techniques carried over to knife technique, and Charlie was good at sword. Better than I was.

And the sheriff had seen my car filled with training swords, and Charlie inside it.

CHAPTER THIRTEEN

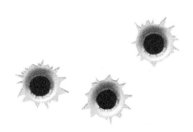

"CRAZY, HUH?" CHARLIE SHIFTED on Lilyanna's lap, and her armor groaned. He angled his head against the SUV's roof. "You never know what'll happen in the MBS."

"We were lucky he didn't ticket us." I pulled onto the mountain highway.

"Oh, come on," he scoffed. "For having three people in the front seat?"

"Three people and two dogs." I gnawed my bottom lip. If he'd wanted to, the sheriff could have caused us problems. Why hadn't he?

Fredo growled, and Lilyanna shushed the dog. To my surprise, the gray dog quieted.

"You sure you don't want Fredo?" I asked her. Fredo hadn't tried to bite Waffle once. That had to be a good sign.

She turned her head, the helmet groaning. "Nice try."

I made a few more feeble attempts to unload the dog, but Lilyanna didn't bite. *Heh.* She *did* take the archery equipment when we dropped her at her apartment building.

I aimed the car toward the theater to drop off the remaining weapons.

"So you got a dog," Charlie said. "Does this mean you're staying?"

"Uh, no." I laughed shortly. "The dog's temporary, and so am I."

His shoulders hunched. "If you hate this place so much, why did you come back?"

"I don't hate it. I never hated it. It was just... small."

"And that's why you left? Because it was small? Dad wanted you to stay."

Heat flared at the front of my skull. "Well, Mom told me to go, okay?"

"What are you talking about? When did she say that?"

I clamped my jaws shut, shame heating my face. What was wrong with me? I shouldn't have lost my temper. *Again.* "Never mind." Charlie didn't need to know. It was my issue, not his.

"No," he persisted. "What do you mean? I don't believe Mom would have told you that."

I didn't respond.

He lightly punched my arm. "What do you mean?"

"You were young," I finally said. "You didn't see what was going on."

"What was going on?"

I twisted my hands on the wheel. "Mom... She wasn't happy here. She told me to get out while I could before I suffocated." She'd told me that a lot—well, shouted—when I was growing up. "And then when she..." A lump hardened my throat. "After she was gone, I just had to go."

Charlie folded his arms. "I don't believe it."

"I was a kid," I muttered. "Maybe it all seemed bigger than it really was." But I was pretty sure it hadn't. Our mother had been an unhappy woman.

And I was regretting my confession.

Charlie and I were adults. We should be able to have hard conversations. But that wasn't why I'd brought it up. I'd wanted to punish my brother for making himself a suspect, for putting himself at risk. I'd let fear turn me into a jerk.

"If you don't want the dog," he said, "why don't you take it to a shelter?"

"Look at him. No one's going to rescue Fredo. I'm not going to let him be put to sleep." My hands tightened on the wheel. I might not have been able to save Koppel, but at least I could save the dog. "I'll find someone to take him."

"Okay then," Charlie said. "It's up to us." He rubbed Fredo's head. "You're in good hands, Fredo."

I laughed unevenly. That was one of the great things about my brother. He'd already forgiven me. Though I was pretty sure I hadn't deserved it. The gray dog belched.

"I need to pick up some dog food," I said.

We sat in the minimart's parking lot, a bag of dog food the lone item now in the back. Fredo snored in Charlie's lap. The steep, black granite cliffs across the highway cast long shadows.

"I'm worried about you," I said, a decision reached. "The sheriff's going to find out you talked about burning down Dad's house. He may connect you to Donald Rigby's murder."

"How?"

"There were full gas cans found by his body." I buckled my seatbelt. "He may have interrupted an arsonist."

"But I never burned anything down or bought any gas cans."

"You threatened to. Publicly. And everyone knew you weren't happy about losing the house to Rigby."

He scratched Fredo's head. The dog's ears flicked. "Yeah, well, my friends aren't going to say anything."

But they would, if questioned. They'd have to. "Even if they don't, there's a PI sniffing around. He's got no obligation to keep your secret."

"Alice, I'm innocent. Innocent people don't get arrested for murder."

How I wished that were true. "I know you're innocent, but I'd feel a lot better if we knew who killed Rigby." I started the car. "So who wanted him dead?"

"I don't know. He was just this guy."

I pulled from the minimart's lot and headed toward town. "There had to be someone. *Someone* killed Rigby. He was the face behind the marijuana resort. What about the people who didn't want it?"

"I guess there's Terrence." Charlie scratched his beard. "He's kind of obsessive about his art. I don't think he liked the idea of it becoming art for stoners. But he's no killer."

"Where can I find him?"

"I'll take you there now."

"Just tell me where to find him," I said. "It's best if I go alone."

"What? No way. You're my sister. I can't let you confront a possible murderer on your own."

"You said he was no killer."

"Well, yeah, but we don't know he's not. That's why we're going to talk to him, right?"

"No, *we're* not. I am."

But of course, we did.

I shouldn't have agreed to bring Charlie. I was still feeling guilty about telling Charlie our mother had wanted out of Nowhere. Because the corollary to that was she'd wanted out of the marriage. And maybe away from us too.

I really wished my mom hadn't confided in me. And I guess I felt guilty about that as well.

Charlie directed me to a ramshackle cabin at the edge of town. Metal art and whirligigs sprouted from its front yard. A sign hung from the traffic barrier blocking the driveway.

SHAMAN PARKING

"Pretty cool, huh?" Charlie opened the car door and stepped onto a giant purple eye painted on the sidewalk. He leaned his head into the car. "See? There are all sorts of interesting things in Nowhere."

I leashed Fredo, and we walked up the crooked stone path to the front steps. Charlie limped up the three concrete stairs and knocked. Footsteps sounded behind the blue door. It swung open, and Terrence peered out.

The artist scraped a hand through his wild, gray hair. "Yeah?"

"Hey, Terrence," Charlie said. "It's us. Can we come in?"

He shot Fredo a wary look. "Not with that dog. He tried to eat my tires." He pointed to a ramshackle blue Beetle. "Keep him away from me."

Yeah, I could totally see Fredo going for tires. "Understood." I dragged Fredo backward, toward the porch steps.

"We wanted to ask about Donald Rigby's plans for the town," Charlie said.

Terrence's face reddened. "His plans? He planned to ruin the town and my art. You can't separate the big art from the town."

"Ruin it how?" I asked. Fredo attacked the hem of my jeans.

"With his pot resort," Terrence said. "Can you imagine a bunch of rich stoners wandering around Nowhere? My big pieces are serious art."

I raised a brow.

Terrence sighed and rolled his eyes. "The distortions in size unsettle the viewer's self-perception and sense of place by disturbing the space," he said in a bored tone.

"Well," I said, shaking the dog loose. "Obviously. Did you talk to Rigby about the impact of the resort on the town's art?"

The artist's face contorted. "He laughed in my face. Said it was *because* of my art he wanted to build here. But he was out of luck. Marques would never sell."

"Oh?" I leaned against the yellow porch rail. It creaked beneath my weight, and I straightened.

"His building downtown, the mixed-use art and living space he's creating. Rigby wanted it, but he wasn't going to get it. Marques had no reason to sell. He didn't want the resort either."

"Why not?"

"He's got his own reasons," Terrence said darkly.

"I thought the resort was going to go forward at another location in Nowhere," I said.

"Where?" The artist snorted. "I mean, sure there are other empty buildings, but they'd have to be torn down and something new built on the site. It would have cost more. The cannery's ready to go."

"Where were you Sunday night, early Monday morning?" Charlie asked.

Oh, that was subtle.

"What is this?" Terrence stiffened. "An interrogation?"

"No." Charlie leaned on his cane. "We're just curious."

"I was home, alone, working in my studio."

"Can you think of anyone who'd want to kill Donald?" I asked.

Terrence rolled his eyes. "Aside from the entire town?"

"Aside from them," I said.

"No." He stepped backward and shut the door.

"I call that a success," Charlie said. "Now we know he doesn't have an alibi."

He also didn't have a good reason for killing Donald. I rubbed my jaw. Had Donald been trying to burn down the building himself? It would have given Marques a reason to sell the lot. But it seemed a little extreme.

We knocked around town for a bit after that, ate dinner, then drove toward my motel, Charlie tossing out murder theories. The sun sank behind the Sierras, night dropping like a velvet curtain.

I parked in front of my cabin and waited at the front door while Charlie hobbled up the porch steps.

"It's great to have you back in Nowhere." My brother brandished his cane, waggling it in the air. "The Sommerland siblings, investigating crimes."

I smiled and shook my head.

"What?" he asked.

"Nothing." I unlocked the door and glanced around the dark parking lot.

Something moved in the trees between the lot and the road, and I stiffened. Fredo sniffed at my shoes. Still staring into the trees, I opened the door for my brother.

Charlie dove sideways, knocking me into the railing. There was a whoosh and a metallic crunch. His cane clattered to the porch.

"Are you okay?" he asked, crushing me against the rail.

I pushed him away. "I will be once I can... breathe." I stared at my SUV.

An arrow quivered from its grill.

CHAPTER FOURTEEN

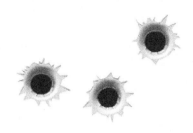

STEALTHY FOOTSTEPS PADDED THROUGH the darkened lot. Gently, I pressed my brother aside, a fluttery feeling in my gut. "Charlie," I said in a low voice. "Step back."

Fredo barked enthusiastically, his squat tail quivering.

Fitch edged around a Jeep and held a finger to his lips and the tension seeped from my muscles. Why he was here was a question for later.

He motioned toward the cabin's open door. I nodded and made a circling motion. The private detective changed direction, slinking around the side of the A-frame cabin.

Charlie leaned over the railing, watching his progress. "Who's—?"

I pressed my hand to his mouth and grimaced. He shut up.

I handed Fredo's leash to my brother and sidled to the cabin doorway. The interior of the cabin was dark. The security light beside the front door illuminated everything on the porch, including me. It also attracted a ton of insects. They batted against the lamp in a hopeless bid to reach the light.

I waited a beat.

Something crashed inside the cabin. I somersaulted through the doorway, coming up in a low fighting stance.

A light flicked on. "It's me." Fitch raised his hands in an I-surrender gesture. "The sliding door was unlocked."

My jaw hardened. "It wasn't when we left this morning."

"We?"

"My brother, Charlie's staying with me."

He nodded. "Oh, yeah. You mentioned that."

Charlie stuck his head in the room. "All clear?"

My gaze dropped to the chair Fitch had knocked over. A crossbow lay beside it on the laminate floor, beside the remains of my knitting.

I swore. "Dammit, Gert." I was never going to finish that sweater. I knelt and looked without touching. A string ran from the trigger to the front doorknob. I grabbed up what was left of my red sweater—now missing its needles—and tossed it on the bed.

"A booby trap?" Charlie hobbled inside on his cane. "Cool."

"Cool?" I looked up from the crossbow. "One of us could have been killed by that arrow."

"Technically, it's a bolt, not an arrow." He shrugged. "Just another thing I learned in the MBS. It's educational."

I pressed my mouth shut. But okay, I might have been a *little* jealous he knew something about weapons I didn't.

"Bolt or arrow," Fitch said, "your car's not looking too hot."

"It's not my—" I strode to the open door and groaned. Steam shot from the grill.

I should have gotten the rental insurance.

Fitch appeared beside me and whistled at the SUV. "She's dead, Jim."

"Can I keep it?" Charlie asked.

I turned, and we walked inside the cabin.

Beside the coffee table, my brother cradled the crossbow in his hands. "I've always wanted one. Oh, hey." He nodded to Fitch. "Aren't you that gardener?"

Fredo trotted around the cabin, sniffing for clues.

"Keep it? You…" I pinched the bridge of my nose. My brother's fingerprints were now on the crossbow. Sure, neither of us were PIs. But anyone who watched TV should have known better.

"This crossbow is in great condition." My brother motioned toward the open door, and the car beyond. "I mean, look what it did to your SUV."

Fitch pulled his phone from the rear pocket of his jeans and snapped a photo of Charlie holding the crossbow. "Are we calling the cops?"

I hesitated.

"No way," Charlie said. "It's Gert. We can't narc on Gert."

"Someone tried to kill you," Fitch said.

"Someone? I'm telling you, it was Gert." Charlie scratched his beard. "And he's not really trying to kill us. If he was, we'd be dead. Or at least Alice would be. He's got nothing against me."

I blew out my cheeks. If we took this to the cops with Charlie's prints on it, they might start looking harder at my brother. They might even think we'd set this whole thing up. But I didn't see how we could *not* report this to the cops.

"Gert?" Fitch asked. "The old guy who runs the antique shop?"

"He's got the best weaponry," Charlie said.

"That explains the crossbow. Why is he trying to kill you?"

"It's a long story," I said.

Fitch raised a brow. "I can't wait to hear it."

Charlie rubbed his bandages and frowned. "You can't call the cops on Gert. He's harmless."

My gaze flicked to the beamed ceiling. "That crossbow was not harmless."

"Look, Gert's going through something, okay?" Charlie said. "Just cut him some slack."

I raised my brows. "Cut *him* some—"

"Hey," Charlie said to Fitch. "Did you drive here? Because I'm not sure if I can walk to the theater tonight, what with my leg and all."

My fists clenched. "This isn't the—"

"You want a ride?" Fitch asked.

"Yeah." Charlie dropped the crossbow to his side. "It's the late show, but I can't be late. This one's not as hot as the 1920s mafia divorce, but I'm still the one-eyed man."

I tried again. "But—"

"What's going on?" The elderly motel manager peered through the open door into my cabin. She adjusted her reading glasses on their beaded chain. "I heard a ruckus."

"No ruckus," Charlie said. "I just knocked over a chair."

"Are you having a party in here?" she asked, querulous. "You're not allowed to have parties."

"No, no parties ma'am." Charlie steered her outside and shut the cabin door behind them, leaving me alone with Fitch.

"Why is a geriatric antiques dealer trying to kill you?" Fitch asked.

I sighed. "Like I said, long story. What were you doing here?"

He rubbed the back of his dark head. "I need your help."

"Oh?" I asked cautiously.

"Marques Washington. How well do you know him?"

"I knew his kids, but not him. And as soon as I was old enough, I left town. So not very well."

"Then you wouldn't mind breaking into his office?"

Oh, this was interesting. "Are you wearing a wire? Because breaking and entering is illegal." And I was really curious about how it was done.

"Yeah, I could lose my license if I got caught. Which is why I want your help in not getting caught."

"You think he was the one who tried to frame you for Donald's murder," I said, catching on. "But you said it was a woman who hired you."

Fitch shrugged. "There could be more than one person involved. And Marques hired me off the street to landscape the plots around the Big Things."

I folded my arms. "Yeah, how exactly did that come about?"

"I was in the Sagebrush Café, watching Rigby. Marques struck up a conversation with me at the counter. I told him

I was an underemployed gardener. He told me he needed a gardener. I got the job."

"That was convenient." I braced one hip against the foot of the twin bed.

"It gave me an excuse to be here, and in a small town like this, I needed one. Strangers stick out. Marques has the most to lose if that pot resort opens. He's invested big bucks in Nowhere."

"I'm not sure he loses," I said. "The value of his investment may increase if that marijuana resort goes through."

Fitch raked a hand through his thick hair. "I'm not sure either, which is why I want a look at his books. None of this is really adding up."

"So why do you need me exactly?"

"I saw him let you into the building earlier. I figured you might have noticed the door code."

"I might have," I admitted.

"Can I have it?"

"No."

He gave me a disappointed look. "You picked a fine time for ethics. So are you helping me or not?"

"Let me get this straight. You think since I let a sleazy client get killed, I'm the sort of person who won't blink at breaking and entering?"

He sucked in his cheeks. "That's not—"

"Well I am. Let's go."

We dropped Charlie off at the dinner theater. He pressed two tickets for tonight's show on us then vanished into the theater's rear door.

We'd left Fredo in the cabin, and I wasn't feeling good about it. I didn't worry about Fredo, but I did worry about what he might do to the motel.

Fitch and I strolled down Main Street. The shop windows were dark, and the tour buses long gone, the sidewalks empty.

"No wonder no one noticed Donald getting stabbed," I muttered. "This place is *still* a ghost town after dark. You know what time Rigby was killed?"

He shook his head. "All I know is he left his house after eleven. So he died sometime between then and when you found him Monday morning."

We passed the giant corkscrew.

"You were following him?" I asked.

"No, I got that intel from Carmel. I figure he was killed not long after that, probably around midnight. He told her he'd be back around one."

"That's what I figured too." *The infamous midnight nachos.* "Is there anywhere that even sells nachos in Nowhere at midnight?"

"Oh, yeah," he said. "The Viking bar."

That was good to know. And it sounded like Fitch had gotten more out of Carmel than I had. My insides squirmed. It was only a matter of time before he pegged Charlie as a suspect. If he hadn't already.

"All right," the PI said, "we'll keep it quick. In and out. No lights. No one will know we've ever been there."

I rolled my eyes. No *lights*. As if I'd flip on a light switch. I was a bodyguard, not a chump. "Right, low profile. Gotcha."

"Whoops," he said. "Act natural."

"Wh—"

Fitch pulled me into a kiss. Suffice it to say, the man knew what he was doing. So much so, I forgot about the why's and just enjoyed it. It had been a long time since I'd been kissed like that. I wasn't sure I'd ever been kissed like that.

"Ow." He jerked away and rubbed his chest. "You stuck me. What's that on your jacket?"

I adjusted the pin Charlie had given me. "I'm an honorary knight."

"Yeah, well your lance is—"

"Hey, Baby Alice!" a man shouted.

I jerked free and turned, my face heating. Mr. Washington stopped on the sidewalk and waved.

"Baby Alice?" Fitch whispered gleefully.

"That's Marques's father," I snarled. I could kick Fitch. This was going to be all over town by morning. "Act innocent." It was a silly thing to say. We were way beyond innocent.

"No," Fitch hissed, "I think I'll act guilty. What do you take me for? Of course I'll act innocent."

We crossed the street.

The elderly man waited for us to approach. "I guessed it was only a matter of time before you youngsters met up." He leered. "Are you two out for a romantic stroll?"

My cheeks grew hotter.

Fitch took my hand. "Yep, just a walk around town."

"Perambulating is good for the heart." Mr. Washington winked. "In more ways than one." He ambled down the sidewalk.

"So much for low profile," Fitch muttered. "Baby Alice."

I yanked my hand free and scowled. "Call me that again, and I'll hurt you."

He grinned. We circled the block and approached the brick cannery from the rear. The buildings behind it were deserted. We were less likely to encounter Nowhere's residents from that direction.

"I've been thinking about those gas cans," I lied. I'd been trying *not* to think about that kiss. Fitch had obviously had lots of practice. "Either Donald interrupted someone, or he came to burn down the cannery himself. But why?"

"Revenge?" he said. "To break Marques's spirit? Marques is pinning his hopes for economic development on that cannery. If it's gone, maybe he'll be less of an obstacle to the resort."

"I just get the feeling there's something else going on."

"Says the woman whose client got pureed by a tomato truck."

"I know it sounds unlikely," I snapped, "but it's what happened."

"What I can't figure out is why you were the only BG there." He turned to me, his chiseled face a study in shadows. "What happened to the rest of Koppel's team?"

My annoyance evaporated, replaced by a thick weight that pressed upon my lungs. "I don't know." I clawed my hands through my hair. "They were with another company." Or had they worked for his brother? Could they have been mafia?

"I was undercover," I continued, "doing countersurveillance, sometimes close, sometimes at a distance. At Koppel's request, his other team didn't know I was there..." But *had* they known, or at least figured it out? I rubbed my bottom lip. *Someone* had pointed the press in my direction.

His square jaw set. "And you took the fall."

"I wasn't blameless," I said. "I did let him steal my car. Not intentionally, but it happened."

"And speaking of cars, Rigby wasn't carrying two gas cans to fill up his. He had a half tank when they found him."

Impressive. Fitch had checked. And I hadn't thought to. But I was personal protection and not a PI.

"I'm betting there's plenty of flammable material inside the cannery," he continued.

"And Marques caught Rigby and killed him?" I shook my head. This was a lot of speculation.

"A knife is generally a man's weapon," he said.

I didn't bother calling him sexist. In my experience, Fitch was right. Men *were* more likely to use knives. They were messier.

I pulled from my back pocket a pair of leather gloves I'd brought from the motel and put them on. Waiting for Fitch to look away, I punched in the building's code. The lock beeped. We crept inside.

Fitch flipped on a red-light flashlight, the kind campers used so they could see where they were going and still admire the stars. I unclipped mine from my belt and clicked it on.

"A red-light?" One corner of his mouth quirked upward. "Where have you been all my life?"

I shook my head and tried not to smile. "The office is on the fourth floor."

We crept across the floor, dirt and construction material crunching beneath our shoes.

"Now will you tell me why Gert Magimountain wants you dead?" he asked.

"No." Was breaking and entry a misdemeanor or a felony in Nevada? Either way, we couldn't afford to get caught. The sheriff was already giving me the stink-eye.

"Why not?" he asked.

"It feels a little personal."

CRASH. The metallic blast reverberated through the building.

Fitch shoved me sideways, pressed me against a wall. He exhaled slowly, his breath soft against my throat. "So much for my catlike stealth."

His muscles were iron against mine, and he'd pushed me as if I hadn't weighed anything at all. I swallowed.

He eased away from me, and I shined my red light on the floor. A metal table lay on its side next to a heavy, circular saw. Fitch levered the table upright. With a grunt, he returned the saw to its top. We continued up the stairs and to the office.

Fitch rattled the doorknob. "Locked."

"Someone smashed a window to get in here two days ago," I said. "Marques must have gotten more security conscious."

In the darkness, the silhouette of Fitch's head tilted. "There was a break-in? Interesting."

"They took the gas cans."

"Why didn't you mention this before?"

"I wanted to see where the evening went," I said.

He choked back a laugh.

"The gas can theft implies Marques doesn't have anything to do with it," I continued. "Unless he has a partner and performed the entire charade for the sheriff's benefit."

Fitch knelt and pulled something from his pocket. "Give me some light on this lock?"

I aimed my red light at the office's doorknob. Fitch slid a bent piece of metal followed by a lock pick into it. He fiddled with the pick.

We didn't use these things in my business, and I watched, interested. That was a skill I wouldn't mind learning. I did know how to hotwire a car—something I'd learned in college during a brief relationship with a mechanic. But since I could only hotwire older models, this wasn't particularly useful.

"Question," he said. "When you decided to go into hiding, why did you choose your hometown? Doesn't it seem a little obvious?"

"Everyone thinks my hometown is Reno."

"There *are* records, you know. I'm just saying, as a PI..."

Annoyed, I brushed back my hair. "I didn't think I'd be big news. I wasn't protecting Koppel. And Nowhere was close."

He shrugged. "Investigative journalism is dead. All reporters do is regurgitate press releases written by the people they're supposedly investigating. It's why they all use the same language."

I shook my head. "That's cynical." The phone rang in my pocket, and I winced.

He looked up. "We're committing a B&E, and you forgot to silence your phone?"

"You knocked over a circular saw." I checked the number in case it was Charlie. But it was a number I didn't recognize. "Probably a telemarketer."

"At this hour?"

Palms damp, I declined the call, turned off the ringer, and pocketed the phone.

The lock clicked, and Fitch turned the knob. "We're in."

Fitch edged into the room, and I followed, checking over my shoulder. I wasn't really worried about that crash being overheard. It was a big building, and not many people were on the street at this hour. Odds were we hadn't been noticed. But my skin twitched, my stomach knotting.

I found a filing cabinet, and Fitch booted up the desktop computer.

After five minutes, he grunted. "I'm in."

"Are you a hacker too?"

"I guessed the password, one-two-three-four. Easy to remember and easy to crack."

I thumbed through the manila files. My hands were steady, but my pulse raced. Receipts. Invoices. Nothing screamed of a motive for murder.

"It looks like Marques is heavily mortgaged."

I returned a file to the narrow wooden cabinet. "That's not unusual for an entrepreneur like Marques."

Fitch's head turned, the computer screen casting craggy shadows across his face.

"I was on a team protecting some guys in construction over in the old Soviet Union," I explained. "Leverage is the name of the game. It's how they make money. They borrow it and risk it."

"Judging by these numbers, a fire in this cannery would have been a blow." He squinted at the screen. "Though he's paying insurance premiums."

"Got it." Triumphant, I pulled out an insurance contract. "The building's insured for fifty thousand."

"Doesn't sound like enough."

"This isn't Hot Springs. Property values here can't be all that high."

Fitch shook his head. "It won't be hard to verify." He pulled a zip drive from his breast pocket and stuck it into the computer. "I don't want to spend more time here than we need to. I'll look the computer files over back at my office."

Where I wouldn't get to see the results. But we'd been here long enough, and I nodded. We closed up and slipped from the building. I returned the gloves to my back pocket, but I kept the flashlight in my hand. They made good weapons too.

"So what do you think?" Fitch asked. "Want to go to the dinner theater?"

"Why?" I asked, glancing at him sidelong. What was he up to?

"Don't think this is a date or anything. We just committed a crime. We need an alibi. Besides, I like dinner theater. And we have two tickets."

I laughed. Who didn't like a good mystery? "Fine. Let's check out the dinner theater."

We walked down the quiet street and turned the corner. Gas lamps flickered outside the dinner theater's old-west building. The gravel lot beside it was filled with cars.

"I've heard of this place," Fitch said. "It's getting popular."

"There's not a whole lot to do in Nowhere after hours."

"No, I mean, I heard about it in Reno." He opened the door for me. "The theater's becoming a destination."

I ran my hands through my hair. "Really?"

I handed over our tickets at the window while Fitch perused the murder mystery role-playing games for sale.

FLAPPERS AND FALL GUYS
A Mystery Roleplaying Game
By Charlie Sommerland
Take the Mystery Home!

A woman in a flapper dress took our tickets and ushered us to a small, round table covered in a red cloth. We were seriously underdressed. Most of the other guests also wore 1920s garb. They wandered through the tables, sipping champagne and mingling.

A stage with red curtains closed across it dominated one side of the wide room but the actors weren't on it. They mingled with the guests.

"No, Sir," my brother's voice boomed from the crowd. "I took no part in that dastardly scheme."

"Oooh, this must be the part where the guests interrogate the actors," I said. "The murder must have already happened. Come on. Let's find out who died."

Fitch rubbed his broad hands together. "Don't feel bad when you can't figure it out. I'm a professional detective, after all."

"Just think how embarrassing it will be when I win."

I plucked a full champagne glass off the tray of a passing waitress. Fitch followed me through the maze of tables. A blonde in an emerald beaded dress and matching cloche hat gave a man in a tux and tails a bored look.

"Daring Dan may be rolling in cabbage," she said in a nasal voice, "but I ain't going to the big house for no one. I saw him in the garden with my own two eyes, and there's nothing nobody can say to make me say otherwise."

I blinked at the blonde. "Ivanna?" A wig covered her red hair, and that simple change had been enough to briefly throw me.

"Don't know her." Ivanna looked me up and down. "What sort of get-up is that?"

"Who died?" Fitch asked.

Ivanna dropped her chin and rolled her eyes. "That dumb Dora, Fran Wilson. Where've *you* been?" She pivoted away.

"What exactly happened to Fran?" Fitch asked her.

Ivanna paused and adjusted her cloche hat to dip further over one eye. She glanced over her shoulder at us. "Whaddaya think happened to her? She got fogged."

"Shut your head, Morganna." Charlie, in a white suit and eyepatch, limped through the crowd leaning on an elegant cane.

Ivanna made a negligent motion and moved toward another group of guests.

"Charlie?" I asked, uncertain, because his face looked blockier somehow.

Charlie bowed. "Daniel Darkwing, at your service."

"Nice to meet you, Mr. Darkwing," Fitch said. "We're just trying to get a handle on what's going on."

"The big sleep," Charlie said mournfully. "It comes for us all, but it came for Fran too soon."

"Did you know her well?" Fitch asked.

"She was my wife's maid and a valued employee."

"But nothing more?" Fitch's eyes narrowed.

Charlie straightened. "Just what are you implying?"

"We heard the two of you were seen together before her death," Fitch said.

We'd heard no such thing, I thought, indignant. That was a shot in the dark. One that landed.

"Yes," Charlie said, "because she'd come to tell me my wife's jewels had gone missing. She was worried she'd be blamed."

Fitch rubbed his jaw. "Tell me more about these jewels..."

I sipped my champagne and watched, interested, as the show went on. Charlie was good. Really good. He improvised witty retorts, got laughs out of the guests, and in the end was voted the killer.

But the majority had it wrong. Lilyanna, playing his wife in a heavy beaded dress, had killed Fran in a fit of jealousy. Both Fitch and I had guessed right.

We enjoyed cocktails with the cast afterward. And when we were shuffled from the theater, Fitch and I waited outside for Charlie to get out of costume.

Fitch leaned against a lamp post. "Your brother's a good actor."

"And that's all he is," I said sharply, thumbing through *Flappers and Fall Guys,* the game Charlie had made. Fitch considered Charlie a suspect. *Dammit.*

He shrugged. "I'm just saying."

Charlie, hobbling on his normal cane, emerged from the back door. "So what'd you think?" he asked excitedly. The metal door clanged shut behind him.

"You were terrific," I said. "I had no idea you were such a good actor." My chest tightened. Why *hadn't* I known? Because I'd spent little time in Nowhere since high school. Charlie and I'd had occasional calls but that was no excuse.

"Thanks." Charlie rubbed his beard and plucked out a piece of glue. "Right now, we've got three 1920s scenarios for our shows—Flappers and Fall Guys, Death in the Mines, and

Death at the Adventurer's Academy. That's a sort of 1920s adventurers club. The 1920s are popular for murder."

"How'd you change your face?"

"You put something in your mouth, along your jaw." He bared his teeth. "Back here," he mumbled, his hand pointing where inside his mouth. "Ivanna taught me how to do it. She's amazing." His eyes glowed.

"I knew your wife was the killer," Fitch said. "But I got outvoted."

"I know," my brother said. "People always want me to be the bad guy." He shrugged. "It's the eyepatch."

"There does seem to be an unreasonable prejudice against them," Fitch agreed.

The PI drove us back to my cabin and parked beside my car. It was no longer spewing steam, but the crossbow bolt still stuck from the grill.

Charlie lumbered from the back seat. "Thank you, kind sir, for the lift."

"Anytime," Fitch said.

I opened the passenger door.

"See you tomorrow?" Fitch asked me.

"Not if I see you first." Glancing at my phone, I stepped from the car and checked my messages. A text transcription of a message flashed on the screen, and my stomach plunged. I stumbled to a halt.

"What is it?" Fitch asked from the driver's seat.

"I got a call from a reporter," I said slowly.

"Cool," my brother said. "Now you can tell your side of the story."

"Who?" Fitch asked.

"A guy named Zed Kelley," I said.

Fitch whistled.

I leaned inside the SUV. "You know him?" I rubbed the corner of the cellphone with my thumb.

"He's got a YouTube channel," Fitch said. "He's a big name in the new media."

I exhaled, relaxing. *Online videos.* Zed was small time. But how had he found me?

"You okay?"

"Yeah," I said slowly. So a reporter had gotten my number. It wasn't like he could triangulate off cell towers to find my location.

I shut the car door, jogged up the porch steps, and stopped short, staring. A knife handle stuck from the cabin's door.

CHAPTER FIFTEEN

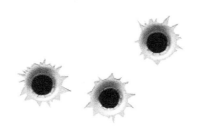

I BRACED MY FISTS on my hips and glared at the knife stuck in the cabin's wooden door. "Oh, this is just—"

"Overkill?" Fitch suggested, stepping from his SUV.

"Ridiculous." Death beside a giant can of peas, a crossbow, a knife in the door. It was too much.

Charlie reached for the knife.

"Don't touch it," Fitch and I shouted in unison.

Behind the closed cabin door, Fredo barked once. A high-pitched yap.

The dog. I smacked my forehead. I'd almost forgotten about Fredo. He must be ready for a walk. I opened the door. The tiny dog charged out, snapping and snarling.

"Hey, buddy." Charlie lifted him up.

Fredo gave him a startled look and fell silent.

Pulling my phone from my pocket, I snapped a picture of the knife in the door. pulled on my gloves again and wrenched the stiletto from the door. It looked a lot like the knife that had been left behind at the murder scene but flimsier and with a bone handle. In fact... I squinted. It wasn't a knife. It was a letter opener.

"What is it?" My brother set the dog on the porch.

Fredo bounded to me and tugged at my shoestrings, his bulging eyes rolling with the effort.

"Gert again?" Fitch asked.

I frowned. "Maybe." It seemed odd he'd return so soon. Maybe he'd come back to make sure I was dead, and when I wasn't, had left the letter opener?

Walking inside the cabin, I switched on the brass hanging lamp. I laid the letter opener on the coffee table.

"Hey, cool," Charlie said. "Can I keep the stiletto?"

"No," I said.

Fitch snapped a picture of the blade. "Who knew small towns had so much drama?"

"Everyone who's ever lived in a small town."

"But seriously," Charlie said, "mind if I keep it?"

"It's evidence." And removing it from the door had been a rookie mistake, especially after scolding Charlie for picking up the crossbow. I might not be a detective, but I should have known better. I needed to start acting like a PI, even if I didn't feel like one.

And Gert needed to back off.

"You admit you and your brother handled the crossbow and the bolt. Your prints'll be all over them," the sheriff said over the phone.

I sat on the edge of the bed and edged aside the cabin's curtains. The morning shadows knifed across the discount cemetery. "But there could be other prints too."

He slurped something, I imagined coffee. Whatever he was drinking, it had to be better than the stuff in my kitchenette. "If you haven't messed those up too," he said.

I winced. He had a point. "What about that letter opener?"

"Letter opener? What letter opener?"

"The knife in the door isn't a real knife," I said. "It's a letter opener."

"So it's even less of a threat."

"It looks a lot like the knife Rigby was killed with," I said, repressing my irritation.

"But you said it's not a knife. It's a letter opener."

"Yeah."

"Then I don't see the point."

"But... Gert said he was going to kill me." I winced. Had that come off whiney? It had sounded whiney.

The sheriff laughed. "Magimountain? That guy's ancient." He wheezed over the phone. "What's he gonna do?"

"He tried to brain me with a flowerpot."

The sheriff laughed harder and hung up.

"Well, I could have been hurt," I muttered and pocketed the phone.

The cabin door creaked open, and Charlie and Fredo strolled in. "What did he say? Can we keep the weapons?" Charlie asked.

I frowned at the crossbow and letter opener on the coffee table. "Sure. Why not?" The sheriff wasn't interested in them.

"Cool. Hey, did you hear a tourist tried to climb the giant flamingo last night? He got stuck, and the fire department had to get him down."

I stared at him fixedly.

"Okay," my brother said, "maybe it's not the first time something like this has happened. But still. The flamingo, right? This place is crazy."

And Charlie thought the town's quirkiness was a reason for me to stay. I smiled weakly. "Yeah, it is."

I spent the next two hours waiting for someone from the car rental place. Finally, a tow truck trundled up to my door, and a bulky man hopped from the cab.

"Hi." I looked around, rubbing my jaw. No new car. Maybe it was still on the road. "Do you have any idea when I'm getting my replacement vehicle?"

He shrugged. "Nope. I'm just here for the car. They didn't tell me about a replacement."

"Okay. Thanks." I backed onto the cabin's porch and called the rental company.

"You're not on the list to get another car," the customer service rep said.

"But I talked to one of your representatives last night. She said she'd send a new one."

"That was before we learned what had happened to your first car."

There was a metallic, creaking sound, and the tow truck lifted the rear of my car into the air.

I sucked in my cheeks. "It's not my fault someone shot it with an arrow."

"It was a bolt," she corrected. "A crossbow bolt. And since your car was parked face-in, it had to have been intentional."

Everybody's a detective. "So? I didn't do it."

"Tell that to Koppel's victims. They won't get their day in court."

"That's not—"

She hung up. *Fair.* I stared at the phone and pocketed it. The barb had hurt more than it should have.

I forced a smile. At some point, people would figure out Koppel's death wasn't my fault. And there were other car rental agencies. In Reno.

The tow truck rumbled through the parking lot and turned onto the shady street.

Stumped, I stared after my retreating car. "How am I supposed to get around?"

Charlie leaned against the wooden porch railing. "You can use my bike." He tapped his leg with his cane. "It's not like I can ride it. It's locked behind the dinner theater." My brother hobbled closer and pulled a set of keys from the pocket of his surf shorts. He tossed them to me.

I grimaced. *A bicycle.* Not only was I hiding out in Nowhere, I was regressing to childhood. But I didn't have the time or energy to get a lift to Reno. I blew out a breath. "Thanks."

Leaving Fredo with Charlie, I walked to the dinner theater. As Charlie had promised, his mountain bike was locked to a lamp post behind it. The orange bike was in good condition, if a little muddy. I climbed onto the bike and wobbled around the parking lot for a few minutes. When I was relatively certain I wouldn't fall off, I peddled to Gert's shop, Magimountain Antiques.

I coasted past a backhoe in the rear parking lot, around the low building, and to the front of the shop. Its dusty windows were cluttered with junk. Yanking open the glass door harder than I'd intended, I walked inside. An electronic chime pinged.

Gert looked up from his counter. In a smooth motion, he pulled a Glock Gen4 from beneath the counter and aimed it at my head.

I blinked, my insides freezing. The eyes of the jackalopes lining the shelf behind him glittered. Overhead, a florescent light made dull, rhythmic pinging sounds. A deck of cards lay on the glass counter, an Ace of Spades face up on top. I'd underestimated Gert. In my defense, it was hard to take seriously a guy who looked like a gnome and tried to kill you with a flowerpot.

I did my calming four-count breath. "Do you really want to shoot me?" I asked and was pleased to hear my voice was steady.

"You're in my store. I've got the right."

"I'm unarmed."

"Your hands are deadly weapons."

"But imagine the mess."

His eyes narrowed.

"Plus," I continued, "how would Charlie feel if he had to bury me in a closed casket?"

Gert cocked his head, considering. "He did re-roof my garage." He lowered the gun.

My muscles sagged, and I released a slow breath. I'd live to fight another day. "Can I ask you something?"

He shrugged. "Ask."

"How many people have you killed?"

"Including you?" He looked up at the stained ceiling. His lips moved silently. "None."

I blinked. "None?"

"I'm on retainer. This is the first time I've been retained."

My heart vaulted into my throat. "Wait. You've—Someone's contacted you?"

"Not yet," he said. "It's only a matter of time. I suppose you're here about the crossbow."

I forced my heartbeat to slow. Okay. This was okay. No Estonian mafiosos were gunning for revenge. And our guess that Gert had set up the crossbow had been correct. "No, I'm here about a knife."

He blinked. "What knife?"

I pulled out my phone and scrolled to my crime scene photos at the can of peas. "Charlie's staying in my cabin until his leg is back in tree-climbing shape. Plan your next attack accordingly."

"Roger that."

I slid the photo across the glass counter. "I wanted your opinion on this knife."

He adjusted his glasses and squinted at the screen. "You've got a picture of the murder weapon?"

I raised a brow.

"The sheriff was here earlier," he explained.

"What can you tell me about it?"

"Looks like a replica of a seventeenth-century stiletto." He tapped the glass counter with one crooked finger. "That's Italian."

"Did it come from your store?"

His eyes narrowed. "It might have."

"Who did you sell it to?"

"Does this look like the kind of place that keeps detailed records?"

I studied the dusty register. No, the shop did not. I lifted my chin toward the rear of the store. "Are you branching out from antiques? What's with the backhoe out back?"

"I rent it. I've got motorbikes too. You look like a motorbike type." His expression turned crafty. "I'll give you a deal."

And sabotage the bike. "No, thanks. Has Carmel Rigby been in here lately?"

He brightened. "Yes, she was in a couple weeks ago."

"Did she buy the knife?"

"No idea. Knives are popular. She was here for a birthday gift for her husband."

"Did Donald like knives?"

"He's from Nevada. Of course he does." Gert pulled out a ginormous magnifying glass on a swivel and frowned at the photo on my phone. "Too bad about the paint."

"What paint?"

He pointed to a tiny brown smear beneath the handle.

"Looks like dirt to me," I said.

"It's paint." The phone buzzed in his hand. "You've got a call." He returned my phone.

I checked the number and stilled. *The reporter from last night.* I declined the call. "What kind of paint?"

"How should I know? Do you see paint for sale here? But look at that smear. It lowers the knife's value."

Paint. I realized Gert was still talking. "Sorry. What?"

"I said, I could probably remove the paint."

I shrugged. "It's a moot point. The knife's in evidence, and it's not mine."

"Was it one of Charlie's?"

"No," I said, too sharply.

He looked up.

"It's not his," I said, my insides rolling. But the antique-looking knife, the gas cans... They all pointed to my brother.

CHAPTER SIXTEEN

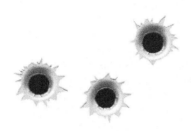

IT WAS ONLY A matter of time before the sheriff brought my brother in for questioning. But the paint on the knife pointed to Terrence, the Big Things artist who did not like the idea of a marijuana resort.

I stopped pacing and stared out the cabin's back windows.

Though Carmel had been in the antique shop too. She could have bought the knife that had killed her husband. If Donald had gambled away their retirement, she'd have motive.

The stag watched me from the other side of the creek. He lowered his head to the water.

"What?" Charlie asked from my couch. His sandalled feet rested on the coffee table, his cane propped beside it. "Something's bugging you, I can tell."

Fredo yipped on the other cushion.

"Who else did Donald owe money to?" I asked.

"How do you know he owed anyone else?"

"Because people stick to their patterns."

"It's a small town," Charlie said. "If he was a deadbeat, people would know."

But my brother might not. He thought the best of people and was oblivious to gossip. "People like who?"

He scrunched his face, thinking.

"Who's the town gossip?" I asked. "Aside from Mrs. Malone."

He rolled his eyes. "That's a stereotype. Not every small town has a gossip. But ours is Mrs. Malone."

Who I'd already talked to with no success. But there *was* a town gathering place, where gossip was likely to wash ashore. I checked my watch. "Lunch?"

Charlie straightened and hitched up his board shorts. "Sure. Uh, are you paying? I'm a little short."

"My treat." I eyed Fredo. He'd destroyed a bath towel last night, but if he went after the furniture... "Is the Sagebrush dog friendly?"

"Yeah, they let dogs on the back patio."

It wasn't ideal, but I'd make it work. "Good enough. I'll call a rideshare."

"Don't bother. I can borrow a bike from the motel manager."

I pointed to the bandages around his leg. "I thought you couldn't ride."

"My leg's feeling better," he said. "I can do it."

I trailed Charlie into the dirt parking lot and watched him hobble to the manager's office. I unlocked his bike from the deck, carried it down the stairs, set it against the porch railing. Stretching, I ambled to the corner of the A-frame cabin.

There was a thunder of hooves, a rush of wind, a blur of motion. I threw myself sideways and landed hard on the dirt. The stag charged past and pivoted gracefully. It stared down at me.

On the dirt, I stared back. I didn't know if getting up or staying down was the better move.

The stag snorted and tossed its head. Turning, it walked away, its tail flicking with contempt, point made.

I changed my clothes, and we pedaled to the Sagebrush, Fredo in my saddlebag. We passed a parked tour bus on the street. We locked our bikes to the diner's wooden fence, and I collected Fredo from the saddlebag. The small dog didn't want to leave. Maybe if I got him a comfort vest, he'd calm down. It worked for Lilyanna.

I held the door for my brother. He limped inside, and I followed. The café was filled with people I didn't recognize, tourists from the nearby bus. Fitch sat at the counter. Ignoring the detective, I led Fredo out the rear door and found a table on the back patio.

Charlie hooked his cane over the metal chair and lowered himself into it. "I'm telling you, it's more than just a game," he said, continuing the lecture he'd begun on our ride here. He pointed at the pin on my jacket. He'd been so happy to give me the pin, I'd decided to wear it for a while. "Being a knight in the MBS is serious business."

"Mm, hm." Worried, I gazed at the mountains looming over the town. How long did Charlie have before the sheriff brought him in? A cloud capped the highest peak, still dotted with snow. But the cloud wouldn't make it to Nowhere. It took a super storm to get past the Sierras in this part of Nevada.

"Knights have duties," he continued. "And the training is intense."

Ivanna set a dog bowl beneath our table. Fredo ignored it and gnawed the hem of my jeans. The wire mesh table cast prison bars across his rolling eyes.

Ivanna cleared her throat. "What can I start you two with?"

Charlie patted his flat abs. "I'll have the burrito con carne."

"I'll have the Buddha Bowl," I said.

"Oh," Charlie said, "and I'll have the loaded fries." He leaned closer to me. "You don't mind, do you? It's a dollar extra."

"No." I could afford an extra dollar. For now. My insides quivered. I *would* get my career back.

My brother smiled, relaxing in his chair. "Cool. Thanks."

"Sure thing." Ivanna tapped her pen on her notepad. "When are you planning on returning to the treehouse?"

My brother lifted his cane off the chair. "As soon as I get off this. The doc says it'll be six weeks."

I stood. "I'll be back in a few minutes. Watch the dog, will you?" I walked inside the café and made for the counter.

Fitch's glance flicked toward me and away. I took that to mean he didn't want to talk right now. But I wasn't here for the detective. The old timers sat on their faded blue barstools and sipped coffee.

I sidled onto a stool beside Mr. Washington, who seemed to be the one fixed star in the counter's rotating constellation of men. "Hi."

"Howdy, Baby Alice."

I winced.

He laughed. "You're not losing that moniker any time soon, especially not riding around on that bicycle."

"You don't forget a thing," I said, morose. If people hadn't forgotten my mutton-busting disaster, what were the odds they'd forget about Koppel?

"The memory loss is coming. I play word games every morning to stay sharp though. I've got an app." He brandished his cell phone. "Marques got it for me."

I lowered my voice. "I need help on an investigation."

"What?"

"I need help on an investigation," I said marginally louder.

"What? Can't hear you." He tapped his hearing aid.

"I need help on an investigation," I shouted into a conversational lull and winced.

Tourists turned to stare. I rubbed my forehead. *I'll laugh about this later. Much, much later.*

"Not sure you'll find any clues as to who killed that Koppel fellow in Nowhere." Mr. Washington adjusted his hearing aid. "Okay. Now I can hear you better."

A plate crashed. The diner's attention shifted to the hapless waitress.

"I'm not investigating Koppel's death," I said in a normal voice. "I know how he died."

"Killed by one of his blackmail victims?"

"Honestly, it was just a tomato truck. I'm asking about Donald Rigby."

Mr. Washington whistled. "That one was always trouble. The only surprise is why he wasn't killed sooner."

I looked at my hands on the sky-blue counter. "I wondered about the timing too. Why kill him now? What's different?"

He sipped his coffee. "That marijuana resort, for starters. The only person happy about that was the mayor."

"What about Donald's personal life?"

The elderly man shrugged. "Let's just say he didn't make friends here."

"Because of the gambling?"

He peered into his white mug. "Right. The gambling."

"He owe money around town?"

Mr. Washington looked around. "Not that I heard." He turned to the old man beside him. "Rigby owe any money in Nowhere?"

The man blew on his coffee. "Everybody knows he owed money in Nowhere."

"But to whom?" Mr. Washington asked.

His friend shrugged. "I thought you mentioned it."

"I thought you told me." Mr. Washington leaned over the counter and peered at the third man, short and round and breaking the crust on a cherry pie. "Bud," Mr. Washington said. "Bud!"

Bud put down his fork and chewed slowly. "What?"

"Who told us Rigby owed money in Nowhere?"

Bud swallowed. "I thought you did."

"But who told me?"

"Am I supposed to keep track of everyone who tells you something now?" Bud grumped.

"Yes," Mr. Washington said. "You are."

"I'll make a note of it." Bud returned to his pie.

Mr. Washington swiveled to face me. "I don't know who told me."

"You said Donald didn't make friends," I said. "Why?"

"Well. He left."

Mr. Washington was carefully *not* telling me something. I hesitated. "If you remember anything else, will you let me know?"

"You know where to find me." He raised his mug in a salute. "Thanks."

I returned to the patio. Ivanna had vanished, and Charlie was feeding Fredo pieces of bacon. The dog ate like a shark, his eyes rolling back into his head with each bite. The other patio diners watched with expressions of disgust and horror.

"Where did you get bacon?" I dropped into my chair. "It can't be good for Fredo's digestion."

"It's meat. So what'd you learn?"

I started. My brother wasn't as oblivious as I wanted to think.

"I figured you were still investigating," he continued. "Ivanna thinks it's totally cool."

"I'm not—" *Why bother?* "I got confirmation that Rigby owed money around town. I just don't know to whom."

Ivanna strode to our table carrying a tray. "Here you go." She smiled and set Charlie's burrito and fries in front of him, and a bowl of tofu and vegetables in front of me.

I eyed the burrito. Its edges touched the rim of the large plate. The rest of the plate overflowed with fries drowning in sour cream, cheese, peppers, and bacon. I hated eating healthy.

"Anything else I can get you?" Ivanna asked. A hank of auburn hair slipped from its bun.

"Yeah." Charlie scooted forward in his chair and dropped his voice to a whisper. "Alice's investigation has taken a turn."

I glared. At this point, everyone might not be a suspect, but they *were* potential gossips.

She fingered her thin gold necklace. "Oh?"

"It looks like Donald Rigby owed money around town," he said. "Have you heard anything?"

She blinked, and her blue eyes widened fractionally. "Seriously?"

"A lot of gossip washes through the Sagebrush," Charlie said. "And we figured you may have heard something."

Her tray dropped to her side. "No one's said anything to me."

Charlie sat back, his face creasing with disappointment. "Oh. Bummer."

"I'll keep my ears open though," she said.

"Thanks." Charlie smiled.

She turned and strode into the brick building, her hips swinging.

"She's great, isn't she?" Charlie asked.

I shook my head, ignoring his question. "No more telling your friends about our investigation, even if you think they might have info. *Especially* if you think they might have information."

"Okay, okay. No more talking to my friends."

The odds of that happening were close to zero, but what was I going to do? He was my little brother.

"So what do you think?" he asked.

I thought this wasn't getting me anywhere. The person who knew Donald best was his wife. She was the one I should be talking to, not random waitresses. It was time I had a real, sober talk with Carmel.

"You know who else might know who had it in for Donald?" Charlie asked.

"Who?" I asked.

"Carmel."

I sighed and dug into my salad. It wasn't going to be easy to keep Charlie out of this. "Yeah, she might."

"We should talk to her." Charlie shoveled burrito into his mouth.

"I'll do it later."

He set down his fork and folded his arms. "Oh, come *on*. You're going to go see her now, aren't you? I'm coming with you."

"No."

"Are you trying to protect me or something?"

"Yes."

"Carmel's not going to hurt me." He pulled a fry, dripping cheese from his plate.

"She may have killed her husband."

"No way." He popped the fry in his mouth.

I tried the tofu. It was mildly spiced and pretty good. "If not her, then who?"

Charlie swallowed. "Honestly? I can't believe anyone in Nowhere killed him. It was probably some jerk from Hot Springs."

"Gert Magimountain has tried to kill me three times."

"That's different. He's having a rough time."

"*He's* having a rough time?" I raised my brows. "He wrecked my car."

"It was a rental. And Gert's cool."

I drummed my fingers on the metal table. *Could* Gert have killed Rigby? I didn't know why he would have, but I couldn't ignore there was a wannabe hitman in town.

"So why's Gert having such a hard time?" I asked.

Charlie shifted in his chair. "I don't think I should say anything. It's personal."

"You told me about Marques."

"That's different. Everyone knows that. I don't think I'm supposed to know this. I mean, I don't really *know*. I just assume. It seems obvious to me. But still. I shouldn't say anything."

I eyed him. When had my brother learned to keep a secret?

We rode to Carmel's house and parked our bikes beneath the big pine tree in the front yard. Charlie and I stood a long moment looking at the ranch house—our old home. A pit formed in my gut. It was only a house, and I hadn't lived in it for a long time. And I'd spent years dreaming of leaving it.

Fredo growled.

"Okay," I finally said. "Let's do this."

I retrieved Fredo from the saddle bag and hooked on his leash. The three of us walked to the front door, and again I paused. How many times had I breezed through this door? Our parents had rarely locked it.

Charlie knocked on the door with his cane. "It's weird coming back, isn't it?"

"Yeah. It is."

He shifted his weight. "I guess if I hadn't lost it, it wouldn't be so weird. It would still be ours."

"Yours."

"Right," he said. "Mine."

But it *would* have been different if Charlie still owned the house. It would have still felt like the family home, even if it hadn't been mine. The low, yellow house blurred. I hadn't realized how much I'd wanted a place to come home to until I'd returned. But *did* I want that?

"You hear anyone inside?" Charlie asked.

"No, I don't." The house had an abandoned air, but a Mercedes sat in the driveway.

"Let's look around."

"It's not our house anymore. We'd be trespassing."

But Charlie had already limped off the porch and to the ungated side yard. I swore and dragged Fredo after him. Charlie was pretty speedy for a guy with a cane.

"Carmel?" Charlie shouted, hobbling in front of me.

"Get back here," I hissed. Was Nevada a castle-doctrine state? Carmel might be within her rights to shoot us.

"Carmel?" he called again and rounded the corner.

"She's not home," I said. "We'll try again later."

"Sure, and you'll sneak off and leave me back at the motel."

"I promise I won't," I lied.

He pressed his face to a sliding glass door, cupping his hands around his eyes to block the glare. Charlie staggered backward. I grabbed his arm to balance him.

He pointed his cane, shaking, toward the window. "Carmel," he croaked.

I went to the window and peered inside.

Carmel lay on the floor beside a fireplace and stared blankly at me.

Carmel was dead.

CHAPTER SEVENTEEN

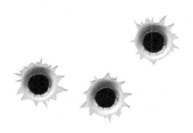

CHARLIE CRANKED BACK HIS cane, as if he were winding up a baseball bat.

"No." I grabbed his arm before he could break the glass. "We're too late," I said, low and intense, pushing down my fury.

Anger was useless. Stupid. But I'd thought I could protect the people of Nowhere. I should have known better.

And I'd *liked* Carmel. She'd given me her Viking helmet and got me on top of that mushroom, which I'd really wanted to do anyway. And yes, all that was silly and shallow, but an ache speared my chest anyway.

The phone in my pocket pinged, and the memory rose of the bleak interior of a gray surveillance van. I'd been in one when I'd gotten the text from Charlie telling me our father had died. I'd come home then, too late to say goodbye. It had been a year since I'd seen my father before he died, and I hadn't even been here for that. The ache rose into my throat.

"But—" Charlie began.

"No." I shook my head, and he dropped his arm.

Fredo growled at the glass door.

"Too late for what?" Fitch asked. We started and turned toward his voice.

Charlie blinked. "Oh, hi. You're... that gardener." He canted his head. "Are you working for the Rigbys?"

"Something like that." Fitch stepped up to the glass door and looked in. He was quiet a long moment. "Did you touch anything?"

"No," I said and looked again.

A fireplace poker lay in a crimson puddle. The blood had spread, staining the carpet. Fredo returned his attention to gnawing on my jeans.

"Have you called the sheriff?" the detective asked.

"I will now." Throat thick, I turned away from the men.

I didn't like being the one to call in another murder. The person who found the body was always an object of suspicion, and now I'd found two. But we *had* found the body. I couldn't pretend we hadn't, no matter who made the call. I called the sheriff's office, and when I'd finished, we waited for the police.

"You followed us," I said to Fitch.

The PI nodded. "I had a feeling I should tag along."

"I'm not sorry you did," I admitted. Fitch had seen us arrive. He'd be able to confirm we hadn't had time to kill Carmel.

Of course, we could have come here earlier, committed the murder, and then returned to "discover" the body. Days like these, I hated having an imagination.

It took an hour for the sheriff and his deputies to arrive. I was trying hard not to be annoyed by that. But this *was* an emergency. This was murder, and time was of the essence.

We gave our statements and were told not to go anywhere. We watched from the sidewalk. Deputies walked in and out of the house. Neighbors emerged from their ranch homes to see the show.

The sheriff ambled from the house, pointed at me, and crooked a finger. He waited for me to meet him beneath the front yard's big pine. "Explain again how you found *this* body."

Keep it brief. "My brother and I came to Carmel's house and knocked on the front door. We saw her Mercedes in the driveway. So when no one answered, we walked to the back and saw her through the glass. Fitch arrived, and we called your department."

"Why?" Sheriff Randall squinted at me.

"Why'd we call your department?"

"Why'd you come here?"

I glanced at Charlie and Fitch, talking quietly on the other side of the tree. "Condolence call," I said and hesitated. "I'd heard her husband was in debt. I thought she might want to talk." And now the sheriff knew about the debt, and another motive for murder, if he hadn't known already.

"Why would she talk to you?" The sheriff adjusted his gray, wide-brimmed hat.

"We met at the Viking bar a couple nights ago," I said, wary. "She taught me axe throwing and we both had a little too much to drink. I got the impression she did that a lot."

"If you're suggesting she got drunk and hit her head on that poker, you've got another think coming."

"That wasn't what I was suggesting."

"What *are* you suggesting?" The sheriff's broad brow wrinkled.

"I meant the axe—Nothing." A bead of sweat trickled past my eye. "I'm only giving you what little background I have."

"That makes three bodies you've found in... how many days is it?"

"If you're suggesting it's all starting to get a little mundane, it isn't."

He stared at me, his brown eyes dull. "Send your brother over."

I nodded and walked to the bicycles. "He wants to talk to you again, Charlie."

"Oh, cool."

My stomach tightened. I didn't bother telling Charlie to keep it brief. My brother would say what he'd say. There was nothing I could do to stop him now. Uneasy, I watched him limp toward the sheriff.

"He'll be okay," Fitch said.

"He talks too much."

"Yeah. You sure you two are related?"

I shot him a look and edged into the shade of a lilac bush. Bees hummed around it.

He shook his head. "Just because Rigby moved into the house Charlie lost—"

"You know about that?" I asked gloomily.

He nodded. "I looked at your brother as a suspect, but the general consensus is that Charlie is too mellow to kill anyone."

The general consensus didn't seem to know my brother had threatened to burn down the house. True, it had been empty and unsold at the time. But if the sheriff found out...

"He's not following proper procedure," Fitch said.

I shot him a startled glance. "Who? The sheriff?"

"We should have been separated so we couldn't get our stories straight."

That was not a good sign. "What have you heard about this sheriff?"

"It's a mixed bag."

I shifted my weight. "You know anything about Rigby's gambling?"

He shook his head.

Charlie gestured beneath the pine. I gnawed the corner of my thumb, a habit I thought I'd broken. I dropped my hands to my sides.

"But," Fitch continued, "where there's smoke, there's fire. If your buddies at the Sagebrush say something was up, then something was probably up."

"Maybe."

"You think they've got bad intel?"

"I think half the country is convinced I'm an accessory to murder by tomato truck. I'm done with relying on rumor."

He winced. "I've got bad news for you. It's more than half the country by now."

"Oh, good." This was going to make it *really* easy to go back to my protection work.

"Hey, I don't believe you had anything to do with Koppel's death."

"Thanks." I jammed my hands in the back pockets of my jeans. "Why?"

"Why what?"

My stomach hardened. I rubbed my eyebrow. "Why do you believe me?"

He shrugged. "I ran a background check on you. You've got a good reputation. I mean, a *really* good reputation, at least until now. You were sort of a big shot in the industry."

Were? I adjusted the MBS pin on my lightweight jacket. "There aren't a lot of women in it. It made it easier to stand out."

"Anyway, there were no unusual deposits into your bank accounts—"

"You got into my bank accounts?" I asked, aghast.

"And no communications I could find between you and anyone who'd want Rigby dead."

"You got into my phone records?"

He shrugged. "I could leak all this to the press, but I don't think it'll help you. You make too good a villainess. Tall, blond, good looking. If it weren't for your muscle tone, you could be o n *Dynasty*."

Misplaced anger heated my face. I wasn't mad at Fitch. He'd been doing what he was made to do. I was angry at the situation. But there was no sense stomping my feet and yelling that it wasn't fair. Even if it *wasn't* fair.

The sheriff grasped Charlie's shoulder.

A heavy coldness weighted my chest. I clutched my arms and straightened. "Oh no."

He walked my little brother to the back of a squad car and guided him inside.

CHAPTER EIGHTEEN

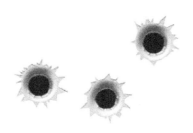

I SAT, STUNNED AND broiling, on the sheriff's station's concrete steps. Fredo panted beside me. Charlie had been brought in for questioning. *This was bad.* I gnawed a fingernail. *Really bad.*

My brother was in jail, and Carmel was dead. And both thoughts made me a little sick. A black van cruised past Perella's Honda Accord. Perella had responded to my rideshare request and driven me to the station, twenty miles outside Nowhere. We hadn't been far behind the sheriff but had now been waiting over an hour. I didn't want to think how much Perella waiting on me was going to cost.

I called Buck.

"Alice." His tone was wary. "How's it going?"

Oh, now he picks up. "I need a lawyer."

There was a beat of silence. Two beats. Three. "Did the press find you?"

"No. And it's not for me. It's for Charlie. He's been brought in for questioning."

"For what?"

"Murder."

Buck swore. "You know what the press is going to do with this when they find out?"

Heat flared in my chest. "And you think I care? Gimme the number."

Buck sighed. "Sorry. Things haven't been easy here, but... Right, the number... Okay, here you go."

My phone pinged. "Thanks," I said. "So what *is* going on over there?"

"Ah, I was actually about to call you."

My heart jumped. "You found something? A risk-assessment gig?" Those didn't involve protection—just analysis and reporting. We did them for companies working internationally all the time.

"No." He drew out the word. "It's about the other team protecting Toomas."

"Did they corroborate my story?" I asked, my chest lightening.

"No. They've disappeared."

My insides went cold. "What do you mean, they've disappeared?"

"Disappeared. Vanished. No one can find them, not even the feds."

I swayed and braced my free hand on the step. *Not even...* Even though the day was brutally hot, a chill seeped from the cement through my jeans. "Hold on. Did the FBI ever interview them?"

"No. It's like they never existed."

For a moment, I couldn't speak. "But they did exist. I have them on video. I handed those videos over to the FBI."

"And those videos are the only reason you're free."

"But—"

"The *press* hasn't seen any evidence that team was working for Koppel. You're not only the BG who let him steal your car and get killed. You're the face of his protection detail."

My voice rose. "But it wasn't my *job* to provide him with close protection. That isn't—" I bit back the word. *Fair.* No one cared. "So what's the play?"

"Just keep doing what you're doing. The feds know where you are if they need you."

My throat closed. It didn't sound like much of a plan. It sounded like Buck didn't *have* a plan. I rubbed my forehead. *Move on.* "There's one more thing."

"Oh?"

The black van drove past a second time, and I frowned. It was easy to be paranoid in the surveillance biz.

"I need a car," I said.

"You can't get a car? Aren't there rental agencies where you are?"

"No. I'm in Nowhere, and the nearest rental car agency is in Reno."

"What happened to your other car?"

"Someone killed the radiator with a crossbow bolt."

"Please tell me it was a hunting accident," he said.

"It was a hunting accident."

"Really?"

"No."

He cursed. "Do you need protection? A safehouse?"

I was ashamed to admit I wanted to say yes. I wanted to be protected. Safe. But taking that sort of help from Buck would not be a good idea. And Charlie needed me here. "No."

"All right," he said. "If you're sure."

I could hear the relief in his voice. I was a problem that wasn't earning him money, and he didn't want to deal with me. Me, his once-wife. To my surprise, I wasn't that disappointed.

"Okay," he said. "I'll have a new car delivered. Where do you want it?"

"Have them leave it outside the Sagebrush Café in Nowhere."

We said our goodbyes. I sat on the sheriff's station steps and thought.

Koppel's personal protection detail hadn't been near the crash scene. I was as close to sure they hadn't been involved in the accident as I could be. But this business about the detail disappearing... I rubbed my damp palms on the legs of my jeans. Either they were involved, or they were scared and running. Or both.

I shook my head. Toomas's death was a problem for the FBI. Charlie was my problem. My focus had to be my brother.

Fitch walked up the sidewalk and sat down beside me. "Carmel's not your fault." He nudged my shoulder with his own. "I wasn't watching her either. I guess one of us should have been."

"I know." Why hadn't I thought to surveil Carmel? It was my specialty. But whether I'd returned to Nowhere or not, Donald would have been murdered. My brother would have been a prime suspect. And Carmel? It felt like her death was my fault. "What are you doing here?"

"Didn't have anywhere else to be." He paused. "You didn't tell me about the arson."

I stiffened. How did he...? Didn't matter. "*Threatened* arson. Charlie didn't do anything. It was only talk."

"But it connects him to the abandoned gas cans found by Donald's body. And it connects him to Donald and Carmel."

"He was connected as soon as the town took his house and sold it to the Rigbys," I growled.

Fredo growled back and grabbed his leash in his teeth, tugging. I tugged lightly back.

"It's weird." The PI leaned back, bracing his elbows on the steps. "I thought someone was trying to frame me for the murder. All along, Charlie made a better suspect. The gas cans. The antique knife..."

"Yeah." My shoulders slumped. If Charlie hadn't shot his mouth off about burning down his house, or argued with Donald...

So why frame Fitch?

The stiletto *must* have been used to point the sheriff toward my brother. That implied the killer was someone in the community, someone who'd heard about Charlie's antics. And that Fitch was either lying or confused.

"Is it *only* Charlie you're worried about?" Fitch asked.

"Fredo needs a good home," I said. "Are you sure you—?"

"I'm sure." A faint smile flickered across his face. "But I wonder if what's happened with Toomas Koppel is bigger than you've been letting on."

I folded my arms. "Explain to me how this is helping."

"I'm just saying you're under pressure."

"I've got an ex-husband who used to say the same thing."

"Maybe it's causing you to react instead of be strategic."

"I'm plenty strategic."

The detective tilted his head. "Then what's your plan?"

"To call a lawyer." I reached for my phone.

"Hey, Al!" Charlie burst through the station's tall, double doors. "You waited for me."

I sagged with relief, then hopped to my feet and hugged him. "They let you go?"

"Sure, they only wanted to ask me some questions."

Fitch's gaze flicked skyward.

My chest squeezed. "Wait. You answered their questions? I told you to wait for a lawyer."

Charlie shook his head. "They weren't exactly hard questions."

My pulse pounded in my head. "Charlie, anything you say can be used against you in a trial."

"Yeah, they told me that. But I'm innocent. It's all good. And see, they let me go."

"I'm going to... get back to work." Fitch backed down the steps.

"Yeah." My brother laughed. "That Marques can be a real tyrant."

Fitch waved and trotted to his blue Ford Explorer.

"You..." I ground my jaw. *Stay calm.* "Charlie, you don't talk to the cops when you're a suspect."

"Sheriff Randall is okay." He looked around. "You didn't bring my bike?"

"It's still at the house. I had to take a taxi to get here."

I motioned to the rideshare, waiting at the curb.

Perella waved from the open window of her Honda Accord. A wisp of her gray hair floated from the top of the window.

"Cool," Charlie said. "You ready to go? I've got another show tonight."

We retrieved our bikes from our family home, and Perella dropped us off at the motel cabin. I left my brother there and walked into town with Fredo to cool off.

The Sagebrush had always been the town's heart. It was where people gathered to meet and gossip. If someone close to Charlie had set him up, I couldn't think of a better starting place in my search than the café.

I tied the gray dog to a lamp post and pushed open the door. The bell above it jingled. Heads turned toward me, the volume in the café dropping.

I sat at the counter. The owner, Molly, flipped over a white mug on the counter and poured me a cup of coffee without asking. "How's Charlie?"

My muscles hardened. Of *course* everyone knew. I shook my head. "The sheriff let him go. He's fine."

"What can I get you?" she asked.

"Blackberry pie. Heated, please."

She nodded and bustled away. I sipped my coffee.

Mr. Washington leaned my way. "Is it true Carmel Rigby's dead?"

I nodded.

"I heard your brother was arrested." He ran his hand over his cropped, curly gray hair.

"No," I said too loudly. I cleared my throat. "The sheriff interviewed him. That's all."

"We all know he didn't do it. He's Charlie." The elderly man sipped his coffee. He returned the mug to the blue counter. "I guess the sheriff doesn't know that though."

"I guess not," I said, morose.

I killed time, talking to the regulars and eating pie, waiting for my new car. No one had anything bad to say about Carmel, aside from the fact she could be a little wild.

I blew out my breath and stabbed the pie with my fork. I assumed it was flaky and delicious, but today, it tasted like sawdust.

Two slices of pie and three cups of coffee later, I got a text. *Car arrived. White Toyota Corolla.*

I sighed. When I'd worked in Afghanistan, white Toyota Corollas had been the car bomb of choice. I should have specified an SUV.

I slid off the faded blue barstool.

A young man in a t-shirt and a black beanie stood in the doorway of the diner. He caught my eye and nodded, strode toward me. "Alice Sommerland?"

"That's me." I stretched my hand out for the keys.

He shook it. "Zed Kelley."

I felt the blood drain from my face. *The reporter.* "Oh." *Dammit.*

He grinned. "Sorry to ambush you. I didn't mean to. I was looking for food. It was dumb luck running into you here."

Another man, slightly older and thinner, stepped inside the Sagebrush and looked around.

My gaze darted around the diner. How had the reporter found out I was in Nowhere? "Look," I said. "This isn't a good time."

"I'd like to interview you for my podcast, let you tell your side of the story."

"Podcast?"

He smiled more broadly. "I'm online. My podcasts are long-form interviews, not soundbites. We can dive deep, get the real story."

The man in the doorway looked down at his phone, frowned, and spotted me.

"Sorry." I hurried to the second man. "Toyota Corolla?"

"Here you go." He handed me a key fob. "From Buck."

"Buck, that's your ex?" Zed had followed me. "He owns the executive protection company you contracted to, right?"

The key-delivery man turned on his heel and left, the glass door closing slowly behind him. I forced myself not to bolt after him.

"Look." I slid the key fob into my pocket. "I've had more than enough publicity. I don't need more."

Zed nodded. "I get that. But your story is being told without any input from you. And I get the feeling no one knows what really happened."

"I don't know what really happened. I mean, I do. It was a tomato truck."

"And the other bodyguards?" he asked.

I sucked in a breath. He knew about that? If he knew, then others must too. So why was I still public enemy number one? "What about them?"

"Aren't you a little worried you'll disappear too?"

An icicle trailed up my spine.

"I don't know what's going on," Zed said. "But there's no way for you to get a handle on this story unless you tell your side. And if those guys were disappeared, maybe telling your side will give you some protection." He handed me a card.

I glanced at it and shook my head. "Sorry. My goal right now is to keep a low profile."

"And I won't give your location away. But I am going to stick around and do some old-fashioned investigative reporting. So I'll be here for a few days if you change your mind."

Kelley strolled to the rear patio.

I cursed. Returning to the counter, I motioned to Molly for the bill.

Someone sat beside me, the stool creaking, and I glanced to my left.

Pete nodded to me. "I heard the news about Charlie," he said, expression serious. "I'm sorry, Alice."

"Thanks. Did the sheriff let you know?"

He shook his head. "The mayor of Nowhere doesn't get that kind of courtesy," he said bitterly. "I learned through the gossip chain. What can I do?"

Warmth filled my chest. It was more than Buck had offered. But how much pull did a small-town mayor have in a murder investigation? I guessed not much.

Molly slid another slice of pie in front of me. "You look like you need it."

"No thanks," I said. I wasn't going to come back from my forced vacation out of shape. "Just the bill, please."

"I'll have her slice," Pete said. "With ice cream."

She bustled away with the pie.

"I have a hard time believing Charlie was responsible for any of this," he said.

"He wasn't. We were together most of last night and all this morning. He's been staying at my motel. If I can find out *when* Carmel was killed, I might be able to give him an alibi."

An odd look crossed Pete's face.

"You think the sheriff won't believe an alibi from me?" I asked.

He flushed. "It's not because of... Your word's good enough for me. But you're his sister. Unfortunately, I don't have much influence over the sheriff. And he doesn't share details of his investigation with me. But you can trust the system."

Ha. People hired bodyguards because they *didn't* trust the system. I wanted to trust it. I really did. But I couldn't afford to.

Molly slid the bill across the counter to me.

"Thanks." I smiled at her briefly.

"I know what it's like to lose someone," Pete said in a low voice. "And I know what it's like to think you're going to lose someone. Let me help."

He *did* know. My lungs squeezed. At least I'd had my dad.

When Pete's father had died in a car accident twenty-four years ago, his mother had descended into alcoholism. The fact that Pete had held it together and made something of himself was impressive. He'd struggled, and he'd succeeded. I guess his mother finally had, too.

And then my father had crashed *his* car. Pete and I had lived parallel lives, and I hadn't seen it until now.

"You're the best," I said, voice thick, "but Charlie's out. I've identified a lawyer for him. Right now, there's nothing to do."

He rested his hand on mine and squeezed. "That's great news."

I lowered my head. "Pete—"

"Can I get you some more coffee?" Ivanna asked at my elbow, and I twitched, pulled my hand away. "No thanks, I'm leaving." I hurried outside and away from the diner.

Fredo barked on the sidewalk. Guiltily, I returned for the dog. I untied him from the lamppost, and we walked toward a shiny white Toyota Corolla with a car rental sticker in the window. Gert leaned against the car, his gnarled hands on his knees.

I slowed, wary. "Are you going to try to kill me again?"

He shook his head. "Not right now."

"Great." I aimed my key fob at the car and froze, arm extended. "You didn't put a bomb in it, did you?"

He straightened. His spectacles flashed with indignation. "That could hurt someone. Someone I don't mean to kill."

"Fair enough." I hesitated. "Are you okay?"

"Just catching my breath."

I unlocked the door.

"I heard your brother was arrested," he said.

"Only questioned and released."

"Let me guess. Charlie didn't keep his trap shut. He never could. I told him and told him you can't trust the cops, but he doesn't believe me." He wheezed. "Bastards."

"This isn't the old Soviet Union. Most police are trying to do the right thing." Some cops got into the job because they liked pushing people around, but I didn't get that vibe from the sheriff. The vibe I got was *disinterested.*

He blinked rapidly. "What do *you* know about the Soviets?"

"I worked in the former Soviet Union after it broke apart." The criminality and general chaos had been great for executive protection firms. Many of the countries were still pretty chaotic. Too bad I couldn't hide out there.

"I returned to Estonia in the nineties." His expression turned wistful. "Such a beautiful country."

"Ever think of moving back?"

He shook his head. "The people who stayed and suffered under the Russians look at people like me, the people who left, like rats who fled a sinking ship. It wasn't my fault I abandoned them. I was a child when my family left." He shrugged. "My life is here now."

I nodded, my hands falling to my sides. I was starting to get an idea of what it might feel like to be exiled. A tour bus chugged past, belching exhaust.

"I was looking for you," he said. "Not to kill you. I've got information. Information that might help your brother."

"I'll take anything."

He scratched his ear. "Rigby was scum. He tried to seduce Marques's late wife. Before she died, I mean."

"I *hope* not after." But this was news. I studied him. "You said Rigby tried. Does that mean he didn't succeed?"

"I don't stick my nose into other people's beeswax. But it put a strain on the marriage. Marques was the jealous type back then—hot headed. Then she got the cancer a few months later." A distraught expression crossed his wrinkled face.

"When exactly was this?"

"Not long before Donald and Carmel left town."

So decades ago. Donald's return to Nowhere might have been Marques's first chance at revenge. But if Rigby had tried and failed, would Marques consider revenge worth it? Marques didn't seem the type.

"What about Mrs. Malone? I asked slyly.

He stiffened. "What about her?"

Okay, I wasn't going to tease him. Maybe they were seeing each other, maybe they weren't. In either case, it was none of my business. "I hear she didn't like the idea of Rigby building a marijuana resort. Did she have any other reasons not to like him?"

"Mrs. Malone's a lady. She's not the kind of woman to commit murder."

Oh, he totally had a thing for her. "Everyone's that kind of person, under the right circumstances."

"Not Mrs. Malone." Gert turned and tottered down the cracked sidewalk.

I stared after him. Fredo strained on his leash. Gert vanished inside his dusty antique shop.

One thing I was sure of. Gert hadn't killed Carmel and Donald. He made a lousy hitman.

CHAPTER NINETEEN

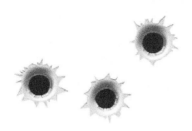

"...LEAVE A MESSAGE."

A waitress brushed behind me. Cool shadows stretched across the Sagebrush's back patio, packed with customers this Saturday morning. The clink of their silverware and murmur of their voices seemed proof of life went on. But it didn't. Donald's memorial was scheduled for this afternoon. And I wouldn't miss it.

"This is Alice Sommerland. I... work with Buck Jackson and he gave me your number." I hesitated. "And yes, I'm that Alice Sommerland. But that's not why I'm calling. My brother is a suspect in a murder investigation in Nowhere, Nevada. I'd like to retain you in case... in case he's arrested."

Ivanna set a ginormous pancake in front of me. She laid a plate of breakfast burritos on the table by the empty chair opposite. Fredo stretched at my feet.

"Thanks," I mouthed and left my number on the voicemail.

I tapped my phone on the table, and it rang, vibrating in my hand. I checked the number. *Zed Kelley.* I declined the call.

Charlie limped out of the diner, and we ate our breakfasts. The Sagebrush was famous for their fluffy, buttery pancakes. My memory of them did not disappoint. These were birthday-cake style, a mid-west innovation that elevated pancakes everywhere.

After we'd finished, Lilyanna swung by the Sagebrush with her car, and she and my brother drove to MBS practice.

I walked Fredo back to my Corolla and opened the door. The little dog shot me a mutinous look and sat on the sidewalk.

"You can't sit here all day," I told Fredo.

The dog scratched behind one ragged ear.

I gave a gentle tug on his leash. "Let's go."

A tour bus rumbled to a halt, boxing in my compact.

"See what you've done?" My grip tightened on the leash. "Now we're trapped."

Eyes rolling, Fredo lifted a hind leg and scratched his other ear.

The doors of the bus squealed open. A man looking like Santa in a Hawaiian shirt waddled out. More tourists followed, milling around my car and making it impossible to leave. I leaned against the compact, got comfortable, and crossed my legs at the ankles.

"Hey," the man in the Hawaiian shirt said to me. "Can you recommend a good place to eat?"

"Sure. Try the Sagebrush Café." I pointed. "The pizza parlor down the street isn't bad either."

His brow, beaded with sweat, furrowed. "Don't I know you?"

I folded my arms. "Ah, I don't think so."

"You look familiar."

Abruptly, I straightened off the Corolla. "I have that kind of face. Fredo, let's go." I pulled on the leash.

It went limp. Fredo raced down the sidewalk, and I swore. Had he chewed through his leash?

"Hold on," the man said. "You're that killer bodyguard."

I charged through the crowd after the dog. He wove around a mailbox. For an animal with such tiny legs, Fredo could move.

I glanced over my shoulder. The tourist stared after me. He said something to a woman in a matching Hawaiian shirt and pointed in my direction.

The dog stopped in front of a shop. Fredo raised himself up on his hind legs, his front paws on the dusty glass door. I scooped him up, opened the door to the antique shop and slipped inside, locking the door behind me. I turned.

Gert leveled a revolver at me from behind the counter.

My insides spasmed. "Oh, come *on*." I set Fredo down and raised my hands, the leash dangling.

His eyes narrowed behind their thick lenses. "Why'd you lock that door?"

"Tourists."

Fredo yipped.

"No dogs allowed," Gert said, gun steady. "Can't you read the sign?"

Hastily, I reached for the door handle. "We'll just leave."

"Not so fast."

I froze.

"You locked that door. You came into my shop in a threatening manner. I have every right to shoot you."

Hadn't we been through this before? "If you shoot me, the dog gets it."

His nose wrinkled. "I've got excellent aim, and I don't kill dogs."

"Mrs. Malone gave me this dog to save him from the pound. Do you think anyone will adopt him? It's a kill shelter."

He frowned. "That *is* one ugly dog."

Fredo growled, eyes bulging.

Gert set the gun on the glass counter, and my muscles unknotted. "Kill shelters." His upper lip curled. "It's enough to make me lose faith in humanity."

"You're older than God and you still haven't lost faith in humanity?"

He eyed me. "What happened to you? You're too young to be cynical."

My shoulders slumped. I couldn't believe I'd said that. That wasn't me. I used to be an optimist. "I know. I'm sorry. It's this business with... everything."

"It's because I'm trying to kill you, isn't it?" he said glumly.

"No, it's not you. If those tourists figure out who I was, it will be all over the internet. They wouldn't care how it might affect me, not when they think I killed your buddy, Koppel."

"He wasn't my buddy. Toomas was a little creep. If anyone deserved a speedy and unexpected exit from planet Earth, it was that guy."

"Then why are you trying to kill me?" I asked, affronted.

He shrugged. "I told you. It's me or the others. I'm doing you a favor."

"It really doesn't feel like it."

"That's your perspective."

Hold on. "And what others? You said no one had contacted you."

"Yet." Someone knocked on the door. "We're closed," Gert shouted.

"This is so unfair."

He braced his elbows on the counter. "You think you got it hard because people don't understand you? Wake up. What do you think happens when you get old? No one cares abo ut..." His wrinkled face spasmed. "All they see is old."

A fluorescent lamp flickered above the jackalope. Its paws were raised as if it were about to leap from the shelf and make a break for it.

"I don't just see you as old," I said. "You're a mafia hitman. What I can't figure out is why you'd want to be one."

"There are dangerous people out there. People who need to be taken care of."

"Like me?"

Gert shifted and straightened. "It isn't fair what happened to you."

"That's for sure."

"But trust me, it's better if I take care of this business." He shuddered.

I stared vacantly at the jackalope. "It's depressing that I'm starting to believe you."

"You're just temporarily disillusioned. You'll get over it. What you need is a boyfriend."

"Seriously?" Did the town know about my divorce too? This was just depressing.

"What about that gardener fellow? He's tall."

"That's not—" I sputtered. "No."

"Why not? He's even taller than you are."

"That's not the point. Have you met him?"

"Sure," Gert said. "He came in here yesterday asking about Renaissance knives."

"Son of a—" Fitch didn't miss a step.

"That gardener isn't to my taste," he said, "but I don't have to date him. He's your problem."

"No, he isn't. And besides, according to you, I'm on a clock."

"That is true," he said. "What about a jackalope?"

"What *about* a jackalope?"

"It'll cheer you up."

"No, thanks." I glanced over my shoulder at the glass front door. A tourist in a flowered hat peered inside.

"You should have a jackalope," he said.

"Where would I put it?"

"On a shelf in your house."

My face warmed. Not having a house hadn't seemed like a big deal until it was the future home of a jackalope.

"Don't you have a house somewhere?" he asked.

I shifted my weight. "I'm in between places."

"What? Are you some kind of bum?"

Someone banged again on the door. Gert snatched up the gun and aimed. I ducked. A muffled shriek came from outside.

"Pushy," Gert said, lowering the gun. "I don't like pushy people."

I straightened. "Ah, maybe you should put the gun down."

"What? You think I don't know how to aim?"

"I'm just saying—"

He swiveled and aimed at a deer's head on the wall.

"Gert, no—"

He pulled the trigger. BOOM. The barrel of the gun exploded.

Fredo started and yipped.

Gert goggled at what was left of the gun. He toppled backward.

A sharp ache sliced through my chest, taking my breath away. "Gert!" I ran behind the counter.

Fredo howled.

The old man lay on his back, his wrinkled hand shaking. Scrapes on his cheek and forehead oozed blood. "What the hell? What the hell!"

"Are you okay?" I asked.

He glared. "I would of hit it. I had it dead to rights."

CHAPTER TWENTY

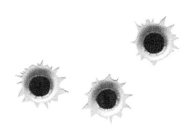

AFTER I MADE SURE Gert didn't need professional medical help, I went to the antique shop's glass door and peered through. A half dozen tourists clustered beneath the mushrooms in the park across the street. Odds were they weren't watching for me to come out. The giant mushrooms were more interesting than me. And I couldn't hide out in Gert's all morning.

"I don't need you watching me." Gert scowled. "It was just a scratch."

"It was just a lot of scratches."

"I'm fine. Don't you have somewhere better to be?"

"Fine." I tugged Fredo's leash. "Let's go."

The animal sat on the linoleum floor and scratched behind his ear.

"Your dog's not that bright, is he?" Gert cackled, bandaging his hand.

I wasn't sure about that. Fredo seemed to know how to get what he wanted. Unlocking the door, I scooped up the dog and strode onto the sidewalk. Head down, I hustled toward my rental.

"That's illegal!" Mrs. Malone's voice floated down the street.

I hesitated, orienting on her voice. It seemed to be coming from the throng of tourists in the park. That was the last place I wanted to go. Setting Fredo down, I gazed longingly toward the Corolla.

"Stop that," she bellowed.

I hung my head and blew out my breath. The tourists were likely in more danger than Mrs. Malone. But I couldn't pretend nothing was going on. Fredo and I crossed the street. The dog tugged on his leash, resisting, his eyes bugging with the effort.

A small boy in yellow shorts and a striped t-shirt stood on top of a mid-sized red mushroom with white spots.

"Those are poisonous, you know," I told him.

Mrs. Malone leaned on her cane and scowled at a red-faced woman. "If that child falls," Mrs. Malone said, "I will personally testify for the town attorneys that you were responsible for putting him up there. The sign clearly states no climbing on the mushrooms. Or on the giant flowers, or on any of the Big Things."

There was a NO CLIMBING sign? If I'd seen that... I still would have gone up there after Carmel.

The woman's mouth puckered. "Don't you tell me how to parent, you old—"

Fredo loosed a flurry of barks. He lunged at the woman, and I tugged him back.

The tourist yelped and hopped away. "Good God, what *is* that?"

The boy stepped to the edge of the mushroom.

"It's a dog," I said. "And you're going to give him a complex with that attitude."

Mrs. Malone snorted.

And then, what was destined to happen, happened. The boy's foot skidded out from under him. His butt hit the edge of the mushroom. He flew off and plummeted downward.

I leapt forward and caught him, swinging him to the ground.

He laughed and raised his arms. "Again!"

"I think not," Mrs. Malone said.

Fredo snarled.

The indignant mother snatched her son's hand. "I'll be registering a complaint with your information bureau."

"Go right ahead," Mrs. Malone said.

The woman stalked away, her son wailing behind her. The other tourists reluctantly followed.

"Do we have an information bureau?" I asked.

"No. That woman *could* try the Chamber of Commerce, but they're closed on weekends." She smiled at Fredo. "Good dog."

He leaned against her stockinged calf and gazed at her adoringly.

"Why don't you keep Fredo?" I asked.

"I can't. I'm allergic. Do you think I would have pawned a desperate animal off on you if I could take responsibility for him myself?"

"No," I said. "I was just surprised. He likes you."

Fredo's eyes bulged.

"I told Marques these monstrosities would cause trouble." Mrs. Malone swung her purse at the mushrooms. "It's only a matter of time before some idiot hurts themselves and sues. Climbing mushrooms. What sort of a fool climbs up on those things?"

I rubbed the back of my neck. "No idea. Is that the only reason you're not a fan of the big art?"

"Art? You call this art?"

The nearby bushes rustled.

"Terrence Madoff does," I said.

"Terrence is a hack. He doesn't even put these things together. He draws them, and some poor fool who works for Marques builds them. These aren't art. They're spectacle."

"But if they bring in tourists—"

"Tourists! When I was young, people came to Nowhere for its charm. We had businesses. Industry. The cannery actually canned things. I worked there when I was a girl, you know."

I hadn't known, and I tried to picture Mrs. Malone as a girl, her head in a scarf, canning peas. "I suppose having Big Things' tourists beats a marijuana resort."

Her face reddened. "Oh, you think so? We wouldn't have even been considered for that awful *resort* if these crazy things weren't here."

"That resort proposal couldn't have made Marques happy. I heard he didn't want it either."

"You'll have to ask Marques about the resort," she said stiffly. "His Big Things plan will never work. Marques wants to make Nowhere new and exciting. You can't make something old new again."

"How long has Terrence lived in Nowhere?"

"Marques lured him in for his ridiculous projects." She motioned toward the mushrooms and painted metal flowers.

A stag with a dark slash of fur over its eyes emerged from behind a cluster of Russian sage.

"He even gave Terrence a house to live in," she continued. "Have you seen what that *artist* did to it?"

"Yes." I dragged my gaze from the deer. "It's—"

"It *used* to be a lovely, Craftsman-style home. Now it looks like a fun house."

I glanced at the deer. "Well—"

"I told Marques he shouldn't have hired him. It's not as if Terrence had a name of any sort. He was toiling in well-deserved obscurity before Marques found him. But Marques has a soft spot for artists."

The bushes rustled. The stag had vanished. Or found a better surveillance spot.

"Are you listening?" Mrs. Malone said.

"Yes." But I'd gotten distracted by the deer. If the big art was all Terrence had, then he had more to lose. But *would* he lose anything if the resort opened? "I stopped by his house," I said. "Terrence seemed—"

"Unbalanced?"

"Intense."

"He's off his rocker, if you ask me." Her eyes narrowed. "Why *are* you asking me?"

I sighed. "I don't know this town anymore."

We gazed at the high wooden fence surrounding the Japanese tea garden.

"I don't know it either," she said in a low voice. "I know things change. I know it's inevitable. But why does change have to be so... disruptive?"

We stood in silence for a long moment.

"Screw change," I said.

One corner of her mouth quirked upward. Her face smoothed, hard as a granite tombstone. Mrs. Malone straightened. Footsteps approached, and I turned.

A woman in her late thirties, her blond hair cut in a glamshackle style strode toward us. She waved. "Hi, you two!"

"Who's that?" I asked in a low voice. She looked kind of familiar.

"A reporter. From *Reno*," Mrs. Malone said darkly.

My stomach clenched.

"Alice Sommerland," the reporter said. "It *is* you."

CHAPTER TWENTY-ONE

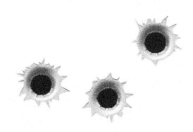

I TURNED TO BOLT. Fredo's leash tangled around my legs. I braced myself on the red-spotted mushroom and unwound myself from the gray dog.

The buxom reporter thrust a digital recorder in my face. "Oh, wow, it *is* you. I didn't think you'd come back."

I reared away. "Do I know you?" The dog grabbed the middle of the leash in his teeth and yanked backward. I glowered at Fredo. "For Pete's sake..."

"Young lady," Mrs. Malone said to the reporter, "this is entirely inappropriate."

The reporter tugged down the hem of her red blazer. "Why was Toomas Koppel in your car alone? Why weren't you with him? Weren't you supposed to be protecting him?"

"I insist you stop bothering us," Mrs. Malone said. "We were having a private conversation."

"Let go." I jerked the leash. Fredo let go, and I staggered backward. I picked him up and tucked him under one arm. "Bad dog." He licked my neck.

"Kitty." The reporter pointed at herself. "Kitty Bannon. From UNR? We shared a dorm."

"Oh." I shook my head. "What?" I graduated from the University of Nevada at Reno before joining the Army.

"At first I thought there was no way you'd come back here. It would be too obvious. But then I realized it wouldn't be obvious at all. You never exactly advertised that Nowhere was your hometown."

"Say nothing," Mrs. Malone snapped.

Warmth spread through my chest. It was kind of sweet that Mrs. Malone was defending me. Even after all these years, I was still a part of Nowhere. And the townsfolk stuck together.

"Nowhere has enough problems without you further tarnishing our reputation," the older woman continued.

Oh. I deflated.

"Let me buy you a cup of coffee," Kitty said. "We need to catch up."

I looked meaningfully at her recorder.

"Oh. Sorry." She turned it off and dropped it into the pocket of her blazer. "Bad habit. I was just so excited that I'd found *the* Alice Sommerland."

I raised a brow. "I wasn't *the* Alice Sommerland in college."

I remembered Kitty now. She'd left the dorm after the first year to join a sorority. I'd crammed into a ratty apartment with three other girls. Kitty and I had barely talked, even when we'd shared a dorm.

The reporter shrugged. "You know what I mean." She edged closer. "What really happened to Toomas Koppel?"

I rolled my eyes, turned, and jogged into the mushroom park, startling the stag. It bounded into a stand of pines.

"Wait," the reporter shouted. "Oof!"

I glanced over my shoulder. Kitty lay sprawled on the lawn, Mrs. Malone's cane tangled between her legs.

I put on more speed, sprinting around the giant shrooms, past the high, tea garden fence, and down a narrow path through clusters of purple sage. Fredo yelped irritably under my arm.

"I have to carry you," I huffed. "You can't run as fast as me. Your legs are too short." The dog growled. "Don't you start."

I darted across the street and found myself behind the cannery. Its door stood open, braced by a stack of boxes.

Setting the dog down, I tied Fredo's leash to a post. I edged inside the brick building.

"It had to have been one of us." Terrence's voice echoed off the metal ladders and paint cans and dusty concrete floor. "But Carmel—"

"No," Marques said. "Come on. You can't believe that. You're talking about *two* murders."

I peered around a forklift. The ground floor was empty. The voices drifted from upstairs.

"I'm telling you," the artist said, "this is getting out of control. If I'd had any idea what I was getting into—"

"You haven't gotten into anything. Look, I don't know what's going on either, but it's got nothing to do with us. Our project is on track."

I shifted my weight, interested. *Project?* Were they talking about the cannery? The Big Things? Or something else? Could they have colluded in the murders?

"How can you be sure?" Terrence asked. "He was killed right here, right by my can of peas."

Something clanked above me, and my muscles tensed.

"That can grapples with the enigmatic boundaries of identity," the artist continued. "It's one of my best works. Now tourists are only coming to see it because that's where the murder happened."

"That's not true," Marques said.

"It is. I heard them. Murder tourism. Was *that* your plan?"

"Of course not," Marques said.

"And I don't want an intern. I don't care if she has an MFA. As far as I'm concerned, it's a mark against her."

"Look we need to play ball." His voice lowered, too low for me to catch every word. "...permits," Marques was saying. "...own big things."

"That isn't going to happen," Terrence said flatly. "There's only one Big Things artist."

There was a long pause. I held my breath.

"We're going to have to replace the can's paper wrapper at the end of the summer," Terrence said. "It's already beginning to fade."

Marques grunted. "I've got a stack of wrappers in my warehouse. Don't worry about it."

"And what about Charlie?"

My scalp prickled.

"Don't worry about him," Marques said. "I've got it under control."

"How?"

My hands clenched. *Yeah. How?*

"What are you doing in here?" a man shouted in my ear.

I jumped. "Ack!"

A ruddy-faced man in an orange vest and hard hat glared at me. "You shouldn't be in here. Not without a hard hat."

Bad tactics was what came of last-minute surveillance. In the normal course of things, I'd have figured out my target's patterns, scoped out places to watch from and understood the patterns and people at those locations. Only then would I have settled down to surveil my client. I wouldn't have wandered into a place I didn't know for impromptu spy work. Little wonder I'd gotten caught. But I still couldn't believe this guy had snuck up on me like that. Was I losing my edge?

"Well?" he demanded.

"Jerry?" Marques shouted from upstairs. "Everything okay?"

"It's fine," I called. "It's me, Alice Sommerland. I came in here to hide from a reporter."

"Reporter?" Marques ambled down the wide stairs.

"From Reno." I crossed my arms.

His expression darkened. "Not Kitty Bannon?"

"The same," I said.

"I told her she should be wearing a hard hat." Jerry jabbed his thumb at me.

"It's fine." Marques clapped my shoulder with one of his work-roughened hands. "So Kitty found you."

"We went to college together," I said by way of explanation.

Marques ran one hand over his cropped, graying hair. "You should have seen the report she did on our Big Things. She all but called us a bunch of rubes catering to more rubes."

"They say no publicity's bad publicity," I said.

He raised a brow.

"Right," I said. "At this point, I should know better."

Marques's brown eyes narrowed. "How long have you been in here?"

"About ten seconds. Jerry here was right behind me."

Marques smiled thinly. "Terrence and I were just hashing over the murders."

"Really?" I cocked my head.

"I was sorry to hear your brother was brought in for questioning," Marques said. "No one believes he did it."

"That's good," I said. "Because he didn't do it."

"I heard he's the only one who was brought to the station for questioning though," Marques said.

I shot him a look.

Marques shrugged. "This is a small town. Everyone knows."

I stiffened. But Marques was right. Of course everyone knew.

"Tell Charlie the job offer's still open," Marques said.

My muscles unbunched. "I will."

Footsteps sounded behind me.

"There you are," Marques said.

I turned.

Fitch grinned. "Like a skunk at a garden party."

CHAPTER TWENTY-TWO

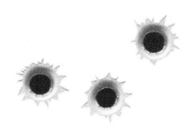

"Looking for me?" Fitch asked me suggestively. His leer was even more irritating because he looked good. His t-shirt stretched manfully across his chest, and his faded jeans accentuated the muscles in his thighs.

"Why would I be looking for you?" I asked.

The PI waggled his brows, and the other men laughed.

"I need to see a guy about a dog." Chin high, I strode out the cannery's back door and untied Fredo's leash.

"Hey," Fitch jogged into the overgrown yard. "I thought you might need an assist with an exit, since you'd obviously been caught snooping."

"*Obviously?*"

"It is what it is."

Heat seared my skin. I'd been under pressure between Charlie and the press, and it had overridden my good judgment. But no matter how I rationalized it, I'd screwed up.

But I'd also recovered. I'd been caught, but I hadn't been burned—at least not by Marques and Terrence. To cover for my embarrassment, I extended Fredo's leash. "Want a dog?"

Fredo sat, wagged his tail, and drooled through his snaggle teeth.

He eyed the dog askance. "Um, no. When I get a dog, it's going to be a real dog."

"Fredo's a real dog."

He yipped to prove it.

"A dog that's useful," Fitch clarified. "I'm not even sure that *is* a dog."

"Now you're just being mean," I said.

"Any word on your brother?"

I sucked in my cheeks. "What sort of word are you looking for? A confession? Because Charlie didn't kill anyone."

The PI took a step backward, his hands raised in defense. "Okay, okay. That wasn't what I... I can recommend a decent PI if you need one. He's not as good as me, but he's good."

"And *you* can't take the case, because you're already working another angle?"

"It would be unethical."

"Thanks," I said. "I'll take that number."

"I'll text it to you." He nodded toward the brick cannery building. "Overhear anything good in there?"

"I'm not sure." Since I couldn't think of a reason not to, I told him what I'd heard.

He rubbed his chin. "I wonder who *us* is."

"Besides Terrence and Marques?" I shook my head. "Not Pete. He's been pro-resort from the get-go. Mrs. Malone? She's always been a big shot in Nowhere."

"I'm having a weirdly easy time imagining Mrs. Malone as part of a murderous cabal. Speaking of which, is Gert still trying to assassinate you?"

"Unclear. When he realized killing me would mean taking responsibility for Fredo, he backed off."

Fitch's mouth twitched. "Gert's no dummy."

"You investigated this company behind the marijuana resort," I said.

"Ye-es."

"How would you feel about sharing what you turned up?"

"Everything I found was publicly available." He shrugged. "So, sure. I'll send it over." He hesitated. "You know, there's a lot of evidence against Charlie."

My pulse grew loud in my ears. "And?"

"And you might have to face the fact—"

"No."

"—that your brother could be guilty."

"And you're in Nowhere today to try and prove that?" I asked.

"Just trying to understand what's what. Besides, it's the weekend. I can go where I want."

"My brother's a patsy, just like..." Like Fitch had been meant to be? I shook my head. This was confusing, and I wasn't a detective. I studied Fitch, who was being a little too helpful.

"You're looking at me that way again," he said.

"What way?"

"Like you were looking at your brother's breakfast burrito. Unless you're trying to keep up the story that we've got something going? Because there's no one around right now to fool."

"Ugh. Email me what you found." I turned and stomped toward my rental car. I couldn't believe I'd even *considered* hiring Fitch. As far as I was concerned, the PI was a suspect too. Hiring him to help clear Charlie would be like hiring Capone to catch bootleggers.

"You know where to find me," he called.

I gave him a single-digit farewell, and he laughed.

Across the street, Kitty and Zed chatted by my compact. I made a sharp left turn and ducked around the back of a brick building.

"Well, this bites," I told Fredo. Because I had the feeling Kitty wasn't going to let anything as piddling as a long wait deter her. If my memories of Kitty were accurate, I'd probably have to run over her to get away. And this town had enough murders on its hands.

I could hike back to the motel. I could call a ride share. Or I could try to figure out who had committed two murders.

"Two murders it is," I muttered.

Keeping off Main Street, Fredo and I made our way to the rear of the town hall. Its back door was locked, but the front was open. Carrying Fredo, I walked down silent hallways until I found the mayor's office.

I rapped on the door, and it swayed open a few inches.

"Come in," Pete called.

I opened the door wider. "I hope dogs are allowed."

He smiled and stood, bracing his hands awkwardly on the wooden desk. "They're my favorite constituents, even if they can't vote."

We walked inside the spacious office, my feet sinking into the deep carpet. Books and binders lined shelves on one side of the room. Photos of Pete with various residents and local dignitaries hung from the opposite wall. A big square window looked out onto Main Street. Fredo leapt onto a leather chair and curled into a ball.

"How'd you know I'd be here?" he asked. "It's the weekend. Town Hall's closed."

"It was a shot in the dark. I remembered how obsessed you could become with your projects." I picked up a book on his desk—*Your Job Doesn't Love YOU*—and raised a brow. It was the second time I'd seen it in Nowhere. "Popular book."

He grimaced. "I guess I haven't changed that much from high school. I'm trying to ease up though, not get burned out." He nodded to the book in my hand.

"I'm starting to think my job actively hates me. And please, don't stand on my account. Your leg—"

"Needs weight on it to heal." He motioned me into the chair beside Fredo, and I sat. Pete sat against the wooden desk, his bad leg crooked. "What brings you here?"

"What else can you tell me about the marijuana resort?"

His hazel eyes widened briefly, and for an instant he was the Pete of my youth, heart on his sleeve and vulnerable. "The resort? I'm not sure there's much more to tell."

"Where exactly was it going to be built?" I shifted, discomfited by the girlish longing that had surged through me. But that girl was long gone. "Was Rigby's company planning on building a hotel?"

"Donald had hoped to acquire the cannery property for his firm. He said it was the perfect location." He adjusted his long leg and winced.

"I suppose those offices could be converted to hotel rooms?"

"Maybe. But Marques didn't want to sell, so Donald was looking for other options."

The cannery was an old, historic building in a town full of old, historic buildings. But the thought of tearing it down physically hurt. I was glad that had never been in the cards. "Like what?"

He shrugged. "There are other abandoned buildings off Main Street. They weren't ideal. But from the town's perspective, well, we'd like to see them occupied or gone."

"How set on the cannery property was Rigby?" I asked.

"I don't think he'd given up, if that's what you mean. But you should ask Marques. He'd be the one Rigby would have to convince to sell."

"Could Rigby have gone to burn the place down, thinking he'd get the lot at fire-sale prices?"

Pete stilled. "That's—"

An older woman in a neat business suit strode into the room, her head bent to a manila file folder. "Mr. Mayor, you asked me to review the funding for the Big Things, and I can't find any room in the budget for another artist. And frankly, given your past involvement with—" She looked up and started. "Oh. I didn't think anyone was here."

"It's fine." He straightened off the desk. "Sorry, Alice. Maybe we can chat later? When an employee chips in on their day off, I don't like to waste their time."

"Of course not. Thanks." I collected Fredo and stumbled over a freshly untied shoelace. Glaring at the dog, I picked him up and walked out.

The woman pulled the door closed behind her. It drifted to a halt before shutting completely. I bent and tied my shoe. Fredo went for the other lace, and I gently shoved him away.

"You can't be seen with her," the woman said.

"With Alice?" he asked, sounding surprised.

"Perception is everything. That woman is political poison. She as good as *killed* that man."

He sighed. "She says she didn't." There was a long silence. "We went to school together," he continued weakly.

"Then maybe you can convince her to leave town. You have reelection to think of. You have the *town* to think of."

Cheeks burning, I stood and strode away, Fredo's nails clicking on the linoleum.

CHAPTER TWENTY-THREE

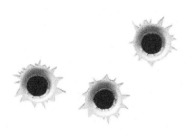

As I'd feared, Kitty was still staking out my rental. And my laptop was in the car. I wanted my laptop, so this was doubly inconvenient.

Pivoting, I walked down Main Street in the opposite direction. The fact that the reporter had figured out the Corolla was my car disturbed me. It wasn't such a reach—the car had a rental sticker. But there might have been other rentals in town. Kitty was not to be taken lightly.

My phone rang in the pocket of my jeans, and I checked its screen. The number registered as one I'd once dialed, so I answered. "Yes?" I walked past the knitting shop.

"Ms. Sommerland? It's Jackson Phillips."

My shoulders tensed. My brother's maybe-lawyer. It was Saturday afternoon. He should be enjoying his day off. But instead he was calling me. Either Buck had called him, or my bad reputation had piqued his interest. Guess which was more likely. "Thanks for returning my call."

"No problem. What can you tell me?"

I explained what I knew.

"Got it," he said. "There's not much I can do for Charlie unless and until he's arrested."

I swallowed. "I know. But there's a lot of circumstantial evidence against him. I think you should be prepared."

"And I think *you* should be prepared. If he's arrested, your notoriety may cascade onto Charlie and onto any officials who prosecute him."

I stopped short beside the enormous lawn flamingo, a dull feeling settling in my chest. "You mean his case would to be higher profile than it normally would." And Charlie would pay the price. I scrubbed a hand over my face.

"I'm sorry, but that's the reality. Does your brother have an alibi? An alibi who isn't you?" he amended.

"I'll see what I can turn up."

"No, I don't think you should. The closer you get to this case, the messier it will be. Hire a PI if you feel you have to, but stay out of it."

"Thanks. I'm working on hiring someone. I'll let you know if anything changes."

We hung up, and I checked my phone. Still no contact info for the PI from Fitch. I pressed the edge of the phone against my forehead.

Charlie had been living in Ivanna's treehouse when Donald Rigby had been killed. It wouldn't hurt to talk to her while I was waiting for Fitch's contact. There was a slim chance she could alibi my brother.

I checked my watch. Ivanna could be working at the Sagebrush, but Kitty or Zed might spot us there. She could also be at home. Or Ivanna could be somewhere else entirely, and I'd be out of luck.

Her house wasn't far, so I started walking. Fredo kept pace, his tiny legs motoring, his tags jingling. I was pretty sure the dog was just trying to get close enough to attack my shoes again. But there was something comforting in having him around.

We turned into Ivanna's driveway. I glanced up at the treehouse and wondered if Charlie had left anything else behind. It was a better reason for coming here than asking about alibis.

I rang the bell. After a few moments, sounds of life emerged from the house.

Ivanna opened the door, her elfin face tight. She smiled. "Alice? What are you doing here?"

"I came to check the treehouse. I don't know if Charlie left anything behind, but I thought I should take a look, just in case."

She studied me through deep-water eyes. "How's Charlie doing? After the arrest, I mean?"

"He was brought in for questioning, not arrested. So he's fine."

She bit her bottom lip. "What did they ask him about?"

That... was a good question, one I should have asked. "Where was he when the Rigbys died, that sort of thing," I said vaguely.

"So he *is* a suspect." She lowered her head. "Dammit," she whispered, and I suddenly liked Ivanna a lot more.

"He's not the only one," I said. "Oh, hey, there is one other thing."

She stilled, one hand on the door.

"We both know Charlie didn't kill anyone," I said, "but he needs an alibi for Donald's death."

Her reddish brows gathered inward, and she rubbed her palm across her chest. "I'm sorry, I wish I could help you, but I can't."

She really *did* like Charlie. My little brother needed to make his move. "Oh. I mean, I figured he'd been in the treehouse, and you'd been home, and if you noticed him at any time that night—"

"That's the thing. I wasn't home."

I frowned. "You weren't?" But we'd seen her when I'd dropped off Charlie that night.

"After I came home from the theater, I went out later, to the Viking bar."

If only she'd asked Charlie to go with her. "What time did you get back?"

"Around one, I think."

A branch behind me rustled. I glanced over my shoulder, half expecting to see the stag. A squirrel bounded from a branch to the treehouse.

"When you came home, did you notice if Charlie was in the treehouse?" I asked. "Did he call down to you or anything? Because if he did—"

She shook her head. "I wish he had."

"Oh." The Viking bar was just down the block from where Rigby had been killed. Though I had a hard time imagining Ivanna knifing a man, unless it was a desperate case of self-defense.

BANG. I flinched and glanced up at the treehouse.

Ivanna rolled her eyes. "It's the squirrels. Look, if it helps, I did see that creepy gardener wandering around after I left the bar."

"Creepy... You mean the guy who's been landscaping around the Big Things?"

"Yeah. Him."

Fitch hadn't mentioned being in town the night Donald Rigby was killed. The omission had to be intentional. But why *wouldn't* he keep things from me? We barely knew each other. But I barely knew Ivanna either.

"I mean, it's weird, isn't it?" Ivanna continued. "He doesn't live here. He's from Reno. And Nowhere isn't exactly a hot spot. What was he doing here so late at night? Why was he commuting to Nowhere for a gardening job at all? It can't be worth the drive."

"That is strange." The PI could have been on a stakeout. But if so, he should have been surveilling Rigby. Or he could have lied to me about everything. "Thanks." I turned to go.

"Don't you want to look for Charlie's things?" She jerked her chin toward the treehouse.

"Oh. Right. Thanks." Tying Fredo's leash to a small pine, I climbed the ladder and stuck my head through the opening in the floor. A canvas bag lay against one wall.

Atop it hunched a squirrel, gripping something fibrous and yellowish between its paws. Flakes fell from its tiny mouth to Charlie's bag.

I climbed higher and waved my hand at the squirrel. "Shoo."

The squirrel ignored me and kept eating.

"Your funeral." I stretched and pulled the bag toward me. It clanked. *More weaponry.*

The squirrel dropped its food and chittered angrily.

"Hey, I warned—"

It launched itself at me. I sucked in a breath and ducked. The squirrel landed on my head, its paws tangling in my hair.

"Get off!" I jerked backward. My shoes slipped off the makeshift ladder. I let go of the bag and clutched wildly at the floor. I slid backward, hands clawing at the wooden floor, feet flailing twenty feet above the ground.

And then one foot touched the ladder. I relaxed and straightened, grasping the open doorway for balance. The squirrel hopped onto a window and smirked.

Shaking my head, I slung the bag, which weighed a ton, over one shoulder. I clambered down the ladder to the ground.

I didn't like the idea of hauling the bag to my motel on foot. And I was tired of hiding from Kitty and Zed. I wanted my car. I slipped the other arm through the bag's straps, wearing it like a monstrous backpack.

"Let's go." I untied the dog.

Fredo hurled himself at my shoes. His teeth caught in the laces. I bent, and the weight of the bag nearly toppled me. Using the pine to lever myself upright, I removed Fredo, and we staggered into town. .

I slowed, scanning Main Street. The reporters were nowhere in sight, and I lengthened my strides. Fredo's tiny legs were a blur, and he made a sort of wheezing pant.

I pointed my fob at the car. The Corolla beeped, lights flashing. Opening the door, I reared away from the waves of heat that emerged. I tossed the bag on the back seat.

"Alice! I'm sorry." Kitty jogged out of a doorway, and my shoulders hunched to my ears. "I know I can push too far," she continued. "It's only..." She slowed to a halt. "Can we talk? And not about Toomas Koppel."

Sure. She wanted the goods on Koppel. But I didn't see how I could extract myself gracefully. "Okay," I said.

Besides, maybe she had contacts inside the sheriff's department I could use. So I guess that made me no better than Kitty. She wanted me for a story, and I wanted her to help my brother.

The blond reporter braced her hand on top of the Corolla. "So. Hi. Long time no see."

My gaze flicked skyward. I opened the car door and set Fredo inside.

"No," she said, "wait. Look, I don't know where to start. I'm working now for a local news station in Sparks."

"I thought you were with a Reno station."

She smiled bitterly. "Fired. It became too awkward with my ex-husband working there."

"So they fired you?"

She made a face. "His new girlfriend, the station manager, did. She said I didn't appeal to the younger demographic."

I felt an unwilling twinge of sympathy. Buck and I had managed to stay civil, even working together. But it hadn't escaped me that Buck was more worried about his company's reputation than mine.

"That stinks." I leaned against the hot car. "I'm sorry."

"No, I'm sorry. Getting an interview with you would have been sweet, sweet revenge."

"It wouldn't do much for me though."

"That's not necessarily true," she said. "People need to hear your side of the story."

"There's nothing useful I could tell you. I wasn't there when Koppel hit that tomato truck. That's in the police report. And the FBI's report."

"But you were on the scene immediately afterward. You were following him. It was your car he crashed. How *did* he get your car?"

I shook my head. "I can't talk about it."

"I haven't told anyone you're here," she said. "Yet."

"Ah." I grimaced and slid into the baking Corolla. So much for my moment of sympathy.

She grasped the car's door. "And since Charlie was brought into custody and released, no one's made the connection between the Rigby murders and you."

"Yet, you mean," I finished for her, and swiveled to face the reporter. She'd figured out my weak spot, I'd give her that. If it was between saving my reputation and Charlie, my brother won, no contest. My jaw set. I knew what I looked like. I'd had a lot of practice with the look. It had scared off bigger and badder people than Kitty.

"I need this," she said quietly.

"Revenge against your old station is important enough to blackmail me over? I know we were never friends. And college was a long time ago. But still, that's low."

"You're not the only one who's starting over."

Heat rose in my cheeks. "Who said I'm starting over?" I'd get my career back. Eventually. "And neither are you. You're still in the news biz."

"And I need this win."

"So what are you saying? You'll tell the world about Charlie and the murders if I don't give you an interview?"

"It's news. Your brother was brought in for questioning on two murders days after the Koppel incident."

"I'll think about it." I reached for the door handle.

She held onto the door, keeping me from shutting it. "Don't think too long. This offer has a twenty-four-hour expiration date."

I yanked the door, and she released it so I could close it.

I pulled from the curb and checked the rearview mirror. Kitty stared after me but didn't follow.

The lawyer's predictions were already coming true. The media was making the connections. And once media attention was brought to bear on a trial, the chances of the defendant getting a fair shake dropped.

My hands clenched on the wheel. I was partly responsible for my brother's predicament.

I had to clear Charlie's name before he saw the inside of a courtroom.

CHAPTER TWENTY-FOUR

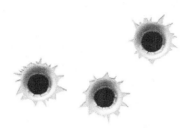

THE BOWLING ALLEY WAS a red and gold high-ceilinged affair from its prior days as a ballroom. I gawked at the crystal chandeliers grazing the top of the giant bowling pin. The scent of nachos and hot dogs brought the tone down a bit, but still. Chandeliers. And the bowling pin had to be nearly forty feet tall.

There was a clatter of bowling pins. A family at the far end of the alley cheered.

A poster-sized wedding photo of a smiling Donald and Carmel Rigby stood on an easel beside a lane. Mourners in brightly colored bowling shirts clustered in small groups, talking in low voices.

An overweight, older man in a red bowling shirt cleared his throat, and we fell silent.

Fitch's PI contact had been a bust. After a bout of initial enthusiasm, when he heard my full name, he'd acted like the case was nuclear waste. He hadn't been able to hang up fast enough.

I hadn't given up on finding a real detective. But I was here, and the wake was now, and it seemed silly to miss it. Fitch must have had the same idea. He lurked beside the two-story bowling pin.

The older man checked a notecard. "Donald Rigby was my godson." He smoothed his wispy white combover. "We all know about his love for Carmel, and his passion for water sports. But when I think of the essence of the man, I think about a man with demons."

My ears pricked. *Demons?*

"We also all know the trouble he got into in his youth," Donald's godfather continued. "Carmel, God rest her soul, saw beyond that. She knew that he could overcome those demons. And he did."

The mourners, who included Gert and Mrs. Malone, nodded and muttered.

I looked around, interested. What trouble had Donald gotten into in his youth? Was it the attempted seduction of Marques's wife?

"We all have our demons," the man went on, his voice rough. "We all know what it means to struggle against them. Donald struggled, and he won. Donald Rigby was an inspiration to me. And so was Carmel, because she had the patience and the enduring love to see him through to better times. They were an amazing couple." He blinked rapidly.

Mrs. Malone stepped forward. "Thank you, Mr. Cartman. Would anyone else like to speak?"

No one stepped forward.

"There are refreshments on the tables." She motioned toward a short flight of steps. "Please enjoy them."

I hurried to Mr. Cartman. "That was lovely," I said.

"Baby Alice." He beamed. "It's been ages since I've clapped eyes on you. How've you been?"

"Uh..." Shame on me, I was more embarrassed by that stupid nickname than by the fact that I couldn't remember him at all.

"We heard about what happened with that Koppel fellow." He patted my arm. "No one blames you."

I grimaced. "Everyone blames me. But that's not why I'm here tonight."

"I know." He turned toward the photo of the Rigbys. "What a shocking thing to happen in Nowhere. I'm glad you're here for your brother."

"He wasn't involved."

"Charlie?" He laughed and shook his balding head, his chins wobbling. "I can't think of a *least* likely evil genius."

"You mentioned something about Donald having demons." Fitch edged closer.

"Oh." Mr. Cartman's face fell. "That was before your time. Or actually, it was during your time, but you were too young to understand."

"What happened?"

He shook his head. "I'd rather Donald was remembered for the man he became instead of the man he was. Like you. You're more than that mutton-busting incident from your childhood." He winked. "Baby Alice."

I sighed. "I hate that name."

He chuckled. "It's strange the way it all worked out, isn't it? You get in trouble and come home. Charlie gets in trouble, and you help him. It makes me wonder if you're exactly where you're supposed to be."

"But about Donald—"

He patted my arm. "I'm glad you're back. You belong here."

Mr. Cartman called a man's name, threw up his hands, and wandered into the crowd. He hugged another mourner.

Mrs. Malone appeared at my elbow. "Donald Rigby didn't owe money around town."

"He didn't?" I asked.

She nodded. "I heard you asking, and I'd prefer you *not* dig up old scandals at the Rigbys' memorial. Bad enough that we had to add Carmel at such short notice. We don't have anyone to speak on her behalf."

I hung my head. I'd violated memorial etiquette. "Okay."

"Besides..." Mrs. Malone sighed. "Donald had a wake-up call."

I looked up. "When Marques's wife said *no* to him?"

She raised a brow. "You heard about that?"

"Is that why Donald left town? Fear of Marques?"

"He left town because his hiking store failed after Norm—" She clamped her mouth shut.

"Pete's father?"

"Feelings were running high after his death. Donald took the blame, especially since he'd been so close with Pete's mother. Where's Fredo?"

"In my cabin. Wait, are you saying Donald and Pete's mother had an affair? No way. Why hadn't I heard about that?"

"It was only a rumor. It may not have been true. And relationships between men and women can get complicated."

"So Donald left out of guilt? For Norm's car accident?"

Her eyes widened.

"Mrs. Malone?" Following her gaze, I turned and found myself nose-to-nose with Gert. He held a bowling ball high above his head. Blinking furiously behind his thick glasses, he swayed beneath its weight.

"Really?" I said. "You're going to drop that on me in front of everyone?"

He gasped. "My hands are slipping."

I took the bowling ball before he dropped it on himself. Wheezing, he bent, bracing his age-spotted hands on his knees.

"I'm starting to think you're not taking my assassination seriously." I set the ball in a return machine and turned back to Mrs. Malone. She was gone. "Where'd she go?" Miffed, I scanned the crowd.

"Maybe she didn't want to answer any more of your damn questions," Gert wheezed.

"Do *you* know why the Rigbys left town?"

"Everybody with any sense leaves."

"You didn't."

He thumped his chest and coughed. "Guess I don't have any sense."

Studiously avoiding Fitch, I asked around some more about Donald's secret past. But either my interrogation skills were terrible—this was probable—or no one knew.

Frustrated and half-hoping Fitch would follow, I left the bowling memorial and walked to the Viking bar. It was Saturday night. The place was shoulder-to-shoulder people. Thunks and whoops emerged from the ax-throwing room.

At the blond-wood bar, I wedged myself between two cowboys and motioned to the bartender. Lucky me, he was the same guy who'd been there the night I'd had drinks with Carmel.

He eased down the bar polishing a beer stein. "Let me guess. You have questions."

"How'd you know?"

He polished the stein more furiously. "It's a small town. Word gets around."

Maybe I should ease into this interrogation. "What brought you to Nowhere?"

"I wasn't on the run from the law." He winked.

I stiffened. "What's that supposed to mean? The police know I had nothing to do with Koppel's death." The cowboy on my left gave me the side-eye and edged away. I took his barstool.

"Sorry," the bartender said. "Bad joke. To answer your question, Marques Washington brought me here. This is his building."

How much town property did Marques own? "How do you know him? Before he became your landlord, I mean."

"He stopped in at bar I was working at in Sparks, and we got to talking. I told him about the kind of bar I'd like to open, and he offered me a deal I couldn't refuse."

"Which was?"

"Obscenely cheap rent. I don't know what he's charging his other tenants, but he's not making any money on me."

I frowned. How *was* Marques managing it? And how far was he willing to go to lure his kids back to Nowhere? "Ivanna Simms," I said. "Was she here last Sunday night? Late?"

"The waitress from the Sagebrush? Yeah. She closed the bar."

"What time does it close?"

"One o'clock."

That tracked. "Do you know if she left any time before that? Maybe for some fresh air?"

"I'm not her keeper. But she was throwing axes with that bunch." He nodded toward a group of middle-aged women sitting at a round, wooden table.

"Thanks."

Bracing myself, I got a beer and strolled to their table. "Hi, can I join you?"

"Sure," said a perky brunette with an upturned nose. "I'm Tracy." She was petite and curvy, and I felt a surge of envy. What would it be like to be that size?

They didn't flinch, didn't nudge each other, didn't check their phones. Could it be possible they didn't know me? Because that would be *amazing* luck.

"I'm... Amy." I pulled out a chair and sat. "It felt a little weird being alone. After the murder last Sunday and all."

They shivered dramatically.

"That was awful," another woman, a platinum blond, said.

"Whoa." I sat back in my chair. "You weren't *here* when it happened?"

They nodded.

"And it happened practically across the street," Tracy said, "at that big can of peas."

"Did you see anything?" I leaned forward, breathless. They shook their heads. "I guess..." I sighed. "Nowhere's a fun town. But I guess walking around alone at night still isn't the best idea."

"We're from Reno," a third woman with gray streaks in her hair said. "We're not stupid."

People *were* coming to Nowhere for fun? It baffled the mind. "What brought you here?" I asked.

"That dinner theater," Tracy said. "The one-eyed man is hot. And then we came by here afterward for drinks, and this woman from the theater talked us into axe throwing..."

"Ivanna?" I raised a knowing brow, and they laughed.

"Do you know her?" Tracy asked.

I nodded. "Oh, yeah. She's super daring. Definitely not the sort to worry about walking around by herself at night."

"Oh," Tracy said, "but she left with us that night. We walked her to her car."

"Really?" That was good news for Charlie's love life.

"She was a hoot," Tracy said. "Honestly, Nowhere is so much more fun than that stuck-up Hot Springs."

I warmed to the woman. We *were* better than stuck-up Hot Springs. Though it would have been nice if Nowhere had hot springs.

"But the bars in Hot Springs have more drinks on tap," Tracy continued.

Another woman snorted. "At twice the price."

I finished my beer and chatted with the women, but I learned nothing more. It seemed odd that Ivanna had gone all the way home from the theater and then returned to Main Street and the bar. But maybe she'd just wanted to change?

Since Fitch didn't turn up for axe throwing, I left and collected Charlie from the theater. The two of us drove to the motel in silence.

I stood a bit to the side as I unlocked and opened the door, more concerned about what damage Fredo might have done than another booby trap.

"All clear?" Charlie asked.

I took a hesitant step inside. The cabin looked undamaged, though it smelled like Fredo funk. "Clear."

The dog looked up from my bed, gave a snaggle-toothed yawn, and returned to dreamland.

———*ele*———

The next morning, Sunday, the cabin smelled a lot funkier. This was because Fredo had peed in my trail running shoes the night before.

Annoyed, I began to toss the shoes into the garbage bin, then hesitated. There was something about shoes... *Whatever.* I dropped the shoes into the waste basket. I never was my best in the morning.

Charlie yawned and stretched beneath his blanket on the couch. "This is great. I haven't slept on a couch in ages."

"Yeah." I sat on the bed across from him. "But I'm worried about you."

"Hey," he said. "I'm not the one wanted by the Estonian mafia."

I tugged on the skin at the base of my throat. "What did the police ask when they questioned you?"

"The same stuff they asked at the house. What did I mean when I said I'd burn down my house?"

My chest caved inward. *They knew?*

Charlie rolled his eyes. "What did I have against the Rigbys? Nothing. And where was I Friday between nine AM and when we found Carmel after lunch? I was with you. So they had to let me go."

So nine AM to noonish was the window when Carmel had been killed. Good for the local coroner for figuring that out. Unless Carmel been seen by someone around nine?

"What happens at nine o'clock on Friday morning?" I rose and let Fredo out to do his business.

"Garbage pick-up," Charlie said. "The timing was great. I didn't have to get up at six AM to put the garbage out like some people."

The garbage bins hadn't been in front of her house. If they'd been empty, Carmel must have brought them back into her garage after the pickup.

He yawned. "Now are you going to demand everyone's alibis between nine and twelve?"

Fredo yipped at the glass door.

"Something like that." I let the dog inside.

Charlie shook his head. "I'm telling you, it couldn't have been anyone from Nowhere. This town isn't like that. People care about each other. I mean, look at Marques. Everything he does is for the town. And Pete. He may have been a real jerk about my house, but it was for the town. And—"

"It's most likely someone close to the Rigbys killed them. And that means someone here in Nowhere."

He threw off the beige blanket and swung his feet to the floor. Never one for pajamas, he'd slept in his board shorts and a white tee. "No way."

"Speaking of Marques, he says he's still got that job for you."

"See?" He slapped his hands on his bare thighs. "He cares. People care. You care."

"Because you're my brother."

"And you're an awesome bodyg—personal protection agent or whatever. We're going to figure out who killed the Rigbys."

"It would be easier if you didn't talk to the police without a lawyer," I said.

He pulled on his tennis shoes. "Water under the bridge."

"Promise me. If they pull you in again, no talking without the lawyer I've found."

He groaned. "Fine. I promise. And now, I've gotta go."

"Where are you going?"

"I'm staining Mrs. Malone's back porch." My brother hopped to his feet, then winced and rubbed his thigh.

"Charlie, there's something else."

"What?"

"There are some reporters sniffing around," I said, "looking for a story on me. If any reporters approach you—"

"No comment."

I smiled. "Thanks."

Charlie left on his bike for his painting job. I scoured the cabin for more evidence of Fredo's revenge, but my shoes seemed to have been the only damage.

Since it seemed the sort of thing a detective would do, I searched the internet for intel on my suspects. But I kept getting diverted by speculation on Toomas Koppel's death. Koppel's name was everywhere.

Muscles tight, I typed my own name into the search engine. Before I could hit *enter*, an email pinged into my inbox from Fitch. I opened it.

Here's what I got on the resort. See attached.

—F

I opened the files and saved them to my computer. I reopened the search engine. Should I? I shook my head. Better to know than not know. I typed in my name.

Thirty minutes later, hands shaking, I shut the laptop. I stared blindly at the couch, covered in Charlie's rumpled blankets. The things people had written...

Fredo leapt onto my lap. Absently I stroked the dog's back.

The person they were writing about wasn't me. I wasn't a killer. I wasn't a conspirator. I wasn't...

It was like I didn't exist anymore. An awful stranger with my name and face had taken my place, and everyone was talking about her. No wonder Buck hadn't called.

Blinking, I shook my head. This was stupid. They were only words. I'd faced real, physical danger, real threats. Words were nothing. I had to stop thinking about this. I needed to get out of the cabin, to talk to real people.

I slid the computer into my backpack, gathered up Fredo, and drove to the Sagebrush.

Inside the doorway, I scanned the bustling diner. Kitty wasn't inside and neither was Zed. I had four hours until Kitty's deadline. I still wasn't sure what I was going to do.

In a sense, her threat had been empty. Once she got her interview and other reporters found out I was in Nowhere, the others would descend. They'd learn about Charlie and the other murders.

Molly bustled past. "Just grab a table on the patio, hon."

"Thanks." I found a corner table near the gate and sat with my back to the high, redwood fence. I tied Fredo's leash to a chair leg, set up my laptop, and ordered brunch.

While I waited for the food to arrive, I wandered inside the diner and to the counter where the old-timers sat. If Mrs. Malone wouldn't tell me Donald Rigby's old secret, someone else might. "Hi, Mr. Washington."

Marques's father swiveled to face me on his barstool. "How's it going?"

"It's going. Say, do you remember the year the Rigbys left town?"

He set down his coffee mug. "That was a terrible year."

"Why?"

"The ballroom caught fire. Remember? That scouting group let things get a little out of control."

"Oh, yeah." It was the first time I'd been glad I'd never become a scout.

"That was also the year Norm died."

"Norm? Pete's father?"

"You should know. He saved you from that runaway lamb. He had an accident in that same ravine where your father lost his life five years ago. They put better warning lights up after your father's passing."

My chest hollowed. Dad hadn't had a chance. "Why didn't they put up lights after Norm's death?"

"Ah." The elderly man stared into his coffee mug. "You picked up on that."

My guts twisted. "Was Norm's death... an accident?"

"There were no skid marks where Norm went over." He sipped his coffee. "But there's no sense dredging all that up, is there?"

My gaze dropped to my shoes, my belly knotting. *Poor Pete.* "No. I guess not." How could I not have known? This explained so much about Pete's withdrawal. Hard enough losing a father, but to lose one like that... *Did* Pete know?

"You were close to that family, weren't you?"

"Not that year," I said guiltily. "Pete sort of went into his own solitary confinement that year."

He angled his gray head. "Well, his mother *was* doing poorly."

My hands curled. I should have been there for Pete. His father dead, his mother drowning her sorrows... He'd needed a better friend. But fourteen-year-old me couldn't handle his chilly indifference and had put up a shell of my own.

I was starting to see a pattern.

And then summer came and went, and we were back in school and back to normal, and I'd been too relieved to question it. But of course, nothing was normal when your parent was gone. I hadn't learned that hard lesson until my own mother had died two years later. Maybe that was what had brought us back together, for a time.

"I hear his mother's doing better," Mr. Washington said. "Living it up in Florida."

"What else happened the year the Rigbys left?"

"The five-and-dime went belly up." He took another swallow of coffee. "It was the beginning of the end for Nowhere. Or maybe the middle, before our Renaissance." Laughing, he motioned toward the window and the giant mushrooms across the street.

"And that's it?"

"That's all I can think of. Why? Do you *want* more bad news?"

"No. It's nothing. Thanks."

I returned to my patio table and dug into the financials Fitch had emailed. The company behind the marijuana resort *seemed* solid. But my old college business classes didn't qualify me as a financial analyst.

The company also had resorts in other states, including Colorado. And they were public, so they were regulated by the SEC, for whatever that was worth. Had Fitch seen anything in their numbers that I hadn't?

I finished my huevos rancheros and checked my watch. What was I going to tell Kitty? At a loss, I put Fredo in my car and drove toward the motel.

I checked the rearview mirror. No tails. I was still in the clear.

I slowed in front of the motel cabins, I slowed, and my chest hitched. News vans filled its parking lot.

No one had to follow me. They already knew where I was.

CHAPTER TWENTY-FIVE

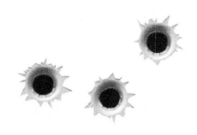

HORRIFIED, I CRUISED PAST the A-frame cabins. The manager shouted at a news van blocking the parking lot and raised her fist, the sleeve of her oversized pink sweater sliding up her bony arm.

On autopilot, I drove by our old house. A news van sat outside that too. I didn't think Kitty had blabbed about my location. She wanted her exclusive. But it didn't matter how they'd found out. They'd found me.

I kept driving and wound up on Main Street. Two news vans were now parked outside the Sagebrush Café. I circled the block and parked behind the antique shop. Fredo growled. My phone rang, and I pulled it from my pocket. *Buck.*

Relieved, I answered. "Hey."

"What the hell? You're giving interviews now? I told you to lie *low*."

"No one's interviewed me."

"That's not what some reporter in Sparks says."

I closed my eyes. *Kitty.*

"And a rabbit?" he bellowed. "You're protecting a rabbit? Are you trying to make me look like a fool?"

"Yes. That's been my plan all along. To destroy my career to spite you."

"If you want to salvage your career, you've got to get out of Nowhere," he snarled. "Now."

"I can't. Charlie's—"

"Charlie's got a lawyer, hasn't he? You don't need to be there."

"Hanging the people who matter out to dry is your play, not mine." Furious, I hung up. Buck hadn't had his reputation destroyed, and he didn't seem to be helping much.

My chest heaved. That damned, dog-faced confession. Me, standing in our bedroom, and holding my shoes by their straps after the company holiday party. There'd been bits of red glitter in his hair from the cheap Santa hat he'd worn. The bed unmade, because we'd been running late, and Buck had pulled me back into it that morning. And the words, the words dropping from his mouth like stones, and the rushing in my ears, the inability to comprehend what he was saying so that he'd had to say it twice.

The phone rang again. I turned off the ringer. *Compartmentalize.* I eyed the rear of the brick building. Metal doors lined its wall. I hauled a resisting Fredo from the Corolla and tried one of the doors. It scraped against a concrete floor, emitting an earsplitting squeal.

"Gert," I shouted. "It's me. Don't shoot."

He stormed into the hallway. "What are you doing here?"

"The press found me. They're at my motel, our old house, even the Sagebrush."

His eyes bulged behind their thick glasses. "So why'd you come *here*? I'm your arch enemy, your nemesis. I want you dead."

"Exactly. They'll never look for me at your shop."

"Why not? No one knows I'm going to take you down."

I lifted a brow. "Are you sure? You used to have quite a reputation. An enterprising reporter might figure it out."

"Don't try to make me feel better." He turned and shuffled down the hall.

"Feel better?" I trailed after him. Fredo snapped half-heartedly at my ankles. "What's wrong?" I asked.

He slouched behind his glass counter. "I thought I'd have more time. Now you're all over the news again, you and your brother." He picked up a remote and aimed it at a TV on the wall, surrounded by hula hoops and velvet paintings.

A local newscaster frowned in front of the Sagebrush Café. "Brother connected to two more murders. And people are asking, could the recent murders be connected to the death of Toomas Koppel?"

"What people?" I asked the screen, exasperated. "Which people are asking? The only people asking that are you."

"There's no sense yelling at the TV," Gert said reasonably.

I swore.

"Tell me about it," Gert said. "Now the Estonians are coming to Nowhere, and how am I supposed to kill you with them underfoot?"

"The Estonians aren't coming. They're a small operation with bigger fish to fry." I twisted Fredo's leash around my hand.

"That's what *you* think." He braced an elbow on the dusty counter. "On the bright side, I hear Zed Kelley's in town."

"How is that a bright side?"

"Haven't you watched his channel? The kid's terrific. A little excitable, but... youth."

"Look," I said. "I just need a quiet place to think. And maybe a place to stay tonight."

"You can't stay here. If the Estonians find you, they'll think I've betrayed them."

"They're not going to find me. Because they're not coming." Though I'd said the same thing about the media. I shoved my hands in the pockets of my jeans. "They've got nothing to do with me," I said less certainly.

"Nothing to—What do you think happened to Toomas's other bodyguards?"

My hands grew damp. "They're lying low?"

"They're lying six feet under. They failed. You don't fail these kinds of people. And my shop will be the *first* place they come. Why do you think I'm closed?" He motioned toward the front door. A metal door brace held it shut.

"You left your back door unlocked," I pointed out.

He cursed and lurched to his feet. "Why didn't you lock it?"

Metal screeched on concrete. A draft of warm air wafted down the hall. Gert and I stared at each other, dismayed.

"Gert Magimountain?" an accented voice called.

"Get out," Gert whispered frantically, waving toward the front of the antique shop. "Go."

A news van glided past the front windows.

I shook my head. "But—"

"Gert?" a man's voice boomed.

"Go," Gert hissed and shoved me toward the glass door. "I'll take care of this."

I walked, legs stiff and jerky, to the door, and fumbled with the lock. Fredo and I darted outside. The Estonians were here. This was real. They really wanted to... I gulped.

A black panel van screeched to a halt in front of me. Zed rolled down the window and leaned out. He adjusted his navy knit cap. "Need a lift?"

I grabbed Fredo off the sidewalk and sprinted to the van.

"I take it that's a *yes*," Zed said.

I opened the van's sliding door and glanced over my shoulder. A tour bus rumbled up Main. I jumped inside, and Zed pulled from the curb. He made a sharp turn in front of the bus, and its horn blared. Swaying, I grabbed a handle in the ceiling to keep from falling.

We zoomed down the street. I peered through the rear windows. No one was following. Exhaling slowly, I made my way to the front of the van. It was packed with recording equipment, two small green chairs, and a bed and a hotplate set up.

"Cool van," I said. Fredo whuffed, and I held him closer.

"There are solar panels on the top," Zed said, "so I can power the equipment."

I clambered into the passenger seat.

"Where to?" Zed's brown eyes widened, and he jerked away from Fredo. "Oh my God, what *is* that?"

"It's a dog."

"Yeah, no."

"What else could it be?" I said, annoyed.

Zed raised a hand in surrender. "Where to?"

I shifted my feet. I couldn't go back for my car. If Kitty had found it, others would too, and the Estonians... I wiped a bead of sweat off my upper lip. Okay, forget the Estonians. It would be safer to leave my car and lie low.

But where? I'd run out of clues to follow, people to interrogate. Or had I?

"Well?" Zed asked.

Fredo curled at my feet.

"The park behind the cemetery," I said.

"Sure thing." He turned the van down a rutted road.

"You know Nowhere's shortcuts already?"

"I have a photographic memory." He adjusted his knit cap with one hand. "So, have you given any more thought to doing my podcast?"

"This is colossally bad timing."

"Here's the thing. If you wait until the news cycle has moved onto the next scandal, no one will care what you have to say. Your image as the bodyguard who looked the other way while her client got killed will be locked in."

"That's not what happened," I said.

"What *did* happen?"

I pressed my lips shut.

"The rest of those reporters just want a soundbite they can twist for clicks," he continued. "And to get clicks, it's going to have to be something dramatic and bad."

I sighed. The press had found me. The Estonians were here. Things couldn't get much worse. "How much do you know about the personal protection business?"

"I've worked with a few bodyguards. I know they aren't fond of that word, but not much more."

"There are different types of protection. There's close personal protection, where the bodyguard stays near the client. There's also covert personal protection, where the BG keeps a distance and watches for watchers."

"Countersurveillance," he said.

"Exactly. I was covert countersurveillance."

The van bumped over a rut, and we rocked in our seats.

"That tracks." Zed nodded. "The heavies he kept around him, the ones who disappeared, were the close protection."

"Right."

"Did his other team know you were there?"

I cut a sideways glance at him. "How did you know about his other guys?" I asked. "I haven't seen it reported on."

"I took a job at Koppel's hotel and got in good with the housekeeping and other staff. I asked around. So? Did they?"

"No," I admitted. "At least that's the way Koppel said he wanted it."

"So, Koppel didn't trust his own men." He nodded. "Any idea why he took off with your car?"

"I imagine he wanted to go somewhere without anyone knowing," I said, sarcastic.

"But you knew."

"There was an anti-theft tracker on my car that I have—had access to. I followed it."

"And you didn't alert his other team, because they weren't supposed to know you were there."

"Right." It was a relief to tell the story. I'd told the cops and the FBI, but they'd been trying to poke holes in it. *Like a good reporter should.* I angled myself to face him. "Are we being recorded?"

"No. That would be unethical and probably illegal since you haven't given me your permission."

The van swayed again, and the dog looked up at me nervously.

"Stop here," I said.

Zed pulled up to the curb. "We're not at the park."

"This is far enough. Thanks for the lift."

"No problem. Thanks for the insight."

I opened the door.

"Hey," he said. "As far as the world is concerned, you're a blank slate to slap an identity onto. If they heard from you directly, they might listen to your side of the story."

"Thanks for the ride," I repeated and stepped from the van to the sidewalk in front of a petite, blue-gray Victorian. We were in my old neighborhood, not too far from what used to be the family home.

"It's your funeral." Zed drove off.

I watched his rear bumper vanish around the corner. My fists clenched and unclenched on Fredo's leash. He sniffed a mailbox.

Zed was right. All anyone could do was assume I was the person the press had painted me. And all Nowhere knew me as Baby Alice. In my quest for travel and adventure, all I'd left behind were bad impressions.

The dog lifted his leg over my shoe.

I hopped backward. "Don't even *think* about it."

Fredo and I stuck to back alleys too narrow for news vans. The alley behind my parents' old house was unguarded, the yard half-hidden by lilac bushes.

The dog and I crossed the lawn to the pergola at the back of the house. Before my father had died, he'd installed easy-to-clean windows. They were also easy to remove from the outside if they weren't locked properly. And you had to work to lock them properly.

I tied the dog to one of the pergola's wooden posts, near the back door. Keeping him in my peripheral vision, I went to the window with the trickiest lock and popped out the screen. My insides writhed. Breaking and entering wasn't how I usually operated. But desperate times.

Fredo tilted his head. Drool slipped sideways through his teeth and to the dying grass.

I pressed my palm against the glass and lifted up. The window levered out of its base. I reached my fingers beneath it and shoved the bottom inward. Tilting it this way and that, I maneuvered the window out of its frame.

Fredo wagged his tail and strained at his leash. I set the window on the lawn and peered through the opening. Inside, a desk sat beneath the window.

I hefted myself through and crawled onto the desk, knocking over a cup filled with highlighter pens and a sheaf of plain paper. Using the hem of my t-shirt, I wiped the desk and the window frame where I'd put my hands. I kept one hand wrapped in my t-shirt as I returned the pens and paper to the desk.

Unbelievably, the sheriff hadn't taken Rigby's computer. Or maybe it *was* believable. I turned it on. No password. My luck really *was* turning. I opened Rigby's email, and his password logged in automatically. This run of good fortune should have made me suspicious, but I was too enthralled by things finally going my way.

Sometimes, people got killed because they were in the wrong place, wrong time. And while I despise victim blaming, sometimes people were murdered because they'd set the wrong guy off.

When people put themselves in high-risk situations, bad things could happen. Since I was often in high-risk situations, I had strong feelings about this. Ultimately, the person to blame for a murder was the murderer, not the victim. Period.

But *had* Rigby been up to no good?

I skimmed past the emails for male enhancement drugs and Nigerian Central Bank scams. FYI, I *had* been to the Nigerian Central Bank. The place was rundown, but the people there had been friendly and professional.

CREAK.

I looked up, heart thumping, and cocked my head, listening. I shook my head. It was just the house settling. I returned my attention to the screen. On the left side, Rigby had organized files by subject. I clicked on a file titled *Nowhere*.

Emails between Rigby and his company, discussing plans. He said he'd found a perfect spot, but there were alternates if it fell through. Nothing specifically about the cannery. A few emails from Pete's nowhere.gov address discussing zoning and support Rigby's firm would get from the town.

Near the bottom of the file, I clicked on the first email from Pete, addressed to Donald. It invited Donald and his company to Nowhere. The lure was free living space while they evaluated the town's potential.

My jaw clenched. The Rigbys had been living in Charlie's house rent free? I blew out my breath. It wasn't my house anymore, and it wasn't Charlie's. And it wasn't Pete's fault my brother had forgotten to pay his taxes. But it still burned.

Something scraped inside the house, and the back of my neck prickled. Wood groaned, as if someone was prying a door open.

I sucked in a breath. Someone *else* was breaking in.

CHAPTER TWENTY-SIX

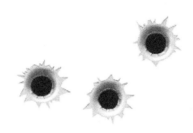

SHEESH. CAN'T A GIRL *break into a house in peace?* I shut down the computer and reached for the office's window. Fredo, leashed to the pergola outside, whuffed.

My hand clenched. No. I wasn't going to run. I'd come here for evidence to help my brother. I needed to know who was trying to get inside the Rigby house.

I crept across the beige carpet toward the wooden door. It stood ajar.

A floorboard creaked in the hallway. It wasn't the cops. A cop would have announced himself. This person was moving too stealthily.

Another floorboard creaked. Whoever this was they were also moving slowly, like they suspected they weren't alone.

That *wasn't* a good thing. They'd be ready for a fight, something I'd rather avoid. I evened my breathing. I sensed someone moving close to my door. Edging against the wall, I raised my elbows, readying for the attack.

Fredo howled.

A dark shape burst into the room. I slammed my forearm into the side of his neck, and he went sideways. Before he could recover, I jumped backward and grabbed a wooden chair to bash him with.

Fitch straightened and rubbed his muscular neck. "Ow." He shook his head. "Nice one."

I held the chair at the ready. "Have you been following me?"

"No. I came here to look for evidence." He nodded toward the computer. "The cops didn't take it? That's not a good start to their investigation."

No, it wasn't. I couldn't trust the cops to figure this out, and I didn't trust Fitch. Not after what Ivanna had told me.

"Find anything interesting?" he asked.

"Nothing. You?"

"Nothing since we last talked." He eyed me. "You okay?"

"Why wouldn't I be?"

"I don't know. But you haven't put that chair down since I got in here."

I shrugged and set down the chair. "My brother's a suspect. The press are all over me, and his lawyer thinks my problems are going to rebound on Charlie."

He grunted.

I glanced around the home office. Bookshelves. A printer on a stand. No likely filing cabinets. "Hence my last-ditch attempt to find out why someone else would have wanted to kill the Rigbys."

"Maybe I'll have better luck."

I racked my brain for a pithy exit line as I clambered out the window. "That's what he said."

My comeback had lacked a certain something, namely wit. Fortunately, I dropped to the ground before Fitch could respond.

Fredo and I walked into town, and I retrieved my Corolla from behind Gert's antique shop. Since I still didn't know where to go, I drove to Snitz Woods. It was press and MBS-free.

Keeping an eye out for resentful deer, I walked Fredo to the picnic area. I dusted pine needles off a table, found a spot with minimal sap, and opened my laptop. Tiny, flying insects flocked to its light.

Fitch might be a suspect, but he was also right. I hadn't been thinking strategically. I'd been reacting to events instead of anticipating them, and that wasn't how I'd operated in the past.

I shook my head. In surveillance, I planned, analyzed. I hadn't been doing any of that lately. I'd also learned how to stick with my plan, my training, even when I was terrified. Lately, that had gone out the window.

I swatted away a mosquito, pulled up a blank security incident report form, and began filling it out. Incident Type: murder of Donald Rigby.

Name—Role—Contact of suspects...

I didn't need the contact info. They were all within walking distance. I scratched out the contact info line and revised it.

Name—Role—Motive—Opportunity

Terrence Madoff—Artist—Motive - Wants to stop pot resort/Opportunity - ???

Marques Washington—Contractor—""—""

Mrs. Malone—Retired—""—""

Fitch Rhodes—Detective—Motive - unknown—Opportunity - Downtown at time of murder and with me at theater when knife stuck in my door.

I needed to find out where the others were at the time of Donald's murder. I skipped down the page to the witnesses section.

Pete McGregor—Mayor—Brought Rigby to town—Pro-resort.

Ivanna Simms—Waitress and Charlie's "landlady." Witnessed Fitch downtown— At theater when knife stuck in my door.

I killed a mosquito on my arm, smearing my own blood, and cursed. Fredo scratched his ear. I drummed my fingers on the sappy picnic table then listed Gert and Lilyanna, aka Captain Rabbit, as possible witnesses too.

Lilyanna wanted to clear Charlie's name. She might know something that could help. I was reaching, but at least I had a list and some direction.

But not quite enough direction. I pulled out my phone and studied my photo of the murder weapon. That paint... It jiggled something in my brain, but what? There'd been plenty of paint cans lying around inside the cannery. I shook my head. No, the cannery wasn't it.

Terrence? As an artist, he was an obvious candidate for splashing paint on a murder weapon. But that didn't seem right either.

I opened a new file and filled out the same form for Carmel's murder. And then I opened a third file and drafted a situation analysis.

A situation analysis included lists of external factors I couldn't control, internal factors I could control, lessons learned, and the gap between where I was now and where I wanted to be. The last was easy. I wanted Charlie cleared and the real murderer caught.

It was a depressingly big gap.

CHAPTER TWENTY-SEVEN

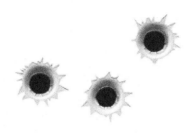

THE NEXT MORNING, I lay still in the sleeping bag. Tree branches creaked beneath me, and for a moment I was a kid again, spending a night in a tree with my brother.

Then a ghastly stench warmed my face, and I gagged, cracking open one eye. Fredo licked my chin, one of his snaggle tooths nicking me.

"Gross." I lifted Fredo off my chest, sat up, and clawed my fingers through my hair.

Something small scampered across the treehouse roof. In the sleeping bag beside mine, Charlie snored. With the media staking out my motel cabin, I'd bunked with Charlie. He'd had a little trouble with the ladder on his bum leg, but my brother was improving.

Figuring the dog could wait another couple minutes, I rolled up my sleeping bag and tossed it to the ground. I shrugged into my jacket and climbed from the treehouse one-handed, dog beneath my free arm.

I checked my watch. *Six-thirty.* Ivanna wasn't up yet. This was a good thing, since we hadn't asked permission to spend the night. I guess my ethics were getting more flexible. But I didn't trust Ivanna not to blab, and last night, the motel cabins had been surrounded by unfriendlies.

"Alice?" a woman called, and I started.

An elderly woman ambled across the lawn. She was broad and hunched in her pink house coat, and she carried a plate covered with a tea towel. Her gray hair was done up in curlers. "I thought that was you."

"Ah, hi," I said, wary.

She smiled. "You don't remember me. I'm Mrs. Yarrow. I live next door." She motioned to a tan ranch house on the other side of Ivanna's lawn. "I baked extra scones and thought you and Charlie might like some." She handed me the plate. It was still warm. "I saw you get in last night," she confided.

"We're trying to lay low."

She pressed a finger to her wrinkled lips. "Mum's the word." She ambled into her house.

I took the plate up to the treehouse and grabbed a scone. Charlie didn't wake up.

Then Fredo and I hiked to Snitz Woods. We went for a run. I cooled down with Tai Chi, then grabbed my binoculars from the car and peered across the cemetery. A lone news van stood beside my cabin.

"Dammit." They weren't giving up.

But it was true about new dawns bringing new perspectives. I'd successfully evaded the press and broken into a house. A local PI might be an ally. Gert would try to hold off the Estonians. I was still on my feet and moving forward. I'd call that a win.

Fredo at my side, I drove downtown and parked the car behind an abandoned building. Keeping with today's down-low theme, I snuck into the Sagebrush via the back gate. Fredo and I settled in on the diner's back patio, my laptop bag braced against my ankle. I ordered pancakes and bacon for me, a bowl of chicken for Fredo.

Tugging my baseball hat lower on my head, I leaned back in my chair. I peered through the open door into the diner's interior.

Zed, in his navy knit cap, sat at one of the tables. Pete sat alone in a booth. Two tall, muscled blond men I didn't recognize sat hunched at the bar. Mrs. Malone sat between them, chatting animatedly.

I jerked forward, my heart thudding. *The Estonians.* What was Mrs. Malone doing with them?

Keeping an eye on the door, I ate, paid the waitress and slung my bag over my shoulder.

Lilyanna stepped in front of me. "How's Charlie?" She wore a beekeeper's suit, her white, netted hat beneath one arm.

"Things are looking up," I lied.

Her shoulders sagged. "Thank God. I can't imagine him in jail."

"It's not going to go that far. Don't worry, he won't miss any of your medieval reenactments."

"It's not just medieval," she said. "We do Renaissance too."

I pulled up the photo of the murder weapon on my phone and handed it to her. "Does this look like one of Charlie's knives?"

She frowned at it and shook her head. "It could have been one of his, but I can't be sure. There's a lot of chaos at our practice. We're always trading weapons." She laughed shortly. "Sometimes I think we have too many people. But how can I help? I mean it. I want to. I heard there's too much evidence against him."

"Where'd you hear that?" I asked sharply.

"It's in the news." She gestured toward the diner's interior. I couldn't help myself. I leaned sideways and glanced inside. The Estonians and Mrs. Malone were gone. On the TV, high in one corner of the room, Koppel's mugshot dissolved and was replaced by photos of Charlie and me.

My stomach spasmed. "Well, the evidence is just..." I trailed off. "It's not wrong, it's just..."

"Just what?" Lilyanna asked.

There *was* too much evidence. "Charlie's going to be okay," I said, lightness spreading through my chest. *Too much evidence. Too many people.* More than one person was involved in the murder. "It explains everything."

"What?"

"Thanks, Lilyanna." I clapped her shoulder and hurried out the patio exit and walked into the cool, brick alley, Fredo on his leash.

Gert stepped in front of me. He held a Glock 9mm in his bandaged hand. It was aimed at my gut. More adhesive bandages decorated his skull. The ropy muscles in his neck were corded, and behind his glasses, his blue eyes had a wild, desperate look. After seeing the other Estonians, I sympathized. But I was also a little offended. I'd thought we'd reached an understanding.

"I'm taking you in," he said.

"Okay." I dropped Fredo's leash, stepped to the side, and slammed one palm into the back of Gert's wrist while grabbing the top of the Glock with the other and pulling it toward me. There were other gun takeaways, but they all depended on where the attacker was standing and aiming. This one worked on handguns. Gert yelped and released the weapon.

I quickstepped back and aimed the gun at him. "What the hell, Gert?"

He rubbed his wrist. "They've got Artemisia."

"Who?"

Fredo shot me a worried look.

"Mrs. Malone," Gert said in a strained voice. His gaze darted around the alley. His fingers twitched. "I have to bring you in."

I lowered the gun. "Oh my God." *Mrs. Malone.* All those hours Charlie and I had spent in her house. Anger flared in my chest. "Those sons of—"

"The good news is she doesn't know she's a hostage yet." He ran a shaky hand over his head. "She thinks she's giving foreign tourists a history of Nowhere."

I retrieved the end of Fredo's leash. "Where are they?"

"They're taking her back to my shop."

There was no way we could do this alone. We needed help. Something hard and sharp pricked my chest, and I winced, looked down. The pin Charlie had given me had come undone, spearing me.

"You need to come with me," Gert pleaded.

I re-hooked the pin's clasp. "I will."

I returned Gert's gun and walked to the street. The Estonians and Mrs. Malone disappeared into the antique store. A new crowd of tourists ambled across the street toward the massive mushrooms.

"Alice Sommerland!" Heels clicked on the pavement behind me.

An ache crawled up my neck. My old dorm mate was relentless and now was not the time. I looked at Gert. "I'll come to your shop. Give me twenty minutes."

I scooped up the dog and bolted down the sidewalk. He wriggled, snapping at me.

"Cut that out," I said.

Two more reporters charged from the opposite direction. "Alice Sommerland!"

I raced for the Corolla, set the little dog inside, and peeled down the street. I rounded a corner, stopped behind the bowling alley, and phoned Fitch.

"Alice? What's going on? Are you in trouble?"

"Why would you think—?" Okay, I *was* in trouble, but that was neither here nor there. "Where are you?"

"In Doyle."

"Why—?" I bit back a curse. "That's hours away!" And I was on my own. The thought of calling the sheriff didn't even enter my mind. They'd never get here in time either, even if I could convince them to help.

"You *are* in trouble," he said.

That was a colossal understatement. There was no getting out of this unless I ran. My insides hollowed out. I rubbed my thumb across the pin, the grooves of the knight and his charger scraping across my skin. The cheap metal was already starting to tarnish.

I couldn't run. I couldn't fight. There were too many and they had Mrs. Malone. But fighting had never been my first move. My first move had been negotiating, talking people down. The odds I'd succeed in that were low, but they beat my other options. And at least I could help Charlie.

My jaw set. "I need to tell you who killed the Rigbys and why," I said, my voice low and steady.

He was silent for a beat. "Okay. Thanks, I guess. But why me and not the police?"

"It's complicated. Are you listening?"

"Listening and taking notes."

"I'm sending you a text now. So, here's what I think..."

CHAPTER TWENTY-EIGHT

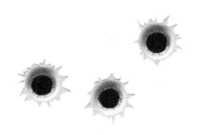

IMPASSIVE, THE BLOND MAN stared across the table at me in my chair. Kaarl Koppel was a bigger, scarier version of his brother Toomas. He didn't have the layers upon layers of muscle as the even bigger Viking-type goon standing behind Kaarl's chair, but Kaarl was solid. On the whole, I preferred his weaselly younger brother.

Phony antique knives, chipped China, and the world's biggest supply of stuffed jackalopes lay in pyramids around us.

Shoulders tight, I kept my hands on the table, and tried to look nonthreatening. My heart jackhammered. "Where's Mrs. Malone?"

"Safe and explaining the history of Nowhere's silver rush to Artur." Kaarl angled his head toward the storeroom's cinderblock wall.

"All right." Gert rubbed his wrinkled hands together. "As long as we're clear I brought Alice in—"

"You can go, Magimountain," Kaarl barked.

Gert slipped from the office.

"You too," Kaarl said, motioning to the man behind him. The cement-truck sized Estonian unfolded his muscular arms, shot me a threatening look, and followed Gert from the cramped room.

I swallowed. "I'm sorry for your loss."

Kaarl nodded and said nothing.

A nigh irresistible urge to babble my innocence flooded my system. I resisted anyway. "Your brother was a... real character."

Kaarl's arctic eyes narrowed.

Shut up, Alice. Just shut up.

"Tell me about that night," he said.

My hands turned clammy. "The plan was to stay in San Francisco. Toomas's plan, I mean. There was a Chinese restaurant he liked—"

"The White Lotus." Kaarl nodded.

"We had dinner there, in Chinatown, then returned to the hotel. I was pretending to be his girlfriend that evening. We had a drink in the hotel bar—"

"Did he meet anyone there?"

"No," I said. "There was a man he seemed to recognize—a broad-shouldered brunette, six-foot two, 225 pounds. They made eye contact and nodded but didn't talk. The man left the hotel. Toomas stayed in the bar and had another drink—a mojito."

"His favorite," Kaarl said glumly.

"I drank club soda. We went upstairs to his room. I double checked it after his team had done the same and didn't find any bugs or cameras." I hesitated. "Your brother told me he was tired and was going to bed."

A ghost of a smile flickered across Kaarl's face. "He fooled you."

"Yes," I said, relief and fear twining inside me. Maybe he didn't think I'd gotten his brother killed. Though getting suckered was reason enough for execution with this crew.

"I understand you were at the scene not long after the crash," he said.

"Yes. We had a connecting suite. He'd spiked my orange juice with sleeping pills."

"You drink orange juice at night?"

"Yeah," I said. "I know it's weird, but—"

"Forget the orange juice."

I swallowed. *Forgetting the orange juice.* "I didn't hear him leave, but I knew something was up when the pills kicked in. I threw everything up then went after him."

"And?"

A crow landed in the high, open window in the cinderblock wall.

Just the facts. Don't apologize. "I didn't want to spook him. So I got a cab and had it hang back, give him space. There was an anti-theft tracker on my SUV, so I wasn't going to lose him. He was moving fast—"

"Toomas loved to drive."

"We followed him across the bridge and to Sonoma. The police say he ran a stop sign—"

"He trusted you."

My insides turned to ice. Toomas had drugged me and stolen my car. He *hadn't* trusted me. "Maybe. He was his own man."

"He trusted you."

I pressed my damp hands harder into the table. Black spots swam before my eyes. This was it. They were going to kill me. This had been a bad, bad, bad idea. I clamped my mouth shut.

"You don't talk much," he said, "do you?"

I didn't respond.

He leaned forward. "You got anything else to say about my little brother?" he asked, voice hard.

My leg muscles tightened. I glanced at the closed door. "Only that again, I'm sorry for your family's loss."

We sat that way, frozen, for a long moment. The crow flapped from the window, and I twitched.

Kaarl sat back. "Good."

Good? We sat in silence for another week or two.

"I've got a brother," I finally croaked.

"Ah, yes. The murderer."

"He didn't kill anyone. I only need one more day to prove it."

"Families can be complicated."

"If I could have one more day—"

"You'll have plenty of time to sort it out," he said unpleasantly. "Toomas liked you. He liked you a lot."

My mouth fell open. I shut it. "He did?" We'd known each other for all of three weeks.

"You were the only one he drugged."

"And that's a... sign of affection in Estonia?"

"He didn't bother with his bodyguards, the men who were supposed to be protecting him. Instead he drugged you, the woman watching for watchers, and he stole your car so you couldn't come after him. But you came after him anyway."

"Those other bodyguards—"

"Are not important. You haven't said anything to the police?"

"Only what I told you," I said, baffled.

He nodded. "Good. Keep it that way."

"I will." Since there was nothing more to say.

"And that's *all* you say to anyone. Nothing more gets to the press, to your friends, to your brother." He stood, his chair scraping on the concrete floor. "He told me you would keep his secret." Kaarl held out his hand.

I blinked at it for a moment, then hastily stood and took his hand.

"Keep his secret, Alice."

"Ah..." *Secret? What secret?*

He squeezed my hand, my bones grinding. I thought I managed not to wince. I definitely didn't squeak like a little girl. He released me and strode to the door.

I wobbled and slapped my hand on the table to steady myself. The sound echoed in the cinderblock room.

He turned. "Yes?"

Oh, crap. "Is Gert really a hitman?" I blurted.

He smiled. "He smuggled my family out of the Soviet Union. He smuggled many Estonians out. We owe him a debt and keep him on retainer, but..." He shrugged, turned, and strode through the door. It slammed behind him.

My knees folded. I collapsed onto the folding chair. What had just happened?

Gert scuttled into the storage room. "You're alive. I told you I could fix this."

I nodded, mute.

"You still have all your fingers, that's good," Gert continued. His expression turned anxious. "Did he take a toe because you're a woman? Kaarl's thoughtful that way. He wouldn't want to make it harder for you to attract a husband."

"No," I said, thinking hard. Why was I still alive? "My toes are all there."

"I have to keep an eye on you," he said proudly.

I shot him a look.

"I've still got it," he said. "I thought I was losing it. Getting old isn't for pansies. But I've still got it."

Maybe I did too. Not the way I had it exactly. My career might be DOA, but I wasn't. "Congratulations. But when I blow this pop stand—"

"Oh, you can't leave."

"Excuse me?"

"That's part of the deal," Gert said. "I don't kill you, and you stay in Nowhere."

My lungs squeezed. I couldn't breathe. "That's... No." *You'll have plenty of time to sort this out.* "No."

"How else am I supposed to watch you?"

I shook my head. This was fine. Gert was the world's worst hitman. He'd have even less luck trying to kill me outside his home territory.

"If you leave," he said, "they'll come after you."

"The Estonian mafia," I said flatly.

"No, the Russians. You think the Estonians got any juice here? They'll call in a favor with the Ruskies."

My brain seemed to freeze. "The Rus..." *The Russians. The freaking Russian mafia.*

Now *that* was a threat.

CHAPTER TWENTY-NINE

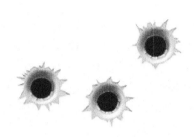

THE SUN SLANTED BEHIND the brick building, casting the alley in shade, and I shivered. It was nearly sundown, and the temperature had dropped like it did in the mountains.

Fitch and I were meeting two blocks off Main Street. We were still waiting on Charlie. An enterprising reporter cruising the back streets could have found us. I guessed most reporters weren't that enterprising.

Leaning against his blue SUV, Fitch pocketed his phone. "I can't believe I didn't see it before." He rubbed his square jaw. "But we've got no evidence."

"Yet," I said, wrapping Fredo's leash around my hand. The dog growled.

"The circumstantial evidence adds up," the detective said. "But I can't promise I can link it together."

"Link what together?" Charlie ambled toward us.

Circumstantial wasn't good enough. "Don't worry about that," I said.

Fitch quirked a brow. "Okay, *that* makes me worry."

"You do your part," I said, "I'll do mine."

"What's your part?" Fitch asked.

"Take my dog for a walk."

"Whoa," Charlie said. "Fredo's your dog now?"

"No," I said. "He's not my dog. This is a temporary thing."

My brother folded his arms. "Uh, huh."

I wrapped Fredo's leash more tightly around my hand. "Okay, well, give me a call when you learn anything."

"Will do. If you're right..." He nodded at Charlie. "Your brother's either the unluckiest guy on the planet, or I'm the luckiest. And I know I'm not the luckiest."

"Maybe your luck's turning," I said.

Fitch watched me load the dog into the Corolla. Charlie and I drove away. I turned a corner.

"So we're meeting gardeners in dark alleys now?" Charlie asked. "That was a little weird."

I glanced up. The sky was darkening. "He's not a gardener. Fitch is a private investigator."

"Oh." Charlie's brow wrinkled. "So why was he gardening?"

I parked behind the theater. "A woman hired him to investigate Donald Rigby."

"And then Donald was killed, and he stuck around to figure out why," he said excitedly.

"Exactly."

"So who was the woman?"

"Can you get into the theater after hours?"

"Sure." He pulled a key from the pocket of his board shorts. "I've got a key." He let us inside.

"I'm interested in the costumes," I said.

He led me to an oversized closet. I rummaged through tightly packed satin and frills to no success.

"What are you looking for?" he asked.

I pulled out a codpiece, put it back. "A wig."

"Most of us keep our costumes at home. There's not a lot of room here. What do you need a wig for?"

I shut the closet door. "Let's go."

Charlie locked up, and we returned to my rental. "Where are we going?"

I started the Corolla. "The treehouse."

"I dunno. Staying the night was one thing. We didn't have anywhere else to go. But I don't want to cause Ivanna any problems."

"I think we're beyond that." I pulled from the parking lot. The sun had vanished, the twilight gray and gloomy. We drove in silence for three blocks.

"I keep thinking about what you said." Charlie twisted to face me, his seatbelt tangling. "You know, about mom not being happy. And then *you* weren't happy. And now you're stuck here, because of me."

Guilt twisted my gut. "No, I'm not. I didn't come home because of you. I came home because I thought it would be a good place to hide." Silence fell between us. "I'm sorry," I said in a low voice. "I should have come home sooner. You're my only family. I shouldn't have been gone so long."

"Yeah, I know." He knotted Fredo's leash around his hand. "But you would have left days ago if it hadn't been for me."

"That's not—"

"I heard what those Estonians said to you."

My heart jumped. "What?"

"The back window in Gert's office doesn't close right," he said. "I saw you go inside and thought something was up, so I listened outside."

I shook my head. "Look, that's got nothing to do with you. It's my problem."

"But they wouldn't have found you if you hadn't stuck around."

"Maybe. Maybe not. Anyway, it worked out."

"And now you're staying to get evidence to help me. I'm sorry."

My eyes burned. I'd do anything to help him. He was my brother.

A few minutes later, we pulled into the alley behind Ivanna's house and parked behind her garage, beside an enormous blackberry bush. Its thorny branches spilled onto the pavement.

"Good thinking," Charlie said. "We won't be seen from the street here. So why *are* we here?"

"I'm looking for the wig Ivanna wore when she hired Fitch."

His face screwed up. "Why would Ivanna need a gardener? I mean, I get that he's really a PI, but we all thought he was a gardener. And I was doing her yard work."

"Not to garden. She hired him to follow Donald."

"Why would she do that? It makes no sense."

"She's involved in the murders, Charlie." My jaw tightened. "I'm sorry."

"No." He shook his head. "No way. Why would she hire a private investigator to follow Donald if she wanted to kill him?"

"To protect you." I stepped from the small car. "Do you know how to get into her house?"

He extracted himself from the Corolla. His jaw thrust forward mutinously. "This is bull. She didn't hurt anyone."

"Where does she keep her spare key?"

His gaze flicked to the garden hose, coiled on a wheel on the side of the house. I strode toward it. He gimped past me. I broke into a run.

My brother put on a burst of speed. "Aaaah!" He shoved me aside. Reaching beneath the garden hose, he extracted a key. "Ha! Got it."

I struggled for calm. "Give it to me." I held out my hand.

He threw the key into the dark mass of blackberry bushes. "Ha. Now you'll never get it. Ow." He grasped his thigh and winced.

Furious, I braced my fists on my hips. "She's not your friend, Charlie."

"Says you." He stomped to the rental car and got inside, slamming the door. Fredo gave a muffled bark.

Fine. I huffed a breath. It was probably better I did this on my own. What I was doing was illegal. And if I found anything... I wasn't sure what I could do with it without ruining the chain of evidence. But we had to know the truth.

I tried the door. Locked. Ivanna did *not* have any of those easy-to-clean windows, but I tried them anyway. Also locked.

The old garage door, however, opened easily. I stepped inside and lowered the door, snapped on my red light, and found the door to the interior. And I was in luck again. It was also unlocked.

I figured she'd keep her costumes in a closet. Her stash was in a narrow hallway closet off her bedroom. The wig was at the back of the high shelf.

I stepped back and stared at the brown tangle of hair in my hands. It might not be it. She could have used a different wig when she'd gone to see Fitch. Fitch might recognize it, or he might not. This could all have been for nothing.

And I'd returned to the problem of what to do next. If I brought the wig to the cops, maybe they'd be able to pull her DNA off it. But would it even matter? She was an actress. She had all sorts of reasons to have a wig. It all hinged on Fitch's memory for women's hairstyles.

I took a photo of the wig, close up and far away. Then realized this just was evidence of my breaking and entering. I was in over my head. But Fitch would know what to do. I started to dial.

Outside, a car engine turned over. I hurried to the garage and walked out onto the back lawn.

My Corolla glided past the blackberry bushes and down the dark alley. Charlie sat slumped in the passenger seat, his blond head pressed to the window.

CHAPTER THIRTY

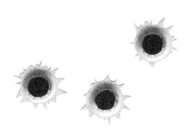

A BLACK SUV glided behind my rental. I raced after the cars, black spots of fear dancing before my eyes. But by the time I hit the alley, both cars had already reached the end of the block.

I whipped my head, scanning the back yards, searching for a solution. A rusting Oldsmobile sat in Mrs. Yarrow's driveway. I jogged to it and tugged on the driver's door. Unlocked.

I slipped inside and shoved aside a wooden cane, crosswise on the seat. My face heated with shame. I was stealing from a senior citizen who'd baked us scones. But she'd get her car back and with a full tank.

Praying I hadn't forgotten how, I bent forward and hotwired the car. It started, and I backed it from the driveway.

The SUV and my rental with Charlie inside were both gone. Clenching the big wheel, I made a pained noise in my throat. I drove down the alley and made a left. At the cross street, I paused. Taillights faded around a bend on the right. I barreled after the car.

Odds were good I hadn't lost them. Nowhere was.. . nowhere, and there wasn't a whole lot of traffic at night. But my heart knocked against my ribs, my palms damp. Running a tail is surveillance 101. But the last time I'd tailed someone, my quarry had wound up dead.

I tried not to think about that.

Fumbling, I found the Oldsmobile's headlight controls, turned them off. The streets had grown dark, light poles few and far between. But I knew these streets. The turns were built into my muscle memory. And the Oldsmobile's headlights were too conspicuous.

I followed the taillights out of town and higher into the Sierras.

The cars rounded a curve. I slowed. A shape bounded in front of the Oldsmobile. I swore, swerving toward the guard rail and whipping back into my lane. The deer I'd narrowly avoided—a stag—pivoted gracefully and leapt up the hillside.

I nosed around the curve. The two cars had pulled over, and ice cascaded through my veins. We were at the ravine where my father had crashed. If I hadn't slowed before that deer had appeared...

Blood pounding in my ears, I pulled to the opposite shoulder and stopped. I grabbed the heavy cane and slipped from the Oldsmobile.

Two voices, male and female, rose and fell. They seemed to be arguing, but I couldn't make out more than a word or two. I could make out the shape of a handgun at Ivanna's side.

Rivulets of rock trickled down the steep hillside, and I glanced up. The stag was silhouetted above me. I couldn't see his expression in the dark, but I don't think I imagined the angry set to his posture. He'd just have to get over it.

I hugged the steep slope, keeping to the opposite side of the road. It was dark, stars blazing above the mountains. But my eyes had adjusted, and I knew theirs would as well. All they had to do was turn, and they'd see me. But they didn't.

Charlie was in the front car, the Corolla, parked beside the guardrail. I forced my breathing to stay slow and easy. A stone rolled beneath my foot. I staggered and froze, gripping the cane to my chest.

The two figures beside the black SUV kept talking. They weren't arguing anymore. That seemed like a bad sign.

Releasing a long breath, I jogged forward, passing both cars. And then I crossed the road. Bent double, I crept back toward the Corolla.

I padded around the hood to the driver's side, beside the guard rail and hidden from view. I ducked and hurried to the passenger seat. Charlie's eyes were closed. His head had fallen back against the rest, his mouth half open.

My limbs trembled. Was my brother unconscious or dead? Slowly, carefully, I set the cane down on the dirt and reached for his door.

Fredo growled from the back seat.

Unfortunately, my desperation to confirm Charlie was alive didn't make me smarter. I opened the door. The interior light flicked on. A masculine shape strode around the front of the car. I lurched from the Corolla and grabbed the cane.

"Alice." Pete smiled slightly. "I thought you might show up."

Heat rushed from my chest to the top of my head. "Charlie's got nothing to do with this, Pete."

He stood four feet away from me. I wanted him at the bottom of the ravine. All his talk of helping me, helping Charlie, and I'd fallen for it. I should have seen sooner that he and Ivanna were a couple. The shared book. The not-so-secret touches. They were a couple, and they'd been hiding it, and all I'd seen was the way I thought she'd looked at my brother. But why the secrets? Had he planned on using her all along?

"Unfortunately," Pete says, "he's involved now."

Because if Charlie went over the ravine in an apparent suicide, the sheriff would stop looking into the Rigbys' deaths. My brother made the perfect patsy.

My grip tightened on the cane. "Your father killed himself because of Rigby. Didn't he?"

Pete's face contorted. "Rigby ran my father out of business, and then he ran himself out of business and left town." Pete glanced behind me, and I focused with my ears. I didn't hear anyone sneaking up on me, but my heartbeat was loud.

"It wasn't Donald's fault. He couldn't have anticipated what your father would do."

"It *was* his fault. He and Rigby had always been rivals. The whole town knew my dad's suicide was why Rigby left. Rigby's business dried up. The town came together and let him know what he'd done. I didn't understand it at the time. But before my mother left for Florida, she told me the whole story."

I nodded. "I couldn't understand why you'd promote a marijuana resort after what your mother went through with addiction. It was revenge. You learned Rigby was working for them, and you lured him here."

His smile was wry. "You were too smart for the Army."

"So what now? You roll us into the ravine and make it look like a murder-suicide?"

"It was supposed to just be Charlie," Pete said.

Footsteps crunched on the gravel behind me. *Ivanna.* I loosened my grip on the cane and shook my head. "I don't think so. Your girlfriend made too many mistakes."

"Shut up," Ivanna said, her voice uneven. I sensed she was maybe eight feet away, near the Corolla's rear.

"What mistakes?" Pete said. He wasn't armed. But Ivanna was. Pete was too close for me to risk glancing over my shoulder at her. I needed Pete incapacitated and Ivanna close enough to take away that gun.

"It was your idea to frame my brother," I said. "That's why you used that ornate knife, and why you brought gas cannisters to the murder. Rigby wasn't going to burn down the cannery. How'd you lure him there?"

"I pretended I was drunk and about to do something stupid. He came to save me. Did you know he apologized for what happened to my father? Right before I stabbed him. He'd no idea what I was about to do."

"You took a risk," I said. "He might have told his wife why he was meeting you."

"He didn't give me away," he said. "But he did tell her too much."

"So you killed her too." My lips flattened. "If she suspected what you'd done, why'd she let you in her house?"

Beside the Corolla, he shifted his weight. "That woman had a self-destructive streak a mile wide. She suspected, but only suspected. She had questions. She was angry. And she wasn't very smart."

My hand grew damp on the cane. "And now you want my brother."

"No offense. I like Charlie. But he made the perfect fall guy. And let's face it, he's not the sharpest knife in the drawer."

Casually, I leaned on the wooden cane. "The problem is, Ivanna tried to frame someone else."

He glanced past me at Ivanna. "What? Who?"

"No one," Ivanna said tightly. "She's lying."

"She used her costuming talents to disguise herself, then hired a PI to investigate Donald Rigby. She figured all his lurking around would make the PI a suspect."

Pete's nostrils flared. "Is this true? I told you it had to be Charlie. You agreed."

"That's not the worst of it," I said. "She's the one who swiped Charlie's dagger that you killed Donald with. You thought it would point to Charlie, since he's in the MBS. But it points straight back to Ivanna." *Come closer, Ivanna.*

"There's no way the police can trace that to me," she said, voice rising.

"Sure they can," I said. "You got paint on it, *Scribe.* Forensics will figure out what kind of paint it was, and I'm willing to bet it's not house paint. It's paint used by artists, like you, isn't it?"

Pete swore. "How could you be so sloppy?"

Inside the car, Fredo barked hysterically.

"Blame yourself," I told him. "You didn't notice the paint before you stabbed Donald."

"This is out of control," Pete said.

"No kidding," I said. "It's only a matter of time before the police arrest you. Don't add more years to your sentence."

"She's lying," Ivanna snarled, her feet crunching toward me on the loose gravel. "Don't listen to her."

My palms grew damp. It was counterintuitive, but gun takeaways are easier than knife takeaways. Unfortunately, Ivanna was too far away for me to do either.

"You were the one who put the letter opener in my door?" I asked Pete and took a step toward him.

"I hoped it might scare you away, that you'd think the Estonian mafia was sending you a warning." One corner of his mouth lifted. "I should have known better."

"Yeah," I said. "You should have."

A warm, electric shudder ran through me, a strange excitement, and I knew it was time. I whipped the cane around my wrist and brought it straight down on Pete's head.

A gunshot cracked. But I was already moving, flinging myself over the hood of the Corolla. I did not slide elegantly across it and land on my feet. I hit the dirt hard, shoulder first, ducked and rolled. I crouched behind the front passenger tire. Fredo's barks grew shriller.

"I'll shoot Charlie through the glass," Ivanna said.

Then Charlie *was* still alive. Relief coursed through me. I glanced at Pete. He lay unmoving in the car's headlights. Blood streamed down his face. I didn't feel bad about that at all.

"It won't look like much of a suicide if you shoot him through the window," I said.

Keeping her gun trained on Charlie inside the car, she walked around the trunk. "By the time the car hits the bottom of that ravine, no one will notice the window."

"Pete's not worth it. He used you. He told you he'd make you a Big Things artist, but he was lying. There's no money in the budget for it. Did he tell you you'd be Terrence's intern first? Work your way up?"

Her face spasmed.

"Terrence doesn't want an intern," I continued. "That was a lie too. He was just putting you off."

Her voice shook. "You're lying. I have a master's degree in fine arts. I am overqualified for the job."

"Why do you think Pete kept your relationship secret? There's nothing wrong with him dating you."

"I know there's nothing wrong with it."

Behind me, Pete groaned and stirred. I licked a bead of salty sweat off my upper lip. "What's wrong is being in love with Pete and with my brother."

"I didn't mean to," she said in a small voice. "But I was with Pete first. He deserves my loyalty."

"He doesn't deserve squat."

Her face hardened.

"Hey," I said hastily, "I get it. It's compartmentalization."

"What?"

"You compartmentalize so you don't have to deal with difficult, conflicting emotions. But eventually, the emotions come out and you have to deal with them, usually at the wrong time." At some point, I was going to have to deal with my divorce and Buck. But not now.

"Just... put your hands up." Ivanna's gun hand trembled, and her finger was on the trigger. Of course trigger discipline was too much to expect. And if I spooked her, she might shoot me by accident.

I raised my hands in surrender. "You don't have to do this. You tried to save Charlie. You don't have to kill us now."

She shook her head and blinked rapidly. "I'm sorry. I just... It's too late. I tried, I really tried, but there's nothing I can do now." An angular shape moved behind Ivanna. "Now just... just get in the back seat."

"Sure. Okay. But... there's, ah, something behind you." I pointed behind her.

She blew out a loud breath. "I'm conflicted, not stupid. I'm not going to fall for that old trick."

The stag stalked closer.

"No trick," I said. "There's a really pissed-off looking deer coming up behind you."

"Get in the car or I'll shoot you now," she said, her voice high and thin. "I'll—"

Head lowered, the stag charged. I threw myself over the hood, fell off, and flattened Pete, groaning and struggling to get up. Ivanna shrieked.

I stepped on Pete's head in my hurry to scramble around the car, but he didn't make a sound. The stag bounded away, vanishing into the darkness. Ivanna lay unconscious on the pavement. The gun lay by the Corolla's front tire.

It made the gun takeaway loads easier.

CHAPTER THIRTY-ONE

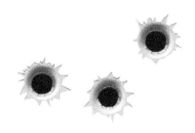

"It would be a bad idea for me to sit down for an interview." Especially since I could barely keep my eyes open. I'd spent a long night with the sheriff, going over things and making sure Pete and Ivanna didn't wiggle out of getting arrested.

They hadn't. Though they'd both had to go the hospital first.

I shifted in the front seat of Zed Kelley's van, parked in the alley beside town hall. "Sorry."

Outside my window, the flamingo loomed. Town hall's spotlights made weird shadows of its spindly legs, stretching across the lawn.

The reporter sighed. "The Estonians got to you, didn't they?"

I nodded. "I've watched your videos. I know I would have gotten a fair shake. But it's just not possible."

"I'm disappointed, but I can't say I blame you. It isn't worth it for me either to tell the world Toomas Koppel was on his way to meet his gay lover the night he was killed."

I blinked. "What?" His lover? Pieces I hadn't quite understood fell into place.

"You didn't know? His brother will go nuts when it gets out." He laughed shortly. "Which is why I'm not going to be the one to break the story."

My jaw slackened. *That* was what the Estonians were so hot to keep quiet? "Who cares if he was gay? This is the twenty-first century."

"Not for everyone it isn't."

How could I have been so... I'd been Koppel's *beard*. *That* was why he'd wanted a female on the team. And that was why he'd kept me separate from the others. He wanted them to think I was his girl, not his surveillance. I hung my head.

"Look," I said, "there *is* a story here in Nowhere, if you're interested."

"The mayor's revenge killings?" He glanced beneath the flamingo's legs at town hall. "It's already old news. Unless you want to tell me what really happened to Ivanna Simms."

"She was hit by a deer."

He raised his hands in a gesture of defeat. "Hey, I'm not judging. That chick totally deserved what she got. I'm just saying, she was a lot smaller than you. Some people might think you weren't playing fair."

Oh, for Pete's sake. "Really, it was a deer."

He raised his brows.

"I nearly hit it before I caught up with Ivanna and Pete. He was probably freaked out by the near miss, and that's why he attacked." And the fact that the stag had had that odd, near-black slash over his brows was only a coincidence.

Zed folded his arms. "Whatever."

"But there is a story for you. Sort of a cold case."

He cocked his head. "I may as well get something from this trip. Lay it on me."

"There's a mob hitman in Nowhere who helped refugees escape the Soviets. Though he was better at smuggling people out of the USSR than as a mob hitman. In fact, I don't think he's actually killed anyone. But he's got stories."

"And he's willing to talk?" he asked.

"You might have to blur his face, but I think I can make it happen."

He shrugged. "I'll talk to him. We'll see where it goes."

I gave the reporter Gert's contact info, then climbed from the van and walked to Main Street.

Fitch stood on the sidewalk talking to my brother. Charlie leaned against the Corolla and held Fredo's leash. The dog lay by his sneakers. Fredo looked dead.

Passing the men, I continued to the antique store. I knocked and went inside. The electronic chime pinged.

Gert looked up from behind the counter, where he was polishing an antique gun. "What?"

"Trouble," I said. "That Zed Kelley's figured out who you were."

He set the gun down. "Damn."

"I know." I shook my head. "I tried to get him off the trail, but... I think he's going to try to interview you."

"I'm no snitch."

I shook my head. "I know. All those stories you've got bottled up inside. He'll never get them out."

Gert's expression turned thoughtful.

"I'm sure you'll figure out a way to deal with him," I said. "But I've got a question for you."

"Yeah?"

"When you said I had to stay in Nowhere... That didn't make a lot of sense."

His white brows angled downward. "You think I was lying?"

"Of course you were lying. What I don't understand is why."

The old man grimaced. "Charlie was listening outside. And I figured you *should* stick around for a while."

"Yeah," I said. "I think you may be right."

Buck had called me last night. It wasn't the apology I was hoping for, and I wasn't going back to work anytime soon. For anyone. I hadn't given up though. But I couldn't sit around waiting for my dream assignment.

I rapped my knuckles on the glass counter. "If you need any help with that reporter, let me know."

"What?" Gert straightened. "Oh, right. It's not going to be a problem."

I nodded and left the cluttered antique shop. I didn't think Gert saw me smile.

"You okay?" Fitch asked on the sidewalk.

"Yeah," I said. "I'm good."

"I was talking to the dog." The PI nodded to Fredo, sniffing my brother's shoes.

"Did you know Fitch is a real gardener?" Charlie leaned on his cane and dropped his voice.

"No," I said. "He's not."

"I sort of am," Fitch said.

"He is," my brother said. "He's a gardener *and* a PI. Ask him."

"I'm a private investigator, and I enjoy gardening," Fitch said.

"Don't complicate the issue." I leaned against the Corolla beside Charlie, and Fredo turned his attention to my shoes. "Things are complicated enough."

"Yeah," Charlie's shoulders drooped. "Ivanna."

"She was trying to protect you, man." Fitch clapped my brother's shoulder.

"Hiring Fitch confused everything," I said. "Pete was trying to frame you. Ivanna was trying to frame Fitch. It was your bad luck the evidence against you was stronger."

Charlie's voice lowered. "I really thought Ivanna was.. . good."

"Ivanna did try to save you, you know." I grasped my brother's shoulder. "She took a big risk, going to Fitch in disguise like that. If he'd seen through it, her game would have been over fast."

"You don't have to defend Ivanna to me." Charlie stared down at his hands. "She tried to kill you."

Fredo flopped onto Charlie's shoe and closed his eyes.

"Not that hard," I said. My brother was doing a good job pretending his heart hadn't been broken, but I knew better. This sort of betrayal was a gut kick.

"Yeah." He rolled the gray dog off his sneaker. Fredo lay limp on the sidewalk. "Well," Charlie said. "Dames. Did you find anything at Ivanna's?"

"The wig she used to con Fitch."

"I wouldn't say *con*," Fitch said.

"It doesn't matter anymore," I said. "Pete confessed." I'd recorded everything last night on my cell phone.

"We're both off the hook," Fitch told him. "And aside from the murders and the threat of jail, Nowhere wasn't a bad gig. Alice, you got a minute?"

"Yeah." I nudged Fredo with the toe of my shoe. He didn't move. "Is he okay?"

"He's just napping. Look." Charlie picked up the dog. Fredo snarled and came to life. My brother set him inside the Corolla. He cranked down the window and shut the door. "I'll watch Fredo."

"Thanks." I followed Fitch to his car. "What's up?"

"What are your plans?"

"I'm taking it day by day."

"That's not exactly a plan."

"Charlie's got a job with Marques Washington helping out with the cannery renovation." Marques and Terrence had big and completely innocent plans for the cannery and Charlie. And my brother had said his time "in stir" had given him a new perspective on life. It was time for a steady gig.

I'd no idea how long that resolution would last, but it seemed like a step in the right direction.

"Good for him." He eyed me. "So. Surveillance."

"Countersurveillance."

"You know," he said, "sometimes I contract out my surveillance work."

"I'm an executive protection specialist, not a PI."

He laughed. "I never said you were a PI. Word is you're not executive protection anymore either."

I sucked in a breath. "I'm great at my job. Just because I lost one client who I wasn't even supposed to be close protecting—"

"And who happened to be America's Most Wanted."

"Technically," I said, "he was out on bail, not wanted."

"Details. Are you sticking around?"

I glanced at Charlie, leaning into the Corolla's open window. Fredo licked his face, and my brother laughed. Staying hadn't been in the plan. But if I stayed, guarding Captain Rabbit wasn't going to pay the bills.

Charlie yelped. Fredo had grabbed his shirt collar and the tiny dog seemed to be dragging him through the car window.

"You offering me a job?" I asked.

He laughed. "Hell no. Contract work. Maybe. If you're around. If you're not..." He shrugged.

Charlie shouted. His legs flailed from the car window.

"It's nice to be wanted," I said.

Fitch clapped my shoulder. He walked around his SUV to the driver's side.

I returned to the Corolla. "Fredo, let him go."

Charlie collapsed onto the seat of the car. Fredo looked up at me from the floor and panted, his eyes rolling.

"I've got to get Mrs. Malone a new flowerpot," I said. "Want to hit the Sagebrush afterward?"

"You sticking around?" my brother asked.

I squinted at the blue sky. "I'll stay until I can find a home for Fredo."

"So. Forever then."

Not forever. Nothing lasted forever. "For now."

Authors Note:

The scene with the deer—including the wrestling over the rail—actually happened at a neighbor's house party. My neighbor didn't expect the deer to go for the wing either, but it happened. No one was injured in the event, including the deer, but the deer was obviously highly irritated. It also got away with the chicken wing, and my neighbor worried about it for days until he learned deer could eat chicken.

And there really is a Big Things town—Casey, Illinois. Its exit is off I-70 and Main Street with its Big Things is well worth the look if you're passing through. The owner of the knitting store there (world's largest knitting needle and crochet hook) told me living in a town like that was... unique. That's when I knew one like it had to be the setting for a cozy mystery.

Alice's adventures aren't over! You can find her in *Big Bad*, coming June 30, 2022!

But before you go... If you're reading on a Kindle, someone recently pointed out a feature to me. A "*Before you go...*" screen pops up and you can leave a starred review, without having to actually *write* a review. Just click the number of stars. And right below that, if it's connected to your Goodreads profile, you can mark the book as read. Anyway, I'd love it if you're on Kindle, I'd love it if you'd leave a starred review. If you're not, I'd love it if you'd leave a review pretty much anywhere!

Click here to pre-order your copy of *Big Bad* so you can keep reading this series as soon as it launches on June 30, 2022.

Hi. I'm Alice, a thirty-something ex-bodyguard. I live to sleep in, but I rarely get the chance now that I'm living above my small-town's dinner theater. Between self-absorbed actors slamming doors at all hours and the theater cat that won't leave me alone... I swear he knows I'm allergic. Also, he led me straight to the corpse of the theater's leading lady.

Thanks, cat.

Now my brother, the murdered woman's co-star, is determined to solve the crime. He thinks his improv and questionable sword fighting skills somehow qualify him as a detective. Whether I like it or not, I'm going to have to solve this murder—and fast—before he gets in over his head. Or gets it taken off.

Big Bad is the second book in the Big Murder Mystery series. If you like laugh-out-loud mysteries, relationships with heart, and stories about figuring out where you belong, you'll love *Big Bad*. Buy the book and start the hilarious cozy mystery today.

Turn the page to find a sample chapter of *Big Bad.*

SNEAK PEEK OF BIG BAD

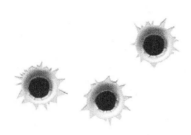

PRURIENT JOKES ASIDE, I really did like to watch.

There was a certain Zen to surveillance. You had to be focused or the object of your surveillance might get away. Worse, you might get clobbered by an unwary driver or by a very wary accomplice.

I liked the challenge.

But on this October morning, I was questioning the life choices that had led me to this Reno suburb. I drummed my fingers on the Jeep's steering wheel. I was back in the surveillance game. Good. Unfortunately, I was working for a PI rather than as part of a personal protection team.

But beggars couldn't be choosers. I'd tried—oh, how I'd tried—to get another surveillance gig with a personal protection firm. They didn't *all* laugh at me. Some had hung up on me. Others simply hadn't bothered to return my calls.

Desperate or not, I still wasn't sure if contracting for this particular PI, Fitch Rhodes, was such a hot idea. Fitch and I had done some heavy flirting before I'd taken this assignment. But the last time I'd dated a co-worker, I'd married and then divorced him. My judgment when it came to men wasn't the best.

I trailed the client's ex-husband down a residential street lined with ranch homes. Pumpkins and plywood witches and blow-up ghosts decorated the wide lawns.

Bulging eyes rolling, Fredo growled in the seat beside me. A string of drool dripped from one of his snaggle teeth. The little gray dog hated all things Halloween—plastic skeletons, jack-o-lanterns, paper ghosts. I had no idea why, but I figured it was going to be a long month.

Taking a dog on a surveillance gig could work for or against you. If your quarry noted the dog, odds were they'd notice the dog a second time—and notice you.

As a blond beanpole, I was memorable enough. Wigs could fix the blond, but there was nothing I could do about the tall. Most women weren't scraping six feet.

Fredo was ugly enough to be memorable. But he was also short enough not to stick above the car window. And dogs made a good excuse for strolling down residential streets where you didn't belong. A confrontation with a paranoid neighbor wouldn't exactly be low profile. The dog, plus my jeans and respectably stylish brown sweater gave me some cover.

Two blocks ahead, my sub's Tesla pulled to the side of the road. I pulled over as well and reached for Fredo, extracting him from his doggy car restraints.

The sub, a tall, good-looking dentist in his forties, crossed the street toward his ex-wife's ranch house. I frowned. According to my intel, the kids were in school, so he had no reason to be here.

The ex-couple was involved in a fresh custody battle. Fitch's client was convinced her ex was drinking and driving with their kids in the car. I'd seen a lot of drinking over the last week, but nothing to endanger his two kids. In short, I'd been a big disappointment to our client. But hey, you got what you got.

I walked Fredo toward the house. My subject rang the bell. After a moment, the door opened. There was a brief discussion, and the sub walked inside. The hairs on the back of my neck stood at attention. Fredo ripped fake spider webs from a nearby bush.

I had no reason to do anything here but wait outside. I was supposed to be catching my sub in the act of drinking with the kids, and the kids were away. But something had pinged my internal radar when the door had closed behind those two. Plus, I was nosy.

I released Fredo's leash. As expected, he ran straight to the pumpkin on the concrete step and lifted his leg. Making a show of it, I hurried after him, recapturing his leash and tugging him away from the Halloween décor.

I took the opportunity to glance in a front window as I hauled the dog away from the house. Neither my subject nor our client could be seen in the elegantly decorated interior.

Something thumped behind the white-painted door hard enough to rattle the doorknocker—a lion with a ring in its teeth. An oily chill slithered up the back of my neck. Insides jittering, I returned to the front door and rang the bell. It buzzed angrily. The sound was out of place, jarring.

If nothing was wrong, this assignment was about to come to a crashing halt, and I could use the money. If my subject saw me, odds were high he'd recognize me later, disguise or no. I'd be made. Fitch would have to bring in someone else, and he wouldn't be happy. But I'd learned not to ignore my bad feelings.

No one came to the door. I pressed the bell again, this time longer. Stomach tight, I peered through the narrow window beside the door. The newly redecorated hallway had been done up in tasteful grays. I rang the bell a third time, waited, tried the door. *Locked.*

"Come on, Fredo." I walked him past the garage and around the corner of the garage. A high, white fence blocked the view of the narrow side yard from the next door neighbor. Trying not to be obvious, my gaze darted around the grassy passage. This was the point where a helpful neighbor with a different view might step outside and bust me.

But no one did as I checked the high gate, which blocked passage to the back yard. It was padlocked shut. I *could* crawl over the six-foot fence, but it wasn't my first choice. Frustrated, I looked for somewhere to tie Fredo's leash and settled on a hose hook beneath a garage window.

I looped the dog's leash as best I could around it and straightened in front of the narrow window. Despite its coating of dirt, it gave me a decent view of the interior. A blue Audi. Behind it, a set of metal shelves full of garage stuff and a door to the interior of the house.

The door bumped open. The sub backed through it, dragging Fitch's client in front of him, his hands hooked beneath her arm pits. He lurched, jostling the shelves, and ricocheted against the Audi.

I darted from the window and bit back a curse. Striding toward the front of the garage, I called Fitch.

"Let me guess," he said. "You're bored and thought, I'll find out what fascinating things Fitch is up to right now—"

"Get the cops to your client's house. She's hurt. Ambulance too."

A car started inside the garage.

"What's happening?" he said, all business.

I was going to have to bang on the window and let the sub know he'd been caught. I really hated that idea, but it might dissuade him from doing anything worse. "Attempted murder."

I swallowed, hoping it hadn't been an *actual* murder. The running car told me my sub was going for the old fake suicide by carbon monoxide plot. TV has given too many wannabe bad guys terrible ideas. But the nice thing about clichés is they're easy to predict.

Without any real expectation it would open, I tugged on the handle of the wide garage door. It flew upward, banging loudly. I sucked in a startled breath.

The dentist and I stared stupidly at each other. He was feeding a hose through the Audi's cracked driver's window. His ex, in the car, slumped lifeless against the door.

Fredo dropped to his stomach and panted. The dog cocked his head, looking interested.

Moving in slow motion, I took the phone from my ear and snapped a photo of the scene. *Busted.* Cell phone cameras really have revolutionized the surveillance biz. "So," I began, "I'm a—"

The dentist dropped the hose and charged, racing down the narrow aisle between the metal shelves and the Audi. At me. I grabbed the top of the metal shelf and pulled. He ducked. The shelves crashed against the Audi and missed him completely.

"Whoops." *Sorry car.* Also, dammit, I'd barely even slowed him down. This is what came from stepping out of my career comfort zone.

Bent double, eyes burning with fury, stumbling over paint cans and plastic toolboxes, he was still moving forward. The dentist emerged from beneath the shelf in a wrestler's crouch. Fredo cocked his head, his ears twitching.

Fear punched my chest. I stepped backward. "Now, let's think about this—"

His arms swung wide, reaching for me. I dropped the phone and skipped backward, but not fast enough.

There was a rule in the dojo where I used to work out—don't go to the ground. Unless you're a jujitsu master, and I wasn't, rolling around on the ground was the last place you wanted to be. This was especially true when your opponent was stronger, heavier, and faster. This was pretty much always the case when a woman was fighting a man. It's why I preferred to stick to surveillance. It's why every move since I'd rung that doorbell had been a big mistake.

He was still bent nearly double, moving fast, head up, his shoulder angled inward toward my gut. This wasn't just a random wrestler's crouch. This guy had obviously trained in actual wrestling, and my insides turned to seawater—not the warm, welcoming Mediterranean, the cold Pacific, filled with monsters with sharp, pointy teeth.

I didn't feel like a trained and toughened bodyguard. I didn't feel like someone who'd once worked in war zones. I didn't feel like a martial arts expert. I felt like a wannabe PI who was in over her head.

"Hell." Grabbing him by the hair, I slammed my knee into his face. Sharp pain pierced my thigh. He grunted a curse and fell flat on the concrete. Then he began to rise.

Being a firm believer 'tis better to give than to receive, I kicked him a couple more times to make sure he stayed down.

He did.

I pulled one of his teeth from my thigh. "Thanks for the support," I snarled at Fredo. The dog grinned, panting.

And then I started shaking.

Can't wait to read more? Order *Big Bad!*

FLAPPERS AND FALL GUYS – A ROLE-PLAYING GAME

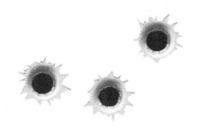

Introduction

FLAPPERS AND FALL GUYS: **A Big Murder Mystery Game** is a mystery role-playing game (RPG) based on the book and characters created by Kirsten Weiss in *Big Shot*. This short mystery is set in 1920s Nowhere, Nevada and is suitable for two to six players, but may be adapted for more. **You can download a PDF version of the game HERE at https://bi t.ly/BigShotGame.** I recommend downloading and printing out the game – it's a lot easier to run, and the printed version includes images and worksheets for the players.

The player most familiar with the game acts as the Mystery Maven, leading the player characters (PCs) through the game by reading through the game story and playing the roles of non-player characters (NPCs). The Mystery Maven should review the game before playing and should also track the life points of the PCs. You may also want to keep the page on 1920s slang and the ice cream recipes out and separate, as you may need to refer to them.

Player Characters choose roles to play (see the Player Characters section). Each PC role has certain advantages and disadvantages when it comes to rolling the die. Players will interview suspects and confront danger in this 1920s mystery set in the imaginary town of Nowhere, Nevada. PCs are encouraged to ham it up—the game's more fun if there's actual role-playing involved! (PCs may read this rule sheet).

You will need one 6-sided die to play this game. Anything *over* a three (i.e. 4-6) is a successful roll. Each character can throw the die once per round, unless there is only one PC playing, in which case they get two dice rolls per round.

Interrogations:

When it comes to interviewing suspects and witnesses, PCs with + charisma may add that number to their die roll during questioning. If there is no more information to be gleaned from an interview, the player(s) who did not have a chance to interview the suspect start play in the next round. PCs may keep rolling, taking turns, until all the clues have been exhausted. Any roll *over* a 3 (i.e. a 4-6) gleans an answer from the witness or suspect. If a PC rolls a six, they get to ask two questions.

Searching for Clues:

When searching for clues in a room or space, a roll over a three (i.e. 4-6) gets players one clue. PCs with + awareness may add that number to their die roll when searching for clues. If there are no more clues to be gleaned in that area, the player(s) who did not have a chance to search for more clues start play in the next round. Players can keep rolling, taking turns, until all the clues have been exhausted.

Fighting for survival:

Players with + strength may add that number to their die roll when fighting. Any roll over three (i.e. 4-6) is a successful defense. A roll of a three loses a PC one life point. A roll of a two loses the PC two life points. And a roll of a one loses a character three life points. When life points reach zero, the PC is dead.

Rounds:

A "round" is one cycle of die rolls. For example, there are three PCs in the game plus the Mystery Maven. The PCs take turns questioning a suspect. After three die rolls (as there are 3 players), one round is completed.

Healing:

Once per round, the doctor can heal one PC by rolling the die and adding the number that appears to the PC's life points until the PC reaches his original life points. I.e. the player's original LPs are six and the PC is down to four points; the doctor rolls a five, and the PC will be restored to the PC's original six LPs. If the doctor rolled a one in the same circumstances, the player would get one LP, bring the PC's total to five. During the same round, the doctor may also roll to search for clues or ask an interview question.

The game's afoot!

List of Non-playing Characters:

Abel Atkinson:

A handsome miner who's down on his luck now that the silver mine has played out.

Burt:

The slow-thinking but goodhearted doorman at the speakeasy.

Clerk:

Works at the cannery. A lover of comic books.

Daniel Darkwing:

Owner of the Nowhere Card Room and mysterious one-eyed man.

Fran Wilson:

Maid to Daniel Darkwing and his wife, Luella.

Gotham Monroe:

Wannabe actor who hangs out at the card club.

Hazel Jannson:

Owner of the Sagebrush Café.

Jack Fandrick:

Owner of the Speakeasy.

Morganna McKeen:

A local flapper.

Susanna:

The Darkwing's maid.

Player Characters

[You may wish to give a copy (or copies) of this sheet to the players in advance, so they can prep for their roles. But if you do, be sure to ask players to introduce themselves to each other in character before game play begins.]

Players will be searching for clues and interviewing suspects. Players will be more successful if they ask open questions which do **not** lead to yes/no answers. Possible open questions include:

- Where were you when... [time of death]?
- What can you tell me about...?
- Who might have wanted to kill [the victim]?
- Who else should we talk to?
- What else can you tell me?

You may find clues in surprising places, so be sure to explore the areas on the map after you get it from the Mystery Maven (you won't get it right away).

To better roleplay your characters, pay attention to the notes in italics at the bottom of the character description. You'll find fun opportunities during the game to let your character quirks shine.

Charlie - Private Eye

+3 Awareness

+1 Strength

Life Points: 6

Cynical Charlie doesn't trust the coppers. Charlie doesn't trust anyone, because nothing and nobody are ever what they seem. Hired to watch the Vaudeville troupe by its owner, Charlie's determined to make sure there's no funny business with the ticket earnings and is watching everyone, including the other PCs. His favorite sayings include: "Don't take any wooden nickles," "I know my onions," and "applesauce!"

Elliot - Doctor

Elliot can heal one life point for any player once per round **in addition to** his die roll (i.e., the healing doesn't take the place of Sawyer's die roll).

Life Points: 9

Elliot is the traveling doctor for the Gulf Coast Vaudeville Players. Having seen so much death in childbirth, Elliot is particularly sympathetic to the plight of women, and is often taken advantage of by them. Elliot will believe whatever a woman says and will boldly defend them against other players.

Parker – Vaudeville Musician

+1 Awareness

+2 Charisma

Life Points: 7

There isn't a saloon or speakeasy that Parker doesn't love. If there are people and booze, there'll be music and fun. Since musicians don't earn much moolah, Parker prefers to spend other people's money, will always suggest going somewhere alcohol is sold, and will be the last to leave.

Emerson – Animal Trainer

+3 Awareness

Life Points: 7

Inquisitive and curious Emerson loves animals more than people, and would rather be outdoors than in a theater. And more than anything, Emerson hates, hates, hates taxidermy, and will tell anyone who'll listen why it's awful. Emerson is a teetotaler, but doesn't want to get left out so will go with the other PCs into bars and speakeasies while abstaining from the devil's drink and loudly disapproving of others.

Quinn – Silent Film Star

+4 Charisma

Life Points: 6

Quinn is more than a little obsessed with looks and stops in front of every mirror. Why not? Appearance is everything in the world of silent films, and Quinn will frequently ask other players how his or her hair and clothing looks (especially after getting roughed up). Though egotistical, Quinn knows how to charm. Quinn is working with the vaudeville players to research an upcoming role, and may mimic them or NPCs to get a better sense of who they are.

Plot

Nowhere lies on the Nevada side of the Sierra Nevadas. The state has recently allowed towns to license card rooms for gambling, which makes Nowhere a lot more exciting. Though Nowhere's silver mine has played out, the town is doing a booming trade in quickie divorces, gambling, and rum-running. It's the perfect place for your struggling vaudeville troupe.

The show has been going well. You just finished your penultimate performance and have been celebrating in the local speakeasy.

Players begin their adventure tipsy and exiting the speakeasy into the back alley. It is 12:30 AM - a little early, but this is a small town, and the speakeasy was getting ready to close.

Download the game at https://bit.ly/Flappers-FallGuys.

Alley Behind the Speakeasy

The alley is narrow and dark, the only illumination thin streams of light seeping past the shuttered windows of the speakeasy you just left.

You notice a woman's white sequined purse lying beside a stack of crates. Curious, you go to pick it up and see the woman herself, in an elegant white flapper dress stained with blood. She lies staring, obviously dead, her back against the brick wall.

PLAYERS EACH ROLL TO SEARCH THE AREA FOR CLUES. Players with + awareness may add that number to their die roll. Any roll over a 3 gets a clue.

Clues:
  • You notice a bloodstained, pearl-handled switchblade in the dirt beside the body.
  • There are footprints of all sizes in the dirt—both men's and women's. You're unable to differentiate between the footprints of innocent passersby and those that might have been the killer's.
  • You can see the butt of a small gun sticking from the open, sequined purse, which matches her dress.

Jack's Speakeasy

Frantic, you bang on the speakeasy door. A small panel at eye-level slides open, and two beady eyes peer out. "Password?" the man behind the door barks. But the person who gave you the password when you arrived left your group hours ago, and you've forgotten the phrase. You're still tipsy, though the sight of the dead woman is sobering you up fast. What is the password?

PLAYERS CAN ROLL TO REMEMBER THE PASSWORD (Anything over a 3 gets them the password: *Giggle Water*).

The speakeasy door opens, and you breathlessly tell the imposing doorman what you've found. He stomps over to the body and studies her for a moment. Scowling, he grabs you and hauls you back inside the speakeasy.

Wagon wheel lamps hang above the rough wood floors and illuminate the brick walls, lined with animal heads. Only a few people remain at the circular tables and long wooden bar.

Behind the bar, the bartender polishes a glass mug. He doesn't look happy when the doorman whispers to him what you've found. The bartender shrugs and tells a busboy to get the sheriff.

"Aren't you, uh, worried about calling the coppers?" you ask, looking around. This is an illicit speakeasy, after all.

The bartender shrugs. "I pay the sheriff not to worry."

How do you respond?

PLAYERS EACH ROLL TO ASK THE BARTENDER QUESTIONS. Players with + charisma may add that number to their die roll. The Bartender will respond to every die roll over 3 (i.e. 4-6)

BARTENDER — JACK FANDRICK

If a player asks you a question and you know the answer (i.e. it's below), you must answer the question honestly. Make the players work for it, and have fun with the character. Ham it up!

Personality: You're acting casual about the murder and the sheriff, but you're worried. You own this speakeasy. Daniel Darkwing, the victim's husband, is paying off the sheriff, and he's got more money than you do. Worse, your friend Abel Atkinson has crossed Darkwing on more than one occasion. He may be in for the third degree when the sheriff arrives.

Objectives:

You keep out of trouble, and you're not your customers' keeper. You don't watch their drinking, when they come and go, or who they spend their time with.

You don't want to cross Darkwing, and the PCs shouldn't either.

Tell the players they should get Abel Atkinson out of here before the sheriff arrives.

Clues:

* "The doorman told me the dead woman is Luella Darkwing, wife of Daniel Darkwing. And the doorman should know."
* "Where do you think this juice joint gets its hooch from? Darkwing. No one knows where Darkwing's giggle water comes from, or where he hides it. It's quality though, I'll give him that. I just wish he would quit raising the price. Not that I'm complaining, see? Complaining has its consequences..."
* "Darkwing owns the card club. He's a real cake eater."
* "The Darkwings live—lived—whatever in that big fancy house on Dead Horse Way."

- "How should I know who'd want to rub Luella out? She was a peach. Just ask Atkinson, over there. In fact, you should get him out of here before the sheriff arrives. Get me?"
- "Where was I all night? Right here, behind this bar. I never stepped outside, and there are plenty of witnesses to prove it."
- "How should I know when Luella got here and who she was with? That ain't my job."

PLAYERS EACH ROLL TO ASK THE DOORMAN QUESTIONS. Players with + charisma may add that number to their die roll. The Doorman will respond to every die roll over 3.

SPEAKEASY DOORMAN, BURT

If a player asks you a question and you know the answer (i.e. it's below), you must answer the question honestly. Make the players work for it, and have fun with the character. Ham it up!

Personality: You're not that bright, but you know trouble when you see it. And this murder is going to be trouble with a capital T. You're just glad Luella's husband, Dan Darkwing, hasn't been around all night. He's *real* trouble.

Objectives: You just want the players out of here and to take Abel Atkinson with 'em.

Clues:

- "The dead woman, Luella Darkwing, was in the speakeasy nearly every night, and boy was she the cat's pajamas. She'd get here around ten and leave at midnight on the dot."
- "The first time I stepped outside since I got to work at noon was when youse lot banged on the door to show me a dead Luella. Poor Luella. She was the cat's pajamas."
- Luella came to the speakeasy alone and she left alone.
- Abel Atkinson's a silver miner. Too bad there's no silver no more. That old mine has played out.
- "Abel was the only one I saw go outside around the time Luella did. He went into the alley to do his business right

before she left and came back in for another drink after midnight. And he was drunk as a skunk."

PLAYERS EACH ROLL TO ASK ABEL ATIKINSON QUESTIONS. Players with + charisma may add that number to their die roll. Abel will respond to every die roll over 3.

ABEL ATKINSON

If a player asks you a question and you know the answer (i.e. it's below), you must answer the question honestly. Make the players work for it, and have fun with the character. Ham it up!

Personality: You like to think of yourself as an honorable man. But lately you've come to realize your friendship with Luella Darkwing might not be all that honorable. Tonight, the two of you agreed not to see each other again— the risk of something happening was too high. You've been drowning your sorrows since that moment two hours ago. Now you're so drunk you can barely stand. You're in no condition to answer questions or understand much of what anyone tells you.

Objectives: Stay drunk.

Clues:

*   "I told her. I saw her at the mine. I should never have told her."
*   "She threw me over. It's over. Everything's over."

The bartender tells you Abel lives in a hut in the corner of an unsold lot, (Lot A on the map). Do you take him home?

[What happens next depends on whether the PCs take Abel home or not. **If they don't take him home**, continue with the section below beginning, "If the PCs don't take Abel home...". If they *do* take Abel home, skip the section below and read the text that continues below it.]

If the PCs take Abel home, they all gain +2 charisma for the next three rounds.

A grumpy and reluctant Abel staggers into his makeshift hut, hidden in the corner of an otherwise empty lot. He won't let you inside and slams the door in your faces.

You turn around and see an irate sheriff. He drags Abel and the players to the sheriff's station and gives them the third degree, roughing up the PCs.

EACH PLAYER ROLLS TO DETERMINE HOW MUCH DAMAGE THE THIRD-DEGREE CAUSES. Players with + strength may add that number to their die roll.

Roll 1 - 2: You are injured, losing 2 life points.

Roll 3: You are injured, losing 1 life point.

Roll 4-6: No injuries.

By the time you're released, it's morning. You're too agitated to go back to your room to sleep, so you go to the Sagebrush Cafe for breakfast.

If the PCs don't take Abel home, they run into the sheriff arriving at the speakeasy. After surveying the body, he drags the players to the sheriff's station and gives them the third degree, roughing up the PCs.

EACH PLAYER ROLLS TO DETERMINE HOW MUCH DAMAGE THE THIRD-DEGREE CAUSES. Players with + strength may add that number to their die roll.

Roll 1 - 2: You are injured, losing 2 life points.

Roll 3: You are injured, losing 1 life point.

Roll 4-6: No injuries.

By the time you're released, it's morning. You're too agitated to go back to your room to sleep, so you go to the Sagebrush Cafe for breakfast.

The Sagebrush Café

Waitresses in short-sleeved dresses, aprons, and white caps bustle across the Sagebrush's checkerboard floor. The tables are full, so you find seats at the counter. The smells of cooking eggs and bacon and the crackle of grease make your stomach rumble.

A waitress hurries to you. "Whaddya wanna chew?"

How do you respond?

[If PCs order meals, one LP is restored to each player. Players cannot end up with more LPs than they originally had.]

PLAYERS EACH ROLL TO ASK THE WAITRESS QUESTIONS. Players with + charisma may add that number to their die roll. The waitress will respond to every die roll over 3.

THE WAITRESS

If the players ask any questions you don't know the answers to, tell them you got no time for this, you're too busy to jawbone, or you're not droppin' a dime on no one.

Personality: The diner is busy, and you don't have time for a lot of questions. But you'll answer them, if a tip is involved. As long as the PCs are quick.

Objectives: Get away from the players to serve better tipping customers.

Clues:

* "Yeah, I knew Luella. Good tipper. Everyone's talking about her murder. Too bad she got the old Harlem Sunset."
* "I figured she'd be more likely to blip off her *husband-*. Darkwing would and *did* chase anything in a skirt. I wouldn't have wanted to be their maid for nothing. Not with that man in the house. And especially not in that *house*. Have you seen it? If that place ain't haunted, I don't know what is."
* "But what's good for the goose is good for the gander, right? Luella and Abel Atkinson weren't any too secret about what *they* were up to. The whole town knew. Abel was crazy about Luella. I guess she didn't feel the same though."
* "My friend Dolly was at Jack's Speakeasy last night, and she heard Luella give Abel the mitten."
* "That Abel's got a real hot temper. Good with a knife, too."

A group of men run past the diner. Curious, you pay and leave to follow. Around the corner, in the alley, men stand in a muttering cluster. You walk closer, straining to see.

Abel Atkinson lies dead beneath a tumble of bricks beside a closed wooden door.

PLAYERS EACH MAKE ROLLS TO LOOK FOR CLUES. Players with + awareness may add that number to their die roll. Every die roll over 3 gets a clue.

Clues:

* Dust is still billowing around the fallen bricks.
* One of the bystanders tells you that Abel must have been on his way to work at the ice cream parlor. The door is the side entrance to the parlor.
* There's a gap at the top of the wall where the bricks have fallen. On the parapet above stands a bucket and stacked bricks, as if work was being done on the roof. But you don't see anyone up there.
* A fire escape zig-zags down the side of the building.
* You check your watch. It's now ten AM.

The sheriff's Studebaker squeals to a halt at the mouth of the alley, and he climbs out, racing toward the fallen man. The sheriff notices you standing there. What do you do?

[What happens next depends on whether the PCs stay to talk or not. If they stay, continue with the section below and ignore the following bordered text. If they *don't* stay, skip down to the section beginning "If players leave to avoid the sheriff..."]

If PCs stay to talk to the sheriff, he drags them to the police station for another round of the third degree.

EACH PLAYER ROLLS TO DETERMINE HOW MUCH DAMAGE THE THIRD-DEGREE CAUSES. Players with + strength may add that number to their die roll.

Roll 1 - 2: You are injured, losing 2 life points.

Roll 3: You are injured, losing 1 life point.

Roll 4-6: No injuries.

The sheriff releases the players. Where do they go next? [**Invite players to now consult the enclosed map** to decide where to go. Players can visit **any** of the places listed on the map, including the mine].

If players leave to avoid the sheriff, they should consult the enclosed map to decide where to go next. Players can visit any of the places listed on the map, including the mine.

Darkwing House

The house where Luella and Dan lived is a white-painted, two-story Victorian. The trim front yard is eerily silent. You climb the porch steps and knock on the door.

After a moment, a young woman in a black maid's uniform answers. "May I help you?" she asks.

How do you respond?

PLAYERS EACH ROLL TO ASK THE MAID QUESTIONS. Players with + charisma may add that number to their die roll. The Maid will respond to every die roll over 3.

THE MAID—SUSANNA

If a player asks you a question and you know the answer (i.e. it's below), you must answer the question honestly. Make the players work for it, and have fun with the character. Ham it up!

Personality: Nervous. You just started this job and don't want to do anything to lose it. You're particularly uneasy today because you're alone today in that big, spooky house. Mrs. Darkwing never came home, and you don't know what's happened to her.

Objectives: Don't get into trouble with the Darkwings.

Clues:

* "Mr. Darkwing got home this morning around one o'clock, which was strange. Usually he doesn't get home until two when he's working at his card room. He left again at sunup, but I don't know where he went or where he is now."
* "Everybody loved Mrs. Darkwing. Well, except for Fran, I guess. Mrs. Darkwing fired her last week.... for *stealing.*"
* The last maid, Fran Wilson, lives at the Brientz Apartment House.

The Brientz Apartments

The Brientz Apartments are in an unremarkable three-story brick building. When you walk inside, you're assaulted by the smell of cabbage. You find Fran Wilson's name and apartment number on a post box and climb the stairs to her third-floor apartment.

You knock on the door. A hesitant voice calls out, "Who is it?"

How do you respond?

PLAYERS ROLL TO TALK FRAN INTO LETTING THEM INSIDE. Fran will open the door for any die roll over three. Players with + charisma may add that number to their die roll.

Fran opens the door and ushers you inside a cramped apartment. She's young and slender, and she wears her hair in a stylish buster-brown cut, though her blue dress is faded and worn. The smell of cabbage penetrates the faded rose wallpaper. She motions you to a threadbare sofa. You sit carefully, feeling the hard springs beneath you.

FRAN WILSON

If a player asks you a question and you know the answer (i.e. it's below), you must answer the question honestly. Make the players work for it, and have fun with the character. Ham it up!

Personality: Scared. You're in trouble and you know it. You let your boss get too fresh with you. His wife found out and fired you for stealing. You didn't steal anything. You never would. But after what happened between you and Mr. Darkwing, you guess you deserved what happened to you. And now you've heard Mrs. Darkwing is dead, murdered. The coppers are going to arrest you for sure.

Objectives: You just want to learn what the PCs know. Like Mr. Darkwing always says, knowledge is power, and you'll need all the help you can get. And you definitely don't want to admit to anything you did with Mr. Darkwing. You get agitated if the PCs ask about your relationship with Daniel Darkwing and refuse to say.

PLAYERS EACH ROLL TO ASK FRAN QUESTIONS. Players with + charisma may add that number to their die roll. Fran will respond to every die roll over 3.

Clues:

- The Darkwings had an unhappy marriage. "They were always shouting at each other. It's not right when married people go out alone instead of with each other."
- "If you ask me, that Morganna McKeen was the problem. At least, that's what Mrs. Darkwing said. Morganna was always hanging around the card club and Mr. Darkwing. That's what Mrs. Darkwing said."
- "Morganna never came by the house, but I saw her in town. Stuck up, she is. I never liked her."
- "I heard Mr. Darkwing was a bootlegger, but he never brought any of that into the house. I never saw a single bottle of hooch at the Darkwing house. Honest."
- Last night, you were home in bed.
- This morning you were out looking for work. You applied at the general store and were interviewing with the manager at ten AM.
- "I didn't steal anything from Mrs. Darkwing. She only said that because—"

The Card Club

Prohibition may have made alcohol illegal everywhere, but gambling in card clubs is legal in Nevada. Daniel Darkwing's club is a long, narrow room. It's filled with card tables manned by professional dealers wearing eyeshades and sleeve garters over their white, button-down shirts. Well-dressed men—and a few women—sit around the tables with stacks of chips in front of them. Taxidermy animal heads line the walls. You're surprised to see they're drinking openly. Darkwing must be paying off the sheriff.

A one-eyed man in a white suit and eye patch swaggers up to you. "Welcome to the Nowhere Card Club. I'm Dan. What can I do for you?"

PLAYERS EACH ROLL TO ASK DAN DARKWING QUESTIONS. Players with + charisma may add that number to their die roll. Dan will respond to every die roll over 3.

DAN DARKWING

If a player asks you a question and you know the answer (i.e. it's below), you must answer the question honestly. Make the players work for it, and have fun with the character. Ham it up!

Personality: Charming. Your wife's just been killed, and the man you thought had done it is dead now too. You'd like to think the latter was a happy accident, but you suspect the person who killed your wife killed him as well. And you've heard these strangers in town have been at the scene of both crimes. Though your wife's death solved a lot of problems for you, you need to know who killed her and why. And why these strangers are so interested...

Objectives: You want to learn what the players know. Like you always say, knowledge is power.

Clues:
- "I was here at the card club last night when I learned of my wife's death. She was a good woman."
- "Before she was killed, I would have said no one wanted to hurt my wife. I guess I was wrong."
- "I've been here all morning. Just ask any of my faithful employees."
- "No, Morganna wasn't here last night when my wife was killed, but she's got nothing to do with this. And I haven't seen her all morning. Check the garage. Her cousin works there."
- "I never believed that baloney about my wife and that palooka Abel Atkinson. He was dizzy with her, but she

wouldn't give him the time of day if she had three watches on and was standing beneath a clock."

- "My wife said the maid stole some jewelry, so I had to hire a new one. Fran swore up and down she didn't do it, but what was I supposed to do? You think she killed my wife? She was plenty mad when I fired her."

You ask around, but although everyone confirms Darkwing's alibis, you can't believe them. It's obvious they're either too devoted or too afraid of Darkwing to cross him.

As you step outside the card room, you hear a man say, "Hsst! Hsst!"

You look around, and a slender young blond man in a straw-hat motions you around the corner of the building. Curious, you follow.

"I heard you asking about Dan's wife," the man whispers. "You shouldn't do that. Dan's not as friendly as he looks, if you get my drift."

PLAYERS EACH ROLL TO ASK THE MYSTERIOUS STRANGER QUESTIONS. Players with + charisma may add that number to their die roll. He will respond to every die roll over 3.

GOTHAM MONROE

If a player asks you a question and you know the answer (i.e. it's below), you must answer the question honestly. Make the players work for it, and have fun with the character. Ham it up!

Personality: Desperate. You want to be an actor more than anything, and you *really* want to get out of Nowhere. All you need is a break. These vaudeville players may be able to help.

Objectives: You'll tell them whatever you know. You just want to make friends with the theater group. You'll do anything for your big break.

Clues:

- "To BE, or NOT to be. That is the question. Like it? Oh, what? Right. Yesterday evening around six, Mr. Darkwing went to resupply his gin. When he got back an hour later, he was furious. I heard him yelling that someone had stolen cases of his best stuff."

• "I don't know where he keeps his alcohol, but he doesn't hide it in the card club. Whenever he goes for more hooch, it takes him at least an hour. And just so you know, I'm not above taking a pie in the face. I don't suppose you've got any work available in your troupe?"

• Morganna's in the club room a lot. It's obvious that broad's got something going with Mr. Darkwing. I see her going in and out of his office all the time.

• "Darkwing's been on edge lately. There's a new player in town, and he's been cutting into Darkwing's business with lower prices and the same quality hooch."

• "To sit in solemn silence on a dull, dark dockin a pestilential prison with a life-long lockawaiting the sensation of a short, sharp shockfrom a cheap and chippy chopper on a big, black block... – That's from *the Mikado*, it is. I know the whole musical."

The Theater

The theater's closed, but the janitor opens the door for you. Aside from the old janitor, there's no one else there at this hour. He leans on his broom and laughs. "You're going about this all wrong. You want a good time, go to the garage and tell 'em Franklin sent you. They'll set you up with some good hooch."

You find no other clues at the theater.

The Cannery

The sounds of machinery whir and clank in the four-story brick cannery. A bored-looking clerk stops you at the door and asks your business. What do you say?

PLAYERS EACH ROLL TO ASK THE CLERK QUESTIONS.
Players with + charisma may add that number to their die
roll. He will respond to every die roll over 3.

THE CANNERY CLERK

If a player asks you a question and you know the answer (i.e. it's below), you must answer the question honestly. Make the players work for it, and have fun with the character. Ham it up!

Personality: Bored.

Objectives: These people might be the most interesting things you've seen all day at the pea cannery, and they're still not *that* interesting. You just want to get back to reading the latest issue of *The Black Mask* magazine.

Clues:

• "I didn't know Mrs. Darkwing, and I don't know Mr. Darkwing. I mean, I've seen him around a bit. I live in the old mining shack out by the mine road, and I've seen Darkwing driving up that road a lot. I reckon he's been meeting a skirt there away from his wife."

• "I saw a tomato in a Nash Touring car traveling up the mining road a few minutes after Darkwing just last week."

• "I've got no idea who might have wanted to kill Mrs. Darkwing. You got wax in your ears? I don't know 'im."

• "I don't know who might have wanted to kill Abel Atkinson either. He was a nice guy."

The General Store

The general store is bustling. Animal heads are above the shelves on the walls. You find the manager behind his cash register. "Yes, I interviewed Fran Wilson this morning. We finished up just after ten. Now do you want to buy anything or not?"

If the PCs buy something at the store, they all gain +1 strength for the next two rounds.

Note: The store only sells Lucky Tiger Hair Tonic, should the PCs ask.

Ice Cream Parlor

You walk inside the ice cream parlor and are surprised to see the counter lined with rough-looking men, drinking from metal glasses. The chalkboard behind the pink counter lists the names of their specials, the bull moose, the buster brown, the tango, and other equally odd-sounding ice cream mixtures.

You squeeze your way to the counter, and a young man in a pink-and-white striped shirt approaches. "What can I get for you?"

[Note: if someone asks what's in the specials, there's an ingredient list at the back of the game. If they want a *special* special, offer them a drink.]

How do you respond?

PLAYERS EACH ROLL TO ASK TEDDY QUESTIONS. Players with + charisma may add that number to their die roll. He will respond to every die roll over 3.

ICE CREAM PARLOR OWNER – TEDDY

If a player asks you a question and you know the answer (i.e. it's below), you must answer the question honestly. Make the players work for it, and have fun with the character. Ham it up!

Personality: Friendly. Prohibition has done wonders for profits, especially when you started adding hooch to the sundaes.

Objectives: Sell ice cream and maybe a little something else...

Clues:

* "Abel Atkinson worked here as a janitor. He was great, especially since I didn't have to pay him. I just let him turn that little closet I never used into a darkroom for his photography."

- "Abel came into work every morning and was done before the customers arrived, so I don't know who would have wanted to bump him off."
- "I knew he was hung up on Mrs. Darkwing. Between you and me, it did make it awkward, what with Mr. Darkwing delivering the... you know." [wink]

PLAYERS ROLL TO TALK TEDDY INTO LETTING THEM INSIDE THE DARKROOM. Teddy will show them the room for any die roll over three. Players with + charisma may add that number to their die roll.

You cram into a small, closet-like space. Teddy pulls a string, and a light bulb flicks on inside. Trays line a wooden shelf. Strings of photos swag the room.

PLAYERS ROLL TO SEARCH FOR CLUES. Any die roll over three will get players a clue. Players with + awareness may add that number to their die roll.

Clues:

- You find a photo of a slender woman in a fashionable coat and hat stepping into a Nash Touring car with the top down. Her face is tilted away, but you can see her hair is bobbed, with short, loose, dark curls spilling from beneath her hat.
- In the photo, wooden boxes are piled on the passenger seat. Stenciled across the boxes are the words: SMITH'S HAIR TONIC.
- The car in the photo appears to be in front of a black-rock cliff.

Barbershop

The barbershop smells like the oil they use on their customer's hair—amber and rum. You sniff experimentally. The rum smell is a little stronger than you expected. Bottles of Lucky Tiger Hair Tonic line the shelves.

The barber in his white jacket approaches you. "Would you like a trim?"

If PCs respond "yes":

The barber tells you that you can buy alcohol at the garage. The garage used to sell bathtub gin, but lately, they've been selling hooch as good quality as you can get at the speakeasy, and for half the price.

If PCs respond "no," they learn nothing at the barbershop.

Town Hall

The Town Hall is closed.

Apothecary Shop

A Nash Touring car sits outside the Apothecary's. Inside the narrow shop, an elderly woman in a black gown from the turn of the century stands behind the counter. She chats with a young woman in a pink flapper-style dress. Bobbed, loose, dark curls tumble from beneath the customer's matching hat. Jars of herbs line the shelves behind the glass counter.

The old woman glowers at you. "We're out of rubbing alcohol," she snaps.

PLAYERS EACH ROLL TO ASK THE APOTHECARY SHOP OWNER QUESTIONS. Players with + charisma may add that number to their die roll. She will respond to every die roll over 3.

SHOP OWNER

If a player asks you a question and you know the answer (i.e. it's below), you must answer the question honestly. Make the players work for it, and have fun with the character. Ham it up!

Personality: You're tired of people coming in looking for rubbing alcohol, when it's obvious they plan to drink the stuff. You're a *real* apothecary.

Objectives: Get rid of the tourists. You don't know anything about the murders. You've got no clues to give them.

Clues:

- "Luella thought she was better than she should have been. But I have no idea who wanted her dead."
- "Look, I just mind my own business, okay? I don't know anything."

PLAYERS EACH ROLL TO ASK MORGANNA QUESTIONS. Players with + charisma may add that number to their die roll. Morganna will respond to every die roll over 3.

MORGANNA MCKEEN

Personality: You are the killer! Some of the below answers are lies. You're smart and always working an angle.

Objectives: Divert attention away from yourself.

Clues:

- "I got no idea who'd want to kill Luella. She didn't mean nothin' to me."
- "Sure I knew Darkwing. He owns the card club, don't he? And he sells the most expensive hooch in town. Why wouldn't I know him?"
- "Everyone knew Abel had a thing for Luella, and that includes her husband."
- "You should'a seen that maid, Fran, after she was fired. She thought Dan would protect her because they had a thing on the side. She shoulda' known better."
- I was having too good a time to know where I was last night.
- I went for a drive this morning. What's it to ya?

Garage

The garage is closed, but you hear sounds inside. You peer through a window.

PLAYERS ROLL TO SEARCH FOR CLUES. Any die roll over three will get players a clue. Players with + awareness may add that number to their die roll.

Clues:

- The men inside are stacking wooden boxes. Stenciled on them are the words: SMITH'S HAIR TONIC.

- On the wall opposite is a photo of a man and woman standing on the running board of a Nash Touring Car and smiling. The woman is young and slender, her hat is pulled low over her eyes. Her dark hair is cut into a bob with loose, dark curls.
- You recognize the man in the photo as one of the men working in the garage.
- "We're short a box," you hear one of the men say. "Don't worry about Morganna," the man from the photo replies. "She hasn't let us down yet."
- "We could go to the mine and get it ourselves," the first man says. The man from the photo slaps him. "Don't be dumb. That's Dan's stash. We got no reason to go up there. And Morganna will be back from the Apothecary's soon."

Lot A

You see a weedy lot scattered with pine trees. Abel Atkinson's shack stands in the far corner of the lot. It's locked. Despite your efforts, you can't get inside.

Lots B, C, and D

You see a weedy, empty lot scattered with pine trees. You find no clues.

Dolan Mine

You drive up the winding dirt road to the abandoned Dolan silver mine, in a black-rock canyon. There's a gate over the mine entrance, and a sign that says: KEEP OUT.

PLAYERS ROLL TO SEARCH FOR CLUES. Any die roll over three will get players a clue. Players with + awareness may add that number to their die roll.

Clues:

- You see tire tracks from a car in front of a black rock wall.
- The lock on the gate is new. You rattle it but can't get inside.
- You shine a flashlight through the gate and see the dim shapes of wooden boxes inside the mine. SMITH'S HAIR TONIC is stenciled on the boxes in black.

Whodunit?

You decide you've gathered enough information. It's time to go to the police with what you know.

Whodunit?

The players should vote now on who killed Luella Darkwing and Abel Atkinson.

Conclusion

Unsure what to do next, you return to the theater. You debate around a card table on the stage. The sheriff might help, or he might just give you the third degree again.

The stage plunges into darkness, and strong arms grab you.

PLAYERS ROLL TO DEFEND THEMSELVES. Anything over three is a success. Players with + strength may add that number to their roll. Players who do not succeed in their rolls are unconscious for the next round. [If all players lose their rolls, then just tell them they're unconscious, and when they come to...]

The lights come up, blinding you for a moment. Morganna stands on stage and aims a derringer at you. "Thanks boys," she tells your attackers, who you recognize from the garage. "You've been snooping," she says to you. "And we don't like snoops. Do we boys?"

PLAYERS ROLL TO STALL MORGANNA BY ASKING QUESTIONS. EACH ROLL OVER THREE GETS AN ANSWER. Players with + charisma may add that number to their roll.

- "That dumb Dora, Luella, thought she was going to tighten the screws on me when she found out I was stealing Dan's hooch. She thought that would make Dan throw me over. He wouldn't have just thrown me over. He woulda fixed me up for a wooden kimono. I had to shut her up."
- "I knew Luella's habits. I was waiting for her in the alley that night and killed her."
- "Why'd I kill Abel? Who d'ya think told her I was stealing? He musta followed me to the mine one day."
- "I knew what time Abel went to the Ice Cream Parlor every morning. I waited on the roof and pushed the bricks on him then skedaddled. No one saw me."
- "My cousin Al sells the hooch I supply out of his garage. We got a nice racket going. Since we're not paying for the giggle juice, we can sell it for half of what Dan does. And we're not going to let you screw things up for us."

Morganna adjusts her aim.

PLAYERS ROLL TO ATTACK MORGANNA AND TAKE AWAY MORGANNA'S DERRINGER BEFORE HER HENCHMEN CAN REACT.

Anything over a three is a successful gun takeaway, and the round ends. If the first player rolls less than a three, he or she is shot and must roll again to determine the amount of damage (see text below). Players continue rolling until the gun is taken away or all players are dead.

PLAYERS WHO ARE SHOT ROLL TO DETERMINE HOW MUCH DAMAGE THE GUNSHOT CAUSES. Players with + strength may add that number to their die roll.
Roll 1 - 2: You are injured, losing 2 life points.

Roll 3: You are injured, losing 1 life point.
Roll 4-6: It's just a scratch. No injuries.

You rush Morganna. She gets off a wild shot and hits one of her henchmen in the leg.

You overwhelm her and aim the gun at the remaining henchmen.

The theater's elderly janitor hears the commotion, and once he sees what's happened, he gets the sheriff. You explain to the unhappy sheriff what happened. He takes in Morganna and her crew, then tells you to leave town. You do, relieved to put Nowhere behind you.

THE END
Download a PDF version of the game HERE.

Ice Cream Recipes

Bull Moose
In a sundae glass add:
- 2 scoops vanilla ice cream.
- Chocolate marshmallow syrup.
- Spoonful of chopped nuts.

Top with a chocolate bud and two cookie wafers placed to look like the horns of a moose.

Tango
In a tall ice cream glass add:
- 1 scoop chocolate ice cream with ½ oz butterscotch syrup and a spoonful of finely ground walnuts.
- On top, add 1 scoop vanilla ice cream, with ½ oz marshmallow dressing and a dash of chopped walnuts.

Top with chocolate syrup and a cherry or slice of fresh peach, plus one cloverleaf wafer.

Buster Brown
In a punch glass add:

- 1 scoop chocolate ice cream.
- 1 scoop pineapple sherbet.

Top with caramel sauce and nuts.

1920s Slang

Broad - woman
   Cake eater - ladies' man
   Cat's pajamas - really terrific
   Croaked - Killed
   Dizzy with - in love with
   Dumb Dora - stupid woman
   Giggle juice/water - alcohol
   Harlem Sunset - stabbed
   Hooch - alcohol
   Juice joint - bar
   Get me? - Understand?
   Give the mitten - break up with
   Palooka - not very smart man
   Rub out - kill
   Tighten the screws - Put pressure [on someone]
   Tomato - attractive woman
   Wooden kimono - coffin

Book Club Questions

- For the person who selected the book: What made you want to read *Big Shot*?
- What did you like about *Big shot*?
- What didn't you like about the book?
- Could Alice have salvaged her online reputation?
- How much does social media and the internet influence your life and opinion?
- At what point in the book did you begin to piece together whodunit?
- What hidden clues did you find in the book?
- How important was the small town setting to the book?
- How did you feel about how the story was told? E.g., was it too fast? Too slow?
- Was there any line or passage that stood out to you?
- Have you read other books by Kirsten? How did they compare to this book?
- Which recurring themes did you notice throughout the book?
- Did Alice and Charlie feel real to you?
- How would this story change if it were told from Charlie's perspective?
- If you turned this book into a movie, what sections would you cut?
- What did you think about the ending?

- After reading *Big Shot*, would you read other books by Kirsten Weiss?

MORE KIRSTEN WEISS

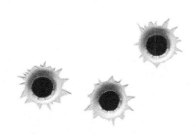

THE PERFECTLY PROPER PARANORMAL Museum Mysteries

When highflying Maddie Kosloski is railroaded into managing her small-town's paranormal museum, she tells herself it's only temporary... until a corpse in the museum embroils her in murders past and present.

If you love quirky characters and cats with attitude, you'll love this laugh-out-loud cozy mystery series with a light paranormal twist. It's perfect for fans of Jana DeLeon, Laura Childs, and Juliet Blackwell. Start with book 1, *The Perfectly Proper Paranormal Museum*, and experience these charming wine-country whodunits today.

The Tea & Tarot Cozy Mysteries

Welcome to Beanblossom's Tea and Tarot, where each and every cozy mystery brews up hilarious trouble.

Abigail Beanblossom's dream of owning a tearoom is about to come true. She's got the lease, the start-up funds, and the recipes. But Abigail's out of a tearoom and into hot water when her realtor turns out to be a conman... and then turns up dead.

Take a whimsical journey with Abigail and her partner Hyperion through the seaside town of San Borromeo (patron saint of heartburn sufferers). And be sure to check out the easy tearoom recipes in the back of each book! Start the adventure with book 1, *Steeped in Murder.*

The Wits' End Cozy Mysteries

Cozy mysteries that are out of this world...

Running the best little UFO-themed B&B in the Sierras takes organization, breakfasting chops, and a talent for turning up trouble.

The truth is out there... Way out there in these hilarious whodunits. Start the series and beam up book 1, *At Wits' End,* today!

Pie Town Cozy Mysteries

When Val followed her fiancé to coastal San Nicholas, she had ambitions of starting a new life and a pie shop. One broken engagement later, at least her dream of opening a pie shop has come true.... Until one of her regulars keels over at the counter.

Welcome to Pie Town, where Val and pie-crust specialist Charlene are baking up hilarious trouble. Start this laugh-out-loud cozy mystery series with book 1, *The Quiche and the Dead.*

A Big Murder Mystery Series

Small Town. Big Murder.

The number one secret to my success as a bodyguard? Staying under the radar. But when a wildly public disaster blew up my career and reputation, it turned my perfect, solitary life upside down.

I thought my tiny hometown of Nowhere would be the ideal out-of-the-way refuge to wait out the media storm.

It wasn't.

My little brother had moved into a treehouse. The obscure mountain town had decided to attract tourists with the world's largest collection of big things... Yes, Nowhere now has the world's largest pizza cutter. And lawn flamingo. And ball of yarn...

And then I stumbled over a dead body.

All the evidence points to my brother being the bad guy. I may have been out of his life for a while—okay, five years—but

I know he's no killer. Can I clear my brother before he becomes Nowhere's next Big Fatality?

A fast-paced and funny cozy mystery series, start with Big Shot.

The Doyle Witch Mysteries

In a mountain town where magic lies hidden in its foundations and forests, three witchy sisters must master their powers and shatter a curse before it destroys them and the home they love.

This thrilling witch mystery series is perfect for fans of Annabel Chase, Adele Abbot, and Amanda Lee. If you love stories rich with packed with magic, mystery, and murder, you'll love the Witches of Doyle. Follow the magic with the Doyle Witch trilogy, starting with book 1, *Bound.*

The Riga Hayworth Paranormal Mysteries

Her gargoyle's got an attitude.

Her magic's on the blink.

Alchemy might be the cure... if Riga can survive long enough to puzzle out its mysteries.

All Riga wants is to solve her own personal mystery—how to rebuild her magical life. But her new talent for unearthing murder keeps getting in the way...

If you're looking for a magical page-turner with a complicated, 40-something heroine, read the paranormal mystery series that fans of Patricia Briggs and Ilona Andrews call AMAZING! Start your next adventure with book 1, *The Alchemical Detective.*

Sensibility Grey Steampunk Suspense

California Territory, 1848.

Steam-powered technology is still in its infancy.

Gold has been discovered, emptying the village of San Francisco of its male population.

And newly arrived immigrant, Englishwoman Sensibility Grey, is alone.

The territory may hold more dangers than Sensibility can manage. Pursued by government agents and a secret society,

Sensibility must decipher her father's clockwork secrets, before time runs out.

If you love over-the-top characters, twisty mysteries, and complicated heroines, you'll love the Sensibility Grey series of steampunk suspense. Start this steampunk adventure with book 1, *Steam and Sensibility*.

GET KIRSTEN'S MOBILE APP

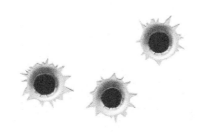

Keep up with the latest book news, and get free short stories, scone recipes and more by downloading Kirsten's mobile app.

Just click HERE to get started or use the QR code below.

Or make sure you're on Kirsten's email list to get your free copy of the Tea & Tarot mystery, *Fortune Favors the Grave*. You can do that here: KirstenWeiss.com or use the QR code below:

About the Author

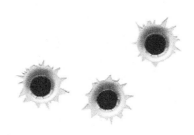

I WRITE LAUGH-OUT-LOUD, PAGE-TURNING mysteries for people who want to escape with real, complex, and flawed but likable characters. If there's magic in the story, it must work consistently within the world's rules and be based in history or the reality of current magical practices.

I'm best known for my cozy mystery and witch mystery novels, though I've written some steampunk mystery as well. So if you like funny, action-packed mysteries with complicated heroines, just turn the page...

Learn more, grab my **free app**, or sign up for my **newsletter** for exclusive stories and book updates. I also have a read-and-review tea via **Booksprout** and is looking for honest and thoughtful reviews! If you're interested, download the **Booksprout app**, follow me on Booksprout, and opt-in for email notifications.

Connect with Kirsten

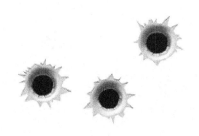

You can download my free app here:
https://kirstenweissbooks.beezer.com
Or sign up for my newsletter and get a special digital prize
pack for joining, including an exclusive Tea & Tarot novella,
Fortune Favors the Grave.
https://kirstenweiss.com
Or maybe you'd like to chat with other whimsical mystery
fans? Come join Kirsten's reader page on Facebook:
https://www.facebook.com/kirsten.weiss
Or... sign up for my read and review team on Booksprout:
https://booksprout.co/author/8142/kirsten-weiss

Made in the USA
Monee, IL
21 July 2022

10094438R00184